**Praise for**

# MICHELE HAUF

"Dark, delicious and sexy."
—*New York Times* bestselling author Susan Sizemore on *Her Vampire Husband*

"Adventure, intrigue, and a voice like no other—
Michele Hauf is a force to be reckoned with!"
—*USA TODAY* bestselling author Emma Holly

"Cleverly engrossing dialogue, overwhelming desire and intriguing paranormal situations are skillfully combined to make this an irresistible read."
—*Cataromance.com* on *Moon Kissed*

"A novel twist on a vampire tale...
Hauf mixes well-developed characters and sparkling dialogue with a paranormal tale and comes out with a winner."
—*RT Book Reviews* on *Kiss Me Deadly*

"With dangerous encounters, a myriad of paranormal beings and even some subtle humor, *The Highwayman* is an enchanting love story packed with riveting adventures."
—*Cataromance.com*

"In this action-packed delight, Hauf's humorous writing and well-developed characters combine for a realistic story—in spite of its supernatural basis."
—*RT Book Reviews* on *The Devil To Pay*

**Also available from Michele Hauf**

**HQN Books**

*Her Vampire Husband*
*Seducing the Vampire*

**Harlequin Nocturne**

*From the Dark*
*Familiar Stranger*
*Kiss Me Deadly*
*His Forgotten Forever*
*The Devil To Pay*
*The Highwayman*
*Moon Kissed*
*Angel Slayer*
*Fallen*

**LUNA Books**

*Seraphim*
*Gossamyr*
*Rhiana*

# MICHELE HAUF

# FOREVER VAMPIRE

HQN™

ISBN-13: 978-0-373-77572-9

FOREVER VAMPIRE



This edition published by arrangement with Harlequin Books S.A.

For questions and comments about the quality of this book please contact us at Customer_eCare@Harlequin.ca.



www.HQNBooks.com

**Printed in U.S.A.**

This story is for YOU.

You, who may have read something I've written before,
and decided to check out this book (I hope you like it!).
You, who saw the word "Vampire" in the title and grabbed
the book to add to your growing paranormal collection.
You, who doesn't really believe in creatures of the night,
yet secretly wonders what it would be like to meet one.
You, who does believe, and yes, you even have the
fangs and kick-ass clothing to prove it. You, who loves vampires
in all forms, be they dark, sexy, brooding, bloody, young,
old (really old), menacing, romantic, a warrior, a lover,
scarred, perfect, sparkly, pale, angsting, powerful—
but most of all, someone you can relate to and love.

# FOREVER VAMPIRE

# *CHAPTER ONE*

LYRIC SANTIAGO STEPPED into a pair of diamond-encrusted Louboutins. They merely twinkled as if they were paste jewels when compared to the fabric hugging her body. A sexy gown shimmered over her skin with her movement. It felt like a summer breeze had wafted through the closed bedroom window. Lyric smiled at the unexpected sensation.

That was about the only thing that could make her smile today.

"Gorgeous," Charish said.

Charish lingered by her daughter's bedroom door, observing. The matriarch of the Santiago clan looked as young as Lyric, but had lived as a vampire for over a century. Her blond hair was pinned up in a 1960s beehive hairstyle with a tiny pink bow attached front and center.

No matter how many centuries she lived, Lyric swore she would never get stuck in a fashion decade.

"I'm so glad you decided to try it on before you leave for the exchange," Charish said.

"How could I resist something that is probably a dream to most?"

Striding before the floor-length mirror framed upon the closet door, Lyric gasped at her first sight of the gown on her body. It dazzled. She could not see her reflection, but the dress conformed to her shape in the eerie manner she'd become accustomed to when viewing clothing on her body.

The gown had been made and was treasured by Faery's Seelie court. Fashioned from thousands of faery-mined diamonds, each of them no larger than an ant's head, it had been sewn together with spider silk. The silk was almost invisible, and it looked as though the diamonds that lay upon her skin were droplets of water under the sun, until the skirt swung gracefully about her ankles creating swishy waves of blinding brilliance.

It was rumored to give the wearer unimaginable magic should a faery don the gown. Holes could be torn in the sky to reveal other worlds. Entire faery clans could be leveled. Love (an uncommon sentiment to the fickle sidhe) could be annihilated or made pure.

On Lyric, a vampire, it would grant no such power save the sensual prowess to make men drop their jaws, stumble over their own feet and profess true lust for one promising wink from her.

She turned sideways and looked down her figure. Slender and toned, thanks to her gymnastics hobby, the gown clung to a taut stomach and her lean thigh muscles. The bodice slipped along the sides of her full breasts.

She liked the tease, and yet only wielded it when necessary.

A twist to check her backside showed the gown plunged to just above her derrière. Were the plunge an inch lower it would reveal things even she preferred to keep covered.

The gown, while revealing more than enough, could never keep all her secrets. Tugging her blond hair forward to cover her left ear, she made sure her mother had not been aware of the move.

"You should take it off now," Charish suggested in her quiet yet demanding tone. "Wouldn't want to muss it."

"Of course. It does feel…powerful."

"That could be the faery dust. Take it off, dear, before you get a contact high. Leo wore gloves when he handled that thing."

The gown had once belonged to the Seelie court, yet had been stored in a security safe by Hawkes Associates, a firm that represented the paranormal nations and acted as a sort of bank and store-all for their assets.

Priceless, the gown was a huge coup her brother, Leo, had stolen a week ago after her mother had requested he do so. Lyric had been surprised at Leo's easy submission to the one person he complained stifled his freedom. Yet at the same time, Charish Santiago could squeeze a tear out of the most stalwart warrior: she was master of manipulation.

Fact was, the Santiago clan was nearly bankrupt. Charish needed money. Fast. Pity, the domineering fiancé Charish claimed to love couldn't provide financial support. Lyric thought him worthless, but her mom did seem to genuinely love him.

If it would help her mother, Lyric was in for the ride tonight, even with the danger it promised.

Another glance in the mirror stirred up the frustration Lyric had thought she'd long pushed aside. She hadn't seen her reflection in nearly two decades. Sure, she'd seen it until puberty, when bloodborn vampires came into their blood hunger, but her memory was of a towheaded young waif whose love for summer camp and horses diametrically opposed what stood before the mirror.

She teased a strand of hair over her shoulder. Nothing good had come of that final summer before she'd completely transformed. Tonight brought up memories that she must vanquish once and for all. But would she be successful?

"The demon guards are prepared?" she asked her mother.

"Yes, three of them. Don't worry, Lyric."

"I'm not." Yes, she was.

"The guards will accompany you to the handoff site, and have been instructed not to allow the Lord of Midsummer Dark to take the exchange into Faery. You'll be safe."

Safe? Lyric sighed. If only.

The handoff site was at a known doorway to Faery. One wrong step and Lyric would never return. But she couldn't express her worries to her mother. She'd kept it a secret for so long, it was best she continue. If things went tonight as planned, it would be the beginning of the end.

"Give me a bit to get changed."

"Certainly. The driver isn't scheduled to leave for another hour, so take your time, dear."

"You going to wait with Connor?" She couldn't summon enthusiasm into that question. If the fiancé would show some initiative toward supporting Charish, she could at least bless her mother's choice.

"I wish you'd give him a chance, Lyric," Charish said. "He loves me. I need someone to take care of me. It's been difficult heading the Santiago clan since your father's death. People rely on me and expect certain rewards and contributions in exchange for an alliance. I can't do it all."

"I wouldn't expect you to, Mother."

Lyric wished Connor wasn't so...devious. She suspected he was at the root of the pilfered Santiago fortune—it had literally run empty over the past year—but she couldn't prove it.

Five decades earlier, Charish had married a thief, and a damned good one. John Santiago had not aligned himself with a vampire tribe, and had instead created a sort of mafioso ring of unaligned vampires across Europe. He had sought power and money, and all the blood a vampire could drink. Lyric wasn't sure exactly what had brought money into the family, but it did—or rather, had—flowed generously. Her father had died when Lyric was eight, but not before teaching her older brother, Leo, the skills of the trade.

Since Leo had left the family nest two years ago, Charish had faltered, taking on the weight of her deceased husband's responsibilities as if a blow to her soul. Until this newest opportunity had presented itself.

Maybe she could convince her mother to keep the reward she'd win from the exchange and ditch the fiancé? The exchange tonight was not for cash, but the return payment, if handled correctly, could prove profitable.

Lyric ran a finger along her ear, tucking her hair behind it, which was a habit she'd developed when she was thirteen. *Last year of summer camp…*

"I'll see you in a bit, dear." Charish blew her daughter a kiss—actual physical affection was not in the matriarch's arsenal—and backed from the room, her high heels clicking on the tiles as she went in search of her lover.

Another sigh could not be helped. Tonight would decide her fate. Running her palm over the diamonds felt as if she had skimmed a cool stream. The gown fascinated her, but much as she adored fashion, Lyric preferred a more subdued look. She didn't like to stand out in a crowd.

Behind her, a glass-on-glass scraping noise cut through the twilight. The floor-to-ceiling bedroom window, secured at each upper corner by a large rubber suction device, popped inside the room.

Lyric backed toward the mirror, slapping her hands

to it as two figures in dark clothing stalked toward her. Just as she was about to scream, one of them punched her across the jaw, knocking her out.

Her body wilted in a glitter of priceless faery diamonds. The intruders opened up a black body bag and stuffed the vampiress inside.

THE GRANITE-COLORED Maserati GranTurismo convertible squealed around a corner in the tenth arrondissement, clipped the bumper of a parked BMW, yet continued onward at twice the speed limit on the narrow, cobbled street. The driver spied a parking space and swerved, hitting the brakes, which swung around the tail of the vehicle and nestled it between two parked cars. Neither car sustained damage, which surprised the hell out of the driver.

He was still mastering the mortal means of transportation.

Killing the ignition abruptly cut off Johnny Cash's voice from the CD player. Vaillant tugged a pair of dark sunglasses from the rearview mirror and slipped them on. He checked his reflection, still not used to the fact he could not see his reflection in the mortal realm—sunglasses hovering above a coat collar was just wrong.

Snakeskin boots hitting the tarmac (fake—you gotta respect the wildlife), he stretched to his six feet six inches and nodded at a passing mortal woman who pushed a pink baby stroller. Her blush amused him.

It was rare Vaillant walked the streets before noon. He was a late sleeper. The nights were much cooler here in the summertime, which decided his preference, though his bad vampire self could walk in the day, longer than most due to his heritage.

"Heritage? Ch'yeah," he muttered as he hopped the curb and marched inside the five-story business complex nestled within view of the train station. "Lot of good family blood has served me."

In truth, such blood had only hindered every step he'd ever taken.

Addicted to the sensory marvel of touch, Vail ran his fingertips along the black marble walls leading up to the elevator bays. The iron rings on his fingers clattered. His boots clomped nastily on the marble floor. The unfastened leather buckles on his right thigh swayed like banners.

Chipped black nail polish from a night he couldn't remember caught the eye of an elderly security guard. Vail didn't usually go in for mortal adornments, but he liked the grungy look of the polish and he wasn't sure how to remove the clingy stuff.

He nodded at the security man, an elderly mortal with a thick crop of gray hair under his official cap. Running fingers through his hair, Vail then stopped before the elevator and punched in the digital code Rhys Hawkes had provided him.

Hawkes Associates was the last place he wanted to visit. He'd been here once, days after arriving in the mortal realm. He'd left with a new bank account, a new car and a new uncle—but no answers.

Now, three months later, he suspected what Hawkes wanted from him. Vail had no intention of working for his pseudostepfather, who was officially his uncle. But Rhys Hawkes—half vampire, half werewolf—was interesting enough for Vail to give him another chance.

He'd swing in, listen to what the centuries-old half-breed had to say, suck down the five-hundred-euro-a-bottle wine Hawkes kept on hand, then breeze off to the Lizard Lounge where he could slake his thirst for faery ichor. It wasn't FaeryTown, but close enough.

The elevator doors slid open to reveal a lean young man with shoulder-length red hair, freckles and muscles that would intimidate a bouncer at a biker bar. The man nodded his head to the tunes blasting through his earbuds. He took one look at Vail and lunged for him, vising his hands about the vampire's neck.

Not about to be taken down, and judging his strength equal to his attacker's, Vail shoved the red-head against the wall. With a glance aside, they were both aware the security guard stood nearby, but the mortal with a pistol secured at his hip belt didn't make a move. Smart guy.

"What the hell are you doing here?" Trystan Hawkes growled. He released his hold on Vail and tugged out the earbuds. The werewolf sneered, and spit, "Longtooth."

"I love you, too, brother. Just come from talking to Daddy?"

"He's not your father." Tryst set back his shoulders and assumed a modicum of calm, but his adamant sneer told Vail what he wouldn't say. He had already said it all, so why bother again? "You slumming with the normal folk?"

"Your daddy called me here." Vail waggled a brow in a malicious tease. "Maybe he likes me better, eh?"

Tryst chuffed. "In your demented sparkly dreams."

Vail did not sparkle, though the faery ichor he had imbibed had seeped through his pores and left a sheen on his skin. It had freaked out Tryst the first and only time they'd met right here in this building. Things had gone downhill from there.

"Glad to see there's no love lost," Vail countered. "Wouldn't want my werewolf brother to go all mushy on me."

He wanted to punch the bastard, but a frustrating sliver of need inhabiting his hardened black heart also wanted to pull the creep in for a brotherly hug. *What a wib you are, Vail.*

"You must be a force, brother," Vail said. "But wait. You don't run with a pack. Just a sad little omega wolf—"

The wolf wielded a sneak-attack high kick. Tryst's hard rubber sole landed on Vail's jaw and ratcheted back his skull on his spine. He saw stars for a few seconds.

Rubbing his jaw, Vail smirked. "Nice one."

"You keep her insane," Tryst said forcefully.

"She's my mother, too. Like it or not," Vail said, but he couldn't get behind the retaliation. *Did* he keep her insane?

"You." Tryst stabbed Vail in the chest. The wolf reeked of aggression. "Stay away from our family."

"Seems your damned family keeps wanting to pull me in."

"You have no right being here!"

"Yeah?" Vail slammed Tryst against the wall, pushing his anger through his brother's shoulders. "I paid your father's damn blood debt! A debt you should have paid."

Trystan's pale blue eyes went soft. He blinked and looked aside. Vail felt the tension in his brother's muscles slacken under his grasp. He stepped away from the werewolf.

He'd spoken the truth. Neither could deny it. Tryst and Rhys Hawkes, and perhaps even his mother, Viviane, owed him more than they could ever give. But Vail knew the blood debt was one bargain for which he'd never know reciprocation.

"Gentlemen?"

The security guard knew they were brothers.

"It's cool, Harley," Tryst said to the guard. "All in jest. Brotherly love, and all that crap."

The guard nodded, but his smile didn't express amusement.

The lanky wolf nodded once, an odd acknowledgment, which either agreed that, indeed, he should have paid the debt himself, or that he didn't care what Vail had suffered.

Vail didn't have to guess at his brother's meaning.

Tryst curtly waved him off and strode toward the entrance, calling, "Stay out of my life, vampire!"

Vail flipped off the werewolf and jumped inside the elevator as the doors closed. Releasing his breath, he then shook out his fists, working his tense muscles loose.

The surprise of learning, three months earlier, he'd a brother could never top the innate desire to connect with Tryst. Vail didn't know where that feeling came from, but he'd fight it to the death, if he had to. Tryst hated him without knowing him. Vail had best accept that.

*You are unwanted in Faery. You will be unwanted in the mortal realm.*

Tough words to hear from his enemy. But not difficult to believe they were true.

Landing at the top floor, he assumed calm as he slicked back his hair and strode into the marble hallway. The place always smelled like leather polish, and that disturbed his respect for nature.

The receptionist, a petite, strawberry blonde with a sexy librarian's penchant for tight, tailored clothing, adjusted her glasses at the sight of Vail and sat straighter behind her desk, offering a bright red cupid's bow smile.

Vail winked at her, and she noticeably swooned.

Mortals. They were too easy.

Hawkes was on the phone, and gestured him inside the sparely furnished, large corner office.

Swinging by the bar, Vail nabbed a goblet of the expensive wine and sucked it down. It tasted like fruit warmed by the sun, but could never match any faery vintage.

He walked to the window that wrapped the two corner walls of the office. Spreading out his arms, he felt the sudden daring desire to jump through the glass, to discover the exaltation of flight. Despite growing up in Faery, the closest he'd come to flying was a raging orgasm. Not to be disregarded on the list of adventures one must constantly pursue.

Yet any attempt at flight would result in a vampire smashed on the tarmac—not dead, but aching and damaged for weeks, surely. He'd save it for desperation.

Rhys Hawkes showed his age with sublime protest. Pushing three centuries, Hawkes had told Vail his hair had once been black with a gray streak striping one side. Now it was gray with threads of black here and there. His harsh European bone structure battled for notice but the man's whiskey eyes were always what garnered observation.

The man was the father of Trystan Hawkes, Vail's brother. Vail and Tryst had the same mother, Viviane LaMourette. He and his brother had been born on the same day; Vail first, then Trystan not two minutes later.

They were not twins.

Vail's father was a vampire who had once been Rhys Hawkes's nemesis—and his brother.

Viviane LaMourette was all vampire—bloodborn in the sixteenth century—but also insane.

What a twisted web woven through this family's history, Vail thought with a mirthless smirk. Made for interesting coffee table talk, if one owned a coffee table. Well, he did own the coffeemaker.

Mortals and their curious habits.

Vail had never met his father. He would, as soon as he could get Hawkes to cough up information on how to find him. If anyone knew where to find Constantine de Salignac, it had to be his own brother. Yet Rhys had been evasive the first time Vail had begged the information from him.

Vail needed to see the man who had driven his mother insane. To look into his eyes, and to know whether or not his own eyes were the same. And then? Well, then.

Hawkes hung up and gestured for Vail to sit on the other side of the sleek stainless-steel desk before him. The man wore a comfortable gray sweater and dark jeans, and a silver wedding band on his left hand. He looked more Aging Rock Star than Vicious Half-Breed.

"I'm pleased you've come. It's been months, Vaillant. How are you getting on in the mortal realm?"

Vail slouched onto the chair and propped an ankle across his opposite knee. He shrugged fingers through his hair, liking the scrape of the iron rings he wore on most fingers against his scalp. He noted Hawkes zoomed in on the rings.

Cracking a lazy grin, he tilted his head. "I'm assimilating. But it's got nothing on Faery. So what's up, Uncle?"

"You feel ready to visit your mother yet?"

Hell, not this scam again. Vail leaned his forearms onto his knees and shook his head.

No, he'd never met his mother. He was too freaked to know she was literally a loony after his father had buried her in a glass coffin under the city of Paris for over two centuries. Rhys had told him the tale when he'd first visited.

What was even freakier? Thanks to a warlock's spell, Viviane LaMourette had been kept in a stasis for those centuries, alive and aware, yet frozen.

But the freakiest thing yet? She had been pregnant beforc being buried alive, and the stasis had also affected the embryos in her womb. She'd given birth to Vail and Tryst nine months after Rhys had finally found her in the twenty-first century. Two hundred and twenty-five years after she'd been buried.

Talk about a long gestation period.

He eyed Hawkes. Did the half-breed look hopeful? What was it with the paranormal breeds in this realm? They were all so…emotional.

Vail should have never left Faery. Not that he'd had much choice.

"A visit to my mother is not on my radar."

Rhys tilted his head, nodding with weary acceptance. Vail could smell the man's feral nature, and it reminded him of open fields dotted with summer blossoms, edged by verdant forest. And he could see a faint, red, ashy aura surrounding him, which proved there was vampire somewhere inside the man.

"That all you want from me, old man?"

"What's that stuff?" Rhys pointed to Vail's eyes. "You go out to a nightclub last night?"

"I do the clubs every night." Vail smeared a forefinger under his eye, smudging the black ointment he wore. "It's for the faeries. I need to be able to see them."

"Hmm." Hawkes nodded. "I suppose." But he could never understand why.

When a mortal wanted to see a faery they smeared an herbal ointment around their eyes. When a vampire wanted to see one in the mortal realm, he did the same. The magical, mythical elixir never worked for mortals. It worked for Vail because he'd come from Faery and knew the right ointment to use—the ingredients could only be obtained from a sidhe healer.

"Makes you look like a rock star with a heroine addiction," Rhys commented.

"I have no addictions," Vail said, but was ashamed his voice faltered on the word *addiction*.

"Right." Rhys leaned back in his chair, assessing Vail to the very marrow. A certain faery, Mistress of Winter's Edge, had utilized the same assessing gaze on Vail. He had never liked that look, and so openly defied the man by stretching back his shoulders and looking down his nose at him.

"I need you to come to work for me," Rhys said, repeating the same words he'd spoken the last three times he'd phoned Vail.

"Not this again—"

"This time it's different," he rushed out. "No office

work. No pickups. This is a recovery mission. Actually, it's a private investigation thing."

Vail lifted an eyebrow. He had no such skills. "You lose something?"

He glanced to the wall where a large safe door hung open. The firm stored smaller items here in Rhys's office, with a massive storage area in the basement of the building, which was entirely owned by Hawkes.

Inside the safe were priceless artifacts, totems, magical objects, currency in all denominations (and from all centuries), and other collectibles. Hawkes Associates was a security house for the paranormal nations, and took in objects of value and stored them for as little as a week or as long as centuries. If you were an immortal, it was a good thing to have a storage facility that would be there as you walked through the centuries. This Paris office was one of about half a dozen locations all over the world.

"As a matter of fact, something was stolen from us about a week ago. But that's not the assignment. Well, it is, but not."

"Don't have time for this, old man, just spit it out."

"Charish Santiago, kingpin for a splinter group of vampires unaligned with any tribe, wants me to find her daughter. She's been kidnapped."

"You want me to track a missing vampiress?" Vail thumbed his chin. "You know I don't do vampires."

"Yes, you can't stand them. And yet you are one. How does that work again?"

"They disgust me." Vail leaned forward. "They

are weak, reek of mortal blood, and are unworthy of regard."

Rhys sighed heavily and tapped his fingers on the desk. They'd had this conversation before. Vail didn't need to convince the man of his prejudices. Hell, he knew it was a ridiculous prejudice. But when a vampire was raised in Faery, he developed certain dislikes, and vampires were one of them.

"What if I told you this mission isn't going to benefit the vampires, but rather Faery?"

"I don't get it."

"A valuable Seelie court gown was also taken, along with the vampiress. Her name is Lyric Santiago. Seems she was wearing the gown at the time because she was about to hand it over to the Unseelie prince, or some dark lord—I don't recall his title."

"Lord of Midsummer Dark?"

"Yes, that's him. I believe Zett is his name. You know him?"

The muscles strapping Vail's jaw tightened. Zett had been his nemesis since childhood. But Vail had had the last laugh before being banished from Faery months earlier. Zett had been outraged. Heh.

"Ever wonder where the title Vail the Unwanted came from?" he tossed out.

Rhys nodded. "I see. So you don't like the guy."

Vail blurted out a huffing chuckle. "To put it mildly."

"More reason to help me recover the gown."

"And the vampiress?"

"Yes, her, too. But it's the gown I'm focused on. Up

until ten days ago, that gown was in the safe here in the office. We'd taken it in from the Seelic court as a means to cleanse it of some dark sidhe vibes. Something like that. I don't understand it, only that it needed to be in the mortal realm a fortnight. They intend to reclaim it after that fortnight. Which is marked four days from now. Someone stole it from me, and I'll give you one guess who that someone was."

"The Santiago clan?"

Vail had heard the name muttered in the dark nightclubs as a connection to deeds even he could not fathom. The Santiagos were old-school vampire mafia, a self-styled tribe that followed none of the legitimate tribes' ways. Thieves, cutthroats and murderers populated their ranks.

Vail avoided tribes—he didn't require any modicum of family, no matter the form—but most especially he avoided the vampires.

"So why steal the thing, then put it on her daughter and hand her off to the Unseelie lord?"

"I'm told she was merely trying it on, and had intended to take it off before the exchange. I'm guessing the gown was leverage for something."

"Not the daughter? What, is she ugly and has a snaggle-fang?" Vail chuckled to imagine a vampiress with such an affliction.

"She's known as the ice princess, and I'm told she is stunning. Well, I've a picture here." Rhys thumbed through a row of files in his bottom desk drawer and tossed a photo across the desktop to Vail. "I'm not sure what sort of deal was made between Santiago and the Midsummer darkness—"

"Lord of Midsummer Dark."

"Yes, whatever. All I know is I need to get that gown back before the Seelie representative returns for it. The sidhe are the last nation on this earth I want to piss off."

"You are not a wib, old man."

"I don't know Faery speak."

"It means you're not stupid."

Vail leaned forward to glance at the photo. He wasn't about to touch it—that would show too much interest—but then he did. Bright white teeth. Brilliant whites surrounding blue eyes. And long ribbons of white-blond hair. She was a stunner. And he could appreciate a gorgeous woman.

But not a vampire.

"So how is this not helping the vampires?"

"You find the woman and retrieve the gown," Rhys explained. "We give the woman back to her mother, but—oops, we couldn't retrieve the gown. The mother is happy to have her daughter back. And I have the gown in hand, ensuring the Seelie court is pleased with my work."

"And Zett is left empty-handed."

"Exactly."

Vail thought about it. Why would a faery lord make a bargain with a vampire? Vampires stayed away from faeries because their ichor was addictive, and faeries generally regarded bloodsuckers as unclean and not worth a glance.

Something didn't figure.

"You in?" Hawkes prompted.

"No."

Vail stood and shoved a hand in his pants pocket. The pants were soft and well worn; buckles circling one thigh hung unbuckled here and there (though most of the unbuckling had been done by random women). So he was still wearing last night's clothes. Sue him.

And yeah, he probably did look like some drug-addicted rocker, but he couldn't deal with how vamps in this realm tried to appear similar to mortals just to fit in. Had to be exhausting.

"Vail."

"I know the drill," he rambled off quickly. "You need to do something with your life, Vaillant. You can't walk about pissed at the world because you didn't grow up with a mother and father. When will you claim your rightful power? You're bloodborn! You could be so powerful in the vampire community! Did I get all that right, Hawkes?"

The man nodded.

"What power?" Vail challenged. "You say both my mother and father are bloodborn? Well, where is he? How am I to win this power without challenging him to what you say is mine?"

"Vail, Constantine is—"

"I know. A vicious old vampire who harmed you irreparably and drove my mother insane. Why didn't you kill him when you had the chance?"

Hawkes lifted his chin, his lips compressing.

After a moment's heavy silence, he said, "He is my brother."

"Right. Blood being thicker than water, and all that crap. Tell that to your son, who likes to slam me around every time he sees me. Blood means nothing. I know you think keeping my father's whereabouts a secret from me is a means to protect me, but it's not, Rhys."

"I don't know where he is!"

"How can you not?"

"It's a long story."

"Well, find him. I need to face him. I need to see where I came from."

"The son is not a product of his father, Vail. You are what you were raised to be."

"A fucked-up vampire who inhales faery dust like cocaine and wouldn't touch one of his own kind if you paid him?"

"You still do dust?"

"No, just ichor." It kept him alive. Mostly. "It is my breath. Without it I die."

"It keeps you in a haze, Vail. You've never taken mortal blood. How do you know you will not like it? It would clear you. Only then will you see what you can become. Only then, can you claim the strength that is yours."

Vail snorted. "I think I saw that movie. Use the force, Luke!" He shook his head and stomped toward the door. He'd known this visit would result in more of the same bullshit.

"All right!" Rhys called. "If you find the Santiago

woman and return the gown safely to Hawkes Associates, I'll tell you everything you want to know about your father."

Vail paused before the glass door and pressed the silver toe of his boot against it, testing its strength until he heard the glass creak in the hinges. "All I want is an address," he said.

"Done," Rhys offered. "I'll start looking for him immediately."

Vail glanced over his shoulder and met the man's tired gaze. Constantine de Salignac was Rhys Hawkes's half brother. They too shared the same mother, but different fathers, though Rhys had been born ten years after his vampire brother.

The man had lived what Vail was now enduring. He knew what could hurt, harm and irreparably change Vail. Rhys just wanted to keep him safe.

Screw safety.

Vail wanted one moment with Constantine de Salignac. That was all he required to shove a stake through the bastard's heart.

"Deal," Vail said.

## *CHAPTER TWO*

VAIL EXAMINED THE cleanly cut edge of the glass window. Charish Santiago stood behind him at the door, quietly observing. Her presence echoed louder than her voice. The bold red flower in her oddly poufed hair, the bright red nails and lips, and that short flounced white skirt screamed slutty vampire.

Slutty vampire who headed an evil clan of thieves and murderers, Vail corrected his thoughts. He was so not going to give her another glance.

Something more precise than a glass cutter had been used on this window, but he guessed the device had been silent, allowing the woman who had been in the room little time to realize what was happening after the window was pushed inside.

But shouldn't a vampire have sensed the intrusion? Heartbeats? Breaths? A scent?

He sniffed. Expensive chick perfume tinted the air. And it wasn't cheap cologne, because he didn't pick up the note of alcohol, but instead a deep, ripe cherry infused with jasmine petals. If he passed by a woman smelling like this anytime soon, he'd know it was the missing vampiress, Lyric Santiago.

"The meeting was scheduled for six," Charish explained. "We checked her room at five-fifteen and found her missing. I had talked to her a half an hour earlier."

No footprints out on the balcony, or on the manicured lawn edged with hawthorn shrubs. Vail had walked the perimeter before coming inside. Whoever had jumped the viciously thorned shrubs had to have bled. Which meant nothing. All sorts of paranormal breeds could lighten their steps, or jump or even fly, depending on what had taken the woman.

Assuming the kidnappers had not been mortal. No, a mortal kidnapping a vampire made little sense. On the other hand, Vail knew little about The Order of the Stake. They were always a possibility.

"What makes you think the Unseelie lord *didn't* take her?" he ventured, his attention on the glass, because he didn't want to look at Santiago's red highlights.

"The faery? Why would he kidnap my daughter when I was going to hand the gown over freely to him?"

"Maybe he wanted her, too."

"But we had a—"

Vail swung toward the vampiress, an inquiring expression on his face. A deal. They had a deal. So why hadn't mommy dearest delivered the gown? Had she been afraid to make the handoff, so had sent her daughter in her stead? What had made her believe her daughter would be in no danger?

"Maybe Zett didn't like the terms of your deal," he ventured, "and decided to cut out the middleman, and any reason for him to pay his portion of the deal? Take the girl, get the gown, and extort more money out of the Santiago clan in return for the daughter. Sounds far-fetched," he examined the idea out loud. "The sidhe have no need for mortal money. What could Zett want beyond the priceless gown?"

The vampiress tightened her jaw. "Nothing. I expected my daughter would return safely."

Shoving both hands in his pants pockets, Vail strode along the wall where a full-length mirror was hung. The vampiress must have stood here admiring herself in the gown, perhaps while the kidnappers had cut through the window.

No, that couldn't be right. He doubted the vampiress could see her reflection any more than he could see his. He hated seeing the bodyless clothing in mirrors, so did not keep them in his home, and avoided them, going so far as to take out the side mirrors on the Maserati. A rearview mirror served to see who was behind him. But seriously? Other drivers should watch out for him.

Charish's bright red toenails were visible when Vail looked down at the floor searching for debris. Man, she stood too close, and her perfume reeked of a more masculine scent that startled his expectations.

"We've already gone over the room," she offered. "There are no clues here."

"That you can see." He scanned the carpeting, seeking one small glint of faery dust that would prove his theory correct. Nothing. Not even a twinkle. "There were no faeries here."

"Exactly." Santiago pressed her hand high along the door frame. The position boosted her breasts higher and he wondered if she was trying to flirt with him. He hadn't dialed into vampiress seduction techniques yet, and didn't want to. "You're cute and all, but what makes you an expert?" she asked. "How do I know Hawkes sent the right guy for the job?"

"You don't."

Vail wasn't a detective by any definition. But he could wear any mask he was handed, because he never wanted to be doubted by a mere vampire.

He picked up a pillow from the bed and sniffed it. More cherries and jasmine. If he were a werewolf like Tryst he could hop on the scent trail and follow the vampiress to wherever the kidnappers were keeping her. But he was not. And while vampires could recognize by scent, they were lousy trackers. Heartbeats and blood scent were the easiest to follow. But no blood had been spilled in this room.

Why hadn't Rhys asked his real son to do this job?

No matter. After thinking about it a few hours, Vail had decided doing the job for Rhys would serve as means to repay him for the kindnesses he'd given him. One did not get along in the mortal realm without a car and cash.

"I want her found within forty-eight hours,"

Santiago said, exhibiting the sharp edge that must see her respected by her kind. "The Unseelie are pressuring me."

"What the hell for?" Vail had lived among the Unseelie. He knew Zett. Which is why this incident baffled him. "What, exactly, did the Lord of Midsummer Dark promise you in exchange for the gown?"

"I'm not at liberty to say." She stroked her red nails down her throat. "Doesn't matter, because my daughter is gone and neither she nor the Unseelie lord got to make the exchange."

The woman didn't care if her daughter was found, dead or alive, Vail decided. This sexpot of an aging vampiress was only concerned about the goods. Whatever those goods may be.

Interesting. Why involve the daughter in a deal with the Unseelie if it had all been about the gown in the first place? If she'd been so concerned for her daughter's safety, wouldn't the mother have sent a man or thug to make the exchange?

A cell phone jingled, and Santiago excused herself to take the call. Her sharp voice echoed down the hallway in tandem with the clicks of her high heels until Vail could no longer hear the erratic tune.

He toed out from under the bed the cell phone he'd noticed while Santiago had still been in the room. Snagging it, he clicked it on and scrolled through the call log. The phone had not been used a lot, but one number showed up three times the day of the kidnapping. It didn't list a name, but Vail didn't need a name. He pressed Call.

A sleep-laced male voice answered, "Lyric?"

So they knew to expect her from this number. That was helpful.

"No," Vail replied. "Lyric's assistant. Just checking in, making sure things went as planned."

"What assistant? Lyric never mentioned no assistant. You call her and get your story straight before you bug me, man." *Click.*

"And how can I call her if she's been kidnapped?" Vail rubbed the phone along his forearm, working the scenarios. "Unless she wasn't kidnapped? Had she worked something out with Zett? Possible."

If her family was into thievery, that made the chances of her being a thief high. Had she stolen the gown? Why? It wasn't as though she could fence such an odd and valuable item to any in the paranormal nation without someone finding out. Faery, most especially, had a way of knowing when things were missing.

"Has to be Zett," he muttered. "That's the only way the gown could still be out there and not draw attention. The two of them must be working together."

Which didn't explain a thing. Zett had been about to have the gown handed over on a silver platter shaped like a gorgeous blonde vampire. He didn't need to steal or kidnap a thing.

Vail could not overlook the huge white elephant sitting in the middle of this bizarre incident—Zett hated vampires. So why kidnap one?

It had been three mortal months since he'd spoken to Zett. Much longer according to Faery time. Vail did not relish seeing the obnoxious Lord of Midsummer Dark anytime soon. Zett would remind him of Kit.

Vail whispered blessings the sweet young kitsune/cat shifter was happy now with her intended husband.

"Her apartment was clean, too," Santiago said as she reentered the room.

"Apartment? Your daughter kept a place apart from this home?"

"Yes, in the second arrondissement. It was close to a gym where she likes to practice the silks with a coach. My men have gone through it. It's clean."

The silks?

"You don't know everything," Vail said. "If you did, I wouldn't be talking to you. Give me the address." When Santiago balked, Vail provided angrily, "I can see things, find evidence your men couldn't dream of finding. Now write it down. You want your daughter found? Learn to cooperate."

HUMMING A JOHNNY CASH TUNE about ghost riders in the sky, Vail strolled the tiny apartment that belonged to Lyric Santiago. His thoughts strayed. What was a ghost rider? Was it an incorporeal being? What did it ride? He'd like to meet one, and go for one of those infamous rides.

"Yippi-i-oo," he sang the chorus from the song.

The apartment was indeed clean. Too clean. Vail had never seen such a Spartan living space—save his own—and suspected the vampiress could not have used it much. Three pieces of furniture—bed, couch and the requisite coffee table—and a few items in the closet. That was it. No personal touches or monogrammed towels in the bathroom. It looked as though it was a new place that had not yet been staged for sale.

If she had used it because it was close to a gym, it was likely only a stop-off of sorts. Silks? He really should have asked what that was about. Sounded kinky. And he did like some kink.

He stuck around a few hours after casing the apartment. Parked across the street from the building, he listened to the car radio while keeping an eye on the place.

When two vampires approached the building, Vail grabbed his sunglasses and got out and crossed the street. He knew they were vamps because of their ashy-red auras. Something he'd tried countless times to see on himself in a mirror but could not. Did he not have the red aura, or was it just that a man could not see his own aura?

For the love of Herne, he was one fucked-up vampire.

The vampires noticed him striding determinedly toward them and veered from the door of the building and around the side. The streets were tight and this one ended at an inner courtyard shaded with overhanging vines and fragrant honeysuckle.

Fingertips trailing the brick walls, Vail walked right into the center of the courtyard and flipped a nod at the vampires. "Nice day, messieurs. Sun is out. Looks like you got your one thousand SPF sunscreen on."

One sneered and lunged toward him, exposing fangs. His buddy caught him by the shoulder. “Who the hell are you?”

“Miss Santiago’s assistant. I’m sure I spoke to you earlier.”

“I thought I told you—” The man realized he’d just given up his identity, in a manner.

“What are you looking for?” Vail asked. He put back his shoulders, flaunting his broad frame and imposing height. The faeries had thought him a freak. Vampires tended to take a step back from him. These two wibs did not. “Did Lyric ask you to get something for her at the apartment? It’s been picked over by her mommy’s thugs.”

“Damn it,” the one who had lunged said. “I knew we should have come here right away.”

They were definitely her allies.

“So where is she?” Vail tossed out. “I didn’t get the final destination.”

“In the seventh—”

The bigger one slammed his arm across the smaller’s chest. “You’re not her assistant. That cold bitch ain’t got no friends. He’s working for the old lady.”

The smaller one, unleashed from the bigger one’s restraining hold, rushed toward Vail, fangs down in warning.

Normally, Vail got into mortal combat. It kept his adrenaline flowing, and he liked to do damage to people who pissed him off. But exerting himself over these two was a waste of breath. He had a few tricks up his sleeve.

Vail rubbed his palms together, loosening the faery dust ever embedded in his skin. Tilting his palm flat, he blew dust in the face of the attacker just as he moved within touching distance.

Faery dust penetrated the vampire's pores, traveling up his nostrils and into his throat, instantly rocketing him to a methlike high. The vampire grinned widely, staggered—and dropped.

"You want a taste?" Vail teased the other, who stood with arms out at his sides in bewilderment.

"What the hell was that? You got some voodoo mojo going on?"

"Ch'yeah. Here's a taste." Vail blew another cloud of dust and the thug batted at it, but succumbed as quickly as his cohort.

Standing over the two fallen bloodsuckers, Vail shook his head. "Vampires. They're so weak."

He licked his palm and inhaled deeply. Once upon a time he could get just as quick and massive a high. He'd give anything for that high now, but since he'd come to the mortal realm he'd shed the haze he'd once lived in, and was becoming clearer by the day.

He wasn't sure how he felt about that.

He bent over the vampires. "FaeryTown is in the eighteenth, guys. You'll find more of what you now crave there. Tell 'em Vail sent you. They'll hook you up with a sweet little number."

He straightened and scanned the area. "The

seventh?" Across the river, the quarter boasted the Eiffel Tower and the Invalides museum. "Big area to search, but I'm on it."

THE TWO MINIONS who'd succumbed to his dust clued him in that something was fishy in Paris. Where would a vampiress who had been kidnapped, or maybe not kidnapped, hide? It had to be someplace close to a food source so when she went out for sustenance she did not risk being seen.

Of course, that could be anywhere in the vast city of Paris. The buildings were close, the streets narrow and labyrinthine. Easy enough for mortal or vampire to move about unseen. Even if her minions had narrowed it down to one particular quarter, it would take Vail hours to cover it all.

One thing he had learned since arriving, the vampire tribes, while they kept to themselves, communicated from tribe to tribe in an amazing network. If you were a tribe member, you were accounted for. But even those unaligned with tribes were known. It was in the tribes' best interest to keep tabs on everyone. A sexy, blonde ice princess like Lyric Santiago would surely be recognized by at least a few.

He did have a tribal contact, but would give the search a go first. Besides, that's *if* anyone knew she was missing. The family was keeping this hush-hush.

He folded the picture of the vampiress and stuffed it in a back pocket. Appealing to any man with a healthy sex drive, certainly, with her high breasts and come-on-let's-kiss white teeth and flirty, long-lashed eyes. But beyond the surface glamour, he wasn't interested.

Vampires did not appeal to his palate. Sure, that was like calling the kettle black, but he'd grown up knowing that vampires sustained their lives through the heinous practice of imbibing on mortals. They drank their blood!

Vail would never succumb to such a base appetite. He didn't need it. Faery ichor sustained him. So why bother succumbing to something that horrified him?

*As if you don't do the same,* his conscience screamed. *You sink your teeth into faery necks. How is that different than taking a mortal?*

"They're filthy and poisoned by their food," he muttered, and walked onward.

Thinking of which, he was a bit peckish. It had been over a day since he'd fed. He should have fueled up for what he suspected would be a long night.

Striding the streets in the seventh arrondissement, he didn't attempt to quiet the clicking beats of his boots. He wanted to be heard, to be seen tracking through the twilight haze.

*Let them know what they can't get away from.*

Every so often the street was cobbled, a remnant from Paris's earlier centuries. Vail liked that. And then he didn't. He knew his father had been around since the mid-eighteenth century, as had Rhys Hawkes and his mother, Viviane.

Rhys and Viviane had fallen in love a few years before the French Revolution. Had they walked these very streets?

"Don't care. They didn't care enough about me. I don't care about them."

Jumping and hitting the bottom of a low, rusted tin sign with his knuckles, he set the ancient thing into a creaky swing.

Eyes followed him as he cut through the twilight; he could feel their regard prick at his spine. Some were mortal, peering out from windows as their televisions blared monotonously in the background. What a mind waste technology was.

Yet other eyes were Dark Ones, unwilling to test his strut. And woe to those who did employ the bravado to try him.

"Yippi-i-oo," he sang lowly. "Where are you?"

A glimmer in the corner of his eye told him a sidhe lurked in the shadows, slithering along, following his steps. Curious, but not threatening. His hunger stirred. He sensed it was a lower imp or perhaps a sprite. Sprites were nasty and he didn't care to go toe-to-toe with one of them. Their ichor was acrid, and he always ended up spitting it out.

Couldn't be a sprite. Their iridescent sheen never allowed them to blend completely into the shadows.

As he turned a corner, Vail twisted his head quickly to spy the sidhe before it realized he'd been aware of it. The ointment he wore around his eyes gave him that sight.

He dashed forward, grabbed the thing about its narrow chest, and sank his fangs into its neck. Just a quick bite, something to take the edge off the jitters he'd felt tweaking his muscles. Hot ichor glittered down his throat and soothed his pangs. He dropped the faery in a collapse of pale violet limbs. It wobbled in a giddy daze from his bite. The swoon was good to mortal, vampire and even the sidhe.

Thumbing the corner of his mouth, Vail walked on and thanked his ability to see the sidhe. He hadn't been well loved in Faery, and suspected if any of his former rivals were in the mortal realm of Paris they would not hesitate to call him out. Zett held the top position on that rivalry list.

"Come and get me," he muttered—then stopped abruptly.

Ahead, a mortal male moaned. A pleasurable utterance that curled Vail's smile smartly. Right out here, in the street, and not tucked inside a bedroom. Such moxie!

He didn't hear a responding female voice, but he did smell cherries and jasmine. "Gotcha."

Racing forward on the balls of his feet—now he wanted the element of surprise—Vail swung around the corner and into a dark alley cluttered with stacked terra-cotta flowerpots.

The man stood shoulders and back to the wall and the female was running her hands up his thigh and over his obvious hard-on. She wore a black scarf that covered all her hair, but Vail bet what was tucked beneath was long and blond. Clad entirely in black, the only spot of color was the red pointed shoes peeking from beneath the pant hem.

She leaned into the mortal's neck, fangs glinting—then sighted Vail.

Palming a huge flowerpot to leverage his strides, Vail pushed it aside and behind him. It cracked and clattered on the cobbles.

The mortal man landed against Vail's chest, groping to stand yet utterly confused about why he'd been pulled from the high of arousal. The scent of sex and cigarettes shrouded him.

Shoving him off, Vail tripped over the man's legs and plunged forward, landing on the cobblestones. He looked up. The vampiress paused at a turn at the end of the alley. She flashed a defiant smirk at him and took off.

"It's not going to be that easy to ditch me."

Charging up from all fours, he performed a racer's dash and made the corner, careening around it in time to spy the vampiress's long legs slip into the open maw of a warehouse.

Taking in the building's structure as he approached, he decided it was abandoned. The missing windows and flat, pebbled roof would provide her an easy escape while he wandered about in the dark trying to sense her. He could see well enough in the dark, but preferred to track her heartbeats.

Sniffing, he noted the jasmine and cherries. "You're the one I want," he said. "But I think I'll let you come to me. Always prefer to be the one in control."

He turned right and walked along the side of the building, tendering careful footsteps so he would sense any noise from inside. She wouldn't be so stupid now she knew someone was after her.

At the opening to a main street, Vail got another

whiff of jasmine. He eyed the stretch of apartment buildings and walk-ups directly across the street. Older, and likely lower rent, though this area was nothing to sneeze at. But dark. No streetlights to expose anyone's secrecy.

"Perfect."

"FUCK."

Shoulders glued against the corrugated iron warehouse wall, Lyric listened for the stranger's boot steps.

Why had he run after her? Who was he? And what a way to spoil supper. She hadn't a chance to sink in her fangs and now she was beyond hungry.

All the adrenaline pumping through her system over the past twenty-four hours had stripped her energy and weakened her. In fact, she breathed heavily and panted. What was with that?

She'd gotten a quick look at him. Hair darker than Himself's heart, slicked back like some kind of goth Elvis. Dark clothing and dark eyes. Really dark, like he used guyliner and smudged it.

Could be a druggie. Mortals, when high on meth, were strong, and if hurt or wounded, could still function without noticing the pain. That had to be it. He was a junkie who'd stumbled onto the scene of her trying to get the mark off, and decided he'd wanted a piece of her for himself.

Which meant she may get lucky and he'd forget what he'd witnessed and be diverted to a quest for more drugs.

Daring a peek around the doorway, she scanned the alley. The room she was squatting in was down the street. She could make a dash for it if she kept to the left side of the street in the shadows that hugged the walls. So she did.

Taking the back stairs up the side of the building to avoid the lobby, she then had to jump onto a neighbor's balcony and lean over to slide through the window she'd left open a few inches. Years of training with Leo and her acrobatic skills aided her as Lyric mastered the leap and slipped into the apartment.

A twin bed with a lumpy mattress sat below the window. She landed on it in a roll and came up to sit on the edge of the mattress. The apartment, a recent acquisition, was dark. The full moon had cruised behind nasty gray clouds that promised rain before morning.

Could she do this? Actually pull it off? It wasn't as though she'd ever spent time away from the family mansion. She possessed some facsimile of a social life, went clubbing and made dates, and hunted. But to *live* on her own?

Lyric sighed and wondered how long it would be before she dared go out again to look for supper.

"So, this is how the young and the kidnapped live."

A tall, dark-haired man strolled out from the bathroom, leaned against the kitchen wall and hooked one foot up on the side of the butcher block.

Double fuck.

## *CHAPTER THREE*

CAUGHT.

Eyes wide and mouth gaping. Blond hair tumbled from beneath the black scarf. Unbelieving. Now that was a look Vail would cherish.

"Who are you?" She backed toward the window, but he didn't think she would bolt, because her body language said *I want to listen* instead of *I'm out of here*. "Who sent you?"

"Ah, now that is the question, isn't it? Who sent me?"

"I just asked that. Got a hearing problem?"

"I found you by sound and smell, sweetie. That perfume is sexy, by the way."

She rolled her eyes.

"And what's a pretty little vampiress doing away from her kidnappers like you just were? They give you a long leash? Where are those rascally kidnappers, by the by?"

"Get out of here. This is private property."

Vail looked toward the front door, where he'd had to break a security lock to get inside. The smell of jasmine wafting out from inside had told him this was the right place. Yet the fact he could enter without a proper invitation told him a lot. Vampires could only freely enter *public* property. Yet another frustrating hazard of living in the mortal realm.

"It may be private, but it's not your property. Which makes it vacant, and that falls under the public category. You always come through the window?"

Standing and marching across the room, the vampiress tugged off the scarf and tossed it aside. She was trapped and, like prey, paced in abandon like they always did when seeking an escape. She worked it, though, her long strides swinging her narrow hips, which revealed a peek of sexy skin between waistline and the hem of her shirt.

Vail maintained his position.

"Who are you?" she demanded again in a remarkably authoritative voice, considering her slender physique and those gorgeous cheekbones. And look at all that hair. It wasn't mussed at all, spilling like ribbons of white gold over her shoulders. "I need a name."

"Vaillant," he offered freely. "But you can call me Vail."

"What kind of name is that?"

"Apparently, it's the one my mother gave me."

She pointed at his face and twirled her finger before her. "What's that stuff beneath your eyes? It sparkles." She gave him a sideways sneer. "Are you a freakin' faery?"

"Such vitriol drips from your pretty mouth. What have the sidhe ever done to you?"

“Nothing.” She paced some more. “Everything! Just get out, will you? This is my place. Go find your own hovel.”

Vail leaned his elbows onto the butcher-block counter behind him and smiled as sweetly as he could manage. He didn’t do sweet, but he could get close to amiable if he tried.

“I don’t think so. I’d like to hang around and have you introduce me to your kidnappers.”

“If you know I was kidnapped, my mother must have sent you. Did you come to rescue me? To bring me back to Mommy and lay me before her sacrificial altar?”

Vail tutted. “You have mother issues?” Even saying it cut into his heart. If anyone had issues regarding their mother…

“I’m not telling you anything.” She stopped before the bed, stared at it a few moments as if it might bite her, then plopped onto it and, shoulders high and straight, fixed an innocent gaze on him. “Get out, Vail the faery.”

“I’m not sidhe. I’m vampire.”

She scoffed. “Could have fooled me.”

“Why, thank you. I take that as a compliment.”

He strolled toward her. The efficiency apartment was small and open, so it was but ten strides to stand before the bed. Squatting, he clasped his hands between his bent legs. “Now, about your kidnappers. I assume the introductions are not going to happen, because the guilty party is sitting right here, before me.”

She looked aside. A pale beam from a distant

streetlight glimmered through the window and highlighted her long, elegant nose, narrow face and chin. Vail believed the ice princess label; she wore it gorgeously. Her eyes were deep blue, almost—no, not violet. That was a color he had only seen on faeries.

"There are no kidnappers," he ventured. "Are there?"

"You think you're so smart?"

"Actually, let me lay it out for you."

"Oh, please do. I'm all about the faery tales tonight."

"Then look at me, please."

He waited, but she tilted her head away from his gaze. Vail slid a palm along her cheek, the light getting trapped in his iron rings, and forced her head up. He gripped her chin firmly, and she flinched, but not out of his grasp.

"We can make this rough," he warned, "or we can do this nice and sweet. Which do you prefer?"

If she said rough, he'd lose it right here. Vail was not immune to an attractive woman. Very well, so she was sexy. It was those damned white teeth, clear eyes and a touch of impudence. Nothing else. Couldn't be the soft, panting breaths that indicated she was still winded from her adventure eluding him. And it most certainly was not her scent that seemed to curl into his brain and dally with the smarts he'd claimed to possess.

The fact she was vampire kept him from shoving her onto the mattress and drawing his tongue down her long, slender neck and to the full mounds of her breasts that peeked above the low neckline of her shirt.

"Tell me what you think you know," she said through a tight jaw. She shoved his hand from her face, and fixed her hard gaze on him. "Vail."

"I work for Hawkes Associates," he said. "You know about them?"

She nodded, but stiffly. She wasn't about to drop the tough-girl act. If she was a thief, like the rest of her family, then she'd probably honed some excellent avoidance tactics.

"Your mother hired us to track down her kidnapped daughter. Seems she—that is, you—had been taken from the Santiago mansion only minutes before you were to meet the Lord of Midsummer Dark for some kind of exchange. Taken, in a valuable faery gown. Mommy wants back her daughter and the dress. You following me so far?"

She jutted up her chin, defiant, but gave a curt nod.

"Seems you, Lyric Santiago—" he liked that she flinched when he recited her name "—were supposed to go along with the Lord of Midsummer Dark, the dress, I assume, being some sort of pseudodowry."

"Where did you hear that? I was only delivering the thing. There's no way I'd go near him again…" She shut her mouth.

Again? She had been in Zett's presence before? A fact to note. She wasn't going to make it easy for him. And he didn't want her to do so—it was more interesting this way. He liked watching prey squirm.

"Funny thing, though." He thumbed his jaw, drawing out the moment and also inhaling her scent, which had deepened with her rising anxiety. Uncomfortable? She may be an ice princess, but he could thaw her out quick enough. "That dress was stolen from Hawkes Associates not ten days ago. Now, who do you think is tops on the suspect list?"

"You think *I* stole that ugly gown? Ha!"

"Ugly?" He stroked the side of his thumb along her cheek. She did not flinch, but he felt her muscles tense under his touch. Something about this scenario didn't feel right, but he couldn't pinpoint what, exactly. "I was told it was fashioned from faery diamonds, the most incredible and dazzling gemstone in the known world. Or unknown world, matters as they are."

His thumb strayed to her lips, full, pink and soft, worth a kiss— Vail suddenly realized what he was doing.

What the hell was he doing? That had not been a harsh touch, but one of—admiration? *Wib.*

He stood, shoving his hand in a pocket. "You don't like diamonds, Lyric?"

"They're not so spectacular."

"I imagine so, for one of your profession. You can steal them if you want them, eh?"

"I'm not a thief."

"That has yet to be proven. What happened to the dress?"

"It's a gown."

"Gown. Dress." Vail leaned over her. A tendril of blond hair swept his hand. It felt like summer. He fisted that hand behind his back to keep from touching her again. "What did you do with it?"

"They took it from me. And left me here."

"'They' being these imaginary kidnappers of yours?"

She nodded. *Liar.*

"So you didn't steal it?"

She shook her head.

"Nor did anyone in the notorious Santiago clan steal it?"

More negative head shaking.

"And now someone else has the *gown,* namely, your kidnappers."

A positive nod.

Vail shoved her across the bed, pressing her shoulders to the mattress, which reeked of mildew and dust. Pinning a knee across her thighs, he prevented her from the anticipated sneak attack of her knee aiming for his jewels.

"You're lying," he growled at her. "There was no sign of force or struggle in your bedroom."

"Force? The whole damned window was taken out!"

"But you expected that to happen, which is why the rest of your room was pristine. As well, the gown has not been sold because that is something the entire Faery realm would be aware of—"

"If Faery is so aware, why don't they go right to the ugly thing and get it?"

"It's not…" Like that.

Faery sensed the thing, but couldn't pinpoint it.

Not without expert trackers, and someone had to actually be wearing the gown to give out the strongest vibrations. And apparently the Seelie court was not currently aware it was anywhere but at Hawkes Associates.

"You plotted your own kidnapping to steal the dress yourself. Admit it!"

"It wasn't for the gown—it was to get away from Zett!"

Vail pushed from the bed and walked a few steps away. Breathing out and raking his fingers through his hair, he then chuckled. He'd gotten the truth from her much quicker than he'd expected.

But seriously? The chick thought Zett had planned to take her to Faery with him? Vail doubted that very much.

On the other hand, he wasn't privy to all Zett's devious kinks. It was possible the bastard wanted Lyric for reasons unknown. And she had intimated they'd met previously.

"I get it," he said. "You saw an opportunity and took it."

"You're not going to take me back to my mother, are you? I need time."

A touch of measured panic warbled in her voice. She didn't want to go back, but at the same time, she was not afraid of such an outcome.

"Time for what?"

The vampiress looked aside, giving him her silence again. The streetlight adorned her profile, glistening off fine cheekbones in a tempting tease. It reminded him of the constant glimmer in Faery, and of what made him most comfortable.

"I am going to return you to your mother," Vail said, forcing away the image of light-kissed skin, "but the deal was you *and* the gown. Where is it?"

"I fenced it already."

"Liar."

"Junkie vampire."

"Junkie?"

"You sparkle. Around your eyes and at your neck. It's in your skin. I know what that's from. You're a dust freak."

He laughed again and pointed at his eyes, which were neither bloodshot nor clouded, which is what happened to dust freaks. "You think so?"

She nodded, knowingly. The vampiress could not begin to know him. Ever.

"Think what you wish. The faster I can get this damned assignment wrapped up the sooner I can be rid of you."

"Just walk away. That'll take care of your problem, like that." She snapped her fingers.

Vail leaned over her. "So who's the fence?" She gave him the side of her face again.

After her false accusation, he had no patience. He gripped her chin and forced her to meet his gaze. He considered enthralling her, but the little he knew regarding vampire-to-vampire relations was that a vamp couldn't enthrall their own kind. Since arriving in the mortal realm, his power of persuasion had been frustratingly absent. And if he dusted her, she'd be worthless.

"I don't have a name," she offered.

"How do you contact him?"

"He calls me."

Vail swung a surveying look around the small apartment. The place was merely a safe house, he suspected. It was empty, save the bare-mattress bed. Just a place to hide out until… Until? "Where's your phone?"

"I…lost it."

He narrowed his brows—then remembered. "I think I can help you with that." Reaching into his back pocket, he drew something out and slammed the phone on the kitchen counter. "I guess I'm staying the night."

"No! Where'd you get that?"

"Found it under your bed when I was looking through your room for clues." He crossed his arms and kicked out a boot to put his weight against the counter. "I'm here until your fence calls, sweetie."

"I hate you!"

"Not feeling much love for you, either."

"I hate it all. I hate this place. I hate this awful, smelly bed." She stood and kicked the bed frame, slamming the entire twin bed into the corner.

"Hey now, that's no way to treat those pretty red shoes of yours, is it?"

"And I hate you again," she retorted. "And I'm starving, which, thanks to you, my supper got off but he didn't get me off."

"Frustrated?" Vail ran a hand over his crotch.

She understood the signal. Tiny fists formed beside each of her thighs. Her plan had backfired, and now he would drag her home to her mother, kicking her pointy red shoes and screaming hate and damnation to high heaven. He couldn't wait to do it.

The petulant vampiress stomped into the bathroom.

"Where you going?"

"Where does it look like?" She slammed the door shut.

Vail hiked himself up to sit on the kitchen counter. After a few minutes had passed, he heard the shower turn on. Seemed kind of strange to strip with a stranger so near and to just…get clean.

If she thought to parade out naked in an attempt to seduce him, the ice princess had better rethink that plan. He was not interested. Despite the erection he'd run his hand over moments earlier.

*Seriously, Vail? You did not get hard over a vampiress. It was…adrenaline. Yeah, that's it.*

This was going to be a long night. And he did not like the idea of sitting around, waiting for the fence to contact Lyric. She had to know the name of the fence. To assess the mental capacity of her minions, the vampiress was definitely the brains of the operation.

How to get the information from her?

Maybe if he brought the starving vampiress supper? Dangled a tasty mortal before her? Slashed its wrist and dribbled blood into a wineglass?

That would be too much fun. But not practical, and

he wasn't into the horror of mortal blood. And besides, a tough little chick like Lyric Santiago would probably grab the mortal from him and sink in her teeth before he got anything from her.

Subtlety was required. How to appeal to a woman he had no desire to connect with on an intimate level?

*Really? You're going to stick with that attitude?*

Vail blew out a breath. So he was attracted to her. Hawkes hadn't given him any rules on how to gain the prize. So, he'd wing it.

LYRIC TURNED ON THE SHOWER and put the toilet cover down and sat. The running water provided a white noise barrier between her erratic thoughts and the overwhelming presence of the arrogant vampire who stood on the other side of the door.

She had expected a search party—the demon guards Charish had hired to accompany her to the hand-off site. She hadn't expected that search party to be only one, and so…efficient. And sexy. So sexy, in fact, that she had sat there on the bed like an idiot, instead of escaping out the window behind her.

She was supposed to have more time. A day or two to get her thoughts in order and then hop a plane to climes unknown. A place to hide, yet exist without the worry that the faery lord would ever find her. And Leo, her brother, was supposed to track down a means to free her completely. She needed to contact him.

Had she been stupid to believe such a plan could work? All she wanted was to live her own life. To not be sent to make an exchange, which would become so much more than Charish could ever imagine.

Because really? The faery lord wouldn't simply take the gown and bid her adieu; he'd kill her. Lyric knew that as well as she knew the vampire out in the kitchen was not going to leave her alone anytime soon.

She had never thought her life would come to this.

Sure, her dreams as a little girl had been similar to those of other little girls—mortal girls. Until the blood hunger had emerged at puberty. She'd always known she was vampire—had been born that way—and that the hunger for blood was a given. But she hadn't expected it to erase all those dreams of living happily ever after with the prince in his castle in an enchanted land far, far away.

"You idiot," she whispered. "The prince doesn't want to marry you, he wants to kill you."

She laughed softly at the ridiculousness of it. In a manner, the little girl *had* been promised to a prince of an enchanted land. However, Charish was unaware of that devastating detail.

"So I guess I can't deny dreams don't come true. Does that mean I should accept it?"

No. She wanted to ride away from the castle and forge a new story. Something that didn't involve faeries.

"You okay in there, sweetie?" the vampire called from the other room.

*Sweetie.* Ugh. Why did men think it was okay to

call women cutesy names when they didn't even know them? She'd give him sweet.

"I'm not going anywhere," she called over the patter of the shower. "Keep your pants on."

"Oh, they're on. But not for long."

Lyric caught her forehead against her palm. Did he think she'd allow him to get close enough for some kind of rough play, as he'd implied? He wouldn't get any information from her by raping her. He didn't seem the type, though. She'd met rapists. Her family ran with a vicious lot.

Vail was scary looking, but not as mean as he wanted her to think he was. When he'd stroked a palm over his erection she'd caught the subtle quiver of his lower lip. He was not immune to the sensual tease. If she were to put the moves on him, she could wrap him around her little finger and toss him over a shoulder.

Lyric bolted upright. Now there was an idea. But could it work?

This smelly apartment was getting smaller the longer she had to sit in it, with him, and wait for the fence to call. Which would never happen. And she was hungry.

She would seduce a frog if it would help get her out of trouble.

Tugging out a soft jersey pullover dress from the packed duffel she'd planted in the apartment two days earlier, Lyric switched from the dark shirt and pants to the cozy red number that clung nicely to her semimoist skin. The shower had given her a nice steam bath.

She put the red high heels on again, because Vail had definitely noticed them.

Slicking on some lip gloss, she pressed her lips together and nodded. The vampiress had a plan.

"And it will work."

The vampire jumped from the counter and stood, legs spread at a cocky stance as Lyric approached.

He stood well over her six feet two inches, which was impressive, considering she wore heels. And his frame was tight and muscled like an athlete. His clothing was classic black leather pants, his black shirt shot through with silver threads, which dazzled as much as the silver studs and rivets embellishing his jacket in a menacing death-metal kind of look.

She stopped before him, red-pointed toes to steel-toed cowboy boots, and made a blatant show of looking him from his face, down over the tight shirt, which hugged his muscled chest like a lover, and then lower. Leather pants with buckles here and there scuffed down one thigh. No visible hard-on, but she intended to change that.

She guessed the dark appearance and wardrobe were not a fashion choice but a means to keep most at a distance. Though some vampires took the dark lord thing too seriously, a wise vampire blended in with mortals and did not stick out like a goth club kid.

She couldn't see any faery dust on him now. Had it been a trick of the moonlight when he'd leaned over her earlier? Or maybe it was a fashion choice, and the dude was into glitter?

Clear whites in his eyes, and his deep blue irises

held her as if he'd clutched her shoulders. His dark glamour appealed to her careful, pining heart. She'd always been attracted to the bad boy, and Charish and Leo had always been too protective. She'd tended to date family friends.

She wondered what this compelling man's dark glamour tasted like? She wasn't above biting fellow vampires. As long as she didn't share the deep bite and sex at the same time. That was a bonding ritual she would only share with the one vampire she loved. The Prince Charming she counted on finding one of these days.

Vail smirked. A killer move. It tugged his mouth higher on the right, and revealed a sneak of white fang. The bad boy wanted some fun.

He grabbed her by the hips and pulled them hard against his groin where Lyric felt a buckle impress her flesh below her belly button.

"Well." She skimmed her palms up the silken weave of his shirt, her fingers touching his skin at the base of his neck. He was cool. Most vampires were warm thanks to frequent infusions of blood. They must both be hungry, she figured. "I guess I gave you time to come up with a plan, eh? Seduce the girl and get her to talk?"

Always make them believe they are the ones in control, and the ones with a plan. Seduction 101.

He dipped his head and landed a hard, firm kiss on her mouth. It was so unexpected that Lyric could only accept it, breathing in his breath, tinted with mint. Men did not take a kiss from her. The ice princess always kept them at arm's length. And she would prove it by…

Well, maybe a little longer. No sense in stopping what felt so good. Bad boys took what they wanted. She was willing to experience what she had always desired.

Too quickly, he broke the unsettling yet sigh-worthy contact. "Seduction tastes pretty good to me."

"Me, too."

Without thought, she returned his kiss but remembered she was playing a role. *Get smart, Lyric. Or you'll never ditch this guy.* This kiss must be the money play.

Lyric nudged open his mouth with her tongue and traced his clean, white teeth. Strong hands at her hips crushed her against him. His hard-on, thick and long, lay diagonally against her hip. Encouraging his arousal, she rubbed her hip against his erection and ran one hand down his back to press him even closer.

He moved deep within her, tasting her mouth, teeth and tongue, giving her the urgent intensity of contact she gave him. It was as if they were starving and had found sustenance in an enemy masked by desire.

Thinking of satisfying her blood hunger brought down her fangs. Amidst the crush of their mouths, Lyric's fang pricked her lower lip. She pulled from the kiss, wiped a finger over the blood, and then traced it along the inner side of Vail's lower lip.

He pushed her away, and she stumbled awkwardly to land against the wall, arms dumbly slapping it. "What the hell?"

Vail sucked at his lip and spit her blood onto the floor. "This isn't going to work."

"Seriously?" She followed his pace toward the window. "I get that we were both screwing with each other right now. But you…spit out my blood? I thought you were vampire?"

He spun on her, his overwhelming height shadowing the moon framed in the window. "I am."

Lyric touched the flesh beside his eye. "No, you're not. This isn't club glitter. You said you were familiar with Faery? You really are a dust freak."

## *CHAPTER FOUR*

FAERY ICHOR TO VAMPIRES was like meth to mortals. And once the vamp got a taste, he needed more, more and more. Lyric knew, because a dust freak had once worked for Charish, and had caused chaos for the few days he'd resided at the Santiago mansion.

"I just…do it to maintain," Vail said, with a stroke of his thumb across the black stuff smudging his eyes.

"Maintain?" Lyric didn't hide a shake of her head. "That's what they all say while they're lying in some dust den, sucking in the ichor. It's so obvious now. You have sparkle issues."

"Is that so? Well, you're avoiding the real issue. Like the fact there is no fence, and you expect I'm going to wait this out forever. Don't be stupid, Lyric."

"I'm not stupid. But neither am I willing to trust a dust freak."

He gripped her shoulder and spun her about. It hurt, his fingers digging into her skin, but she wasn't about to let him see her pain. Lyric pulled the ice princess on and stiffened her spine.

"I'm immune to dust," he said. "I've spent a lot of time in Faery. Now that I'm in the mortal realm, I need to take dust every now and then to maintain it in my body—otherwise I'd go through withdrawals."

"Sounds like an addict to me." She shoved him away.

A flash of moonlight glinted at the corner of his eye, like a beacon calling her to fix on his dark glamour. It wasn't worth the risk if he was a dust freak.

"This little dance we're doing is getting old, Vail. I'm tired, but most of all, I'm hungry."

"You tell me where to find the gown, and I'll let you out to scam for some blood."

"You won't offer me your own?"

"Would you take it?"

"No. Wouldn't want to have to *maintain* because of you."

If even a trace of faery ichor scurried through his veins, she'd taste it and she'd become addicted *like that*. Addiction was not something Lyric was willing to risk simply because the blood hunger currently tightened her veins and made her jittery.

"Let's make a deal," she said, smoothing a hand over her thigh to distract from the burgeoning shakes. "There's a club down the street. They play heavy metal and the blood is always hyped with adrenaline. Let's both go out and have a drink, then I'll tell you whatever you want to know."

"You tell me what I want to know, I'll let you out on a leash."

"Bastard."

"Ice princess."

"Oh, you use that tired old title, too? And here I was beginning to think you weren't like the rest of the male vampires. I'm going."

She started for the window, but he beat her to it, sliding across the bed before she could touch it.

"Fine." Vail parked himself on the windowsill, blocking her escape. He clasped his ringed fingers together and narrowed surprisingly compassionate eyes on her. "I know what it's like to hunger. You're not going to give me anything until you're satiated, relaxed."

"You got that right."

"I'm not a complete creep. I'll let you feed."

"Thank you."

"But we're not going inside the club. I need to keep you close. You try to get away, you're going to regret it."

"Ooh, you going to dust me with your sparkle juice?"

"You willing to take that chance?"

She met his steely blue gaze. Faery dust glittered about his eyes and in his hair. It must seep from his very pores. She wondered now if she'd gotten any on her hands, but did not look, because she didn't want to give him the satisfaction of seeing her flinch. A little skin contact wasn't going to make her high—the dust had to enter her veins. She hoped.

"I'm sure we can find a nice mortal couple in the parking lot. One for each of us," she said.

"I don't do mortals."

Comment wasn't necessary. That was apparent. The guy was fucked up, and that would make her escape a breeze. She just had to play along for a while. "Let's go."

HE DIDN'T TRUST HER as far as he could blow dust into the eyes of his enemies. And that was about five, six feet maximum.

After a five-minute walk they stood outside Club Vert. Hard, growling music pounded through the brick walls, and patrons danced outside the back doors, which were curvy and appealing, designed after the Art Nouveau style.

Vail and Lyric sat on the hood of a black Renault Mégane, watching the crowd shift in and out of the club. The interior was decorated in more Art Nouveau and plenty of green, Lyric explained. The club offered absinthe that mortals inhaled through a long straw, à la freebasing, as opposed to drinking. Provided a faster, cleaner high. Vail favored absinthe himself, but not extracted from mortal veins.

"Those two." Lyric jumped from the car and smoothed palms over her hips and down her backside.

Vail couldn't help but appreciate the tight curve of her derrière. The soft red dress conformed like skin on skin, emphasizing the slight cleft and the sexy dimples at the base of her spine. Those long legs had to end somewhere in the vicinity of her armpits. Legs like that could wrap around him and hold on for the ride.

Legs like that could also kick him in the jaw, which

he entirely anticipated should he put the moves on this wicked vixen.

"Not going to happen," he muttered, as he watched her approach the mortal pair who, hand in hand, searched for their car. They chatted with Lyric. She pointed over her shoulder at him. Vail offered a nod, hiding his disgust. The woman, a redhead sporting a nose ring and a bare midriff, smiled drunkenly.

He suspected Lyric had done this before. Not getting two mortals to succumb to a vampire foursome, but rather, lying to achieve a goal. She was lying to him about the fence. Had to be. But he could play her game. He must if he was ever to get the answers he needed.

The trio approached, the man's arm around his girlfriend's waist, and the other arm draped across Lyric's shoulders.

"Nice," Vail said to them as they walked by, leading him toward the end of the parking lot where the streetlight flickered and a dented black van sat parked in the corner.

Chain-link fencing surrounded the parking lot, bent up here and there to admit a person or a stray cat through the overgrown weeds that probably never saw a mower's blade. Security lights beamed over the entire lot, but here, the van shadowed their encounter.

Lyric was already cozying up to the man by the time Vail rounded the back of the van. The sight of her running her hands up the man's arms and whispering in his ear increased Vail's heartbeats. But for the life of Herne, he wasn't sure if it was arousal or—no, couldn't be jealousy.

The mortal woman threaded her arms about his shoulders and tugged him around toward the front of the van. She breathed whiskey onto his face. "You're sexy," she tried, enunciating carefully as drunks often did when they thought they could conceal their inebriation.

"And I love redheads," he replied, allowing her to kiss the corner of his mouth sloppily. Mortals. No attraction whatsoever.

Keeping an eye on Lyric, he nudged his nose along the woman's jaw, following the rapid pulse that did not call to him. It was just a heartbeat.

He bent closer to her skin, drawing in the acrid scent of whiskey, yet beneath that something deeper lingered. Life. It gushed and throbbed. So unique how mortal blood took on the scents and taint of the things they consumed and put on their bodies, which was why it did not attract him. Ichor remained pure, no matter what the sidhe had consumed.

Remembering his captive, Vail glanced aside, pushing curls of red hair away to better see. His ice princess hadn't bitten her mark yet; she was prolonging the tease, working the mortal to a sexual frenzy. Spiced with adrenaline, it must make the blood hotter, perhaps even tastier.

And yet, it was just a tease. Vail maintained the staunch insistence ichor was the only sustenance for him. And it was. But a weird part of him, something he didn't want to examine too closely, suddenly tilted his head down to inhale the scent of mortal blood. It didn't smell awful. Actually, it smelled appealing, whiskey and all.

What was that about?

The woman read his subtle exploration incorrectly, and palmed his cock through his leather pants. That both pissed him off and pushed him over the edge he'd been toeing since kissing Lyric earlier. The vampiress had gotten under his skin, and he had wanted to get under, into and all over her skin—until she'd touched her blood to his mouth.

He'd never take vampire blood.

Moans slipped from Lyric's mouth now, her mark matching the sensual tones. Scent of jasmine and cherries distracted Vail from the mortal woman's whiskey perfume. She kissed the edge of his mouth, but he didn't want her sloppy attempt at intimacy.

"Swoon for me," he whispered, penetrating her mind with persuasion. *You feel so good. Better than you've ever felt.*

"Kiss me back," she murmured. "Don't you want me?"

The persuasion was not working. Why couldn't he utilize the thrall in the mortal realm? Was it akin to the power Hawkes insisted he claim?

He considered dusting her, but mortals didn't drop like vamps, they usually went into a swoony kind of reel.

Pressing his fingers along her neck, he found the subclavian nerve below her clavicle and increased pressure. Just a second or two... Sleep took her quickly. She relaxed in his arms.

He dropped the woman noiselessly at his feet. He glanced to the van—the mortal man hugged the rear fender, delirious. Blood ran from his mouth.

The vampiress was gone.

Vail leaped over the sprawled female and tilted the man's head to the side. "Did she bite you?"

"Bite me? Dude, she punched me. Think she knocked out a tooth. What's up with that?"

What was up was that the wily vampiress had been waiting for him to drop his guard so she could escape.

"Stone-headed vampire!" he cursed himself.

Trotting along the row of parked cars, he spied a large gap in the chain link. Ducking through, Vail emerged in the pristine parking lot of a car dealer. Hundreds of cars were parked row after militant row. Perfect place for a vampiress to hide.

Vail kicked a tire and swore again. His cell phone rang and he angrily tugged it out from a front pocket and answered. "What?"

It was Rhys Hawkes wanting an update. At one o'clock in the morning. Their kind did keep odd hours.

"I had her. Yes, the Santiago chick. But I lost her." His eyes scanned the cars, searching for movement. She couldn't have gotten far. "Yes, I know. I'll get her back. But she says she fenced the dress."

"We need that bloody gown," Rhys muttered.

"When you find her, you put the screws to her to get her to talk. Torture her if you have to."

"With pleasure. I'll call you tomorrow, Hawkes," he said, and snapped the phone shut.

Torture, eh? This job was turning into a real riot.

A rail train rumbled by, the horn blaring as it passed a nearby crossing. Ducking and eyeing the cars at hood and trunk level, Vail didn't spy anything out of place. So, he lay on his back, looking heavenward. He turned his head left. No feet or crouched bodies tucked behind a wheel. And then right. A pair of red heels peeked out from behind a rear tire. "Gotcha."

LYRIC WOKE AND WRINKLED her nose. Mildew. Smelled like that damned awful bed in the apartment where she'd been squatting.

Her wrists stung and her jaw hurt. Then she remembered looking up at Vail's kick-ass snakeskin boots. He'd found her crouched behind an SUV. Thanks to a passing train, she hadn't heard his approach. Asshole.

She worked her jaw back and forth, wincing. When she tried to reach for the painful spot, her hands tugged against something that wouldn't budge.

She tilted her head back. Her wrists were bound to an old iron headboard with a leather belt. She lay on the bed. Bound.

## *CHAPTER FIVE*

"GET ME OFF HERE!"

"Now, now." Vail's teasing grin appeared above Lyric's face. He must have been sitting right beside the bed the whole time. He stroked her cheek. "We've fun stuff to do before I release you. I'm going to make you sing the name of your fence."

Letting out a frustrated growl, Lyric blurted, "Never happen."

"We'll see."

He produced a knife from inside one of his boots and flicked out the blade. Like that was supposed to scare her? Pressing the tip to the neckline of her dress, he performed a deft move that opened the jersey to reveal her breasts.

"Pretty. And no lacy things to hide them. Bet you like to have them licked, eh?"

"If you touch me…"

"What? You'll succumb to my command? You'll cream in the pretty little panties I know you're not wearing? How easily do you come, Lyric? Just a few licks?"

The arrogance of him!

He leaned down and lashed his tongue across one of her nipples. Despite her anger, Lyric gasped. His slick, wet tongue sent shivers through her breasts and arms. Mercy, that felt good.

She twisted her head away from his keen observation of her every flinch. "Don't do this."

"You want me to stop?" Blue eyes sought hers, his mouth but a breath from her wet nipple. "Tell me your fence's name."

"Never."

His tongue lashed slowly about her nipple, taking exquisite time in circling it, and then he sucked it in.

Lyric squeezed her eyelids shut and held back another breathy gasp. Nothing felt better than this. If this was his method of torture, she could get behind it one hundred percent. But the only talking she'd be doing was a bold cry when she came.

His teeth grazed her other nipple. Her chest hummed and the tingle of want shot down to her belly and lower. She tugged against the restraints. This was not fair!

A languorous suckle drew up a moan to her tongue. She arched her back to receive further torture, but when she didn't feel the next lash of heat, she opened her eyes to find him waiting for her.

"You want it?" he teased.

"Hell, no." She sank into the bed. Two could play this game. But the air cooling her wet nipples only worked to tighten them more and increase her desire. "Thought you didn't like vampires?"

"I don't drink their blood. But I can appreciate a gorgeous woman, vampire or not. And your breasts are—stone me, they are perfection. I guess that makes me a breast man, eh?"

Hallelujah! *Oh, Lyric, don't succumb.*

The next lash devastated her stalwart resistance and Lyric lifted her chest to accept his exquisite punishment. Her fingers curled about the leather strap binding her hands, but being bound no longer frightened her—it turned her on.

His tongue was hot and masterful, and he made it soft and then firm to draw it expertly across her flesh. So close to some kind of giddy release, she pressed her legs together but couldn't quite achieve the squeeze that would make her come.

"Not a tough torturer, if you ask me," she said on short breaths.

"Torturers, by nature, get off on their jobs. I'm no different. This is really getting you off, isn't it?"

"Bloody Mary," she swore.

"Uh-uh. One shouldn't invoke the name of the dark prince's girlfriend unless they wish Himself to pay a visit."

"I'd prefer him over you right now."

"Oh, I doubt it."

True. Himself was *the* devil. No vampire ever invoked his name three times unless they wanted to deal with Hell.

Vail sat back and hooked a finger at the vee in her dress where the cut ended just above her belly button. With a tug, the jersey parted down to the hem. "Doesn't take much to get you wet, eh?"

Lyric struggled against the belt. She was strong, but so was leather.

She held her thighs tightly together as his fingers trailed the crease formed between each leg and her mons. The soft tickle of his fingers felt—damn, it felt great. And the skim of his cold metal rings stirred her flesh to goose bumps.

Her hard, ruched nipples pleaded for more attention, and he noticed. Vail flicked his thumb over one of them. Much to her horror, Lyric gasped. She couldn't stop from showing her arousal. Damn her. And damn him.

"I like the taste of your skin," he said, and lowered his mouth to her breast again.

He suckled her as if he was enjoying a dessert, rolling her nipple between his lips and tonguing it rapidly, then more slowly, then tending her entire breast. He kissed every curve of each of her breasts until she wondered if a woman could come simply from breast stimulation alone. It was beginning to feel possible.

And she didn't notice she'd relaxed her legs until she felt the soft trace of Vail's finger mount the apex of her thighs. Testing, teasing, taunting her with his presence, the promise of something more.

She moved her legs together, but a slap of his palm to her thigh stopped her.

"Keep them open," he said around her nipple. "You want this, Lyric."

She shook her head. *Oh, yes, you do.*

A lift of his eyebrow provided the sexiest expression she had ever seen on a man. And the curl at the right side of his mouth was this bad boy's signature move. Devastating. "Then stop me," he said.

Stopping him meant giving him the information he wanted. Not as easy as he imagined it could be. Especially if no name existed. But she wasn't about to reveal that little white one.

Because that would make him stop.

Letting out a moan, Lyric didn't care if the ice princess mutinied. Desire undermined her resolve and weakened her concern for secrecy. Besides, without a secret name to reveal, she needn't worry about shouting it out at the brink of climax.

And, oh…there. She sucked in her lower lip as Vail's finger slowly entered her wet depths, and then moved back out to slick across her clitoris. Softly exploring. A rub back and forth, and a slow but firm slide in the other direction. All sensation hummed at her core, bringing her closer…

He needed to press deeper, to focus on her ultrasensitive apex, yet he merely teased. Around in circles, and along her folds, and returning to her swollen clit to demonstrate what she could have if only…

If only.

"You like this, Lyric?"

"Yes," she gasped, then closed her eyes and shook her head. She didn't want to talk. Satisfaction. That's what she needed. Why wouldn't he give it to her? "You do, too, Vail."

"Of course I do. Your body is amazing, your breasts

so full." He kissed each one, following with a lick. "Your nipples are so hard I could suck them for hours, devour them like the cherries of which you smell."

Please do, she thought. Don't ever stop. She was still so hungry, having forgone the mortal's blood. Climax would be a fine replacement for what she craved.

"And you're so wet. You like it when I put my finger inside you?"

She nodded, breaths coming as rapid whimpers.

"Right here," he whispered, his lips against her neck now, right over the vein. Still his finger merely circled the spot she wanted him to master. "A little harder?"

"Please," she chirped.

"Pretty please?"

"Mmm," she managed. "Vail, please."

And then his finger was gone. The tingle at her nipple ceased. The heat of his mouth left her skin.

Lyric breathed, waiting. Her body hummed, wanting, desiring, needing.

"Name," he said sternly.

Fuck. No. She couldn't. She didn't have—

She wanted. She needed to get off. Squirming on the bed, she couldn't manage to bring her hips up to meet his hovering hand. The bastard wouldn't bring her to the brink like this and then walk away, would he?

So the torturer did know his craft.

If her hands were free, she'd finish herself off and not be the least ashamed. Pressing her thighs together, she mined the sweet hum of orgasm. It remained elusive, demanding Vail's direct and firm touch.

"Uh-uh." He nudged her thighs apart. "Not that way, sweetie. You want to come? Name."

"Vincent Lambert," she blurted out. Hell, she'd seen the last name on a movie poster recently, and the first name was common enough.

The mattress jiggled as Vail stood and strode to the counter. Grabbing the cell phone, he punched in some numbers.

Lyric crashed, heaving and gasping as if tears would spill free. The high of arousal withered away and her flesh prickled again, not from desire, but from the lack of touch, of expected satisfaction. Her wet nipples cooled and the aching loss of heat softened them. She pressed her legs together.

*No.* Not worth it now without him directing the fireworks. And she wouldn't let him witness her weakness. God, how had she managed to get herself into a situation like this? So vulnerable!

She twisted her wrists within the leather strap, to no avail.

Vail asked the operator to give him the address of Vincent Lambert.

Good luck with that.

"Thanks," he said, and hung up. "You're in luck. There's a Vincent Lambert in the fourteenth quarter. Got the address."

Seriously? Whew.

Vail walked to the bed and loomed over her, hands propped at his hips. "Now, what to do with you?"

SHE'D GIVEN HIM what he'd requested. He should head out for the fourteenth and nab the gown from the fence. Return the damned thing to Hawkes, hand over the girl to Mommy, and then he could finally get the information he wanted from his uncle.

One problem.

The naked woman lying on the bed before him writhed and gasped with the need to get off. And he wanted to help her with that. Because those soft, round breasts surely required more licking. And her molten hot body demanded he fill her with the hard-on he'd suffered for the past twenty minutes.

What had become of his hatred for vampires?

*You don't have to bite her.*

And there was nothing wrong with a vampire in general, just their nasty blood. Right? He'd never slept with a vampire. Had avoided them since arriving in the mortal realm.

But he didn't have to bite when he had sex. It was a great accompaniment to the whole shebang, but unnecessary. And besides, who would know if he screwed a vampire this one time?

Vail unbuttoned his shirt and tossed it aside.

She squirmed and tugged against the leather belt strapping her to the headboard. "Too late, you junkie asshole. I don't need it anymore."

"Yeah?" He flicked open the button on his pants and tugged down the fly. His heavy erection sprang out. Her eyes widened—and not in anger. "We'll see about that."

Retrieving the knife from his back pocket, he sat

on the edge of the bed. Knife in his fist, he skimmed his knuckles over her taut stomach, toying with her fear and desire at the same time. He let the hard ivory handle of the knife rub her nipple as he moved higher.

She reacted with vicious struggles. He'd lost her when making the phone call—a necessary delay from the torture—but he could get her back.

"Settle, Lyric, you don't want me to cut you."

"You wouldn't," she retorted. "Wouldn't want to get any of my nasty blood on you."

She was smart. But he could be smarter.

He pressed his other hand over her mons, fingertips lightly brushing the soft wet folds she kept shaved bare, and her body reacted by arching her back. Much as she thought she didn't want this, her body did. She straddled a tightrope, and one wrong step would send her reeling into the stratosphere or crashing to earth.

He preferred the reel, because that would make it good for him, too.

He slid the blade under the leather belt securing her wrists. This particular blade had been forged in Faery and was sharper than any mortal metal could be honed. Her wrists, unbound, fell to the bed and she grasped for one to ease her fingers about it.

"Sorry, if you lost the feeling in them," he muttered.

Vail dropped the knife on the floor and placed his fingers between her thighs. He pushed them deep into her while, with his thumb, he found the soft swollen heat he knew controlled her entire body. It was command central, so to speak, and he knew how to operate the controls.

Before she could struggle away, he flicked out a finger and rubbed it over her slick clitoris, sweeping the sensitive bud until he heard a gasp, followed quickly by a surrendering sigh. Her fingers clutched at the tattered old mattress. Her legs opened wider.

"Good girl. Now let me taste how sweet you are."

Ignoring the aching pulse in his erection, he told himself patience would win him the reward as he slid down to kiss her cherry jasmine skin.

The first lick started a shudder in her thighs. He dipped his tongue around her clitoris and played with the hard bud of it, making his tongue pointed to trace it firmly.

It was the right move because her fingers released hold on the mattress and clutched at air. She moaned, "Yes," and her fingers found his hair and gripped hanks of it tightly. "Right there."

Steadily, he played her, stroking and dashing his tongue against softness, then hard, to follow with a firm lick. She smelled like a jasmine garden here, and he was reminded of the faery ritual before the bride walked down the aisle. The bride-to-be would spend the day being pampered and perfumed, at one point squatting over an incense burner to infuse all parts of her skin with heady scent.

*Don't think about that stolen moment. Concentrate. Or you'll begin to regret.*

Kicking the door shut on memory, Vail soared back

to the present and into his captive's lushness. Lyric's scent dizzied him. It was almost better than a dust high.

The vampiress cried out boldly. Her hips bucked and the fingers in his hair tugged painfully before releasing him.

He had pleased her. The hot spill of her over his fingers thrilled him. He sucked each digit clean, but was jumbled upon the mattress as she sat and reached for him.

She pushed down his pants and gripped his erection. "Now. Inside me. You know you want it, vampire."

He sucked one last finger clean. "Just waiting for the invitation to cross your threshold."

"If that's the way you ask for an invite, you'll never be turned down."

Kicking off his boots and slipping down his leather pants, Vail then plunged into her depths and the dull mortal world changed colors. The faery dust highs he was accustomed to grew shallow and insignificant when immersed within Lyric. So tight, she hugged him as he moved in and out of her. Grasping him. Claiming him. It wasn't going to take long for him to come, but he wanted to prolong the exquisite torture.

She'd turned the tables on him. Apparently, this seductive brand of torture could be sallied back and forth. He didn't mind. This was all about finding the sweet spot. Mastering the moment.

Winning her trust.

Vail's muscles clenched and his body trembled above Lyric's gorgeous limbs. Her skin glowed pale under the moonlight. Her lips, so red from kissing, parted. She was his. He'd challenge any man who claimed differently.

Tensing his jaw, he waited as the orgasm focused in his muscles and segued at his core. He released, ramming himself deep within her to ride the wave.

SUNLIGHT TEASED Lyric awake. She hated the sun. It would burn her if she stood beneath direct rays. Prolonged UV exposure could drive a vampire mad. Even this pale stuff beaming through the dirty window could prove deadly with longer exposure.

She rolled away from the obnoxious light and her body hugged against Vail's naked form. He lay on his side, facing her, his eyes open. He touched her mouth. A lash of her tongue in the wake of his touch tasted sex and salt and something sweet that she thought might be faery dust.

"You going to track down the fence today?" she asked.

"No reason to bother. It's a ruse. You made up the name. I knew it before I even made the call."

"Then why—why can't you let me go?"

"Told you." He gripped her around the nape of her neck, but not threateningly. His finger touched her behind the ear, and she cautioned herself against making a fast move. Some secrets were best kept. "I need the gown, Lyric."

This guy had a one-track mind, and the replay was growing old fast. "If you had the gown would you let me go?"

"Do you have a gown to give me?"

She rolled to her back, wincing at the sunlight. He thumbed her nipple, but she batted his hand away.

"That was the best sex I've had. Ever," he said, sitting and reaching for his pants. "Thanks."

She closed her eyes. Men were not supposed to thank a woman for having sex. That was wrong on every imaginable level. So much for bad-boy fantasies. He'd used her.

But she had used him, too.

The best ever? Poor guy, didn't get around much, did he? On the other hand, it had been so freakin' good. Her best ever? She wouldn't admit it to herself.

"I suppose if I take a shower, you'll dodge out the window."

"You know it," she answered.

"I need to go home, shower, and change my clothes. After lying on this bed, I feel…crusty. Which means you'll be coming with me, sweetie."

"I'm not your sweetie."

"No, you're not." He exhaled and stood.

Lyric gazed at his bare back and ass. The hard muscles that flexed with his movement defined the dimples at the top of his buttocks. Nice. Without warrant, she imagined him inside her again, pumping hard, filling her, his jaw clenched, and bringing her to climax. A shiver traced through her system.

"Yeah, it was as good as you remember," he commented over his shoulder.

Lyric leaned up on an elbow. "You know you just had sex with a vampire."

"I know."

"You ever do that before?"

"Nope."

Wow. Most vamps socialized with one another, and a lot dated vampires exclusively and used mortals for sex only when biting them.

"Any regrets?" she asked.

Shimmying up his pants and carefully tucking away his semihard penis as he zipped, Vail shrugged. "Actually, no, no regrets."

"You seem surprised."

He picked up her dress and tossed it over her breasts, then leaned in and kissed her on the mouth, slow, delving, most definitely not a regretful kiss.

"I am," he said. Another quick kiss. "You've only just met me, but I'm sure you've determined a vampire would not be my first choice to bed."

"Faeries first?"

He shrugged. "Anything but vampires."

Way to make her feel sexy and appreciated. Not.

"We were just using each other," she felt the need to say. It was an ingrained response.

No man had ever looked at her and seen Lyric, the girl who wanted to live in a faery-tale castle. The girl who wanted to travel the world, and live on a tropical island where the houses had no walls and the sand was white. The girl who spent her free time tucked away in a quiet gym in the second arrondissement, suspended upside down from silken fabric because joining the circus was also a real dream.

No, suitors had always seen the advantages to

aligning themselves to the Santiago clan. Lyric expected others to use her.

"Don't sweat it," she offered by rote.

Vail grabbed her hands as she inspected the torn dress. "Don't sell yourself short."

His dark eyes were still smudged with black liner this morning and it drew her focus to the gorgeous blue irises. "What we did last night started out as a means to get what I wanted from you," he said. "But do you seriously believe fucking a woman is the wisest way to conduct an investigation?"

The kiss touched her at the corner of her mouth, sweet yet lingering, as if wanting to imprint his mark for the world to see every time her smile curled.

She'd been imprinted once already. Lyric twisted her head away from Vail's touch. She didn't want another imprint, and needed one like a bullet through her brain right now.

"It was good, Lyric. But I don't think either of us should beat ourselves up trying to figure the whys and hows of it. It happened. We enjoyed it. Now we step back into our roles."

"You bad guy, me fleeing you?"

"Something like that. Let's go."

"Where?" The dress was a loss. She scanned the floor for her shoes. "Oh right, your place. Why do I have to go along?"

"You think your place is so swanky?" he teased. "The bed was…fragrant."

She slid off the thing, stunned she'd made love on it, and had snuggled next to the man for a good part of the morning. Yuck. Well, it had been a means to hide out. It wasn't that she'd intended to live here.

"Fine. I'll go along for the ride. But you're not going to trick me and drive me home to Mommy, are you?"

"Can't. You're staying with me until I can figure out what deal Charish Santiago made with Zett. Unless you want to make it easy and just tell me?"

"Can't tell you what I don't know. Why is knowing the deal important?"

"Because I know Zett," he said, walking into the bathroom to retrieve her duffel. He dug out the shirt and black pants she'd worn last night and tossed them to her. "The Lord of Midsummer Dark has no interest in vampires. Vampires are the lowest of the low to faeries."

Lyric tugged the shirt on, then bowed her head. Lowest of the low? Tell her about it.

"Which makes me wonder what mommy dearest was supposed to get in return for the dress. I can't imagine Zett would have been too generous, even for such a valuable dress."

"Gown."

"Whatever."

Lyric was about to explain that her mother had gotten the immunity to step into Faery and take as she pleased, but then she stopped herself. As Vail had mentioned, faery items were of little value in the mortal realm.

Why *did* the Santiagos need to steal from Faery? True, they were nearly bankrupt, but it wasn't as though any item taken from the Faery realm could be fenced to any but the sidhe. And sidhe currency had no value among the mortals.

"What's going on in that pretty skull of yours?" Vail asked.

Lyric turned a discerning gaze to him. "I'm not sure anymore. I think you're right. My mother is up to more than I can imagine."

# *CHAPTER SIX*

IT ALL HINGED on Vail gaining Lyric's trust so she would eventually give him the gown. He knew shc had it. An item so valuable as the gown would definitely stir up talk if it should surface with a fence or in the hands of a buyer.

Unless the vampiress had faery contacts? Hmm… he doubted it. Lyric and Zett as allies didn't jive. And yet, what if they had previously met?

Why she was so tight-lipped about it was not hard to figure. She must view the gown as a bargaining chip or a means to a new start. Hell, from what he knew of the Santiago family, it wasn't a place for anyone to grow up, let alone survive.

He could relate.

Which meant Vail had an idea how to win Lyric's trust. Because sex was just that, a means to let off aggression and steam. To get off. It wasn't going to enamor him to her. And anyone who believed trust was gained by sharing a bed and a few throaty gasps of pleasure was fooling himself.

Though he wouldn't mind another round—in a clean bed. That woman's skin…yippi-i-oo!

He opened the car's passenger door and Lyric got in. Swinging around to the driver's side, Vail hopped inside, slid on a pair of Ray-Bans and switched on the engine. The Maserati purred, and he wanted to pat the dashboard and tell her how sweet she was, but the sexy leg distracted him.

Lyric kicked off her high heels and put one bare foot up on the dashboard. He wished the clingy black slacks were a skirt, but he could still recall those legs wrapped around his hips. She leaned back in the seat and closed her eyes, making herself at home with a contented hum.

Vail slid a palm along her leg and the vampiress purred as sweetly as the car. She didn't open her eyes, and he suspected she'd let him touch her as long as he wanted to. Maybe even higher…

He shifted into gear and rolled the Maserati into traffic, before returning his hand to her thigh. He teased a fold in the thin fabric with his smallest finger.

"So you want to know what's up with my mom and the Unseelie lord?" she asked, eyes still closed. The windows had been shaded and treated against UV rays before Hawkes had given it to him, but he figured she was tired after last night's adventures. "Why? I thought you wanted to find the ugly gown and drop me off on Mommy's doorstep?"

"To gain your trust," he said. No reason to sugar-coat things.

"Learning what secrets lurk in my family will gain my trust?"

"I'm giving you a bone, Lyric. I haven't taken you to Mommy's doorstep, which should gain me some points." Turning at a light, he headed toward the tenth arrondissement, where he lived. He didn't signal, and a passing Smart Car laid on the horn. Vail nodded at the driver, but ignored the nasty hand gesture. "And because I'm a curious guy when it comes to anyone from Faery making deals with a vampire. You have no clue what the deal was?"

"Nada."

"How is that possible when you agreed to do the exchange with the guy? You had to have expected something in return."

She grabbed his hand, stopping his constant strokes, but didn't move him away from her thigh. "I've already told you I had ulterior motives. When Charish told me she'd made a deal with Zett to trade the gown for services—"

"Services?"

She shrugged. "That's all I know."

Ch'yeah—no. She was lying, but if he let her talk, sooner or later she'd get trapped in her lies and reveal the truth. Because, apparently, torture worked for neither of them.

"Anyway, after they'd made the deal, the faery lord insisted I deliver the gown."

"And his reason was…?"

"Mother assumed he wanted to keep us on our toes and add the element of danger. Send a helpless woman instead of some capable demon thugs. And it also provided the added threat of locating the exchange site next to a faery portal."

"And you had no problem with that?"

"Like any sane vampire, I freaked. I refused."

"And yet…?"

She toyed with the rings on his fingers, and he liked the soft tickle of it, and that she hadn't moved his hand from her thigh.

"I thought about it a few days," she finally said, "and realized this was an opportunity I couldn't pass up. I planned the kidnapping to take myself out of the equation."

"Why didn't you just refuse?"

"Zett was adamant. And my mother really needed this."

Curious. "Yet your plans, beyond getting out of the house with the gown, seem to have stopped right there."

Lyric sighed and turned to face him. He smoothed his palm along her leg, reassuring—yet she tugged him right back to the sweet spot high on her thigh where he didn't mind being at all.

"I had the apartment," she said, "and had intended to decide on a country or state where I could go hide out for a few years. Leo, my brother, was going to help me. It's not so easy to disappear when your mother runs a network of thieves that stretch across Europe and the United States. I was thinking either Russia or the Arctic."

He twisted to gape at her.

Lyric laughed. "I know! I couldn't be happy in either place. I need to be around people who are modern and, well, I'm still working that part of the plan out. Joining the circus was another option. You ever see the Demon Arts troupe? They are fantastic."

"Really? You? The circus?"

She nodded enthusiastically. "Actually, a tropical island would be my number-one choice, but I don't think there are too many available for sale."

"You'd be surprised. I bet you could buy your own little island, if you wanted to."

"What a dream. One needs cash to buy freedom. The Santiago family is broke. Don't get me wrong, I've got my mother. And, hell, I should have stayed to help her out, but she can't see beyond her fiancé Connor's influence. I hate to see her lose her freedom…."

Her sigh entered his pores and scurried about inside his chest. She wanted to get lost on a deserted island? Didn't sound like such a good life if she was alone, without anyone to please her.

"So why did you feel the need to get away from Mommy? I mean, it seems like the faery lord should have been your only worry."

"There are just some things I haven't told her. I… didn't know where to begin. And this all happened so quickly. Escape seemed the easiest option until I could work things out."

He tapped his fingers gently over her mons, and she tilted her leg out to give him better access. Vail slid his hand between her legs where it was warm. The car swerved. He avoided missing another stoplight by pulling a sharp right turn.

"So you didn't expect anyone to look for you?" he asked.

"I figured Charish would send out someone to find me, but I didn't think you'd find me so fast. I'll be at Mommy's soon enough, thanks to you, so why bother with the dreams?"

"You're giving up that easily?"

"Not giving up. Just…so ready for a little respect." She sighed and dropped her foot to the floor. At the same time she brushed his hand away, and he retreated.

She didn't say more, and Vail felt pushing wasn't the right move at the moment. The woman wanted something everyone should have. He could relate, in a manner. But when he felt he didn't get respect, he took it. Not the smartest way to do it, he knew. People like Lyric's mother took things and expected others to respect them for it.

Probably Constantine de Salignac had been cut from the same cloth.

*I need to find the gown if I ever want to find that bastard.*

Taking a sharp corner, the Maserati nipped the concrete sidewalk pole on the corner.

"You are the worst— Do you even know how to drive?" she asked.

"I've been driving for three months. I think I do pretty well."

"Three mon— Did you take lessons?"

"Ch'yeah right."

Lyric shook her head. "That explains all the dents in this pretty baby."

"She is my baby," he agreed, finally comfortable with patting the dashboard. "And she doesn't mind a little rough handling."

"You're not so rough as you like to think, vampire."

His jaw tensed at that title. He was not vampire, he was…just not.

Vail pulled into the car park below his building, wondering how this vampire ice princess was able to get under his skin with such ease.

"THE BATHROOM IS DOWN THE HALL," Vail said as they entered his loft apartment and he handed her the duffel he'd carried in. "You can shower first. I have a call to make."

Lyric dangled her shoes on her fingers and padded about the space. "Nice. Very…industrial."

Indeed, all the furniture was gray velvet, the floors were high-gloss black marble, and the walls and appliances were burnished steel. Vail liked the hard edges of it all. It wasn't cozy or homey, just there. Completely the opposite of most things in Faery. A serviceable means to exist in a world he'd not yet decided if he preferred over Faery.

"What I expected from you." She wiggled her toes and inspected her shadow dashing across the marble floor. "Especially since you like to work the goth-vampire-lord look to the hilt."

Vail ran a hand over his hair. "Far from it."

"Right. Because you don't like vampires. And yet, you are one. I don't even want to figure that out." She sauntered down the hallway to the bathroom.

Flicking the window shade switch activated the electrochromic shades and gave a calm, gray tone to the room. Vail plopped onto the sofa and waited until he heard the water spatter the bathroom tiles before dialing up Hawkes Associates.

"Vail, you find her again?"

"Yes, I have her in hand."

"For how long this time?"

He rubbed his forehead. The old man knew how to go right for the jugular. Damned half-breed vamp. "Until it comes time to bring her in."

"What's wrong with right now?"

"What's wrong is, I still don't have the gown. I need to gain her trust, because I know she's got it hidden somewhere."

"Torture didn't work?"

Oh, how it had worked. He'd never had a taste for torture after witnessing it a few times in Faery, but the kind he'd used last night? Hallelujah, to the mortal Christ! And that was saying a lot for someone raised with sidhe spiritual values.

"Torture proved ineffective in getting me closer to the ultimate goal. I think the key is to learn what deal Santiago made with Zett. Santiago gives Zett the gown, and Zett hands over…something. Whatever that something is, is the key."

"Why did the daughter have to deliver the gown? I thought faeries didn't like vampires?"

Why, indeed? That was the part where Vail sensed Lyric began to weave her lies. But knowing she'd never had any intention of going peacefully to Faery gave her a little credit.

"It baffles me," he said simply. "I need to investigate further."

"We're not a detective agency, Vaillant," Rhys cautioned Vail in a fatherly tone that irritated him. "We store valuables. If one of those valuables gets lost, we find it. Don't get in over your head. Find the gown and bring it in, along with the girl."

"I'll gain the girl's trust by learning her mother's secret. I know it. I'm going to ask around the faery clubs later. See if there are whispers."

"Be careful."

"Don't worry, old man."

"I do worry."

Vail closed his eyes. Rhys had a certain tone of truth that touched his core like no one had ever touched him before. As if he was trying to play the father role when he had no right. No man had that right, not even his real father.

"Don't let the vampiress pull the wool over your eyes, Vail. Remember who her family is."

"Won't happen. I can see all, remember."

"Faeries, yes. But backstabbing vampires?"

"I see their red auras when they are coming."

"Really? Vail, I didn't know you had the Sight."

"What's that?"

"Vampires can't tell one from the other without feeling the shimmer. But if you can see their auras, that means you've the Sight. Usually only witches have it."

"I've always seen the auras. Yeah, okay. Talk to you later."

He set down the phone and closed his eyes. The Sight and the shimmer? He knew what the shimmer was. It was a tingly sensation vampires were supposed to feel when they touched one another, confirming they were in the presence of another vamp. Now he thought about it, he hadn't felt it when touching Lyric.

Had she felt it when touching him?

Come to think of it, he hadn't noticed her aura, either. That was odd.

The water had stopped and Vail jumped as Lyric tiptoed into the room. She now wore a tight-fitted green dress that looked as if it had been sewn to her curves, no shoes and a tumble of dry blond curls.

Still no ashy, red aura. Weird. On the other hand, all his vampiric senses had altered slightly since stepping into the mortal realm.

"I just took a quickie. Your turn, if you want to shower," she said.

Vail grabbed her arm and spun her about to sit on the chrome barstool. Opening the drawer under the bar, he took out the handcuffs and, before she could question what was happening, secured her to the metal rail edging the bar.

"What the hell?"

"I don't trust you're going to sit tight while I'm in the shower."

She tugged against the wooden handcuffs. "Are you serious? I'll break these like a child's toy."

"I wouldn't try. They're fashioned from the wood of wild roses."

"You asshole!"

Wild roses, when planted by a witch, were excellent vampire deterrents. Or they could be used to contain a vampire, if needed. Vail had been schooled in Faery, and Other Societies 101 had covered all subjects, including the paranormals of the mortal realm.

"If the wood is broken or slivers," he warned, "you get a nasty sensation of thorns prickling through your entire body. If you think the torture I gave you last night was rough, contemplate that."

"Did I mention you are an asshole?"

"Sorry, sweetie, just taking precautions." He kissed her nose, paused to inhale her cherry perfume, and then touched her chin. Nope, no shimmer. "Do you…?"

"What?"

"Never mind." He strolled down the hall, and called, "I won't be long."

He'd wanted to ask if she felt his shimmer, but suspected with his reduced abilities he possibly did not send out such vibrations to another vampire.

He wanted to feel Lyric's shimmer. More than he wanted to solve this mystery.

WITH HER FREE HAND, Lyric gripped the vampire by his crisp black shirt collar after he strode around the corner and gave her a wink. "Not long?"

"What?" He had the audacity to feign innocence.

"That was the longest shower in the history of mankind *and* the paranormal nations. I thought you'd fallen and knocked your head and were bleeding out on the tiles."

"It was twenty minutes, tops."

"It was forty-five freakin' minutes!"

"Why so upset?"

She tugged at the handcuffs—carefully. Just thinking about what the rosewood could do to her had kept her fuming over his nerve, his utter lack of compassion. They had shared some great sex. Shouldn't he be a little softer on her?

Vail retrieved a key from the drawer—that had been right in front of her—drawing out the action nice and slow, then unlocked her.

"Bastard." Rubbing her wrists, which were not abraded or sore in any way, she stomped to the gray velvet couch and sat down.

"I thought it was *asshole*," he volleyed. "Does *bastard* move me up or down the scale of unsavory villains?"

"It's about equal. But you do that again and you'll definitely slide down."

"I'll remember that. Though, sliding down before you would not be a burden."

He stepped over to the couch and stood in front of her. "What do you say?"

Lyric sucked in her lower lip. He slicked back his moist hair with both hands, which spread his open silk shirt to reveal the hard abs and pecs she'd licked only hours earlier. Silver snakeskin pants hugged low on his hips to reveal the delicious, defined cut of his abdomen muscles and a dusting of dark hair. Bare feet rocketed the sexy level of his look right out of this world.

Had he just said something about sliding down before her?

*Yes, please.*

And that quirk of his eyebrow was so dangerously sexy. The sexy rocker with a dark glamour look worked for her. Frustratingly, Lyric couldn't stay angry with him, because the whole package was too enticing. If not strangely sparkly.

He buttoned up his shirt and took a step back. Not about to slide down to his knees now. Bummer.

"How long does a guy have to live in Faery to sparkle like you do?"

He strolled into the kitchen and flicked on the coffee machine. "All his life."

"Really?" Lyric moved onto her knees and leaned her elbows on the back of the couch. "Why Faery? How'd you get there?"

He pressed the grind button and the noise obliterated the quiet for five long seconds. Slipping a glass pot into the machine, he pushed Start.

"I was taken to Faery two days after my birth by a faery named Cressida, Mistress of Winter's Edge."

He regarded her curious look. "I was payment for a boon."

"No way. Like a changeling child or something?"

"Sort of. Not really. I don't call myself a changeling, because I'm not. Those things are mentally unbalanced."

And this vampire, who hated vampires and feared drinking their blood, and who had such a bad-boy appearance, wasn't a little touched in the head?

He leaned a hip against the kitchen counter and crossed his arms over his chest. "You really want to hear this?"

She nodded eagerly. "Your plan was to gain my trust."

Vail bowed his head, considering. Lyric had the distinct feeling she tread in dangerous emotional territory, and that it was too soon to do this with a guy who only had plans to use her. But right now, with the two of them alone, she felt a connection to him. And she wanted to learn all she could about the mysterious vampire whose kisses made her squirm in delight.

"Fine." He heeled the counter behind him with the pad of his foot. "My mother gave birth to me and my brother at the same time. But we're not twins. We each had a different father."

"How does that work?"

"I don't want to think about it too much, but I know my mother slept with two different guys within a week of each other. It happens. Children born from the same womb, at the same time, but with different fathers."

"That's interesting. So your brother is a vampire, too?"

"Werewolf." He chuckled at her dropped jaw. "My brother's father is Rhys Hawkes, a half-breed—half wolf, half vampire—who owns Hawkes Associates. He's the guy who hired me to track you and the gown. But I'm sure you know a lot about Hawkes Associates, don't you?"

She didn't respond. The things he thought he knew about her and her family were close, but not quite on the mark. No reason to make it too easy for him.

"Hawkes is also my uncle. My father..."

His entire frame stiffened, and Lyric noted his jaw pulsed. This was the pricking point. And man, did she ache to know more.

"Well, let's just say he was a bloodborn vampire," Vail said quietly. A heavy sigh, and he switched feet against the counter. He was so obviously uncomfortable revealing information about himself. "My mother was bloodborn, as well. So there you have it."

"So are your mother and father close? Does she live with him or with Rhys Hawkes?"

"She is married to Hawkes. My father is not in the picture."

"Oh. But you and he get along?"

"Me and my father? Never met him. My mother is insane," he stated flatly, and turned to tend the coffee machine, which didn't need tending; it was still brewing. "And my father made her that way. I've been in the mortal realm three months, and I've never met him, or my mother. And that's the end of that story."

"Your father made your mother insane? How?"

"Done talking," he called over his shoulder.

"Sure, but not done prying over here." The side view of his face revealed a grin, so Lyric dared to push further. "Pretty please? I told you about my mother."

"Not much. As for you and your history…"

"You don't need to know anything about me until I get more about you."

He left the coffee cups on the counter and strolled over to where she leaned on the back of the couch. "I know one important thing about you."

"And what's that?"

Leaning in close to her face so his lips brushed her ear, he said, "When I put my fingers inside you and curl them forward, back and forth, slow and fast, you come loud and proud."

He returned to the coffee machine. And Lyric's heart hovered somewhere around throat level. His breathy whisper had achieved a partial result to what he'd just described. Her core throbbed for his expert touch. The man had talent. And yes, she had never come like that for a man before.

Something about Vail melted her icy exterior, and she didn't feel her self-imposed guardrails so necessary. Yet she knew he could possibly be the most dangerous opponent she had faced. Because if he thought she held only the one secret, he was sadly mistaken.

She should have never made love with him. Because now they did have a connection, and disregarding that wasn't going to be easy.

"Coffee?" he offered.

What had the man asked? When he smiled like that the one side of his mouth curled up and his dark eyes glittered mischievously. It was a devastating mix of innocence and tawdry. Naughty thoughts going on behind those eyes, for sure. And her body reacted by softening even more, aching for his attention.

"Lyric?"

"Er, I don't consume mortal food."

"Not at all?"

"Not even chocolate wine, though doesn't that sound tempting? You don't eat, do you?"

"No, but some mortal liquids offer a treat from my usual diet."

"That would be ichor? Why do you keep drinking from faeries if you're no longer in Faery? To maintain? What if you went cold turkey?"

"I'd go through withdrawals."

Says the man who claimed he only did it to maintain. "But you'd come out clean."

"Clean is all in the point of view."

"Apparently your point of view is hazed by faery ichor."

"You don't understand me, Lyric, and don't try."

She understood that when a person avoided the topic of their addiction it truly was an addiction. Last year, one of her mother's best men had succumbed to an ichor addiction. Charish had allowed him to stay at the house a week before Lyric had convinced her to get rid of the dust freak. It had taken two strong demons to carry him out, and a warding spell to keep him off the property.

"Fine, I don't understand you," she said. "But I'll still pass on the coffee. That stuff smells nasty."

"Suit yourself. I've absinthe, if that rocks your boat."

"Alcohol makes me dizzy. So what are your plans for me now? I'll have you know your kind of torture only works once."

"I doubt that."

She met his daring gaze over the rim of the coffee cup. He was so full of his own appeal he likely thought he could have any woman he winked at. Which was probably true.

He'd broken his rule against vampires easily enough, though.

"I'm going to head over to the Lizard Lounge," he said, "see if I can stir up some info on the Unseelie deal. You'll come along."

"Of course. You can't have me sitting here handcuffed to your bed all night."

Again, that wicked smile accompanied by a naughty lift of his eyebrows.

Lyric's neck and cheeks heated and she turned her head away from him because she had actually blushed.

What was wrong with her? The guy had manhandled her, bound and handcuffed her, and insisted on keeping her in hand and telling her what to do. And here she sat in a ridiculous state of arousal. She'd welcome him into her arms again in a heartbeat, just to feel his sensual power encompass her.

She knew what it was. Vail wasn't uncaring when he did those things to her. He did it all with an alluring smirk and a deep desire for contact he'd never readily admit to. The guy was as needy as she.

"Isn't the Lizard Lounge a faery club?" she asked.

"That it is, though not a full-on sidhe club like you'd find in FaeryTown. I'd never take you there."

"Why not?"

"Unless you're a dust freak, you wouldn't survive the visit. Er, not necessarily a dust freak…"

He'd trapped himself with an accidental admission to his addiction. Lyric wouldn't press.

"We should stop and pick up some clothes for you," he suggested as he headed down the hallway.

Lyric followed. "What's wrong with this dress? It's club worthy."

His bedroom was styled with more of the steel and gray marble. Who'da thought? Vail stood before the closet, which oozed out darkness from the black clothing within.

"That dress," he said as he pulled out a black jacket studded at the wrists and along the sleeve seams with silver spikes, "would make a man come just looking at you. But we're going to a faery club, sweetie. It ain't no vampire club."

"So what? Do I have to sparkle? Do I get to wear the eye paint like you?

"I wear this ointment to see faeries."

"You can't see them otherwise?"

"Not the ones cloaked in glamour."

"Well, what about me? Do I get some eye stuff so I can see faeries?"

"You won't need to see them—they'll be everywhere."

He pulled the coat over his shirt and then selected a skinny silver tie. It went well with the silver snakeskin pants. It was rock 'n' roll glam, and would certainly fit into any of the vampire clubs Lyric had been to.

"Why aren't we going to FaeryTown? Wouldn't we find a lot more faeries there?"

"It's not where any sane sidhe goes to have a good time. Not that the club is much safer. This might be too dangerous for you. Change of plans. I'll have to lock you in the car while I'm inside."

"Uh-uh, no way. I'm a big girl. I can handle a club full of faeries."

"Faeries who will know you're a vampire and want to lure you to bite them just so they can watch you succumb to their addictive ichor? A high that'll change your life, Lyric. Ruin it, in fact."

"I'm not going to bite anyone. I've seen dust freaks. They are pitiful." She glanced over Vail's hands; a few glints of dust were visible. "But will the dust get on my skin and make me high?"

"A little, but not so devastating as inhaling it or drinking directly from the vein. You sure you want to try this? I can do this myself."

"Are you embarrassed to show up in the club with a vampire on your arm?"

He toed out a pair of boots that sported steel spikes on the backs of the heels. "Nope. In fact, I'll be admired for having you on my arm."

"Tell me how a vampire is admitted to such a club in the first place? Is it because you sparkle?"

"I've a certain aura. They know I'm more their kind than yours. I've never had trouble walking amongst the sidhe in the mortal realm."

"I wish I could figure why you're so set against your own species."

Vail closed the closet door and turned about, eyes dark and serious. "I lived in Faery almost three mortal decades. Never been around my own kind much. Hell, not at all. Faeries believe vampires filthy bottom-feeders who infuse their systems with the tainted blood of mortals who consume chemicals that destroy this Mother Earth. They are a part of the ecosystem that will destroy the planet, sooner rather than later. You still think it odd I favor them?"

"So you're into the whole save-the-world crap?"

"Lyric, it's where you live. Don't you want it to last?"

She nodded. "Never thought about it much, I guess. I understand, you living in Faery all your life, how you wouldn't feel comfortable around your own kind. So I'll give you that."

"Generous of you."

"Well, you did screw a vampire last night."

"That I did. And I still don't regret it."

He held out a hand, and she took it, feeling as though she were being invited to experience a ball set in an alien world by a prince from that foreign land. It would be exciting, and it was spiked with a jolt of danger.

"If you think I need different clothing, where are we going to shop?"

"There's a sidhe fetish store on the way."

"Joy."

"Not into whips and chains?"

"It sounds so unoriginal. And vampirish."

"This store is nothing of the sort. I wouldn't be caught dead doing the vamp thing, sweetie."

Lyric didn't reply. As far as she could see, he was already doing the vamp thing. Was it possible he felt himself a faery more than vampire? That was messed up. Both his parents had been bloodborn, which made him bloodborn. They were the most powerful vampires.

The man couldn't have any idea of the power he possessed. And it was apparent he wasn't willing to recognize it. That was just sad.

On the other hand, maybe, having been raised in Faery, he didn't have any such power.

Could he ever gain the power his birthright promised? What a spectacular vampire Vail could be.

Maybe he just needed a firm nudge toward taking mortal blood.

# *CHAPTER SEVEN*

One would expect a faery fetish shop to look as though a faery had exploded all over the place, and Lyric was not disappointed. So much color hurt her eyes. The spectrum electrified, the rainbow would be put to shame by the vivid color.

No sparkles—the faery would obviously provide that—but plenty of see-through stuff in indiscernible fabrics. The walls and racks were hung with fluttery, slinky, sexy things she couldn't resist touching. Some fabrics were cool, others warm. Some liquefied between her fingers and she dropped the fabric thinking she held water, but the bright material simply dropped in a graceful sweep. Intricate laces in all colors had been fashioned into strange designs that emulated flowers, insects and horned creatures.

The Seelie gown would have been the jewel among this dazzle. She hoped being here wouldn't remind Vail to get tough with her about that. She really needed to contact Leo, see if he'd been successful in his search to help her.

"This one." Vail handed her a weightless bit of

fabric. Truly out of place in his dark attire and sunglasses, he commanded her attention with but a few words. "Over there." He pointed to what looked like a wall of leaves, but when Lyric approached she figured the dressing room was behind all the verdant greenery.

The dress Vail had handed her was thin and felt as if it would tear if she twitched, but it was gorgeous. A deep crimson, it hugged her body as if a second skin. It was too risqué, for her nipples were plainly visible and it had an A-line cut right across her groin that emphasized her flat belly and the place where Vail had enjoyed putting his tongue. It felt snuggly, though, like a sweater, even with its thinness.

She turned and checked out the back view in the mirror. Did her ass really look that good? Her smile reflected back at her.

Wait.

Lyric turned and pressed her palms to the mirror. Her reflection gaped at her. "I can see myself? What the—?"

Must be some kind of magic faery mirror. Or—who cared? She could *see* herself. She hadn't been able to see her reflection since her first blood hunger. And looking in a pool of water, which was possible, always distorted her features.

Tilting her head, Lyric smiled at what she saw. Bright blue eyes and a fine nose. Not so bad, she thought. The moment took away her breath. Even without makeup she liked what she saw.

"Not so bad," she muttered to her reflection. "Kinda pretty."

"*Kinda* pretty?" Vail popped his head in through the leaves, and she stepped aside to invite him in.

"I can see myself in the mirror," she said, pointing out the obvious.

"Yeah, it's a genuine sidhe mirror. But just *kinda* pretty? Lyric." Standing behind her, he slid his palms along her hips, and looked over her shoulder into the mirror. "You are gorgeous."

"It's been so long," she muttered, caught on the reflected image. Was that a tear burning at the corner of her eye?

He slicked back his hair and winked at his reflection. "Pretty damn sexy myself."

The bad boy at his finest. Lyric smirked and he winked back at her.

"So tell me why you don't do a riot of color, Mr. Dark Lord? I can't imagine black is a popular color in Faery."

"True, I identify with Faery." He adjusted his tie knot in the mirror. "But you might say I'm on a protest of sorts. I wear black because it is everything Faery is not. I don't need a reminder of what I once had."

She tapped the spikes running down his jacket sleeve.

"Well," he added, "a little flash is necessary. The mortal realm can be so dull."

She tilted her head against his shoulder. "We make a good-looking couple."

"We do."

They stared at each other's reflection, and Lyric could almost imagine they were a real couple, until Vail stuck out his tongue at them both.

"Here." He reached outside the leaf curtain, and returned to hand her a pair of high heels. "I picked these out for you."

Five-inch stripper heels appealed to her inner nasty. It looked like tooled violet leather, but what kind of animal it had come from was anyone's guess. "Gorgeous," she said. "Too pretty to wear anyplace but..."

"But?"

She whispered, "Only place to wear these shoes is in bed."

"I can arrange for that to happen."

"I bet you can."

"Come out and model for me," he said, and slipped out of the dressing room.

Lyric gave one last glance at her face, winked at her sassy self, then swished aside the dressing room curtain. Striding out in the complete outfit, she posed for Vail. His eyes dropped right to her breasts, and then her slender waist, before traveling down her legs to inspect the bedroom-worthy shoes.

"Passable?" she asked, finding she preferred her reflection expressed in Vail's eyes to that of the mirror's.

He grabbed her by the neck and devoured her mouth in a claiming kiss that perked her nipples hard against his crisp black shirt. Sliding her hand down his chest, she grabbed his hip and pulled him to her, while hooking a leg up aside his thigh.

The man could kiss. Nothing tentative or weak; he took what he wanted and made damn sure she did the same. It was impossible not to like the guy, despite his wanting to ruin her life by bringing her home and, ultimately, right back to the Unseelie lord's hands.

"It's almost perfect," he offered.

"Almost?"

He grabbed something from a wall display. "I think you should add this."

Dangling from the middle of one finger was a thin, red, braided collar with spikes on it. A delicate silver chain trailed three feet in length.

"I thought you said this wasn't a normal fetish store?"

He moved to put it around her neck.

Lyric swiped it from him. "I don't think so, big boy. That's not my scene."

"Come on. It's a look."

"Oh, yeah?" She threaded the collar about his neck and snapped it to a snug fit. A tug of the chain pulled up his wicked sexy sneer. "Can this work for you?"

He flexed his shoulders and his neck strained against the red collar. It looked like a slice of blood above the somber black shirt collar.

The vampire who could scare any mortal shitless, not to mention most other vampires, glared at her. He looked ready to blow, his eyes narrowing viciously—then he nodded. "Works for me."

SINCE DONNING THE FAERY DRESS and still ogling her sexy shoes, which she'd put up on the dashboard of the Maserati, Lyric had let down her guard about her pseudokidnapper. And she had forgiven him for the wild rose handcuffs.

Bolting was out of the question this evening. Her curiosity for the faery club was too high. And to be seen striding through the place with the hunk of gorgeous vampire at the end of her silver chain?

The image stirred the hum of desire, which hadn't stopped since they'd made love. Okay, *had sex*. It wasn't love. But who cared? Sex was hotter. And she entirely expected round two to happen later while wearing these shoes.

"They are beyond sexy," Vail commented as he shifted gears.

Lyric realized she was bent forward over her legs touching the shoes. She ran her fingers along the soft violet fabric, which felt like rose petals, and marveled they could possibly be real flower petals. "Do they make you want to have sex with me?"

"I don't need a pair of shoes to feel like that. But you can poke me with the heel if you want to see if I moan."

His wink felt as if he clutched the inner core of her and blew on it with a hot breath. The man's sensual aim was impeccable.

Lyric tilted her head and noticed movement in the backseat. She reached back and carefully extracted the long green snake, pulling it up against her chest, where it flicked out its tongue, scenting her. "What's this?"

"Oh, that's where he got to." Vail flashed the snake a look, and managed to skim the bumper of a parked car at the same time. "Hey, Green Snake."

"Watch the road, Vail."

"Yes, O Mistress of the Sexy Shoes." He swerved back into the center of the lane. "So you're not afraid of snakes?"

She tilted her fingers and the green mamba glided over them and down her arm. "Nope. This one's poisonous, isn't it?"

"Not to you or me."

"Why do you keep a snake in your car?"

"He likes to get out."

"Uh-huh. You are the strangest vampire I have ever met. Bet this pretty little guy cost you a fortune."

"Who knows? What is a fortune, anyway?"

"You don't know? Do you have any concept of the value of mortal money?"

He shrugged. "Is it necessary? I keep some euro notes in the glove compartment. When I need money, I use some."

Lyric inspected the contents of the glove compartment, startled to find bound stacks of euro bills that must total in the tens of thousands. "You seriously need to get a financial advisor."

The Maserati roared, and then squealed as Vail's erratic driving hugged the passenger side along a parked car, surely taking a nasty scratch in the process.

"Absolutely no concept," she muttered, closing the glove compartment.

She had to laugh. Oh, to be so innocent of what would cause most mortals stress and drive them to the brink. Even vampires got bummed about money. They weren't all rich and handsome, like Vail.

"How'd you get all this money if you've only been in the mortal realm a few months?"

"A gift from my uncle. This car was, too."

Vail drove into an underground parking lot, and decided to wrap Green Snake around his neck and shoulders.

"You're taking him inside?"

"Sure, the bartender always keeps a treat for him. Come on. And whatever you do, don't stare."

He directed Lyric to an elevator that, once inside, felt as if it moved sideways, but when she asked about it, he just grinned.

They emerged in the Lizard Lounge amid fronds of lush plants. Lyric felt as if she stood in a jungle, were it not for the weird techno-synth music that seemed to emanate from the floor, which flashed green and yellow. A tendril of some kind of vine got caught on her finger and clung with sticky filaments. She flicked at it.

"Be cool," Vail whispered against her ear.

He stopped at the bar and high-fived the bartender, whose skin was a pale shade of amber. Green Snake was rewarded with a squirming white mouse. Lyric couldn't watch while Vail fed the treat to the snake.

"That'll keep him happy for days." Vail teased his

tongue along the shell of her ear. She gripped the silver chain, pulling him closer so his lips brushed hers. And so he'd keep his tongue away from behind her ear. Anywhere but there.

"Lead me through the throngs, mistress mine. Let's take a look around."

"What are we looking for?"

"I'll know it when I see it." Green Snake flicked his tongue out, and Vail pointed in the direction the snake had chosen. "That way."

Laughing with the utter joy of leading the sexy vampire about on a chain, Lyric stepped through the crowd and along the dance floor. She knew Vail wasn't near to submitting to her. The chain was a prop, and too flimsy. But she'd work the role to the hilt.

Stopping at the edge of the dance floor, she spread her legs, hands on hips, and looked about. Vail's hands found their place on her hips over her hands, as he did the same. He ground his hips against hers in rhythm to the music.

"You like to dance?" she asked over a shoulder.

"Hell, yes. So does Green Snake. I want to feel the music in you, Lyric. The vibrations between the two of us."

He talked a good game, but the proximity of the snake's bulging form to her face appealed little to her. "Maybe later."

Lyric took in the atmosphere. Colored lights flashed across her skin and the people all appeared normal. Until she really started to look.

Skin tones soaked in the red and violet lights, yet

here and there they did not. Such as the thin woman with the green skin barely covered by strips of sheer lace. Her eyes were violet, and her white hair swept like liquid over her shoulders.

Wings brushed Lyric's skin as she strolled through the crowd. They felt warm and some scratched crisply over her skin. She wanted to touch but dared not. It would be an intimate move on which she wasn't prepared to follow through, because she did know that to stroke a faery's wings was considered a sexual come-on.

Some of the faeries moved in a jerky manner. It was as if a few slices of the filmstrip had been cut out from their movie. "Why do they move like that?"

"Faery time is different than in the mortal realm. Those newer to this realm are still moving as they would in Faery. The longer they are here—" he pointed to a couple of dancers who appeared mortal for their lacking jerkiness "—the more they lose the connection to where they once belonged."

Faery dust shimmered in the air. She rubbed her arm, worried about the effects of getting too much on her skin. Her fear would give her away, but she suspected no one doubted she did not belong.

"It's not all dust," Vail whispered against her ear. "Lots of it is glitter, blown about by the fans. Adds to the atmosphere, I guess. Like I said, this isn't a full-on faery club. Many different paranormals frequent the place to get a taste of what only FaeryTown offers. I see the sidhe I want to talk to."

Vail tugged at the chain, directing her toward a

wooden staircase that wound around a massive oak tree to the second level. It was impossible for a tree to grow inside the building, yet when Lyric traced along its upper branches and leaf canopy she decided it sure felt real.

Realizing she'd dropped the chain leash—or maybe Vail had tugged it from her hand—she skipped to catch up to him, and was stopped by a man with violet eyes and blue lips.

He gave her a dressing-down that did not in any way feel sexy. Could have been the white film that blinked over his eyes or it could have been the tail that Lyric felt curl about one of her ankles. Just as the guy leaned in with the tip of his blue tongue extended, Vail slapped a hand to his shoulder. "Mine," he said.

The faery skedaddled.

"Did I stop something meaningful?" he asked with a knowing wink.

"Maybe you did." Lyric flounced past him, running her fingers down the chain that dangled before his chest.

"I can bring him back," he said. He clasped a hand about her waist from behind. "Did you like that freak?"

"No. Thanks for the rescue." She kissed him, and they turned to the nervous chuckle from an observer.

"Raskin," Vail said, and slapped hands with a particularly thin male. "Long time."

Brilliant violet hair spiked upon his head, a match to his eyes. His cheeks were sunken and the lighting gave his skin a purple cast. He folded his azure wings down as he made contact with Vail.

"And well met," Raskin returned. He gave Lyric a once-over. She could feel his eyes gliding across her skin, and the smirk he ended with satisfied her need for acceptance in this alien world. "Surprising," he said to Vail without taking his eyes from Lyric. "Looks vampire to me."

"You don't get points for the obvious," Vail answered.

He gestured for Lyric to take a seat in the booth beside them. She balked, not wanting to be pushed aside as if a prop.

"She is the one, is she not?" Raskin said. "So you were the one who kidnapped her?"

"Me? Ch'yeah—no." Vail's cocky smirk dropped. Lyric felt his muscles tense in the arm paralleling hers. Dead serious, he asked, "What do you know, Raskin?"

Vail forced the faery backward until he had no choice but to sit in the booth. The vampire slid in after him. With a glance from Vail, Lyric got the hint and slid in from the other side of the booth, the two of them trapping the purple faery in the middle.

Raskin flinched when his shoulder rubbed hers. Weird. She should be the one afraid to make contact with him.

"I'm not going to bite," she offered, then teased her tongue along the tips of her fangs. They weren't down, and she had no intention of willing them down, not with the haze of faery dust floating about. "Maybe."

"Go ahead," Raskin offered, but shakily. "Bite me and we shall see who walks out of here tonight. Bet those pretty little shoes of yours will not take you far with your brain addled on ichor."

Vail gripped the faery's jaw and twisted his head to face him. "Be nice to my girl."

"Chill, Vaillant. Just testing her mettle."

*His girl?*

The slip of a wing over her bare arm tickled. Lyric wanted to touch it, but the glint of dust restrained her. Everything about Raskin smelled springlike and… alluring.

"What do you know about her that you'd ask me such a question?" Vail insisted.

Raskin shrugged. "I know what everyone knows, that the Lord of Midsummer Dark was screwed over by vampires. And you, sir, are a vampire who is strolling with a sexy, blonde vampiress on his arm who matches the description flittering about. Seems pretty incriminating, if you ask me."

"I didn't kidnap her."

"And yet, here she is." Raskin fluttered his violet lashes at Lyric. "With you dangling from the end of her chain. You tupping her?"

Vail grabbed one of the faery's wings and bent it, which turned the faery's face bright red.

"Don't," Lyric said, "you're hurting him!"

"He can take it." In proof, Vail bent the wing farther, which turned the upper part of it bright violet, while the bent half was drained of color, much as if blood had been forced from unseen veins. "Now, what's the deal with Zett? What'd he promise the Santiago family in exchange for the gown?"

"Gown? I know nothing about a gown. What gown? You have a gown? Oh wait, is it the Seelie gown? That has gone missing?"

Vail dropped the faery and slid from the booth as if burned. He gripped Raskin by the neck. "You didn't talk to me tonight."

"But I am right now—" Vail's fingers clamped tighter about the faery's neck. "Oh. Right. Who are you again?"

"Come on, Lyric."

"But we just got here."

"And we'd better leave before all of Faery gets your scent."

"Every sidhe in the city will be after you now!" Raskin called after them. "You know I will not tell a soul, but it is too late. They know. They hear all, vampire!"

"SORRY ABOUT THAT," Vail said as they entered his apartment and neither bothered to click on the lights. It was after midnight, but both were natural night seers. "I think I made a wrong move going to the faery club."

He set the snake on the potted tree in the corner by the kitchen. No longer could Lyric see a lump in his long, scaled body—that was quick.

"It was interesting." She strolled the glossy floor, her heels clicking smartly. She felt light, and her body swayed drunkenly. "But I think that faery was blowing smoke about the gown. How can they know if you only told the one guy? And you didn't tell him. He just guessed."

"They know. Trust me, they know. Come here."

Spun about from behind, she turned into Vail's embrace. He rubbed her cheek and showed her the faery dust on his finger.

"Is that going to sink in and make me high?"

"Shouldn't, but..." He studied her eyes. "You have a little buzz going, don't you?"

"I think I do." She waggled her eyebrows at him. "Wanna take advantage of me?"

He licked her cheek, dragging his tongue to the corner of her eye where he pressed a kiss. When he clasped her head below her ear, Lyric had enough sense to move his hand away.

"You get off on the dust, don't you?"

Vail rubbed his fingers together. "Last time I got high from this stuff I was a kid."

"I don't believe that. You're in a constant state of high. You're...maintaining. Vampires don't need to feed the hunger until puberty. Did you not get a high when you started drinking ichor?"

"Yes, but I think I've forgotten how good it could be."

"You are addicted."

"Never. I think it's because I've always had the dust in me, you know, growing up in Faery."

"Uh-uh." If that's the way he wanted to play it.

She spread her hands up his shirt, marveling at his tight chest. Muscles and might, her bad boy. All the necessary ingredients for a good time. A silly grin felt wrong, but she couldn't stop it. A contact high? Maybe a little. She should probably shower, but why spoil it?

"Raskin said everyone knows about me. So what do we do now?"

"You could go to your mother and ask her about the deal."

"Out of the question."

"What if I force you?"

"You would do that? You, who said you understood my need to be away from my family? If I go anywhere near my mother, she'll contact Zett, and I'll be a goner."

"That's the part I don't understand. I thought you were just making the exchange. And yet, you make it sound as though Zett was going to take you in hand. Why would Zett want you? Do you know? Because I find it incredibly odd a faery would request a vampire."

"I have no idea. The deal was between Zett and my mother."

"And yet you agreed to the handoff. I'm not following why you would do so, knowing that vamps and faeries don't mix, and you have to know it's a literal death play."

"Vail, I told you I'd no intention of ever going to Zett. So drop it, will you?"

Because she wasn't ready to tell him her secret, and if she played her cards right maybe she'd never have to tell. It was so embarrassing.

*You were young. You didn't know better.*

Vail paced the floor. "Maybe I should be going at this from the vamp angle instead of the faery angle."

"Sounds complicated to me. I mean, for a man who is a vampire yet thinks he's a faery, won't that be a challenge? Maybe you need to rest your brain after inhaling all that faery dust?"

"Insult me all you like. I'm not letting you get away until this mystery is solved and I get—"

"You get?"

"You think I'm not getting something out of this deal?"

"Of course not. So what do you get when the gown is found and the vampiress is returned to her family?"

He drew his hands from her shoulders to cup her breasts. The thin fabric felt like skin on skin. "Nothing you need to worry your pretty little shoes over. Right now, I want to forget about what we did wrong, and instead react to whatever comes up. Mmm, like your nipples."

She wasn't going to allow him the easy win. Not this time.

He bent and bit them gently through the fabric.

On the other hand, she really didn't want to waste what little high she may be riding. "Yeah, sounds right. Whatever comes up. Why don't you do that thing you do…"

"I do a lot of things, sweetie. You have to be more specific."

"You know, with your fingers? And me..." She moved his hand over her mons. He tugged up the short skirt and the heat of him against her skin melted her shoulder against his and she sighed.

"Like this?" he asked against her mouth, opening it with his lips and teasing his tongue along her teeth. His fingers teased at her moistness but didn't enter her.

"A little deeper. Please."

He moved her against the wall, and hiked one of her legs up to rest along his hip. She dug in the heel against his thigh and he moaned.

"Hurt me, Lyric." His tongue dove in deeper, but not his fingers. She nudged her groin against his softly stroking fingers.

"Where?" he whispered. "How do you want me to touch you?"

She slid her fingers through his thick, dark hair and pulled him in for a brutal kiss that clicked their teeth and stole her breath, showing him she wanted it hard, rough and now.

"Like that," she gasped, nudging her nose along his, "inside me."

"As my lady commands."

He stretched his hand along the leg she had hooked at his hip and drew it high to rest her ankle against his shoulder. "You're limber."

She tucked her other leg around his hip. "I work out on the silks."

"Your mother mentioned that. What are silks?"

"Aerial silks. It's a hobby of mine I learned years ago."

"Hence, the circus?"

"Yep. We don't need to chat, lover boy."

"Of course not." He buried his face in her hair and found her moist heat with his fingers.

Lyric wasn't sure if it was the faery dust or Vail's expert skill making her woozy, but she touched oblivion a minute later. And as her body pulsed with orgasm and she dug her fingernails into Vail's shoulders, she felt him enter her, hot and hard and heavy. He moaned as her inner muscles clasped him and brought him to a quick climax.

She'd lost this round. So sue her.

## *CHAPTER EIGHT*

LYRIC ROLLED OVER, her feet tangled in the soft gray cotton sheets. Beside her, Vail slept, or at least his eyes were closed. Vampires didn't need much sleep so she couldn't be sure, but she didn't want to disturb him yet.

She studied the hard angles of his face. Square jaw dusted at the edges with a hint of stubble and defined cheekbones emphasized his sure, rugged beauty. That straight, defiant nose must be the first thing people noticed, until her eyes fell to his mouth.

Soft, and slightly open in sleep, she felt a shimmer scurry through her to imagine those lips at her nipple again. It wasn't like the shimmer two vampires felt when first touching. Now she thought on it, that hadn't occurred.

What was that about? When two vampires touched, a tingly sort of shimmer ran through their system. It was the only way they could tell one another without seeing them drink blood or flash fangs. And she hadn't felt it with Vail. Not even now as she traced her fingers lightly down his rock-hard biceps.

Had it something to do with living in Faery all his life? Probably all the faery ichor he'd consumed had worked a real number on this guy. He believed his own kind were filthy and not worth his alliance, and he wore that belief like armor designed to repel any who would challenge him. That was so sad.

And yet, she'd breached his defenses with an ease that still surprised her. She bet it surprised him, too.

Vail's arm was turned to expose the underside. A thick blue vein ran the length. She leaned in, inhaling with closed eyes. He had that compelling sweat-after-sex scent she loved, yet it wasn't salty but sweeter, which she again attributed to the ichor in his system.

Enticed by the thickness of his vein, her fangs descended. She could hear the blood running beneath Vail's skin, a delicious symphony of platelets and cells. It smelled like sin. It wasn't like mortal blood, which reeked of food (though there was nothing wrong with that; she loved drinking from a mortal who had imbibed wine or chocolate).

Vail's sweet allure tingled at the back of her throat and wet her tongue. His pulse thrummed but did not match hers, which tapped faster against her skin.

Mercy, but she wanted to taste him. To feel the liquid heat of Vail sliding down her throat. She bet it would warm her entire body, probably even coax her to orgasm. The man walked, talked and breathed sex, and she wanted to taste the source.

"Go ahead," he murmured.

A glance to the pillow. Deep azure eyes watched

her. She could lose herself in Vail's smoldering gaze—and then she realized she was already lost.

Dashing her tongue along the length of one fang, she averted her attention to his arm. Below her fingertips his blood spoke to her. *Thump, thump.* "Are you serious?"

"I don't mind you drinking from me. I think it would feel great."

The blood swoon, a giddy dash into pseudo-orgasm, was the reward no matter if you were the biter or the bitten. "So you've never been bitten before?"

"Nope."

"Because you don't like vamps."

"Yep."

"So how can you know it'll feel good? And why me?"

"Why are you questioning beyond the sale, sweetie? I said you could bite me. Shouldn't that be enough?"

It should be, but somehow it didn't feel right. His nonchalant invitation felt forced, if not a downright tease. And they did take joy in teasing each other.

Lyric toyed with the thick vein, pressing it with a fingertip. His strong pulse beckoned. "But you won't drink from me."

"You know I'm not interested."

"Not interested, or…afraid you might like it too much?"

He didn't answer, and instead closed his eyes.

"You don't want to taste real blood," she whispered. "Because you're addicted to ichor. You believe nothing can compare."

"It's just—"

"Maintaining, I know. Whatever. The addict is always the last to admit to it."

"Calling me names again? And after I gave you three insane orgasms."

"Actually, it was four." She kissed his vein but resisted its tempting timpani. "I want to bite you, Vail. I'd love to swallow your blood as you are pumping your thick, oh-so-hard cock deep inside me. But I want you to do the same to me."

"Sorry."

"Yeah, me, too. Besides, I couldn't drink from you now if I wanted to. You're full of ichor."

"That's ridiculous."

"I bet if I cut you, you'd bleed ichor."

He rolled to face her and as he did so pressed his wrist to a fang and opened the vein. Thick, red blood oozed out. He held it before her as an offering.

Like dark candy displayed behind barbed wire, the sweetness bloomed, filling her senses. Lyric teased the air with the tip of her tongue. He would taste like nothing she had ever before put to her tongue. All that hot, red life, creaming in her mouth and slicking the back of her throat.

And yet, within the crimson drop that slid over his pale skin she noticed an unmistakable glitter.

She sat at the edge of the bed and turned her back to him. "I mean it. You get clean, get all the dust out of your system, and then I'll rock your world." She looked over her shoulder as a droplet splattered on the gray sheets. "Promise."

Heading for the shower, Lyric forced herself not to look back at what she suspected was an arrogant smirk. But if she took one more look at the tempting blood, she wouldn't be able to resist.

Ichor or no, drinking Vail's blood could prove dangerous to her heart.

"I'M THE ONE who rocks your world," Vail muttered as Lyric closed the bathroom door. Though he had to admit that his world had been on a wobbly course since Lyric had snuck into it on her sexy red heels.

Surprised she hadn't latched on to his wrist the way he assumed most vampires would when presented with fresh blood, he pressed the wrist to his mouth and sucked at it to seal the wound. It didn't taste wrong or disgusting to him. It didn't taste like anything.

She thought he was a dust freak? He felt pity for those vamps who staggered about FaeryTown desperate for the next fix. Abandoning friends, family and life for the one elixir that could grant them a momentary high. He was nothing like them.

How to make Lyric understand ichor to him was like mortal blood to her; it sustained.

What did he care what she thought?

Swinging his legs over the side of the bed, he shook his head to flick away the hair from his eyes. The last time a woman had stayed over at his place—actually, that had not happened here. He hadn't been in this realm long enough to establish a relationship. And his one-night stands always saw him leaving the woman's house before the sun rose. He'd never reveal whether his preference was for faeries or mortal women—a guy had to keep some mystery.

The Santiago chick was harshin' his M.O. He didn't have to keep her around. And he didn't need the blatant denial when he'd freely offered his blood.

Herne's balls, yes, he did need her. Lyric was the key to finding the gown. She had it. And if she did not, she knew where it was. The clock was ticking. He had two days to find it before the Seelie court arrived to claim it from Rhys.

Not that he should care what trouble Rhys Hawkes got into, but this matter wasn't about his half-breed uncle. Vail had taken the job and promised to do it right. A man of his word, he wouldn't stop until it was completed.

Standing and pacing the room, he listened as the shower pattered against the glass tiles. He imagined the water rolling off Lyric's sexy, smooth skin and then wanted to press his tongue in the wake of those droplets, lapping up jasmine and cherries until he'd sated himself.

Heading for the bathroom, he stalled in the doorway when the cell phone on the bedside table rang. He nabbed it and Rhys answered.

"What the hell were you up to last night? Need I remind you this retrieval mission was supposed to be secret?"

"Morning, Uncle. You're up early."

"It's noon, Vail. I've been up since sunrise."

"Guess being half werewolf helps. I, on the other hand, will always be on Faery time."

"What the hell does that mean? I don't care. You were out asking questions last night and now word is buzzing you're looking for the Seelie gown, if you don't already have it in hand."

Vail tightened his jaw and stopped himself before kicking the bedpost with a bare foot. "Where'd you hear that?"

"Does it matter? Word is circulating, Vaillant. Rumor also tells you had the Santiago woman with you. Now how am I going to keep Charish Santiago from finding out we've already found her but have no plans to turn her over?"

"You can explain we need her daughter to find the gown."

"Great. That is if the Seelie court doesn't find out and go apocalyptic on my ass for losing the thing."

"You should have better security, Hawkes."

"Don't start, boy. We have the highest security measures. I just hadn't expected a nonfaery to steal the gown. Damn!"

Vail sighed. He didn't need a lecture. Nor did he need a pseudofather calling him *boy*. But he wouldn't deny Rhys was right. "I'll step up the investigation. I promise I'll have something before tomorrow—ahh!"

"What's wrong?"

Vail grasped the female who had reached around his waist and now clutched his morning erection. "Nothing," he forced out as calmly as possible. "Just stubbed my toe on the bed. I'll be in touch, Hawkes."

He tossed the phone onto the bed and put his arms

back and behind him to slide around Lyric's still wet hips, squeezing her derrière. "You know you're on the wrong side of me, sweetie?"

"Is that so?" She stroked his cock slowly. Water droplets from her hair ran down his chest and torso and served as a lubricant as she slicked the thick head. "Feels about right from where I'm standing."

"You got over our little tiff."

"I did. I'm not one of those women who make demands and who has expectations. Hell, we've only just met. We don't even like each other."

"We don't," he agreed, but couldn't find the right tone to make it sound like truth.

She didn't like him? That was a disappointment, because he couldn't find any reason not to like her. Other than that she was holding out on him regarding the gown.

"So, enemy mine," she said, "who was on the phone?"

Vail gasped as her motions teased climax, and she pressed her breasts against his back. He was right there, ready to come, and her hand didn't slow, slicking faster and faster, up and down.

"Cat got your tongue?"

"More like...the ice princess got my cock." He came, spilling over her hand and his stomach. Her other hand dug into his shoulder, the nails clawing, and it felt angry good, ratcheting up the climax another notch. "Lyric."

"Yes, lover?"

Just. Lyric. That was all his brain could manage

right now. The ice princess Lyric who knew how to get her enemy off, even after he'd vowed never to drink her blood.

He nodded toward the violet high heels tilted at the end of the bed. "Put those on."

TWENTY MINUTES PASSED, and two orgasms later, the twosome stood in the middle of the pebble-tiled bathroom drying each other off with thick black towels.

Lyric asked again who had called, because she was curious like a cat. And she did want to know if some other woman had been calling while she was around. A sexy man like Vail probably had lots of lovers.

"Rhys Hawkes," Vail said as he tugged her to him with the towel around her shoulders. Their bodies fit together, her nipples hugging under his hard pec muscles. "He wants me to bring you in. Rumor is spreading fast we have been seen together, which translates to most as me kidnapping you."

"That's completely wrong."

"Ch'yeah, well, they also think I know where the gown is. It was a foolish move on my part to take you to the club."

So now she'd involved an innocent in her oh-so-unclever foray into escape.

"I predict they're already on the prowl," Vail said. "The Unseelie."

"So correct it. Turn me over to my mother and you're in the clear."

He tossed the towel aside and combed his fingers

through wet ribbons of her hair. "You willing to give up the gown?"

Not until she'd worked one last angle, which involved giving Leo a call. And as long as he was only aware the gown was the biggest lure for Zett, and not her, she intended to keep it that way. Much as she loved getting it on with Vail, the truth was they were more enemies than allies. Vail's alliance was clearly to Hawkes Associates.

"That's what I thought," he said when she didn't answer. "Get dressed."

She tugged on the faery dress, which now felt blatant and too sheer even though the heavy shades to block the sunlight allowed in no light, and she stood in only the glow from the bathroom light.

"I think I'd better go with my green dress." He nodded, but gave a whistle when she stripped off the one to put on the other. That felt better, still snuggly and sexy, but not so exposed.

Vail put on dark gray crushed-velvet pants and tossed a silk shirt over his shoulder. Lyric followed, observing quietly. He strode into the kitchen and opened a drawer to pull out a short-bladed dagger, which he sheathed at his hip. He grabbed the jacket he'd worn last night, spikes rimming the wrists and along the shoulder seams, and headed back into the humid bathroom.

"What are you doing?"

"What are *we* doing," he corrected.

He took a violet jar out from the medicine cabinet and twisted off the cap. A dark, odorless, gloopy substance shimmered inside.

"Is that what you put around your eyes to see faeries?"

"Yep." He dipped a fine-tipped brush into the ointment, and painted it beneath his eyes, doing an expert job without the aid of a reflection.

"I don't understand. You said we were going to do something?"

Eyes lined with the dark ointment, Vail grabbed her hips and kissed her soundly. A claiming kiss. An urgent, quit-asking-stupid-questions kiss. "We're going on the run."

## *CHAPTER NINE*

VAIL DECIDED TO protect the girl rather than turn her in to save his own ass. It hadn't been a snap decision, but it felt more right than anything in his life had felt for a long time.

Had anything ever felt right?

*Not until you met Lyric.*

He navigated a narrow cobbled street in the Maserati, sensing Lyric tightly clutching the door handle as he avoided clipping the back tire of a nearby biker.

While in Faery, he'd always known he was vampire, and had been born in the mortal realm. His stepmother, Cressida, had been forthright with all the details. She'd taken him in payment for a boon, expecting him to be the half-breed son of a vampiress and another half-breed, Rhys Hawkes. Only when he reached puberty had Cressida realized Vail was merely a bloodborn vampire. Cressida had been vocal about her disappointment.

Ever unwanted. Never loved.

*Get over it,* he muttered to his whiny subconscious. He'd survived Faery, and had made a few friends, and had never backed away from a fight, or the malicious eye of Zett.

If anything, Faery had taught him to survive. It had also taught him no one could ever be trusted, and family was just a word. It meant nothing. He didn't need family. He didn't want it.

Except, he wondered about it now. Rhys continued to tease him into the familial folds, and while Vail had initially resisted, he felt his shoulders relax now. The half-breed wasn't so bad. Hell, maybe he could orchestrate an alliance between Vail and Trystan? Having a werewolf as a brother fascinated him, and he'd like to talk to Trystan about this mortal realm and how to exist within it.

One confidant was all he needed. He was ninety-five percent sure Lyric wouldn't bolt on him and take off with the gown, never again to be seen. But the remaining five percent? He wouldn't let down his guard around her.

He pulled the Maserati into a narrow lot behind a cheesy supermarket. The bumper nudged the steel light pole.

He rubbed the dashboard lovingly. "Sorry, sweetie."

"I thought I was your sweetie?" Lyric delivered him a quirk of her brow, then got out before he could reply.

"Oh, you are," he muttered. Then he patted the dashboard again. "Just kidding, sweetie."

Clasping Lyric's hand, because he needed to feel in control after their disastrous club visit, Vail led her inside the supermarket. The fluorescent-lit green Formica floor disturbed his love for nature and all things wild. Hell, most of the city did—save for the royal gardens—but he wanted to get a handle on mortal existence before moving out to the country. And, well, there was no FaeryTown out in the countryside.

And right now too much was at stake, like learning his father's whereabouts.

"You willing to go all the way with me on this adventure?" he asked.

Lyric flashed him her bright smile as they wandered the store. "Hell, yes. But why are you willing to do this for me?"

He stopped in the beauty supply aisle. "Maybe I like you."

"You don't like me. You like having sex with me."

"True. But I like you even when you're not naked. I swear it."

"Liar. You don't like what I am. We're enemies, remember?"

"I may have been quick to label. Perhaps I've been a wib all along for assuming the vampire race is subordinate to me."

"The vampire race? Those faeries worked a real number on you."

"They have no love for vampires, for sure. Though certainly Cressida would have taken a half-breed over me."

"So you said you were getting something out

of the deal. You hand over the gown to Hawkes Associates…?"

"Hawkes gives me information I need."

"Such as?"

"Sweetie, we aren't that close yet."

Pausing in the middle of an aisle stocked with stuff he'd never need if he lived a millennium, he toyed with Lyric's hair, loving the play of her ribbony curls between his fingers. "If we're going to lie low, you need to change your hair color. You stick out like an Amazon in Faery with your height and ice-blond hair."

"Are you going to change yours?"

"I don't think there's much you can do with this dark stuff."

"Probably have to bleach it, and that would be a mess. Would totally screw with your goth-vamp-lord look."

"I am not—"

She pressed a finger to his lips. "I know, you're not a vampire, but you can still be a goth one, maybe even a little emo."

"I don't know what you just said." He should protest her mockery—he did know what the words meant—but he let it slide.

"Do you have glamour? So you can disguise yourself?"

"Nope. But I do have dust in my arsenal, which could come in handy."

"Really? You can dust someone? How does that work?"

"I just blow some in their face. Vamps inhale the stuff and—bam! They're high and out for the count. You okay with that?"

"Truthfully? Yes, I am. All right, I'm in."

"Great." The quicker they got out of this dismal store, the better. "What color?"

They perused the shelves of hair color and Vail was thankful men didn't have to worry about such things. As a vampire, he'd age gracefully. One reason he should be grateful for his heritage.

"What about red?" she said with a tantalizing tease.

Vail imagined Lyric with siren red hair. The image hung in his brain, yet quickly moved through his body as if silk were sliding over his pores, teasing his nerve endings to a blissful memory of their lovemaking. Those shoes had glided down his legs and back up to dig into his hips as he'd slid in and out of her.

He grabbed a box that featured a woman with mousy brown hair and handed it to her.

"That's not red."

"Exactly. You with red hair would be twice as devastating as blond. I wouldn't be able to concentrate around you. Every man you pass would stumble and crash, face-first onto the tarmac. Do you really want to be responsible for all those bleeding faces?"

"When you put it that way…dull, librarian-brown it is."

She walked away with box in hand, and Vail commented, "I think librarians are hot."

"Don't tell me you've a fantasy about tight buns and schoolmarm glasses."

"Works for me. But don't forget the brains, too. I love a smart woman."

"My attempt at ditching my mother and the Unseelie lord was a stupid disaster."

"It was smart, if perhaps underplanned. You don't know how good it will be until we figure out what the hell is going on between your family and Zett."

"Thanks for this," Lyric said as they took their place in line behind a queue of shoppers. "I needed an ally."

"Don't get ahead of yourself, sweetie. *Ally* is pushing it."

"What about business partner?"

"That implies we would work together for a common goal." He kissed her behind the ear, where it was warm and soft and tendrils of her hair tickled his nose. He liked it there. But she pressed her fingers along her ear, nudging him away. Hmm, didn't want him to touch her? Her nerves were beginning to emerge. To be expected. "Okay, that works. But in the end, I'll be getting the gown to hand over to Hawkes Associates. What do you get out of it?"

"Freedom?"

He looked aside so she wouldn't see his falling smile. Freedom could never be possible. Rhys had promised Charish Santiago he'd return her daughter. And if Zett now wanted her for reasons beyond Vail's imagining, the Unseelie lord would step in line.

"I'm not going to get freedom, am I?" she asked

from behind the box of hair color she held to her lips. "Don't say anything. I won't ask you to compromise your job. Just promise me one thing."

"What's that?"

"When we do figure things out, and if we finally find the gown—"

"Or you reveal the gown's hiding spot."

"Ahem."

"All right. What do you want?"

"Five seconds. I want you to turn and look the other way and give me a head start."

Five seconds? He'd be on her ten seconds after that pause. She may be vampire, but he was stronger and faster than she was. Yet part of him wished she'd asked for an hour.

Vail nodded. "Deal."

THEY STEPPED OUT of the supermarket into the balmy evening sky. Before Vail could clasp Lyric's hand, something whisked past his head. "What the—?" He grabbed Lyric around the waist. "We gotta run, sweetie."

"But the car is right—"

"Right where the sidhe is standing."

"A faery? Let me go. I can run."

Vail sensed the noise of the arrow before seeing it, and squatted, Lyric in arm. The arrow skimmed his hair.

She shuffled from his grasp, but he tugged her aside and pushed her into the darkness hugging the supermarket wall as another arrow cut through his pants.

"Damn it, that bastard is accurate!"

"I don't see him!"

He shoved Lyric into a run. "You can't. He's wearing glamour. Just run."

They zigzagged down the alley. The way to survive elf shot was to avoid it. Though Vail had immunity having lived in Faery, he'd still suffer for days from the poison-tipped arrows. Lyric would not be so lucky.

The next arrow splintered into the brick wall, sending shards of ironwood at Vail's face. He closed his eyes as the razored shards cut his cheeks. The poison stung, but better him than Lyric.

Without pausing, he swung Lyric around the corner and onto the busy street in front of a nightclub doorway, which was surrounded by massive, pink neon lips.

Lyric amazed him. She didn't slow, and ran right for the traffic alongside him. Horns honked and drivers slammed on their brakes. Vail jumped up on a trunk and leaped, gripping Lyric's arm as he did, and the twosome soared to the opposite curb, landing crouched.

Elf shot bulleted the concrete sidewalk before them.

"He's relentless," Lyric gasped, clutching the plastic grocery bag to her chest. Her bright hair had to be the beacon the elf followed. "You've been cut."

"It'll heal."

Vail twisted to spy their stalker, standing on the opposite side of the busy street. The tall, bald sidhe with glowing green eyes patted his back in search of another arrow. He wore a carapace of emerald armor that resembled a tenacious insect's horned shell. Mortals didn't give him a second glance, thanks to his glamour shield.

One thing Vail did know—without the telltale luminescent markings, this wasn't one of Zett's men.

"He's splinter sidhe. Has to be." Gripping Lyric's hand, Vail took off down the street.

"What does that mean?"

"He is aligned with neither Seelie nor Unseelie." He dodged in through a DVD rental store swarming with customers. The blue lighting eerily blanched everyone's faces. Weaving through the bins of DVDs, he tugged Lyric after him.

When they reached the back wall, he shoved open the office door and spied the outer door. They escaped into the night, yet Lyric tugged at him to stop.

"We can't stop," he said, then saw her slip off her high heels.

"I can keep up better this way," she said, tossing the shoes aside but keeping the bag of hair dye. "So he's not Zett's man?"

"Something worse. A rogue sidhe who answers to no one but himself. My guess is he's heard the rumor I may have the gown and wants it. That thing will bring in a fortune on the faery market."

"But if he kills you that won't help," she suggested as they raced down the alley.

"He's not trying to kill me, just poison me to put me out of commission. He's out of arrows," Vail called back. "But he'll never run out of energy. His sort feed off mortal energy. In this realm, he is all-powerful. The best we can do is lose him, or hope for a kill shot."

"Kill shot? With what? That little stick of a blade you carry?"

"Exactly."

"Why can't I see him?"

"He's using glamour. Let's go."

Vail turned a corner, taking a breath when he saw the alley was empty and stretched a long ways. Free rein from here on.

Until he heard the warrior's yipping cry. From the top of a building jumped their pursuer, landing twenty feet in front of Vail and Lyric. The lithe, sinuous sidhe loomed a head taller than Vail's lofty height. His neck grew to his ears, emphasizing his small, round, hairless head, and his shoulders were spiked with the horned armor.

"I just want her," the sidhe growled. "Dead."

"The vampiress?" Vail's jaw dropped open. He'd thought the elf was after the gown. Had Zett placed a price on Lyric's head? Why did the faery lord want a vampire?

When the sidhe lifted a hand to indicate that Vail approach him, the iridescent emerald sheen of faery swept across his bald head and face. That indicated he could be a worm wraith, Vail guessed. He knew what the man looked like in his actual form, and it wasn't pretty.

A challenge over who gets the girl? He had only the sidhe blade in his boot. It wasn't designed to poison, but rather maim. And he had to get real close, which he didn't favor against an opponent wielding poisoned arrows. It would be like using a pin against a battle sword.

Vail tilted his head first one way, cracking his neck, and then to the other side. He reached back, touching Lyric and giving her a push. He sensed she moved against the wall. If she couldn't see the danger, she'd never be able to get out of harm's way.

"Get as far from here as you can," he muttered, then turned to face his opponent.

It had been months since he'd been in Faery and had practiced the sidhe martial arts. He'd been talented, and many times had gone head-to-head with Zett, each match resulting in a tie.

But the worm wraith, snarling and gleaming dangerously, gave *imposing* a new definition.

Glancing about, Vail searched for a more worthy weapon than the blade he held. A rusty tangle of iron railing was piled behind the wraith, perhaps fallen from the balcony overhead. Nice, but not where Vail preferred it to be.

He stepped forward and crouched slightly, spreading out his arms in preparation. Blade held ready to strike, he gestured with two fingers for the wraith to bring it on.

The sidhe nodded in confirmation, "Let's do this, longtooth."

Vail's jaw tightened at the epitaph. He could call the sidhe an earth slug but he didn't need to make the thing any angrier than those glowing green eyes already displayed. Faery eyes didn't glow unless their ichor boiled.

Not sure if the sidhe had weapons beyond his depleted cache of arrows, Vail waited to see what the guy would use to come at him.

After a growl and a twist at his waist, the sidhe soared through the air, his horn-armored boot aimed for Vail's head. He saw it coming, but the sidhe moved so swiftly—the mortal realm doubled his speed—that by the time Vail thought to duck, he felt the skull-cracking pain of spiked horn connecting with the side of his head.

He wobbled but did not go down.

Another kick landed on the same spot above his ear. Vail charged forward, using the pain to focus his anger. He head-butted the sidhe in the chest and rammed the blade into its torso. The blade broke off at the handle.

The wraith tugged out the blade with a yowl and tossed it over his shoulder. The glisten of ichor oozing from his opponent's chest brought the saliva to Vail's tongue. The sidhe cracked a knowing smirk. Not the time to feel the hunger.

Vail rushed his opponent and the two went down against the brick wall. Slamming his palm against the sidhe's face, Vail smashed his head against the rough brick. Faery ichor glittered on the bricks. It smelled delicious. It spattered his face. He dashed out his tongue to test the ichor—then spit.

A punch to his gut sent him flying. Vail landed on the tarmac, stumbling but still on two feet. A glance revealed that Lyric was keeping out of the way, peeking around the corner. He wished she had listened to him and vacated the alley.

The sidhe's wings snapped out like crisp leather sails. Sheer green and veined in violet, Vail noted the serrated bone edges. Now those were the weapons he needed to worry about. A wingtip through his heart would prove as effective as a wooden stake.

The sidhe spun, slashing the air with his wings. Vail dodged and rolled, knocking the sidhe off his feet. A wingtip caught him across the chest, opening his shirt and slicing flesh.

"You bleed red, longtooth," the sidhe remarked. "Heh. Nasty bloodsucker." He spit onto Vail's chest. "Give me what I want, and I'll make this easy on you."

"Why do you want the woman?" Vail kicked, clocking the sidhe's face with his heel. The wraith's head snapped, but he came right back to position.

"For the prize," he growled. "She's worth a lot dead."

"Who put the price on her head? Why?"

Vail didn't see the punch coming. Blood pooled in his mouth and spilled down his throat. And the punches continued, pummeling his chest until he couldn't breathe. He managed to swing up, and ground his fist into his aggressor's jaw. The sidhe screamed as the iron rings Vail wore burned into his flesh.

Jaw smoking, the wraith growled and spit. "That little bit of iron means nothing." He slashed forward a wing, catching Vail across the chest, and whipped him through the air. He landed on the tarmac and something poked his shoulder. The crumpled balcony railing.

The sidhe raced toward the brick building, ran up the side of it and, once at the top, flipped over backward.

Vail grabbed a piece of railing, thankful it was long and straight, and came up swinging toward the wraith's legs. He swept out his left arm, iron bar hooked along it and tucked under his elbow. It connected with the falling wraith and upset his intended attack.

The enemy quickly rolled upright, recovering. He acknowledged Vail's weapon with a growl, and charged. Iron clanked against horned armor, putting back the wraith but not stopping him. He charged Vail over and over, and each time, Vail successfully detoured him. The quarterstaff had always been his weapon of choice. He was virtually undefeatable when wielding it.

Suddenly the sidhe was not there.

Lyric screamed. The wraith held her with an arm about her neck.

"Go ahead," Vail said, standing with the bar held defensively, "break her neck. It won't kill her."

Without pause, the sidhe twisted Lyric's neck and dropped her, lifeless, at his feet. He delivered a toothy snarl to Vail.

Bloody Herne. He hadn't expected the bastard would do it.

Lyric lay unmoving, her head twisted to the side.

Was she dead? Vampire death required a stake, and

some had to have their heads cut off to die. Broken bones always mended quickly. Even a broken neck—unless he'd severed her spinal cord. Hell. What had he been thinking to challenge the sidhe to do such a thing?

Something stabbed Vail in the heart, and it wasn't the worm wraith's weapon. It squeezed and compressed until he yelled out a banshee cry and lunged for the sidhe. He shoved the creature by the shoulders against the tangled iron railing. Vail felt a metal bar stab into his gut, cutting through skin. He shuffled away.

The wraith hung impaled on a spike. Didn't matter how strong or powerful the thing was, iron was any sidhe's kryptonite.

The sidhe's limbs shot out as if being drawn and quartered, and his green eyes beamed. Its iridescent sheen began to glow vividly, and then, the body dropped limply and shimmered to a green dust, leaving behind only a powder of evidence the faery had walked the mortal realm.

Vail slapped a hand to his bleeding gut. It would heal.

But would a broken neck heal?

"Lyric?" He lunged to Lyric and lifted her into his arms. Her body draped limply across his knees and chest. "Lyric, wake up!"

Her neck was loose, broken from the spine. He held her head carefully, hoping the bones would heal. They had to. "You can't be dead. I told him to do it. I didn't mean it. Lyric, don't let this be real. I need you."

His heart pounded. He sucked in a reedy breath, gasping. He'd never needed anyone.

"Lyric?" How to revive a possibly dead vampire?

He'd seen a television show featuring a swimmer reviving a drowning friend by breathing air into their lungs.

Vail pressed his mouth over Lyric's and blew in. The breath came out her nose and dusted his cheek. He pressed her nostrils shut and breathed again. Her chest rose. He did it again, and again.

This wouldn't work. She hadn't drowned. She was broken! But he had to try, so he continued. Breathe in, followed by her involuntary exhalation. And repeat.

Suddenly he heard the bones snap. Her neck jerked. The body in his arms reanimated. She sucked in air and clutched his head. Huffing and sitting up, she looked about to orient herself, then stared into his eyes. Her pale blue irises grew wet with unspilled tears. "You told him to break my neck!"

"I wasn't thinking. I'm sorry, but it didn't kill you."

"Have you ever had your neck broken?" She fitted her hands about his neck but was too weak to squeeze. "You bastard. Get away from me."

Vail sat back. He'd saved them from the vicious sidhe warrior. And they should not be sitting in the open, waiting for the next sidhe to come along to claim the prize offered for Lyric's head.

"We can't stay here."

"I'm not going anywhere with you."

"Lyric." He caressed her hair, but she pulled away

from him. "I'm sorry. I don't know how else it could have gone. He would have killed you one way or another. I was trying to find out who put a price on your head."

"Where is that ugly faery?"

"He's gone. I impaled him on an iron bar."

She scrambled from him and stood, wobbling and clutching the tattered plastic supermarket bag as if it were a valued treasure. Her eyes shuffled over the faint shimmer below the tangled railing.

When he moved to help her, she put up her palm. "Back off, Vail. I'm not sure what I think about you anymore."

He hung his head. "You have every right to hate me. But you can hate me and allow me to get you to safety at the same time. Someone wants you dead."

"This is starting to freak me out," she said, nervously rubbing her neck. "I thought I'd be getting away, starting a new life, you know? Hell, I just wanted to join the circus! Now I've got insane faeries chasing after me, and probably the whole Seelie nation, not to mention that bastard, Zett."

She exhaled and her watery eyes found his. "I'm scared."

Vail inhaled and nodded to her seeking gaze. He could feel her fear, and he didn't like that it curdled his blood and made it sit cold and sluggish in his veins. This gorgeous woman should never fear.

"I vow, as long as you stay near me, Lyric, I will protect you with my life."

"Why?"

"Why? You're not supposed to ask why, you should accept—"

"What stake do you have in protecting me? What's in it for you?"

Finding his father. But there was another reason now. For some reason he couldn't stand back and let her do this on her own. "Lyric. Please. I'm trying to do the hero thing here."

"I get that. As distorted as your version of heroic is." She rubbed her neck, wincing. "But it would make me feel better to know what's going on in your faery-dusted brain right now."

"I want to protect you." He gripped her by the shoulders, but immediately loosened his hold. No, he would not harm her or give her reason to think he might. She was too precious. "Because it feels right. More right than anything I've felt before."

She lifted her chin. Her cheek was smeared with dirt. A tear on the shoulder of her dress revealed dirt-smeared skin. She deserved to be put on a pedestal and not blindly worshipped, but rather cherished.

"You think more will come after us?" she asked.

"They will not relent. The Unseelies will seek us, as well as those unaligned, like the worm wraith. And the more we delay, the faster the Seelie court learns of the missing gown. We can't stand around and let the next sidhe lock on to us like a sniper's scope. If it's you they're looking for, we need to get to my place and fix you up." He touched the bag, and took it from her when she relented. "Come with me, will you?"

She slipped her hand into his and he hated that he

could feel her shake. Lyric tugged him to a stop. "You promise to protect me?"

He slid a hand through her hair and bent to kiss her. It was bittersweet, a kiss for the fucked-up hero who would sacrifice his lover's neck to win the fight. He didn't deserve her trust, or this kiss.

"I promise. But I will give you the chance to walk away right now. My methods are unorthodox. I don't know the rules, and so can't play by them. I'm in this for myself, Lyric. First and foremost."

"I suspected as much. But you're not going to tell me why."

"Can't. It's too personal."

She nodded. "I can relate to that. You need to trust me to let me into your heart."

"No, I—"

But she didn't wait for him to summon an excuse. "You promise you won't let anyone snap my neck again?"

"No harm will come to you. I will ram my heart onto the stake myself, if it should come to that."

"It had better not come to that." She sighed and tugged him into a walk. "Fine. We're in this together, enemy mine."

# *CHAPTER TEN*

LYRIC TUGGED THE towel from her wet hair and pulled a thick hank around to inspect because the hotel room mirror wasn't going to help. Her pale tresses had been obliterated, to be replaced with dull, dumpy brown. She'd refused to let Vail help her put the color in, which had proved a challenge, keeping it off her skin. She was still angry with him over allowing her to die.

Had she been dead? Her neck had been broken. She'd lost a few minutes of perception. What if the worm wraith had staked her in that time?

She eased a hand around her neck for the dozenth time. Head still on, so that meant something. And Vail had beat off the bad guy. An attacker, she sensed, who had been much stronger than Vail, and determined to kill them both to get what he wanted—her. She should be thankful.

She was thankful. For the most part.

The sidhe had been after her because someone had put a price on her head? Apparently, she'd escaped her deadly fate only to step even closer to it.

She should tell Vail everything. He would know

how to help her. Or it was possible the truth would piss him off and, tired of her danger, he'd hand her over to Zett himself.

She couldn't risk that happening.

Vail waited out in the main room. The small one-bed, fifty-euro-a-night heap that he'd rented in the twentieth arrondissement was far from city center. And far from the circle of what she knew. Lyric was a city girl and moved and existed where she was comfortable, which was within the circle of the first six or seven quarters.

*You really need to get out more.*

"You can't even fake a kidnapping right." She pulled out the hem of the dowdy T-shirt she'd bought to wear for this procedure. It was covered with dark dribbles of hair color. "I can't believe I didn't plan that Charish would send someone after me so quickly."

It was supposed to go smoothly. She had got out of the house, stashed the gown and contacted Leo about finding someone to remove the mark and, well, then…

But when she'd been ready to throw in the towel, so to speak—she tossed the color-stained towel into the cracked bathtub—Vail had stepped up, grabbed her hand and offered the support she'd needed.

In a manner.

Why? What did he see in her? It couldn't be anything beyond the great sex. Though when he'd grabbed her hand to walk into the store earlier she'd felt special, as if she belonged to him and he was hers. And how weird was that? Just from hand-holding?

"You're not a teenager anymore, Lyric. Men want women for more than holding hands." She sighed. "But I'll take it for what it was. Which felt pretty cool at the time." And so what if her heart still acted like a teenage girl?

Vail had his own reasons for pursuing the answers in this case. He seemed to know Zett. Likely he did if he'd lived in Faery. Was Vail's keeping her in hand some kind of vengeance against the faery lord?

She didn't want to know, didn't want the betrayal. Vail was the first male vampire Lyric had truly got along with, despite his obvious dislike for their breed. The fact he was an amazing lover was awesome, but that he'd developed the need to protect her meant even more. No one had ever stepped up the way he had for her, not even her brother, Leo.

"How's it look?" he called.

Lyric considered pulling off the T-shirt and walking into the bedroom bare breasted so he'd be distracted from the awful hair, but decided it was time she acted as smart as he thought she was.

Vail lay stretched across the bed on his stomach. He whistled when Lyric sashayed in and fluffed at the miserable hair. "Not too shabby."

"*Shabby* is the perfect word for this." She sat beside him, her shoulders sagging. "This is awful. Do I have to have this color forever?"

"Just until we figure out the secret deal and why Zett wants you dead. I think it's pretty."

"It looks like mud."

"Lyric, the color of your hair has little to do with

my perception of you. Nor do your dazzling white teeth, or those bright blue eyes. Or your gorgeous full breasts and soft, sexy skin." He rolled to his back and slid a palm over her heart. "This matters, though."

"Since when did you become all mushy and romantic? Two days ago you wanted to bag my ass and haul me back to Mommy. The sex can't be that good."

"The sex is beyond good. And I am allowed to like you for more than just the physical, aren't I? I like you, Lyric. I like what you're about. Daring, fearless."

She chuffed. If he only knew how desperately fearful she'd become.

"And the fact you trust me, a messed-up bloodsucker who thinks he's a faery, is tremendous."

"We're all messed up. You just show it more. It isn't every day a guy will let the big bad assassin kill his girl."

"How long are you going to hold that against me?"

"Some time close to forever."

"Good thing I have forever."

She touched the corner of his eye where it sparkled. "How long do you think it would take you to get clean of dust?"

"Don't know. Don't care. Because it's not going to happen."

"Right." Because he didn't think he had a problem.

Maybe he didn't. Maybe he did need the ichor to maintain. She hadn't seen him acting high or out of sorts. Dust freaks could rage, act manic and paranoid if not given the high they craved. But seeing his blood all over his shirt now, glittering with ichor, was too much.

They were too different, yet, to be the hand-holding pair she hoped for.

"So what's next?" she asked.

"I put a call in to a friend. He's asking around about your mother's deal with Zett. If the rumor mill is ablaze with me kidnapping you, it's got to contain some spark about your mother's deal. Said he'd call me back."

Should she tell him what she knew? No, the time didn't feel right. And she needed to make a call of her own. "So we're going to sit in this dump until the phone rings?"

His thumb grazed her nipple beneath the thin T-shirt. "We can sit. Or lie down. Or you can sit and I can lie down. Or I can put you up against the wall, standing."

"You have a one-track mind, vampire."

"Don't you want your new brunette self to get laid? Baptism by orgasm?"

She tugged her hair into a ponytail and twisted it. "Sounds like a holy ritual I can get—"

"Bloody Herne!" Vail flew off the bed as if by magical force.

Arms raised behind her head with her hair in hand, Lyric twisted around to see the vampire pointing at her, mouth gaping and eyes wide. "What?" Oh, hell. She dropped her hair.

"You've a faery mark!"

HER DEEPEST, DARKEST SECRET had just been ripped wide open. One stupid moment of basking in Vail's charming flirtations, and she'd let it slip.

All her life Lyric had been careful to never allow anyone to see the thin luminous mark, which swept behind the curve of her right ear. Always she wore her hair long and over her ears. Though she liked the way it looked pulled up, that hadn't been an option since she was a teenager.

How could she have let down her guard?

*You're starting to trust him. You knew he would prove dangerous, you just didn't know the danger would be to your heart.*

The jig was up. And honestly, Lyric felt relief loosen her muscles. Tilting her head and stroking her hair back and aside, she displayed the faery mark for him to inspect.

Vail approached cautiously, but she sensed it was such a remarkable discovery he couldn't be sure how to take it. He didn't get close enough to touch, yet craned his neck to examine what looked like a finger had smeared a trail of bioluminescence on her skin. It was marked at the bottom with a fingerprint, Leo had told her, after he'd inspected his sister's mark. Leo was the only one she'd ever dared tell.

"Whose mark?" Vail whispered. "And…how? Why? Faeries don't…"

"Like vampires," she finished for him in a quiet breath.

"We hate vampires," he said. "I mean—"

"I know what you mean."

She couldn't expect him to side with her. He had decades of ingrained belief to overcome. And why should she expect him to change to please her?

"How'd you get it?" he asked. "From who?"

"It's Zett's mark."

"What?" His shout hurt her ears, and Lyric winced and tugged the hair back over her ear.

Vail stumbled backward, catching his heel on the wooden chair by the broken television, and sat, slapping his palms to the chair arms with a loud crack. The disgust on his face stretched through his entire tense musculature.

It shamed Lyric, and for good reason. She felt as small and helpless now as she had after her brother had initially berated her for allowing it to happen.

"I'll explain," she offered quietly. "It's not what you think it is."

"I have no earthly idea what it could possibly be. Zett would never—" Vail shoved a hand through his hair. "Hell, I don't know anymore. Apparently there is something about you he desires enough to— I wish you would have revealed that little secret right away."

"So you could have turned me over immediately? Not started to care about me?"

"I don't—" He sighed and thumbed his chin. "I do. I just… Fuck, Lyric, do you know what that mark means?"

His voice had taken on an emotionless tone she guessed was not new to him. A means of putting up a wall. She knew that trick. She'd been doing it since she was a teenager.

"Of course I know what it means. It's haunted me every day and night since I was a teenager."

She sat on the bed, careful not to face Vail directly, because it felt like an intrusion into the shield his intense emotions cast before him.

"I met Zett when I was thirteen," she explained. "It was summer, and my mother had packed me off to summer camp, as usual. I hadn't hit puberty yet, so I was just another silly mortal girl to any who would wonder."

She couldn't erase a wistful smile over memories of camp. And the sun. The curse of the bloodborn vampire was they got to grow up as if a normal mortal, eating, drinking, and enjoying the warmth of the sun upon their skin, until the blood hunger took it all away.

"I met Zett one night after campfire, when most of the others were in their cabins readying for bed. I'd gone for a walk in the woods behind our cabin, gathering daisies for a chain—"

She wasn't swayed by Vail's mocking expression.

"He told me he was a faery prince. You can imagine I was enchanted."

Vail grunted and caught his chin against his fist.

"I didn't believe he was a real faery, but my thirteen-year-old, angsting teenage heart wanted it to be true. You probably don't have a clue how a teenage girl's heart works. Suffice to say, it was dramatic and pining and desperate for any facsimile of love."

It still worked that way. Only now it was more cautious.

"Zett was my first kiss."

She heard Vail's quiet intake of breath, but

continued, needing to get it all out while she still had the courage.

"He touched me behind my ear, though I wouldn't know it was a claiming mark until my brother explained it to me, and swore me never to tell my mother.

"Zett apparently had no idea I was vampire. He didn't come for me after that. The years passed and I thought I was in the clear. Leo was relieved. Until last month. I knew I was being followed by faeries and guessed they were Zett's men. They must have witnessed me drinking blood from a mortal and reported back to the Unseelie lord. I received a polite request, by letter, to meet Zett in the forest."

"You went to him?" Vail asked, incredulous.

"Of course not. I'm not stupid. I also wasn't stupid enough to believe the attempt on my life two weeks ago from a speeding car wasn't related. So when Charish told me she'd made a deal with a faery lord, I knew right away what Zett was up to. He'd found a more sinister way to get at me through my mother, who was completely unaware of the mark."

Vail slammed a fist on the chair arm, breaking it from the body of the chair. He stood and paced. "I can't believe this."

"But it's the truth. I had no idea when a faery marked someone it meant that faery intended to someday claim the person as their—"

"Bride," Vail blurted. "Zett marked you as his fucking bride."

# *CHAPTER ELEVEN*

YES, CHOSEN TO wed the Lord of Midsummer Dark.

Lyric hadn't known what the faery mark meant until she'd shown her brother. Both young, they'd decided not to tell Charish because Lyric had suspected her mother would never allow her to go to camp again. Leo had been busy training so he'd left her alone to deal with the knowledge she must keep a secret—or die. Because no faery would ever claim a vampire as his wife. And if Zett remembered his foolish mark, he would kill her.

After that summer, she'd never pined for boys again. It wasn't smart to moon over a handsome man. It could get a girl marked for life.

Vail's voice broke the awkward silence in the dingy hotel room. "Why were you intending to go to him with the gown?"

"I wasn't! I told you, my mother agreed that I would take the gown to Zett, but my intentions all along were to escape. Charish had no idea of Zett's ulterior motives. You think I don't know what fate waited for me should I set one foot in Faery?"

The two held each other's stares for a moment that felt like forever. Lyric didn't want to speak her fate. *Please, let him figure it out.*

Finally, Vail nodded. "I see. Why didn't you tell your mother?"

"Because I was young and didn't want to get in trouble and if you keep a secret long enough it becomes what you are. It is no longer a secret but just that thing you never talk about. And you try to brush it off as insignificant, but then one day it comes back to bite you."

"Zett must have seen this as an opportunity to get to you."

Lyric shook her head. "Yes, and my mother knew only that she was getting a bargain from Faery. Charish had arranged for demon guards to accompany me. She didn't know Zett had marked me, but she was smart enough to guess that he could try something."

Vail walked to the window and beat a fist against the wood frame. The night sky flashed with neon lights. Raindrops pearled down the window.

"That bastard spoils everything he touches," he muttered. "I will kill him!"

Lyric climbed off the bed and embraced him from behind. He initially shrugged to push her away, but she clung, fearful of abandonment. Vail was the only man she trusted right now.

"Please," she whispered against his shoulder.

He turned and clasped her to his chest, drawing her head against his shoulder, and held her so tightly she thought they two would become one. And she wished for such a magical bonding.

*You know you can never bond, not unless he drinks your blood.*

"I won't allow Zett near you," he said. "I vow it."

Tilting her head, he kissed her hard and deep. Lyric lost her breath, but it didn't matter because she took in Vail's breath. They fed each other the vicious hunger for acceptance only they two could understand.

This kiss was everything that fateful summer camp kiss had not been. Intense and defiant. True. It must be hard for Vail to claim he would protect her when he could not abide her kind. For that, she respected him.

"No one knows about you being marked," Vail said. "They can't."

"It's just Leo. But what about that worm wraith? He said he wanted me dead for the price on my head. He must have known something."

"He could have been Zett's man. I thought he was unaligned, but hell, I don't know much of anything anymore. Surely the wraith couldn't have known the *reason* Zett wanted you dead. If anyone learns the Lord of Midsummer Dark marked a vampire as his bride that could destroy him. The wraith would have kept you alive and used you against Zett."

"I know. Which is why I'm trying to stay away from him. You understand now?"

"Yes, but you can't run forever. He will find you with ease. Changed hair color or not." He kissed the crown of her head. "I'm sorry I made you do this. It's not going to matter now. The mark behind your ear acts like a beacon."

"Does it glow?"

"No, but it gives off pheromones I'm sure Zett can track. He'll exhaust all his resources before coming for you personally. I know Zett does not like the mortal realm. It surprises me that he was at a summer camp looking for a wife."

"It might have been spur of the moment for him."

"I doubt it. Zett would not venture to this realm without intent."

"What are we going to do?"

"Move faster than every faery who wants to get their hands on you and the gown. If we can learn what Zett and your mother had arranged, it may give us leverage. You're not keeping any more secrets from me?"

She shook her head.

"What about the gown?"

"What about it? I swear, beyond telling you I thought she was going to get access to Faery, I don't know what mother agreed to with Zett. She wouldn't tell me."

"You never told me that. Access to Faery?"

Lyric sighed. Yes, she must tell him all if she wanted to retain his trust. "Zett agreed to allow Charish into Faery to steal artifacts and such."

Vail laughed. He pounded the wall with a fist. "That's a lie."

"Is not. That's what my mother told me."

"Then she was lying to you, Lyric. I know Zett. He, along with the rest of Faery, would never make such a deal. First of all, there's nothing in Faery that would be worth fencing in the mortal realm."

"There are collectors. Vampires, werewolves, demons. They all want a piece of faery."

"Any faery item brought into the mortal realm would lose its power unless held by a faery. That's the way it works. So there's got to be another reason."

"I'm sorry, that's what she told me." And truthfully, she'd suspected it a lie the moment in the apartment when Vail had challenged her to consider what a faery could possibly want from a vampire.

"She lied to you, Lyric." He kissed her on the crown of her head. "And for that I am sorry."

VAIL'S CONTACT RETURNED his call. He put the phone to his ear, but kept one eye on Lyric's slinky catlike walk as she paced the room, arms crossed. "Santiago and the Unseelie?"

"I don't know what the deal is," Domingos LaRoque said over the phone, "but I'd suggest you check FaeryTown if you want answers. All roads lead there, my friend. But you didn't hear this from me."

"Of course not."

"They're lookin' for you, man."

"I know that. But what *they* in particular?"

"A gang of Unseelie. I heard Zett sent them. They are badass."

Vail smirked at the notion of badass faeries. They came as vicious and fucked-up as any other paranormal, but still, it just sounded fluffy.

"I didn't kidnap her, Domingos."

"Yeah? So why have you been seen with her?"

"It's a long story. Does Santiago know?"

"I don't think so. I have connections with the family

through tribe Zmaj, but since the Santiago clan is not allied as a tribe, they're out of the loop. It's possible Charish hasn't heard anything."

"Let's hope it stays that way. I don't think I can go to FaeryTown without being recognized if Zett has a crew out."

On the other hand, FaeryTown was the last place a respectable faery would go. Not that Zett was in any way, shape or form respectable.

"Safest place for you is Antarctica, man. I heard faeries don't like the cold."

"On the contrary, their blood is cold so they get on pretty much anywhere."

"Tough luck for you, Vail. Is that all you wanted?"

"Yes, thank you." He slapped the phone shut and slunk onto the end of the mattress. "FaeryTown."

FaeryTown hid in the eighteenth quarter, edging a city park. Very few faeries chose to live in the mortal realm, but those who were attracted to the cities, which were the least enchanted places in this realm, tended to gather and develop small towns within the cities. It was a place to mingle with other faeries, but also a place, Vail knew, that vampires frequented. For one reason.

Lyric finally asked, "Who was that?"

"A friend of mine, Domingos LaRoque. He's with tribe Zmaj."

"You have a vampire friend?"

"Don't give me that look. He pulled me out of a fight with another vampire after I'd first arrived. He's a musician. And I know what you're thinking."

"Yes, well, we are your breed. Sooner or later you'll come around."

He already had, thanks to one very sexy vampiress. As *around* as he intended without succumbing to blood drinking.

"Domingos thinks I'll find some answers in FaeryTown."

"I'm sorry I can't tell you more. I can't believe Charish wasn't forthright about the deal. What is she up to?"

She sat beside him, and he kissed her new brown locks and pulled a few strands from her long lashes. They were two alike, both with parents of nefarious means. However, Vail had never met his father. It was easy to hate someone you didn't know.

And yet, part of him wanted to believe that Cressida's tales of his father's misdeeds had been concocted to make Vail not desire to meet the man.

He touched the lily bracelet he'd worn since leaving Faery. The stem was firm and cool. Cressida had insisted he wear it to protect him from the evils of the mortal realm. Could it shield his eyes from his father's truth?

He pressed his forehead to Lyric's. To capture this moment, shared with her, seemed a ridiculous task. Something not meant to survive captivity. A fleeting affair on the timeline of his weirdly inappropriate life.

Soft caresses stroked his cheek and neck. "I don't think you know how much I appreciate you protecting me, and wanting to get to the bottom of all this. How can I make you understand?"

He kissed her fingers and held them against his mouth. "You don't need to do anything, Lyric. I understand. We should stay out of sight until we learn the truth behind the deal. If Zett's men are after us, they may be tracking your mark by pheromones. If it's not Zett, they need to actually see your mark to track us."

"We can go to Leo's place. My brother has it warded with so many different security systems it's not even funny. And I do need to talk to him."

"Or maybe we can give them what they want."

"Me?"

"Or the gown."

"I didn't steal the gown. And that is the truth."

"I trust you, but I don't believe you." Vail clasped Lyric's hand tightly. "Where is it? You have the gown. You can make it all end right now."

"What makes you think that? I told you—"

"Yes, that you didn't steal the gown. Hawkes told me the storage for the faery items had been neatly invaded."

"The security at Hawkes Associates was lousy." Lyric slapped a hand over her mouth.

"Exactly." Vail smirked, but he didn't feel the win like he should. "Still had that one last secret, eh?" And how many more?

"It wasn't me."

"Is that your final answer?"

"My brother stole the gown after Charish gave him

the big sad-eyes treatment. I don't know why everyone is getting so bent over this damned gown. All I know is Zett was going to let Charish into Faery to steal."

"Which was a lie, because vampires don't belong in Faery, and Zett would sooner kill them than allow them in."

"He allowed you in."

"He hadn't a choice. I told you I was taken right after my birth by the Mistress of Winter's Edge." Vail clammed up, turning his back to Lyric.

"Look, I know you've got a past and it's not necessary to what we're doing right here and now, but do you want to talk about it?"

"Just accept I know Zett would not make such a deal with your mother. It has to be huge, whatever the deal is," Vail said softly, "or it wouldn't be worth the gown."

It should have made Vail glad she was finally in a position to understand his world, but it made him sad. For he saw into her heart and got a glimpse of her weakness—family. She would do anything to protect them, even if it meant running for her life.

"I think we should set a trap," Vail said.

"Which is?"

"We need to hand the gown over to Zett—"

"But *I* was supposed to hand over the gown."

"Yes, and I was supposed to turn the gown over to Hawkes Associates. It belongs to the Seelie court."

"So, you're saying you're going to hand me over to the faery who wants me dead?"

"No, I… No." He pushed his fingers through his hair and tugged. "You're mine."

"Is that so?"

He turned to catch her surprised expression. "You know what I mean."

"Do *you* know what you mean? Because I don't think you do."

He did, but he wasn't prepared to admit that, yes, he'd developed feelings for a vampire, of all creatures. "Can we concentrate on the problem?"

"No, I want to know why you think you can claim me as yours when you won't so much as taste my blood. I disgust you!"

"You don't— It's just you're—" He swung a look out the window and fisted the wall.

"Pretty to look at, nice to fuck, but not to bond with?"

"Who said anything about bonding?"

"Right. I get it. I'm yours, some kind of plaything slash prisoner slash deal-bait—"

He grabbed her by the shoulders and kissed her. It was the only way to stop her from taking this conversation to a place he wouldn't be able to navigate. He kissed her hard and she struggled, but it didn't take long for her to kiss him back.

That she trusted him enough to surrender to his insistent lust, and felt safe in his arms, was some kind of wacky gift he didn't deserve but intended to hoard from all others. Lyric in his embrace, and at his mouth, changed him. Or maybe she steered him toward his truth?

"What if we had a fake?" she suggested.

"Zett would see through it right away."

"Well, everyone can see through the dress. It's sheer."

He chuckled, glad for a moment of levity. "I think the only way this can work is to bring the Seelie court in on it. But how to do that without revealing Rhys Hawkes had lost the gown in the first place? Much as the old man pisses me off, I would never put him in such a position. I've got to figure a plan. We can't trust anyone."

"But Rhys Hawkes is the one who sent you on this mission. Surely you can trust him?"

"I don't want to bring this mess to his doorstep. It wouldn't be fair, and I don't want to cause further harm to…" Vail exhaled and sank against the wall, catching his head in his hands.

LYRIC COULD FEEL her lover's exasperation radiate from his body. She hated seeing him collapsed in on himself, defeated by something he couldn't touch. She sensed if he would release his burden he might be able to get beyond it and start thinking about solving their problem.

Kneeling before him, she stroked his hair. It glittered with iridescent dust, more than usual. She wasn't worried about getting a contact high. She hadn't so far and they'd been closer than close. She did trust Vail. He would protect her with his life. If he didn't first lose that life.

"Rhys lives with your mother," she said, remembering what he'd told her. And then she understood. "You don't want to bring this to her."

He shook his head and looked into her eyes. "She doesn't need this. She doesn't need me, to see me and be reminded."

"Of what? She's never known you, Vail."

He pulled her to him and nuzzled his face into her neck. He clung to her and she sensed he simply wanted the connection without the words, the confession she wanted to hear, the tender inner layer stripped away from his hard core.

"I can't understand you never seeing your mother," she offered quietly. "I would give anything to see my father again, just for a day. He died when I was eight."

"I'm sorry." He pulled her around to sit on his lap. His strong thighs paralleled her legs and she felt like a bird sitting within a protective cove. He kissed the side of her neck, below the faery mark. That went a long way toward his acceptance of her.

"Some days I think I want to see my mother," he said softly. "I'm not sure. I don't want to make her worse than she already is."

"How could seeing her son make her worse?"

He clasped her hand and kissed her knuckles. "Rhys describes her madness as frustrating and unpredictable."

"Is she ever lucid?" she asked.

"Rhys claims she is lucid more than not. When she takes blood she is completely sane. She spends all her time at home, though. Doesn't ever want to go out into the world."

"That's so sad."

"Rhys brings blood to her daily. She needs it often to stay sane."

That was a lot. Most vampires took blood about once every two weeks. It was all they needed to sustain, though some drank more often because they liked it, and others less often for reasons Lyric could not comprehend.

Vail's warmth enticed Lyric to snuggle closer to him, but she would not misinterpret this moment for anything other than what it was. A tense balance limned the edge between Vail's desire for acceptance from his family and his fear of that same acceptance. Yet he'd never admit to that.

She tilted her head against his shoulder. "I bet a visit from you would cheer her up."

"Lyric." Now he pressed her hands firmly between his and clasped them to her chest. His lips pressed her shoulder a moment. She felt him nod against her as if coming to a decision. "There's something you need to know about me and my brother, and how we came to be."

"You said you had two different dads, and one mother, but were born at the same time. That's as far-out as it gets."

"My father raped my mother. I was born of that crime."

She twisted to meet his eyes, moved to touch his cheek, but he flinched. How terrible. To carry that stigma? But surely his mother… Oh, hell, it must be the reason she was mad. "I'm so sorry."

"So you see why I think it would do more harm than good to visit her?"

"Is that…is that why she gave you away?"

"She did not give me away. The faery Cressida chose me. Rhys Hawkes owed her a boon after she had enchanted his vampire. Rhys is a half-breed, both werewolf and vampire occupy his body. When he's vampire, his werewolf mind rules. When werewolf, the vampire takes over. And that vampire, denied blood during the month because his werewolf mind doesn't desire such sustenance, is vicious and blood hungry. Centuries ago, Cressida enchanted him so the werewolf would only come out at the full moon, thus lessening the risk during the rest of the month that he may kill an innocent.

"In exchange for that enchantment, she asked for his firstborn. Rhys has told me he was young and had thought he would never have a child—not purposefully, for he feared what the child of a half-breed would become. He had no clue Viviane was pregnant when she was buried alive. Hell, he thought her dead in the eighteenth century."

"Buried *alive?*"

"My father wanted Viviane, and when he couldn't have her because she and Rhys were in love, he had Viviane bespelled by a warlock. The spell rendered her aware yet unable to move. He placed her in a glass coffin and buried her beneath Paris. Rhys thought her dead. He didn't find her until three decades ago after hearing an urban legend about the Vampire Snow White."

"I've heard that one. Seriously? That was your mother?"

He nodded.

"The rivalry between him and your father must have been fierce for one of them to have buried your mother alive. But I don't understand. If she was found two centuries later…"

"She was pregnant with my brother and I when she was buried. The spell kept her frozen yet aware. When she was released from the spell by taking mortal blood, we began to germinate as normal babies. I gestated in my mother's belly for over two centuries."

"Wow."

"Tell me about it. So when the Mistress of Winter's Edge came to claim her boon, Rhys had no choice but to offer one of his children. One must never refuse to pay their part in a faery bargain. At the time, he assumed both of us were his progeny—because how could he know differently?—and couldn't decide, so he let the faery choose.

"Cressida chose me, expecting I was a half-breed vampire/werewolf. Faeries use half-breeds to strengthen our—*their* race. I was groomed as a child, unaware that I was not the half-breed Rhys Hawkes's son. I grew up knowing some day I would be expected to mate with a faery woman. Very likely the Unseelie princess."

"That's a huge expectation."

"It gave me a big head, let me tell you. I strutted around Faery like I owned the place."

"You still have that strut."

"Yes, well, it was diminished when I came into my blood hunger. Cressida was enraged. Only then did she figure my father had been vampire, and that I was bloodborn. And a bloodborn vampire is worthless in Faery. Well, as I've explained, we're considered filth."

Now Lyric understood how Vail could pin that label on all vampires. He knew nothing else.

"When Cressida arrived in the mortal realm to rage at him, it was the first time Rhys knew I was not his son. When the blood hunger insisted, I was forced to feed on ichor. By that time I'd developed an immunity to it, so it didn't make me high."

"Cressida ignored you after that, I suppose."

"Ch'yeah. It was like losing the mother I never wanted in the first place. Because I'd always known I had a vampire mother somewhere, and believed I had a half-breed father. But I'd grown to love Cressida because she was the only parental figure I had in my life. Not that she was motherly in any fashion."

"So how does Zett play into all this? Let me guess," Lyric said. "Zett was supposed to marry the Unseelie princess until you came along."

"Not at all. The prince and princess always marry a mixed-blood breed to further mix the bloodlines and create new breeds. Zett and I were reluctant childhood friends. Cressida was his aunt, or else his sister. I've never been clear on that—Faery family trees are strange, to say the least. She wanted him to play nice with me. Zett would toss me a ball, then when Cressida wasn't looking he'd slap me across the face. He's always hated vampires, even if at the time, he believed I was vampire by half. I think I know why, too."

"Because he mistakenly marked a vampiress as his bride," Lyric decided. "But the timeline doesn't jive."

"Faery time is different from mortal time. He could have marked you when I was yet young."

"That freaks me out." She squeezed his hand. "You had a tough childhood. I'm so sorry for that."

"I survived. I had a few friends, mostly half-breeds taken for boons, like Kit."

"A woman? You had a girlfriend?"

"We were best friends." He pulled Lyric closer and hugged her from behind. "She was a half-breed shifter. Half kitsune, half familiar."

"A fox and cat?"

"Yep. We both knew we'd grow up and be married off someday and bonded because of that common fate."

"And when she learned you were bloodborn?"

"Didn't change a thing between us. Kit is one of those rare souls who doesn't judge, and only sees into a person's heart."

"Where is she now?"

He pressed his forehead to her shoulder and Lyric felt his chest muscles tense against her back. A touchy subject.

"She's the reason I was banished from Faery," he said.

## *CHAPTER TWELVE*

"YOU WERE BANISHED because of a woman?"

Vail jumped up from the bed to look out the window. "They've found us."

Lyric peered over his shoulder. "I don't see anyone. You're just trying to avoid the truth."

Tension drew his frown tight as he moved her to look him directly in the eye. "Look now."

She turned her head, but he slid a hand to her cheek to maintain her gaze on him. "Don't turn your head, look out the corner of your eye."

She did, and— "Something fluttered past the window."

"We should be going," he said.

She clasped his hand, wanting to know about the woman he'd been friends with. The reason he had been banished? It was too fascinating not to learn about, but she wouldn't sacrifice safety for a few juicy tidbits about his life.

They needed to move, to stay safe from vigilante faeries who wanted to bring her to Zett or, worse, kill her.

"We could go to my brother," she suggested. "I swear to you he is a safe retreat. Trust me, neither of us want what the Santiago family has to offer."

He stroked her cheek and in the darkness the fine glimmer on his skin made her feel protected, as if an entire universe surrounded her.

"Being a Santiago hardened us," she said. "Made us something we didn't want to be. All right, so Leo took to thievery well, and hasn't stopped, but he doesn't want to serve Mother's whims anymore."

"Yet he stole the gown?"

"To appease her. He had no idea Charish intended to hand me over with the gown. If Leo had known he may have never stolen it."

He opened the door and headed for the emergency exit. "So you kept the secret because…? You wanted to do this for your mother, didn't you?"

"She's in a bad situation with a lover who thinks he can take control of her and the family. You know how it is when an abused woman stays with the man because she doesn't know how to begin to escape?"

"Sorry, I don't."

"Well, that's my mother. I thought going along with this deal would make her rich. Give her a means to escape."

"Why doesn't someone take out the bastard vampire who's threatening her?"

"He's got a powerful hold on my mother, Vail. He remains in the shadows, yet controls her and, soon, the entire Santiago clan, I'm sure. I hate him. I fear him."

"I don't like hearing that you fear anyone. I'll kill the bastard for you, and end this whole problem."

She tugged him to a stop at the outer door. "Is it so easy for you to take a life to make your own better? Even for my mother, I would never condone murder."

He kissed her. "And that is what I like about you. Your strange morality makes me want to do better."

"So you think I'm strange now?"

"Not so strange as I am. All right, no killing for now. We've faery vigilantes to escape. Let's head to your brother's place."

"Come on," Lyric encouraged. "He'll want to meet the man who's been protecting me."

"Are you going to tell him that before or after you tell him about the broken neck fiasco?"

"Haven't decided yet."

CRUISING IN THE MASERATI through Paris in Vail's usual speeding, careless style wasn't exactly playing it on the down low. Innocent bystanders fled the sidewalks for their life. Johnny Cash crooned about a boy named Sue who'd had to learn to tough it out in the world branded with the awful moniker.

Lyric turned down the music. Vail may have flashed her a wild look, but dark sunglasses shaded his eyes.

"What did you say you get out of all this?" she asked. "After you've handed me and the gown over? I think you missed that part when you were telling me about living in Faery and your mother."

Vail cocked his head to the side and took a sharp

turn that slammed her against the passenger door. She didn't wear a seat belt. After all, a crash wasn't going to kill her. But she got the I-don't-want-to-talk vibe from him, loud and clear.

They drove through a tunnel, which briefly blocked the late-afternoon sun. The mirror flashed brightly in Lyric's vision when they emerged to daylight.

"Your silence does not deflect my curiosity," she said, rooting around in the backseat and finding Green Snake. She allowed the three-foot-long green mamba to curl about her forearm. "It means you're not willing to be as honest with me as I have been with you. Typical."

"I am the furthest from typical," he snapped.

"Physically, sure. But mentally? You're like all the rest of the men. Closed up emotionally, hot to get it on physically."

He shifted and navigated another sharp turn. "We had sex too soon. That was probably wrong."

"Hey, I'm not complaining. I wanted it. I thought you did, too."

"I did. I enjoy having sex with you, Lyric."

"You're changing the subject, yet another typical male reaction to being asked the important questions. If you're not going to spill about the kitsune cat shifter, then I need something."

Another swerve. This time the Maserati clipped a hedge.

"Hawkes is going to give me information to find my father. I've never met him." Short, precise answer. He definitely did not want to elaborate.

"What will you do when you see him?"

He stopped at a sign and tugged his glasses down to look over the rims at her. The faery ointment around his blue eyes was always startlingly sexy.

"I'm going to look into his eyes," he said. "To see if they are mine."

Lyric couldn't remember her father's eyes. "You'll be lucky to have that opportunity."

"Yeah?" He shifted and revved the engine but didn't take off. "After I see what I want to see, then I'm going to kill him."

The Maserati peeled through the intersection. With a flick of his fingers, Vail twisted the music volume to high.

VAIL PULLED INTO an underground lot beneath the building Lyric had directed him to and got out, attempting not to slam the door, but he was riled and—fuck it—he slammed the door. It wasn't Lyric's questions; it was that he'd let those questions get to him. So he had father issues. Mother issues, as well. Didn't everyone?

Apparently, he and Lyric shared virtually the same issues. He should be able to talk to her about them. They'd shared a lot in the few days they'd known each other. So why had he clammed up and acted the asshole?

Lyric strolled around the trunk of the car behind him, tugging self-consciously at the dye-stained T-shirt she yet wore. They both needed a change of clothing.

He scanned the dark lot, seeking anything out of order. Now, more than ever, he had to remain alert, and see everything before it saw him. The ointment would help him spot the sidhe. What he needed was some serious weaponry for when he did see them. His blade had been sacrificed when fighting the worm wraith.

"I don't understand you wanting to kill someone you've never met," Lyric said.

Didn't the woman know when to stop?

"He's your father. Like him or not, aren't you at least going to give him a chance?"

Apparently she did not know when to stop.

Vail turned and clamped his hands onto her shoulders. She took off his sunglasses and propped them atop his head, which he didn't like, but he'd learned she was a female version of him—strong, stubborn and persistent.

"Listen," he said. "I told you my father buried my mother alive beneath Paris for over two centuries, but before doing so, he raped her. My brother, Trystan, hates me because he claims I'm the one who made our mother insane, regardless of the fact I served the blood debt *he* should have paid. Do you really have to wonder if the bastard who fathered me deserves a chance?"

Leaving her by the car, Vail strode off toward the building elevator. He had pushed the button when Lyric whistled and pointed to a door.

"Penthouse," she said, without looking at him. "He's got a private entrance."

Another elevator pinged open and Vail followed Lyric inside.

"Sorry," she said, and hit the single button with the side of her fist. "Won't bring it up again."

She positioned herself to the right of the elevator, staring at the camera mounted above the door. Wanting him to stand behind her, she tugged him over by a belt loop. Vail removed himself from her grip and stood, arms crossed, in the middle of the elevator.

"Suit yourself," she muttered.

The next ten seconds dragged like a century as they silently watched the camera flash floor numbers beside the screen. Vail wished for the drone of Muzak to cover the uncomfortable quiet. She shouldn't have apologized. It wasn't necessary. He was just in a bad place mentally.

When the elevator stopped, she said, "Leo is private. Necessary, as I've explained. You should step behind me."

Vail remained in place, not about to be ordered around by a chick.

The camera blinked on and a red explosion flashed in miniature on the LED screen above the buttons. Dramatics?

The doors slid open to reveal metal doors, and down the center Vail saw the arrows release from a mechanism. From top to bottom, six arrows sprang free.

He dodged right, slamming against Lyric's body, but still managed to take an arrow to his shin. "What the hell?"

"Booby traps," she offered calmly. "I told you to stand behind me."

"Ch'yeah, but you could have given me a reason." The pant leg had been ripped open and the abrasion on his leg bled. "Ouch!"

A man's face appeared on the elevator screen. The long face was capped by bleached white hair that emphasized his slender nose and bright blue eyes, a match to his sister's features. He nodded at Lyric and looked beyond her where Vail stood. "Who's with you?"

"His name is Vaillant," Lyric said into the speaker box. "He's cool. He's with me, Leo."

"Why did that question not come *before* the arrows?" Vail hissed. "Bloody Herne." His leg stung, but the arrow hadn't cut too deep. "I hope there wasn't poison in those."

"Not today," Leo said.

The screen went dark and the elevator doors slid open, left to right, to reveal a wall stocked with arrows aimed at both of them. That wall slid up to open into an apartment.

Vail waited for Lyric to step across the threshold. He wouldn't doubt there were murder holes in the frame of the doorway. When she passed through and landed in her brother's arms for a hug, he limped forward but was stopped at the threshold by the invisible barrier.

"It's good to see you, sis," the man said. "But what's up with your hair? And this awful shirt? This is so wrong."

"I'm hiding from dangerous sorts. Vail had me change my color. It's awful, isn't it?"

"Yes." The man, with an arm about Lyric's waist, turned to Vail. "What the fuck was your name, goth boy?"

"Vaillant," he offered. "Could you invite me in?"

"No—" Leo started. But Lyric said, "Come in."

Vail leaped quickly inside as the doors closed behind him.

"Nice," Leo said in a tone that sounded anything but pleased.

Vail offered his hand to shake, but when the surly vamp looked aside, he said the first thing that came to mind. "I'm charged to bring your sister home to your mother—"

The man was on him faster than a worm wraith. Slammed against the closed elevator doors, Vail huffed out his breath and winced at his aching skull. The man had actually head-banged him!

Leo held Vail firmly against the doors with an arm across his neck. "You're not taking her anywhere. What are you?" He glanced over his shoulder to Lyric.

"Vampire," she confirmed.

"The hell he is. I don't feel the shimmer. What's that scent?" He shoved off from Vail, then bent to smack his palm against Vail's wounded leg. He spread his fingers, covered with Vail's blood. "This shit sparkles."

Leo stood as tall as Vail, and was long and lean, but his muscles impressed him. Had to do a lot of head-banging to get biceps like those. But he couldn't figure how they would come in handy being a thief. Shouldn't he be lean and slender?

"What the hell are you looking at?" Leo swung a fist at Vail but he dodged. "Get the dust freak out of here before he poisons my home with his breath."

"Leo, drop the tough-guy act. I said he's with me. And he's not a dust freak. Maybe."

Vail winced at her need to add *maybe*. He wasn't a dust freak. He just did it to—yeah, whatever.

"You don't like the company I keep?" Lyric pressed the elevator button. "I'll leave."

"Fine, he stays. He's not a vamp, though." Leo squinted at Vail. "He sparkles like a damned faery."

Ready to spout a diatribe in favor of faeries, Vail paused when Lyric stepped before him, hands on her hips, and said to her brother, "His uncle owns Hawkes Associates."

"Ah." Leo nodded, smirking. "That explains a thing or two. But not why he is *with you*. Playing for a new team now, sis?"

"Stop it, Leo."

"So he took the gown?" Vail asked, knowing neither would confirm nor deny it, even though Lyric had already told him as much.

And neither did. Instead, Leo stalked into the living room furnished in modern brown leather pieces, and flipped a suitcase from the floor onto the couch. "I was packing. Got a job in Berlin tonight. What do you need, Lyric? Did you say you are on the run?"

"Yes. From faeries, and creepy worm wraiths. I need a place to hide out."

"Worm wraiths?" Leo whistled. "What have you got her involved in, man?"

"It's my fault," Lyric protested.

"Yeah? Charish thinks you were kidnapped." He kissed the corner of her eye. "I knew better. 'Bout time you got out of there. But if some vampire wannabe thinks he's going to take you back…" Leo smacked a fist into his palm and eyed Vail.

"I had to make a break," Lyric said. "If Zett gets his hands on me he'll kill me. Did you find a way to remove the mark?"

"I'm still looking. I don't have the right connections." His bravado dropped and he tugged Lyric in for a hug, running his hand over her back reassuringly. "I'm sorry, sis, but we'll figure this out."

"Thanks for trying."

Leo looked to Vail, who could only offer a shrug. "How do you think he is going to help you?"

"We have a deal," Lyric said. "After we find the gown—" the siblings exchanged a look Vail guessed was more than knowing "—I get a head start to run."

"Generous of you," Leo said to Vail. "She'll be off your radar before you can remember the scent of her perfume. Unless you've been tapping her. Have you been tapping my sister, goth boy?"

Enraged again, the man approached him with tightened fists and managed a gut punch before Vail could dodge.

"Tapping means drinking my blood," Lyric explained to Vail as he clutched his gut, wincing, "in case you had concluded it meant sex."

"Ah." Vail offered Leo his most charming, and slightly pained, grin. "Well, then, no tapping."

"Why not? You don't like her blood?" Leo smacked a fist loudly into his palm. "But you have been fucking her? Who do you think you are? You can't—"

"Leo!" Lyric insinuated herself between her brother and Vail—which he was thankful for at the moment. "Who I sleep with is none of your business. Now chill, and quit calling him goth boy."

"Does he prefer dark lord?"

Vail caught Lyric's smirk and said, "Vaillant would be the respectful usage of my name."

Leo sneered.

Vail added, "Dark lord is reserved for Zett, I'm sure."

Lyric bowed her head, and Vail put an arm around her waist. He could feel her sigh ripple through his body. He needed something to anchor himself at the moment, yet she felt a bit unsteady herself. "She was doing it to protect her mother," he said.

"Doing what?" Leo snapped. "Oh, no, you didn't?"

Lyric nodded. "It seemed the best way to get the largest payoff for Mother so she could be rid of that bastard trying to control her."

Her brother kicked the couch and punched the air. "That was stupid, Lyric. You should have told me. I would not have stolen the gown."

"And Mother would be in a worse predicament than

she is now. Besides, I had a great plan for escaping Zett by faking my own kidnapping. Until…"

Both siblings looked to Vail—the man sent to take Lyric back to Mommy.

"It's not going to happen," Vail said reassuringly. "I won't take Lyric home, and I sure as hell will not allow Zett to get his hands on her again."

Leo bowed his head and shook it, exhaling through his nose. "The only way she'll ever be safe from that bastard is to get the mark removed. You got a clue how to do that, goth—er, Vaillant?"

"I've only just learned about her mark. My guess is there might be a healer in FaeryTown who can help, or at least attempt to remove it."

The brother nodded, obviously not having a better suggestion.

"You were leaving?" Lyric asked her brother. "Can we stay the night?"

"I've gotta run right now to catch my flight. And yes, you can stay. But he can't."

"Vail will protect me."

The siblings held off in a defiant stance, Leo standing a head taller than his sister, yet Vail noticed how quickly his straight shoulders sagged, and the brother nodded, defeated.

He lugged the suitcase to the door and paused before Vail. "I don't like you."

"Really? I never would have guessed. I don't intend to harm your sister."

"If you think taking her home to Mommy is not harming her, you've another think coming. She deserves to be away from the Santiago clutches, especially with that Connor bastard trying to take over."

"Connor?"

"My mother's fiancé."

"If you hate the man so much why didn't you stay and stand up for your mother?"

"You can't tell Charish what to do."

"Why didn't you take Lyric with you when you left?" Vail defied the brother. "Insist she go along with you?"

"Because I—" The man's jaw tensed. Vail could sense another punch building in his biceps, but he didn't step back.

"He's got his own life. And I'm a big girl who never listens to her brother's advice." Lyric sat on the couch and stretched her arms along the back. "Stop fighting, boys. You both make me feel so loved."

"You are loved." Leo returned to Lyric and kissed her head. "I can't believe he made you do this."

"It's prettier than yours." She slapped his head playfully. "That cut makes you look like a punk rocker."

"Yeah, but remember the time I got my headset stuck in my hair and it fell across a laser beam, setting off the security alarms?"

"It was the one time I had ridden along with you on one of your jobs. I thought for sure you'd be caught."

Watching the siblings reminisce made Vail realize Lyric did have something he wanted—family. Seriously? The camaraderie between the siblings made him pine for the smallest acknowledgment from his brother.

Leo pulled Lyric in for a long hug. Vail could hear what he whispered, and suspected the man did that intentionally.

"You can't trust him," Leo warned.

"I don't," Lyric reassured.

Vail decided not to challenge what she'd told her brother. He wasn't sure he'd earned her trust, or that he deserved such trust. If the vampiress was smart, she would not trust him farther than he could blow faery dust.

# *CHAPTER THIRTEEN*

VAIL TUGGED OFF his shirt and walked into the guest bedroom. Lyric was taking a shower; she wanted to scrub off the color edging her hairline, and the lingering rancid scent from the worm wraith. He'd used a few paper towels in the kitchen to wipe the itchy blood from his skin, both on his shoulder and his shin where the elevator arrow had nicked him.

He wandered the apartment, and walked into the brother's bedroom, which was connected to the private bathroom where Lyric was. This room was surreal. White marble floor reflected his dark clothing like a ghostly shadow. The bedclothes were white, the electrochromic shades were white, and the light was some weird kind of bright that made the whole room glow like the inside of a marshmallow.

He turned off the light and sat on the floor at the end of the bed, because if he sat on the white counterpane, he'd leave a mark surely. Stretching his legs out before him, he tilted his head back onto the bed.

Cressida had a white room in which he'd spent a lot of time. It had been a room, but not a room. Lots of

Faery spaces were outdoors but served as rooms. The entire room had been vast, all white, and tree roots had hung from above.

Part of Faery was underground, so at any time, when a person was in a room, or even village, roots could be hanging from the ceiling or even the sky. The main underground city on Unseelie territory was called the UnderCity. The first time he'd landed in the mortal realm, Vail had searched for roots in the sky.

He had liked to go into Cressida's room and lie beneath the white willow that glittered as the breeze gently tousled its slender, silver-edged leaves. It had been quiet, almost a nonplace, far from the explosive color and noise of Faery.

He'd needed that respite from a world that was dialed to eleven on the sensory scale.

Until he'd come to the mortal realm, he hadn't realized how shockingly vibrant Faery had been. And yet while he'd never worn sunglasses in Faery, now he wore them, perhaps against the dullness of the world. Weird.

He had to hand it to Cressida. She'd known he'd claimed the white room as a sort of sanctuary, and had allowed him his peace. He couldn't deny she'd had her motherly moments.

Now, he closed his eyes and drifted to that quiet, white place, when he had often wondered if the day would come that he'd meet his real parents.

He'd dreamed Viviane would have long black hair and eyes as blue as his. Rhys had offered to show him a picture upon his arrival in the mortal realm, but Vail had refused to look at it. Still fresh from banishment by Zett, he hadn't the heart or the courage to do so because it would mean acknowledging a part of him he had been taught to despise.

As for Constantine, he wasn't so sure. Vail could never quite put a face to his image of the tall, stalwart, vampire lord Cressida had told him about. She hadn't liked Constantine, which was apparent from her biting sneers as she'd spoken of him, but she had respected him in a manner Vail could never figure.

Cressida had been bonded to Viviane during the centuries that she had been buried alive. It had to do with the boon Rhys Hawkes had promised Cressida for enchanting his vampire—handing over his firstborn to the faery. As soon as Viviane had conceived, Cressida had known. She had become connected to Viviane. And when the warlock had bespelled Viviane, and she'd been placed beneath Paris in the glass coffin, Cressida had been tugged underground, as well. The Mistress of Winter's Edge had existed in stasis for two centuries.

It was no wonder she'd hated Constantine.

Perhaps that was another reason to want him dead. Much as Vail would never resolve his issues with his reluctant stepmother, he didn't like it when anyone he cared about had been wronged.

But how to care about a mother he'd never met?

Perhaps because as a child he'd created the image of a loving, smiling vampiress who would play with him and tell him stories and teach him the ways of his kind. Stupid kid stuff. Still, he would never deny his memories—they were all he had.

He thought now his memories must be similar to Lyric's memories of summer camp. Better times. Innocent times. How odd was it they had so much in common, yet were so different?

*You are more alike than you will admit.*

True. But would his mother see his truth? Know him for the child she had never gotten to love? He did want to see her, but feared Viviane would not feel the same way. Much as Rhys tried to convince Vail she wanted him to visit, he sensed it could never be right. Even though Cressida had been the one allowed to choose between him and Trystan, Vail sensed in his heart that Viviane, enmeshed in madness, could not have missed her vampire son.

He bowed his head and thumbed the moisture from the corner of his eye. Stupid thoughts. What a wib. Imaginings, that's all they were. Creations. He could never know the truth. And he didn't want to know. Knowing would offer the hardest challenge, and he'd give it a pass.

"Shower's all yours."

Lyric stood in the doorway in an oversize white T-shirt that dipped to her thighs. Standing on her tiptoes, her thoroughbred gams drew Vail's eye up to the wet fabric that clung at the intersection of her thighs.

Man, he wanted some of that.

"What's wrong, enemy mine?" Lyric cooed, striding forward in a sexy hip-swinging gait.

"Your legs are amazing," he said on a throaty gasp. "They go up to your neck."

"What?" She tapped her neck. "You mean this little ol' broken neck?"

She wouldn't let go of that one. Deservedly so. "Yes, that pretty broken neck. I don't believe I've ever looked upon a sexier sight."

"You don't believe in much." She squatted before him, one knee between his outstretched legs, the other leg sliding straight out to her side. Cinnamon-scented steam haloed around her. "Tell me what you do believe in, Vail."

He reached to cup her breast but she shoved his hand away. "No. You said we'd had sex too early. No touching for you tonight."

He crossed his arms and exhaled. "So it's your turn to torture me? Fine. What do I believe in? I believe no man has control of his life. We are all mere puppets on a predestined path. Nothing we do is going to make the world any better or worse. We're here to experience and try not to screw it all up too badly."

"Cynic." She knelt on both knees, stroking a hand down her ribs and stomach.

Vail's eyes traveled lower to where the wet shirt clung to her smooth mons.

"Want to know what I believe?" she said on a sultry whisper. "You have to take whatever it is you want from this world."

"I can get behind that. We are two cynics."

"Yes, but there's one thing that isn't for the taking."

"Everything can be had if you know the angle or grift to get at it."

"Nope." She waggled a naughty finger before him, and he wanted to suck it—but he'd abide by the no-touching rule, because this kind of torture was fun. "You can't take love. You can only get it by giving it."

Vail cracked a goofy sneer. "Are you in the market for love, sweetie?"

She leaned in so close her breath warmed his mouth. A flutter of her lashes dusted his cheek. Her tongue dashed out to wet her lip. "Nope."

Fuck. He was hard. Vail unbuttoned the top button of his jeans and blatantly eased a hand over his erection.

"Got a problem?" She eyed his crotch, and slid a hand to the apex of her thighs.

"Nothing you can't solve."

"I said no touching. Which includes no sex," she said in a singsong voice. Her fingers flirted with the shirt hem, and Vail could not take his eyes from it. "I meant it."

"Very well, why don't you take care of yourself? You know you want to rub that hot, moist pussy, Lyric. Don't do it for me. You want something, you gotta take it for yourself. Give me a fantasy."

"Fantasy? You know, I do have a fantasy about a bad boy." She flicked out the tip of her tongue, and when he thought she'd lick his face, she tilted her head back and moaned.

"Yeah? Am I a bad boy?"

"You let a faery kill your girl. I'd say that makes you very bad."

"You're my girl?"

"You said as much earlier."

"I did. You are my girl." Nice. "So tell me about this bad boy you dream about."

He spied her fingers slipping under the hem of the shirt. She would undo him.

On the other hand, he could undo himself nicely with this visual tease. Easing a hand inside his pants, he assumed a good grip on the main stick.

"He's tall, dark and likes to brood. Bad boys always brood. I think it's in their DNA."

Shiny brown hair swished over her shoulder, still wet from the shower. Droplets of water pearled on her pale flesh, slowly trailing toward her breast. She dipped her head and eyed him, mouth partially open to expose the soft pink insides.

"His hair is black as sin and he's got eyes like stained glass. But I never spend too much time looking into them because I'm distracted by his mouth."

Her tongue flicked over her lips. "It's all about his mouth."

Vail sucked in his lower lip.

"Sometimes it smirks, a little curl on this side." She licked the edge of her mouth. "His rare smile makes my body stretch out and push up for his attention."

Vail felt a smile wriggle his lips, but he suppressed it.

"He's always smiling when he walks that walk. That sexy, hip-swaggering walk that channels a panther's sure strides. He calls it his strut. Makes me wet to see him coming toward me. I want to match the rhythm of his hips…"

Vail squeezed his hardness, not wanting to come until she did, but he knew women were slower than men, and damn—now she lifted the shirt. Her hips rocked, pushing forward, seeking the rhythm of the bad boy's gait. She still straddled him but, surprisingly, did not touch him.

He gritted his teeth and stopped stroking, squeezing at the base of his erection to prolong the intense force that shuddered for release.

"Take your shirt off," he growled. "I need to see all of you."

"That's what he says to me." The shirt hit the marble floor. Lyric cupped her breasts and thumbed the nipples. "And he leans forward and draws his hungry gaze over my body. I want him, but when I reach for him, he retreats."

She flashed him a wicked grin. "And always that sexy smile. I don't need his touch." She moaned as she squeezed her nipple. "But I'm hungry for it. To feel his tongue on my skin, knowing he'll tease me until I scream."

Vail swallowed. "Mercy."

"He likes to tease. He knows I want him more than he wants me. He can have any woman. Why me?"

"She's all he wants," Vail hastened out, hissing as an intense climax built in his groin. "Finish yourself," he managed. "Please."

"What if I don't want to?"

"Ch'yeah, right. You need to, sweetie." He hardened his jaw. "Don't you?"

"Yes, I do." She began to stroke herself, this time putting her hand over his shoulder to lean against the end of the bed. Her fast breaths hushed against his ear. "Soon," she whispered. "You able to wait so we can do this together?"

"Anything," he mumbled. "If I'm bad—fuck—you're naughty. Oh, Lyric!"

He couldn't wait. But remarkably, when he cried out and released, she did, as well. The vampiress nuzzled her face against his neck to muffle her cry. He felt the tiny prick of fang—she pulled back, grinning like a drunken pussycat, and tapped her descended fangs. "Not going to tap you, goth boy."

She rolled onto her bottom, and teased her wet fingers up his rigid abdomen where his come had splashed. She waggled a finger at him, then licked it clean. "I like 'em bad."

AFTER THEY'D SLEPT a few hours, they stood on the balcony overlooking the city. It was around two in the morning. It was weird she'd slept, but Lyric had been running on empty lately. She needed blood. And while tempted to sink her fangs into Vail's neck after their incredible Jack 'n' Jill session, she was still leery of the faery ichor she knew pulsed through his veins. Good thing the sex controlled the hunger pangs.

"So we're going to FaeryTown?" she asked.

He'd avoided touching her since they'd risen, and

her skin tingled for his touch. But if he could stand not to touch her, she could certainly hold out, as well.

"We're already there," he said, and splayed a hand to indicate the streets below. "Your brother lives at the edge of it. Clever place to hide. Of course, he does have the elevator of death to keep him safe."

"Leo doesn't take risks."

"Apparently."

"So how do you know it's FaeryTown? It looks like the rest of Paris to me."

He went into the bedroom and returned with the small violet glass jar. "They're everywhere, if you know how to see them. You're going to have to see the enemy coming in order to stay away from him." He opened the jar and tilted it toward her. "You willing?"

She nodded and allowed him to trace under her eyes with the stuff using his little finger. It smelled sweet and wasn't so much greasy as viscous, and immediately blended into her skin.

"So, if vampires go to FaeryTown looking for a high, how do they see the faeries without this ointment?"

"The sidhe who service the vampires don't wear complete glamour. They want the customers to find them. It's the sneaky, fully cloaked ones you need to be able to see." He studied his handiwork.

"Do I look like a raccoon now?"

"It's kind of sultry," he said, and tossed the jar up and down in a hand. "Do I get to call you goth girl now?"

"Goth boy was Leo's name for you. But I'll refrain from using it, too."

"Fair enough." With a nod over his shoulder, he said, "Take a look."

She peered down the street, sighting humans walking briskly in the light rain that drizzled onto the cobbled streets and sidewalks, passing in and out of a supermarket with flashing red neon vodka signs.

From behind her, Vail's hands caressed her hips and he pressed his groin against her ass. It didn't take long for him to get hard, and she encouraged his arousal by grinding her backside against him.

So much for not touching. She wouldn't mention the broken pact if he wouldn't.

"Do they look like the faeries in the Lizard Lounge? What am I looking for?" she asked.

His deep whisper tickled her ear. "You'll know it when you see it."

She had slipped into the thin faery dress and now his hands moved around to caress her breasts. Lyric closed her eyes and moaned at the exquisite pain when he squeezed. The man knew how to summon the naughty side of her. Why she'd ever asked him not to was beyond her.

When she opened her eyes the man three buildings down flickered in and out of focus as he walked the street. It reminded her of how they did ghosts in movies, cutting out a few frames to give them a staccatolike movement.

"I think I see one."

Vail crushed his body along hers and, clasping his

arms under her breasts, peered over her shoulder, but he was looking in the direction opposite to where she had pointed. "Yep, that's a sidhe. No wings. Must be under his clothes."

"How do you know? You don't have the stuff under your eyes."

"Looking out the corner of my eye, like I showed you to do earlier. Remember that, if you ever find yourself without the stuff."

He unscrewed the jar cap and put some under each of his eyes, then leaned onto the railing.

"Is he looking for us?" Lyric asked.

"Could be. Could be looking for trouble. See the other? The female?"

While Vail's hands massaged her breasts, Lyric sucked in her lower lip and scanned the street farther up. A woman in a pink dress flipped her long white hair over red and brown wings that hung heavily in the rain. Her image flickered and rain spattered off the luminous wings.

"I can't believe it. Are they always everywhere like this?"

"Yep. But more so in FaeryTown."

"It's so curious how they flicker."

"This realm tends to slow the sidhe's usual movement so they flicker, but it's virtually imperceptible on those faeries who have been here a long time. They adjust after a few months, and that makes them more difficult to see because they blend so well with the mortals."

"I'm not sure I like this."

His ministrations at her nipples stopped.

"No, I mean the sight. Keep doing that, lover."

"Are you okay with this now? I thought we were slowing down? Not touching?"

"That was a stupid idea. I'm always okay with the two of us making love. But wait." She turned and looked him up and down.

"What's wrong?"

"Nothing. Just checking, you know, for wings."

"I'm completely vampire, sweetie. Love me or leave me."

"So now you admit to being a part of my race?"

"I've never denied it."

"True. But you know when you put vampires down for being filthy you're also putting yourself down? You should never do that. You should be proud of what you are, Vail. I'm proud of you."

"Ch'yeah, right. How does that work? I've done nothing worthy of your admiration."

"You've saved my ass more than a few times."

He slid a palm over the backside in question. "It is far too nice to let get harmed. Which reminds me… We need to take a look around FaeryTown. Maybe we can find someone to remove your mark."

"You really do want to protect me."

"I made a vow. And I meant it."

"Then let's do it. But before we go…" She bit her lower lip because his hand stroking her ass felt too good. "Why don't you, um…do that thing you do?"

"With my fingers?" He flicked his fingers before her in demonstration.

She clasped his wrist and lowered his hand to her loins. "Yeah, that thing."

"All right, but you have to look at me." He moved in to kiss her, and as his lips connected with hers, his fingers parted her legs and slid inside her.

His intrusion made her soft and melty, opening her to his dark glamour. Lyric closed her eyes and tilted back her head to moan.

"Eyes on me, Lyric. Right here."

Sucking in her lower lip, she held his gaze, which was sexily defiant. His blue irises were hot with desire, and his stare felt more intimate than what his fingers were doing. He played her well, stroking softly and then more sure.

"Oh, yes." Her fangs lowered and Lyric grinned widely, showing her bright incisors to her lover. "You know exactly how to do that thing you do."

"You ready to come?"

She nodded, and he caught her jaw with a palm, forcing her to maintain eye contact with him. The bad boy's smirk revealed his wicked pleasure. Lyric pressed her mons hard against his wrist and fingers, taking from him what she wanted.

And he gave it to her.

# *CHAPTER FOURTEEN*

LOOKING AROUND FAERYTOWN, Lyric was fascinated by what she saw. Everything was normal according to mortal standards, and the mortals she did see walked through the streets unaware of what existed around them, beneath their feet and above their heads.

Yet with the ointment around her eyes, she saw the fourth dimension that existed simultaneously.

Faeries were everywhere. They walked the same streets as if the mortals did not exist. Occasionally a faery would walk right next to a mortal, its wings brushing their shoulder, and the mortal would flick their fingers as if at a nuisance fly.

The buildings were mortal buildings, but the faeries could enter them on the level of their own realm. It was like parallel realms stacked one over the other. And since this neighborhood was not a popular spot with the mortals, the faeries had taken over.

They passed more than a few bars flashing luminescent signs with wings and a huge V in them. Vail explained the symbol vampires recognized for ichor dens—wings embracing a down-pointed triangle. It wasn't *V* for *Vampire,* he explained, but rather the triangle represented a fang.

"Do you go in those?" she asked, clasping his hand at her hip. His palm felt too warm. Did the ichor house lure him with its offerings, increase his hunger?

"Once in a while. I rarely take from a live faery. Usually from the vial."

"What does that mean? A live faery? Is that like me drinking from a live mortal? Because you know we get no sustenance from blood without a heartbeat."

"Doesn't work that way with ichor. Some vamps prefer their ichor direct from the vein. Some buy a few vials and take it home to enjoy the high in private. Others will buy a faery to take home with them, draining them dry."

"To death?"

"Yes."

He didn't elaborate, and Lyric didn't need him to. The practice was barbaric. Vampires did not need to kill for sustenance.

"But where does the ichor in vials come from?"

Vail tugged up her hand to kiss the knuckles. No answer to that one either. And she knew, without doubt, live faeries were drained to fill the vials.

His habit was awful. But was it any worse than those vampires who insisted the kill was the only way to survive? Lyric had never, and would never, kill. She didn't need that much mortal blood to satisfy her hunger. And the kill would bring on the *danse macabre,* a state in which the vampire relived the victim's nightmares—while awake. Often, if the vampire had killed multitude times, the *danse macabre* ultimately drove him mad.

They passed an ichor house with a stout, indigo-skinned faery guarding the door. He nodded as they approached, and said, "Vaillant."

Vail nodded in acknowledgment but walked by.

He'd been in FaeryTown often enough that he was recognized? That shouldn't surprise her, but after discussing drinking methods that eventually killed faeries, Lyric felt her throat go dry.

"I shouldn't have brought you along," he said. He slid a possessive hand about her hip. His claiming her settled some of her apprehension. "But it's my truth."

She liked that he was willing to show her his truth. Maybe someday he'd step beyond what he'd been taught, and begin to explore life and develop his own tastes. She'd help him if he ever indicated an interest.

"You don't feel compelled to go inside and feed the habit?"

"Lyric, I told you—"

"I know, you do it to maintain. But if we're talking truths here, do you want to stick with that excuse?"

He pulled her to him as he leaned against a wall beneath a neon sign advertising *La Fée Plaisir.* The bustle on the street moved around them, coving them into the hazy blue glow of the neon.

"I may be the sorriest excuse for a vampire you've ever met," he said, whispering into her ear. "But it's all I know."

She kissed him. He let her take as she pleased, not reacting, and she liked the moment. A press of their mouths, an exhalation of breath, a sigh shivering across her lips.

"Learn differently," she challenged. Another kiss to his nose and his cheek. "For me."

His smile was completely lacking in mirth.

She'd pushed too far. The man was not the kind a woman could tame or change or shape into something to suit her designs. That would be cruel to even attempt. Vail was unique, and despite his addiction, she did not want to change him.

But could she reach the untouchable core he guarded so fiercely? They had a connection, but it yet felt too thin, not nearly substantial enough to forge a long and trusting bond.

"I misspoke. I do need you along. Ahead," he said. "See that symbol in the window with the blade and herbs? It's a healer's house. Let's see what we can find."

It was a narrow building, seemingly squished between two surrounding buildings, as if an afterthought; couldn't be more than twelve feet wide. Cozy and intriguing. Violet waves of smoke swirled through the air as Lyric followed Vail through the black-painted halls of the healer's house.

Head bowed and eyes closed, Vail stood outside an open door, seeming to take a moment of peace or thanks. Lyric wanted to blow away the smoke that trailed about his head, but then she yawned.

"Is this some kind of sleeping stuff?" she murmured.

"Smells like poppy flame," he said.

"Opium?"

"Could be. She's inside. We can enter. I feel her invitation."

Lyric had always avoided accompanying Charish's monthly visits to the witch seer, much as her mother had insisted she could craft a love spell for her. She just didn't believe in hocus-pocus.

Vail had felt the invite? Things had just gotten spooky.

Lyric followed as he stepped into the room, which resembled some kind of gypsy tent, hung with colorful silks that upon closer inspection looked like spider webbing. An ivory incense burner trickled out the mysterious violet smoke and Lyric positioned herself on the side of Vail opposite the cloying haze.

Before the bay window on a bed of vines sat a tiny woman with dark violet skin and curious white tattoos. They looked like henna designs, elaborate Indian arabesques, yet all were in white so they virtually glowed against her dusky skin. A crown of what looked like cranberries circled her head, twined within a thorny branch.

Lips as bright as the berries opened and a spill of white smoke curled out and around her neck, then circled her body, calling attention to the tiny wings at her back, the tips barely revealed behind her head.

"Well met. I receive your blessings with an open heart," Vail said, and bowed to the faery. "I have lived in Faery all my life, until three mortal months ago when I was banished to this realm. I revere the sidhe, and wish them no harm."

"And the vampiress?" the faery asked in a curiously deep voice that vibrated at the back of Lyric's throat.

"She is respectful of the sidhe and their ways."

The white tattoos flashed on the woman's skin as she looked over Lyric. Deep violet eyes that were pure color, no dark pupil at all, dug through Lyric's skin and into her blood. Suddenly she felt Zett's mark behind her ear begin to burn.

"You've been marked by the Lord of Midsummer Dark," the healer announced. "Step forward, chosen one."

"No, I'm not—" Chosen? Never.

Vail put a finger to his lips and nodded that she take a step forward to stand beside him.

The healer faery tilted her head, and blew out a wisp of white smoke that crept toward Lyric and curled up behind her ear. The smoke touched her as if a finger, gliding along the mark.

"A vampiress attracted the Unseelie lord to make her his own?"

Lyric looked to Vail for direction. She felt it best he speak because she wasn't at all dialed in to the protocol for communicating with this woman.

"It was a mistake on Zett's part," Vail explained. "Now he seeks to destroy that mistake. We respectfully request you remove the mark from her skin so she will no longer be the Lord of Midsummer Dark's prey."

The healer sniffed. The violet smoke that had filled the hall now wound its way about Lyric's body, twining like rope strands about the white smoke. It tightened, pressing her knees together and clamping about her hips. Her eyelids blinked, and she had to concentrate to focus.

"She is very susceptible," the faery explained. "Perhaps it best she succumb to the Unseelie lord's will."

"No," Vail said, a bit too forcefully.

The healer blanched and her wings snapped out crisply and fluttered. He'd upset her. Lyric reached for Vail's hand, but he eluded her touch.

"She did nothing wrong," he explained more calmly. "Zett has no right to kill indiscriminately. Why should it not be he who suffers for his mistake?"

"To suffer such a mistake would see him taking her as his bride. I sense, vampire, that you would have something to say against that."

"I—" Now Vail's hand did clasp in hers. "Yes. She is mine."

The faery closed her eyes, revealing the delicate white designs tracing her lids. The aroma of flowers and cranberries grew so strong Lyric tasted it as it drizzled down her throat. She wobbled.

Vail caught her across the back and held her against him. The violet and white smoke rope released its tight clutch.

The healer flashed open her eyes and aimed her gaze upon Vail. "No, I cannot help you. Certainly I feel there is a connection between the two of you. I honor that, Unwanted One."

Vail's intake of breath at that cruel moniker reminded Lyric just what he was sacrificing by kowtowing to the sidhe to help her.

The healer continued, "But I cannot risk bringing Zett's wrath upon me. Understand."

"Of course." Vail nodded. "Thank you for seeing us. Blessed be."

She bowed her head and closed her eyes, the berries crowning her head spilling forward like ruby pearls.

Stepping out of the room with Vail, Lyric didn't feel disappointment so much as pride in Vail for having stood up for her, and at least attempting to help. She hadn't expected it would be easy.

When they closed the narrow door behind them, outside air whisked through Lyric's lungs and cleared away the opium fog.

"I'm sorry," he said, and kissed her at the corner of her eye. "I tried."

"I know you did. Thank you for trying."

"We'll find another way."

"Whew! What was all that smoke?"

"Sedative, for unwary strangers."

"I get that. And I think I was unwary. Did it affect you?"

"A little. But the fresh air is helping. Let's head back, shall we?"

He threaded his fingers through hers and led her onward. Lyric sensed he didn't want to discuss what he must feel was a failure. It wasn't a failure to her. It only further cemented their connection.

They strolled down a street fronted by many ichor dens, and Lyric breathed in deeply, drawing in as much of the fresh night air as possible.

"Fancy a bite?"

She startled at the drowsy voice to their left.

"Go away," Vail said to the faery whose jasper wings hung straight and where they dusted the sidewalk were tattered and dirty.

The pale lavender pixy pouted, and teased a finger along her neck. Curious by what she saw, Lyric tilted the frail creature's head aside.

The faery bristled in delight. "I don't charge much. Right there." She tapped the thick, pale vein.

"Do you see that?" she asked Vail. "That tattoo or mark."

Now interested, Vail made to touch the faery's neck, but she tugged away and insisted on cash. He dug in his pocket and handed her a 500-euro banknote. "Just touching," he said. "I don't want to bite."

"Whatever gets you off, pretty boy."

He stroked his thumb along the fine red mark just below her drooping earlobe. It wasn't bioluminescent like Lyric's mark. To Lyric, he asked, "Does it mean something to you?"

Her heart suddenly pounding, Lyric swallowed a scream. Tears heated her eyes. She began to think of the implications, but her mind tugged her back and wouldn't allow her to go down that dark path.

"It's the Santiago family crest," she said.

# *CHAPTER FIFTEEN*

VAIL HASTENED LYRIC from the ichor den. The rain had picked up and they scurried toward Leo's building. Both were silent regarding what they'd seen on the faery's neck. The Santiago crest? That stirred his suspicion.

He wasn't sure how Lyric would take it, but she must have her suspicions now. She'd grown up in the family. Surely nothing they did, or had done, could shock her.

On the other hand, she was on the run from that family. Obviously, she didn't agree with everything they did.

If he could get her to give him the gown he could hand it over to Rhys, and then…

And then? Well, he wasn't prepared to hand over Lyric. She was his.

Yes, his. Zett would never lay a single dust-laden finger on Lyric's flesh. As for Charish Santiago, he knew Lyric wanted to do what was best for her mother. And Lyric, well, she should be able to decide what she wanted to do in her life, not anyone else.

Not even him.

Which was why he wasn't about to tell her what he was thinking as they took the elevator up to her brother's place. She was smart. She'd figure out what her mother was up to.

As for her being his, well, he wanted her to give him a chance. But that was a decision only Lyric could make. Did she want him only for the fantasy, or was there something more, deeper?

After Lyric punched in a seven-digit code, the elevator doors slid open. This time, Vail stood behind her, but no arrows sprang out at him.

"Why didn't you punch in the code the first time we came here?" he asked as they stepped inside.

"It wouldn't have been as fun. And you'd never have known how serious my brother is about protecting what is his."

"I might have if you'd simply told me."

"Doubt it." She strolled through the living room, headed for the guest bedroom. "I want to get this stuff off my eyes. I'll be right back."

Sensing his lover's need for distance, Vail slouched onto an oversize leather chair, swinging a leg over an arm, and closed his eyes. It was almost dawn. He'd gotten enough sleep earlier, but he felt drained.

*You know it's hunger. You wanted to sink your fangs into the faery's neck and feast on ichor. Now you'll have to go back, sooner rather than later.*

He wasn't feeling the jittery cravings yet, but soon…

Lyric sashayed into the room, hips swaying and legs

moving as if orchestrated for subtle allure. Maybe she was looking for closeness rather than distance?

"Hey, kitty. How'd you get such a sexy walk?"

"Must be my gymnastics training."

"Whatever it's from, it's incredibly sexy. I could watch you walk all day. Is it something to do with the silks you've mentioned? What are silks?"

"Aerial silks," she said, "are long strips of fabric that a person swings from and performs acrobatic moves on. It's a great workout. I do it whenever I need to think or lose myself from the world."

"Sounds like something I need to take up. I used to swing like a monkey from the vines in Faery when I was small."

"You Tarzan, me Jane?"

"Huh?"

"Sorry, a movie reference. You probably haven't seen too many of those."

"Use the force, Luke!"

"Just the important one, then."

Instead of sitting in the chair next to his, she sat on his lap and laid her head on his shoulder. Vail got an instant hard-on, but he didn't want the moment to go full speed into sex like it usually did, because he sensed she was out of sorts. Probably running through her brain right now what they'd seen in FaeryTown.

Breathing in her cherry jasmine scent, he noticed the weight of her breast against his chest, the slide of her leg across his. She was so real. Not flighty or vindictive like the faeries with whom he'd had relationships.

And she was like him. *If* he chose to accept he was vampire and not some fucked-up longtooth with a faery complex.

"So what does it mean?" Her pale eyes sought his.

The truth would earn her respect but, as well, her disdain. Her mother had lied to her. He would not do the same, no matter the consequences.

Vail kissed her forehead, lingering until he could no longer prolong the silence. "The only reason that faery, and probably others in the ichor den, would wear the Santiago crest is because they are owned by the Santiagos. I suspect your mother is trafficking in faeries with Zett, Lyric. It's the only conclusion. Makes more sense than Zett allowing a vampire into Faery to steal artifacts."

She nodded, her gaze avoiding his. No denial?

"Half an hour ago," she said, "I would have been angry and come to my mother's defense. She'd never do anything like that. But standing in the bathroom alone, thinking about it a moment, made me realize I can't deny my family has always been involved in underhanded and vicious dealings. And she's been so pressured lately."

"By the fiancé?"

"Yes, Connor. But I don't understand how trafficking in faeries can further his plans to take over the Santiago clan."

"He may not be involved. On the other hand, it may be profitable."

"So you think my mother promised Zett the gown in return for faeries to put to work in the ichor den?"

He nodded and stroked her hair. "Maybe she did it to get away from the fiancé? Get some quick cash and start anew?"

"No, she loves him. Unfortunately." She snuggled in closer, hooking an arm across his chest. "If your guess is true about the trafficking, that's a crime punishable by the Council. And the only people who know about it are you and me."

Honest eyes studied his. Wondering, touching and knowing. He would give her honesty in return.

"I'm going to finish my job," he said. "Zett has no right to the Seelie gown, nor do you. But I don't work for the Council. And I can't stop you from keeping secrets from me."

"I've no more secrets. Promise. And I understand you have to do what you have to do. You won't report my mother?"

"No need to."

"Then I will. Leo will stand beside me. It's not right. Sure, we're a family of thieves. And once in a while another bad guy gets hurt when dealing with the Santiagos. I love my mother. But participating in an illegal operation that harms innocent faeries? It makes me sick to think of it."

"What do you care for the sidhe?"

"I've always been frightened of them. Of the addiction they bring with one bite. Because I fear something doesn't mean I wish it harm. They are living beings, like you and me. They've done nothing wrong."

Vail swallowed and looked away from the sincerity in her eyes. He'd never taken a faery as a slave to drink from and drain dry, but certainly he used them to maintain.

Maintain. *You still hiding behind that excuse? She's sees the truth of you, man. Own it.*

"How can we stop it?" she asked. "There's got to be a way."

"As long as Zett hasn't received the gown, he's not going to hand over any faeries."

"Yes, but for those who already live in FaeryTown to fulfill the sick pleasures of addicted vampires. How to help them?"

"I'm not sure. Aren't you concerned about yourself? Zett is after you."

"Can we use this as leverage? We don't report him and he forgets I have a mark?"

"It's a tricky situation. I… Hell."

"What?"

"I just had the thought I should talk to Cressida."

"Your faery stepmother? Would she be on your side?"

"Not sure." He turned the delicate May bells about his wrist. Another flower had fallen away. Two remained. "I can't return to Faery. It would be deemed a malicious affront to Zett, who banished me. Besides, I'm sure there are wards to keep me back."

"You haven't tried to return?"

"Haven't had a reason in the few months I've been in the mortal realm. I left behind more bad memories than good."

"About that banishment. What did you do to the guy? You said it had to do with a fox shifter?"

"Kit. I...shouldn't tell you this." If anything would drive a wedge between them, it was the thing he had done in Faery.

"Be honest with me, Vail. You've told me about your father and wanting to kill him, which I don't agree with. What could be more hideous to hide?"

"It's not hideous. Kit, she..."

He grasped Lyric and squeezed her in a hug, wishing life were easier, that words were not required to gain trust, and actions could be his voice. They'd been his voice for Kit. And, much as he wished it could have been different, he didn't regret those actions.

"Was it a fight over a girl?" she guessed. "Between you and Zett?"

"Not so much a fight as a mastery."

"That's sounds seedy. I don't understand the ways of Faery. But if you don't want to tell me, I understand."

He sensed she would let it drop, but at the core of him, Vail wanted to release it, to bring her into his heart by granting her entrance to his most shameful secret.

*Not shameful.* Depended on the mood he was in when he thought about it.

"Kit grew up with me," he began, twisting a hank of Lyric's brown hair about his finger. "We'd both expected to be married off when we reached majority. Cressida never hid anything from me, and explained she'd taken me as a boon and the reasons for it, early on. Kit was excited about her husband-to-be. She'd met him. He was a wood sylph who gave her pretty ribbons and composed songs about her. Some men are born natural romantics, I guess."

"Had you met your fiancé?"

"No. Cressida had bargained for me before puberty, and you know what happened following. After discovering I was a bloodborn vampire she did a swell job of making me feel smaller than a worm, worthless, and generally a pariah."

Lyric's hug deepened the warmth of their connection. Vail realized he felt safe with her, and that conclusion made him relax more. No one in this realm felt more like family to him than Lyric, and he would try to keep the bond now that he recognized it.

"There's a ritual Faery observes," he said. "I've learned it mirrors a medieval mortal rite. When a couple is to be married, the lord of their particular Faery sect, in this case, the Midsummer branch of the Unseelies, has first right to the bride."

"I don't understand?"

"That means the Lord of Midsummer Dark can have sex with the bride the night before her wedding, if he so chooses."

"That's awful!"

"It is. But it is an accepted practice in the sidhe culture. And Kit, well, it wasn't so much she feared Zett—he isn't known as a tyrant who harms females—only she did not want him to be the man she gave her virginity to. And she couldn't risk going to her fiancé. He was an upright sidhe and abided by the rules, even if they weren't rules, but rather a shameful ritual."

"Her fiancé wanted Zett to have her?"

"It's not that he wanted it to happen, only he would not speak against Zett."

"What did she do? Oh, I don't want to think about it. How sad that happened to her."

"Actually." He kissed her forehead, and brushed aside the hair to trace behind her ear where the faery mark glowed. Wincing, because Zett had touched so many, and in ways Vail could not fathom, he continued. "Kit wanted her first time to be with someone she could trust, so she asked me. And I agreed, because I loved her. We made love as friends, not as lovers, but it was what she wanted, and I could not deny her."

"That's strangely honorable of you."

"Strange, certainly. I'm not sure how honorable. No matter that I gave Kit what she desired, the fact remains, I took away her husband's right to claim his wife."

"But if you had not, Zett would have."

"Yes." He sighed. Sort of a Robin Hood of the maidenhood, he had figured at the time. Not something to be proud of.

Zett had been outraged when he'd gone to Kit's cabin that evening and found her bed empty. She and Vail had gone to the briarwood and had spent a few hours in each other's arms. They'd returned at dawn, when the wedding nuptials were to take place. Kit and her intended exchanged vows and danced about the toadstool ring.

Vail had, for a moment, thought they'd pulled one over on Zett. Until he was followed home and Zett's men entered forcibly behind him, tearing everything apart, including the clothes from Vail's body. Of course, he hadn't bathed since making love with Kit and evidence remained of his climax, which an ugly demi-troll had sniffed out.

Zett had Vail, naked, brought to his quarters and beaten.

"So then Zett banished you?" Lyric asked.

Vail nodded, wiping away the image of his humiliation in the midst of a strangely bittersweet triumph. "Banished that instant. Forced to leave Faery with but the possessions I held at that moment."

"Which were?"

"Nothing." Not even his clothing. But she didn't need to hear that. It was too humiliating to speak.

Cressida had come to him, as he'd stood in the middle of a mortal forest, naked yet proud of what he'd done for Kit, and had given him the lily bracelet and wished him good stead.

At that moment he'd felt both the utter hatred Cressida had for him—the unwanted bloodborn had proved his lack of worth—and her love, for Cressida had understood his motivations behind sleeping with Kit and congratulated him for the rebuff against Zett.

Faeries. Ever contrary.

"Cressida gave me this." He displayed the lily bracelet and Lyric touched it carefully. "May bells are supposed to protect me against my lacking glamour. When the last flower falls away, the bracelet has lost its power."

"May bells? Looks like lily of the valley to me."

"I believe that is another name for them."

"So when all the flowers are gone she'll give you a new one?"

"I hope so. I'm not sure what will happen when the last flower has fallen."

"You can get another from her?"

"Yes, but she must come to me. Banished, remember."

"I hope you're not ashamed of what you did for Kit. That was an unselfish act, Vail. I don't even know Kit, but I'm glad she had a friend like you. You consider her family, don't you?"

He'd never thought of that, actually, but… "Yes." He smiled. Truly Kit had been family, and still was, even though he might never see her again. He was pleased to know she had married a man she adored, and that her life would be happy. "You make it easy to talk about the tough things."

"I'm going to make it harder. I want you to visit your mother."

"Where did that come from?"

"You didn't have real family in Faery."

"I had the closest thing to family I'll ever want. Don't worry about me, Lyric."

"I don't. You're a strong man who doesn't need anyone for support. You've learned the mortal realm quick enough, though I do wish you'd take driving lessons."

He chuckled, tilting back his head, but Lyric did not lighten. "I know what it's like to pine for a lost parent. And your mother is not lost. I want you to see your mother once. I'll go with you to talk to Rhys Hawkes. I think it may be good for both of you."

Vail sighed and stretched out his legs. Lyric was a comfortable weight against his chest. "You think?"

She nodded.

"But we've faeries to avoid. They're out there, tracking us."

"I suspect they won't think to look at Rhys Hawkes's home. That's the last place you want to be, yes?"

"Yes," he agreed with a tousle of her hair. "Sometimes you're too smart for your own good."

"Only if I've convinced you to visit your mother."

"What's in it for me?"

She sighed. "Don't give me that faery bargain crap. What's in it for her? Have you ever wondered if your mother thinks of you?"

"Every day of my life," he said softly. It was a wound that would never heal.

And with a nod, Vail confirmed he would do as she suggested. It would be painful, and it would go against every morsel of hatred and angst and irrational fear he'd built up against his real family, but life wasn't worth it unless it hurt a little.

Or so Zett had told him as he had plucked Vail up by his beaten and bruised arm and flung him into the mortal realm.

JUST AS THEY WERE locking up Leo's apartment to leave, Vail's cell phone rang.

"Trystan?"

"Yeah, who else is going to call you, longtooth? What the hell is going on?"

"What do you mean?"

That Trystan had made himself dial up the brother he hated was huge. Yet Vail's hopeful anticipation sank as his brother explained.

"I've been worked over by a bunch of freakin' faeries. Faeries! Their damned wings cut like knives. I'm still bleeding. But I did take that skinny one out. You tear off their wings, they turn into babbling babies, you know that?"

"What did they want, Trystan?"

"They wanted you! Is this your idea of forging family ties? By bringing all this bad shit into the mortal realm with you? Because if so, I think you and I need to go mano-a-mano, brother."

"They're looking for me."

"Ya think?"

"Because of a mission your father sent me to do."

"Yeah, I figured that one out. Which is why I didn't tell them where to find you."

"Like you would know."

"I called to warn you, but if you're going to be an asshole—"

"I'm sorry, brother. Can you tell me what they looked like?"

"Ugly with wings."

That described a good portion of Faery. "Did they mention who had sent them?"

"Yes, some Zett dude sent them. The leader, the one who cut me across the nose—this is going to take a week to heal—said you were wanted for crimes against the Unseelie nation. And can I say, dude?

Crimes against an entire nation? Way to go! I didn't know my little brother had it in him!"

"Big brother," Vail corrected. "By two minutes. Thanks, Trystan. I'll be on the lookout, but I'm already aware Zett is after me. Hell, you don't think they'll go after Rhys and Viviane?"

"You'd better pray not, longtooth. If anyone harms my family, I will tear out their hearts. And then I'll go after the reason for it, which is you."

The phone clicked off. Vail shook his shoulders to shed the harsh vibes that always accompanied talking to Trystan. But his brother was right. If any faery caused harm to his family—be they blood or pseudofamily—he too would rip out their hearts and nail the bloody muscle, beating and dripping, to a tree with an iron stake.

Wow. He'd just thought about protecting his family. What was up with him?

"Vail?"

He focused on the beautiful woman who stood by the elevator door, waiting expectantly. She was a part of his family now and he considered her part of his inner circle. Worth protecting with his life.

If Zett laid one finger on Lyric, the sidhe lord would not inhale another breath.

"We need to hurry. My brother thinks the sidhe may go after the rest of my family, like they did him."

"Your brother, the werewolf?"

"Tryst. Zett's gang worked him over. I'll call Rhys, while you drive there."

## *CHAPTER SIXTEEN*

THE MASERATI IDLED outside a trendy boutique on the Champs-Èlysées. Vail had declined accompanying Lyric to buy some clothing less risqué than what she'd rummaged from her brother's stash of ex-girlfriend discards. If she was going to meet the parents, she wasn't going to look like a harlot.

And she sensed he needed to stew by himself after his werewolf brother's call.

Lyric had smelled the acrid anger on Vail. He wanted to charge the vanguard, not visit his mother. But she suspected he needed this visit more, right now, than he could imagine. If he could connect on the smallest part with his mother, it might set him on the right path. Who knew, it could focus him for the inevitable battle.

And he did need to ensure his family was safe. She smiled to think Vail thought of them as family. Bet the misplaced vampire hadn't quite realized that. He was coming around.

The soft pink dress, with cinched waist and fluttery red ruffles at the back, was perfect. Not too uptight, but not too sexy either, because the neckline stopped above her breasts in more ruffles.

No longer fearful of revealing the mark she wore, Lyric pulled her hair into a bun and stuck an ivory hair pick through to secure it. "He did say he liked librarians."

HE DID NOT WANT TO DO THIS.

He did want to do this.

He had to do this.

Rhys wasn't answering his phone, and Vail needed to warn him about the Unseelie. He hoped this visit didn't lead the sidhe right to the Hawkeses' front door.

It would be difficult walking into the home of the mother he had never met. As long as Lyric stood beside him, her hand clasped in his, Vail would find the courage to walk across the threshold.

The Hawkes couple lived an hour east of Paris in a Regency-era two-story mansion that boasted one hundred leagues of surrounding forested land. Vail suspected Rhys did like to run as a wolf; a forest was a requirement. The foyer opened to a vast circular main room with a sunken pit entertainment area. An inner balcony all around led to private bedrooms and guest rooms. A hi-tech kitchen curved along the right wall, and straight through, Vail saw the glint of blue water in the pool.

After extending an invite to enter his home, Rhys introduced himself to Lyric when it was apparent Vail was too busy distracting his nerves by looking around.

He had worried only a moment about bringing Lyric along. Though Hawkes Associates was in deep shit, Vail trusted Rhys to give him the benefit of wanting to figure everything out, after he explained their latest discovery regarding faery trafficking, before turning Lyric over to her mother.

"You're looking good, Vaillant," Rhys said after shaking Lyric's hand.

Vail nodded, speechless. He hadn't worn the eye ointment and Lyric had suggested he wear a crisp white shirt and dark trousers—which he'd borrowed from her brother's closet—so he wouldn't appear so scary to his mother.

Lyric thought he looked scary? Hell, he looked usual. Yet what would his mother think?

His mother.

Maybe he should leave.

*No, you're stronger than that. You'll only let yourself and Lyric down if you leave now.*

"You didn't answer your phone," he said to Rhys. "I tried to call."

"Sorry, I was out on a run. This is fine, you stopping by like this."

"No, I came here because I need to warn you," Vail insisted. "Trystan was worked over by the Unseelie. Zett's crew. They could come here next."

"They'll not find us," Rhys answered confidently. "The mansion is protected by wards against virtually every creature that walks the land."

"Then how was I able to drive up unannounced?"

"You think I'd put up a ward against you?" The

werewolf shook his head sadly. “Interesting to finally meet you, Miss Santiago. I’m sorry I can’t say *nice* to meet you, but, you know.”

“I understand. I’m the cause of your troubles, Monsieur Hawkes. Believe me, I hadn’t expected things to get so out of hand. All I wanted was to avoid going near the Lord of Midsummer Dark.”

“Vail insists he’s got a handle on things. I trust him.”

“Why?” Vail intruded with spread hands. “You don’t know me, old man. I could be working against you.”

The elder half-breed took a moment to sum up the two of them and, with a smiling nod, said, “You are not. And I do trust you. You are family, Vaillant. I look forward to the day you finally start believing that.”

He remembered Rhys telling him he’d believed him his own son for thirteen years—until Cressida had told him otherwise. Could love sustain after such a betrayal? Doubtful.

“I’ve spoken with Viviane,” Rhys said.

“I don’t know if we should do this now,” Vail said. Odd how his heartbeats increased. Nervous? Not him. “There’s so much going on. We have to be careful—”

“You’re safe here, Vaillant.” Rhys laid a hand on Vail’s arm. The connection was firm and quiet, married with a flash of the shimmer. It cemented the word *safe* in Vail’s brain. Yes, he was safe here. He did trust Rhys. He had to trust him.

Lyric clasped his free hand and, standing between

the two of them, Vail did not feel as though they were ganging up on him, but instead offering support.

He sucked in a breath and nodded. "Yes. I will see her."

Rhys spoke quietly as he led the couple around and to the kitchen counter where a bottle of wine decanted in an ice bucket. "I've explained to Viviane that you've come home from Faery."

"You didn't tell her about this months ago, after my arrival?" Vail wondered.

Had he been the secret no one talked about?

"Of course, I did. But she tends to forget." Rhys offered a goblet to Lyric and she shook her head. "You are bloodborn," he said to Lyric.

"Yes."

"Vail is bloodborn, too."

"She knows." Vail grabbed the proffered goblet and tilted the full-bodied sauvignon back in one swallow. "I didn't figure you for a matchmaker."

The old vampire grinned. Hawkes was always vampire in human form, yet his werewolf mind directed him; when in werewolf form his vampire insisted on blood. "I've always said you possess great power, Vaillant. You stop drinking ichor and take vampire blood and you will come into that power."

"Just a guess, old man. And please don't talk about Lyric as if she's some object to be bartered around for marriage. There's enough trafficking in innocent lives going on lately."

"I'm sorry, Lyric," Rhys offered. "So you figured out the Santiago secret?"

"You knew?" Vail asked. "And you didn't think that would be helpful in my investigation?"

"Vail, you found the missing woman four hours into your investigation. What help did you need?"

"You could have warned me Zett had made a deal with Santiago. That he'd marked Lyric—"

"What?" Rhys tilted a curious look on Lyric, who noticeably blushed.

"You didn't know that?" Vail pulled Lyric into a hug and kissed her forehead. "I'm sorry."

"It's okay," she said. To Rhys she explained, "Zett marked me as his bride when I was thirteen, before he could know I was vampire, and before I'd developed the blood hunger. He wants to get his hands on me now to do away with his mistake."

"I see." Hawkes set down his goblet. "May I…see the mark? Just curious, and always wanting to learn as much as I can about the sidhe nations."

"Of course." Lyric turned and tilted her head for Rhys to inspect.

As the old man moved closer to his woman Vail tightened his grip about the goblet. The wolf didn't touch her, but he was too close.

The goblet cracked. Wine spilled over Vail's hand.

"Sorry," Rhys said, stepping back. He grabbed a towel from the sink and tossed it over the broken glass. "If I can recognize such things, it serves as a valuable tool, especially in my business."

"Ch'yeah." Vail stalked out from the kitchen toward

the open patio doors, needing a breath of air. And some distance, not from Rhys, but Lyric.

When had he become so possessive of her? It shouldn't have mattered to him that Rhys had wanted to inspect the mark. The old man hadn't even touched her! But he'd been close enough to smell, and werewolves were all about the scent.

Vail stepped into the sunlight and tipped the sunglasses from his forehead and down onto his nose. Hawkes was not a wolf now, his conscience reminded him, he was a vampire. Which made it ten times worse, because that meant the old man's werewolf mind now directed his actions.

"You want to go say a few words to Viviane?" Rhys called from the patio doorway. "She's in her gallery, painting."

Lyric had joined him at his side. When had that happened? Her fingers twined within his, a connection that bolstered his courage and made him feel as though his heart was strong enough to endure anything. Hell, he'd survived Faery; he could do this.

"I'll go in with you," she offered, bright blue eyes beaming hope at him.

He bowed to kiss her, and the whisper of her breath emboldened him. He needed that. Truly, he needed her.

"You stay here. I should do this alone." He eyed Rhys. "Can I trust you with her alone?"

"What do you mean?"

"If you think to turn her over to her mother—"

"He's not going to." Lyric hugged his arm and her

calm voice notched down his irritation. "I'm a big girl. I'm not going to let that old guy tell me what to do." She and Rhys exchanged smiles. "I'll be right out here. You take all the time you need."

"Fine." He rubbed his palms over his thighs. "Do you need to tell her I'm here?"

"Just came from her room when the butler announced your arrival," Rhys said. "She's expecting you. Go on."

WHEN VAIL HAD BEEN banished from Faery—ousted from a world that was not normally a vampire's environment, yet still his home—into the mortal realm, he'd lost his breath. The mortal realm, while lesser and not so vibrant as Faery, possessed a pulse of its own, and had breathed the life he had often felt missing back into him.

Now, as he entered the grand art studio, lined along the far wall with bay windows that looked over a colorful garden, he lost his breath again. Within this room, a different realm existed.

Touching the lily bracelet, he connected to what he'd known, and then, with a heavy exhalation, he released the anxiety over what he could never have again. Faery was not his place.

Where was his home?

Taking everything in, the unbleached pine walls blurred out of his focus and he saw dozens of canvases in all states of the creative process stacked and propped and hung. The pictures depicted women in gorgeous eighteenth-century gowns that twinkled as if decorated with real jewels, so much so, Vail felt he could reach to a painting and draw away the necklace glinting at the model's neck.

And there, a fine, dark-haired lord in silver damask frock coat and lace, revealed fangs within his wicked grin. Could that be his father?

The woman who had created these images, his mother, would know. She had known Constantine de Salignac, for good and for evil.

Had it ever been good for her?

Vail swallowed and ran a palm down the front of his shirt. He felt naked without the usual spikes on his clothing and faery ointment. Despite the lily bracelet, he had no armor to protect himself from this truth.

A truth he desperately wanted.

"Hello?" he called.

Rhys had said at her worst, Viviane would wail and beat her fists against the ground and then get lost in a silent stare. Those states were rare, and only if she had not fed the blood hunger for days.

He didn't want to startle her. But what could be more startling than meeting the son you gave birth to twenty-eight mortal years ago after being buried alive for two hundred and thirty years?

He heard faint, musical humming, and guessed she stood behind the canvas propped on an easel to the left and at the back of the room near the bay windows.

"Viviane? It's uh…Vail. Vaillant." *Your son.*

No, he couldn't say that. It didn't feel right. He didn't own that title. Not until his mother brought him into her arms and hugged him.

"Vaillant is a princely name," came a soft voice. Melodic and bright. She sounded like the mother he had dreamed about.

"It was given to me by my vampire mother," he offered, stepping closer but still uncertain about broaching the distance. His pulse pounded at his temples.

Was it too late to turn and dash out of here? Run into Lyric's arms and hope she would forgive him his cowardice? She knew what it was like being at odds with her mother.

How could a man be at odds with someone he didn't know?

"Rhys told you I wanted to see you?" he tried. Now the soft strokes of a brush across canvas touched his ears. "I've only been in this mortal realm a few months. I'm sorry I've stayed away. I didn't want to do anything to upset you..." *Mother.*

No, it didn't feel right. Viviane?

"Is it okay? Do you mind that I'm here?"

A clatter, perhaps a brush hitting the easel tray, made him flinch. And then a woman swept out from behind the canvas. A beautiful woman dressed in flowing black silk and with long curly hair as soot-black as his own. Her bold azure eyes were lined with kohl, and Vail smiled a little because the similarity struck him.

She stood proudly, shoulders straight and countenance demanding awe. Gorgeous and youthful, she appeared no older than he. A diamond hummingbird glittered in her hair. She'd stepped out from one of the paintings.

Vail's heartbeat clattered, surprised and overwhelmed yet uncertain.

"You are Constantine's son?" she asked, arms crossed, her nose tilted up. Not about to let down her guard. To be expected.

He nodded. He'd hoped to avoid mention of his father's name. It couldn't bring good memories to her.

"Step closer. Let me look at you."

He took a few steps, too quickly, for she hissed and backed toward the canvas.

Vail stopped, putting up his palms. "Sorry."

He tried a few slower steps until he stood about six feet from her. Now her fingers flexed at her sides, unsure. As did his. He should have worn a jacket, something to protect—

*You don't need protection from your own mother!*

"Your paintings are incredible. You are talented."

"Of course."

Not chatty, then. What had he expected? That she'd wrap her arms about him and coo that everything would be all right?

*Yes.* Oh, yes.

"I'm Vaillant." Duh. *You said that already!*

"Vaillant." And then so softly he had to lean forward to hear, she murmured, "My dark prince."

Vail swallowed. She had claimed him in some small way. Or did she mistake him for someone else? His father? Did he look like him? Dare he ask?

"Why have you come to me now?"

"I..." He had expected this reaction, but to stand

here receiving her vitriolic question confused him more than he could have imagined. His sweaty fingers and racing heart gave away his nerves. At once he wanted to pull her into a hug, and yet keeping his distance felt wiser. Safer. "I wanted to look at you." *Mother.* "To know where I came from. Forgive me."

"Forgive you what? You've done nothing to me."

"No, but…"

"That bastard." She hissed and snarled at him. The diamond pin in her hair flashed angrily. "You look like him."

"I do?" If he reminded Viviane of the one man she must despise most…

He could sense her agitation. The scent of anger always hit the center of his tongue with an acrid bite. He should leave. "I'm sorry."

"You apologize too much. I hate you." She flung up her arms and declared loudly, "I love you!" She slyly eyed him from over her shoulder. "You are pretty, my dark prince. Like me. You think me pretty?"

"Very."

"Your eyes are bright."

"Never so bright as yours…" *Mother.* The word dallied at the tip of his tongue. The notion to step forward and pull her into his arms—

"Go away from me. I don't want to see you."

Vail stiffened. For a moment his heart stopped beating. *Go away* echoed between his ears in a screeching red tone that scratched at his soul.

"Now!"

"I will." He nodded and stepped back, grasping for

security, yet his hands found nothing. He was stepping away from a tragedy he wanted to fix but could only further break beyond repair.

She did not want him. Could not stand to look upon the man who reminded her of her rapist.

"Sorry. Goodbye, Viviane. Mother."

She hissed and clawed at him.

Vail retreated, leaving the gallery door open. The breeze from the patio wafted chlorine into his nostrils. He winced at the sudden plunge back to reality. Marching into the kitchen, he swerved as Lyric put out her arms to embrace him.

"I have to leave," he growled.

"It'll take a while," Rhys tried. "She needs to get to know you."

"She doesn't want to know me!" He gained the foyer and turned, unable to look either of them in the eye. "Will you drive Lyric to her brother's home? It is the only place she can be safe. I need to be away from here."

Rhys nodded. Vail didn't meet Lyric's eyes, because to do so would reveal to her his failure. She'd had such high hopes for Viviane and him. He'd let them both down.

Turning and entering the cool night air, Vail's boots dug into the pebbled surface as he raced toward the car. He shifted into gear and peeled out of the driveway. The security lights flashed on as he peeled down the long curved driveway.

He had to get away from it all.

Turning onto the main road, Vail jammed his foot on the accelerator and raced the car into the night.

LYRIC STOPPED HERSELF from running after her lover when he made his hasty retreat. She knew better. He needed to get away.

She glanced beyond Rhys, who leaned against the kitchen counter, then to the gallery, from where Vail had charged out as if hellhounds snapped at his ankles.

Was Viviane LaMourette so much the monster, then? To have made her son, a powerful, confident man, flee as if the devil Himself were on his heels?

"Sorry," Rhys offered.

"He just wanted to know his father," she blurted out, feeling defensive for her lover. "Why won't you give him the information to find him?"

"We have a deal."

"A deal? You sound like the sidhe who won't agree to anything without a return reward. You want the gown? I'll hand it over."

Rhys's eyebrows lifted. Of course, both he and Vail had to have guessed she had the gown all along. Wasn't as if she could have fenced it in the mortal realm.

"He's in love with you," Rhys stated.

"No, he's not."

"You are in love with him."

A statement she couldn't find words to deny, so she kept her silence.

"It would be a betrayal of Vail if I allowed you to hand over the gown."

"How so? It would end this stupid deal the two of you made. End of story."

"He needs to hand it over to me. To complete the quest, so to speak."

"But I insist! I'll go retrieve it right now. Don't you see how hurt the man is? He wants connection with a family he's never known."

"He has family. I am his family. His mother—"

"Just sent a grown man racing out of here. What kind of monster is she?"

Her comment struck a painful chord in Rhys, and he turned away from her.

"Sorry."

Rhys sighed and shook his head that it was all forgiven. "Do you know when I first met Vail, he sat down before me in my office, and said as a means of introduction, 'I'm Vail the Unwanted.' Just like that. And he believed it. So, no, I will not make this easier for him by taking away his opportunity to learn that he is truly loved and can become the vampire we all want him to be."

"Thank you for telling me that. He's getting better."

"I hope so. He's a fine man. Honorable in ways even he isn't privy to."

The front door opened and in marched a wild, red-haired man sporting two black eyes and a split lip. A gash cut across his nose, but he managed to smile with a wince and at the same time blatantly ogle Lyric.

"Who is this fine bit?" he asked Rhys, who had moved alongside Lyric protectively.

"She's vampire," Rhys stated.

The man stepped back and put up a palm. "Oh." That one word dismissed her to the ranks of something vile and of small regard.

"What happened to your face, Tryst?"

"Tryst?" Lyric looked from him to Rhys. There was resemblance about the square jaw and eyes. "You're Vail's brother?"

"Who are you?" the werewolf asked defiantly.

"I'm Lyric Santiago," she said, holding out her hand, which he almost shook but, at the last moment, flicked his hand away from her offer. "Vail told me the Unseelie got to you. I'm sorry."

"Yeah, man, faeries are after Vaillant. Because of her. I can see why, too. Nice. For a vampire."

"Tryst, mind your manners. Lyric is a welcome guest in my home."

"Yeah? I thought she was the one you were supposed to find for the client? Aren't you going to hand her over and end all this?" He pointed to his bruised face.

"You can't handle a few cuts and bruises?" Rhys chided teasingly.

"You know I can. But do you see the trouble my brother has brought to us? Where is he, anyway?" The werewolf sniffed. "Did he abandon her here like yesterday's baggage? Because if he did, that bastard is luring the faeries right to my home, and I warned him not to."

"That's not it at all," Rhys said. "He came here to warn me after I missed his phone calls. As well... Vaillant finally met Viviane."

The wolf stilled and shoved his hands in his front pockets. "Oh."

At that moment, Lyric sensed Trystan Hawkes was much more receptive to the idea of having a vampire brother than he wanted anyone to know. He didn't hate Vail; he just acted the role he assumed others expected of him.

Rhys cleared his throat. "I was going to offer Lyric a ride into the city, but if you are able?"

She exchanged looks with the werewolf and suspected the last thing he wanted was to spend a moment with her. Yet she wanted to get to know the brother better. To determine the accuracy of her assessment of the brothers' relationship.

"Good, then." Rhys shuffled Lyric toward Trystan. "He can give you a ride into the city. Don't worry, his bark is worse than his bite."

"But I just got here," Tryst said. "I was going to sit with Viviane."

"She's in a mood," the old man said lowly.

The werewolf sighed, and cast his gaze down the hallway toward the gallery.

"Return tomorrow, why don't you?" Rhys offered his son. "Bring her some of those white chrysanthemums she favors so much."

"I can do that." He flicked a gesture toward Lyric. "Come on, faery bait."

THE MASERATI SKIDDED on loose gravel. Vail pulled up the emergency brake. The vehicle spun. The back tires left the ground.

He opened the door and flung out his body, hitting the gravel with a bounce. Stones spattered his face, hands and skull. The car door narrowly missed shaving his scalp. The car spun and went over the edge of the riverbank.

Water splashed over Vail's dirt-dusted face. He tilted back his head to laugh.

## *CHAPTER SEVENTEEN*

RHYS HAWKES CLOSED the door behind Trystan and Lyric and turned into his wife's embrace. Her frail limbs trembled against his body. It had been too much for her to see Vail. It tore his heart open that the two could not have a relationship.

Perhaps it needed time and patience. God knows, he had learned patience in this marriage. He'd once thought her dead, and to find her alive decades ago had put back together the pieces of his broken heart. He adored Viviane, even when she raged.

"You told me Constantine was no more," she said, her voice warbling. "You told me, lover. Did you lie to me?"

Sometimes it had been easier to allow Viviane to believe what she wanted. He'd never told her as much, only that he had no idea where Constantine was—which was true.

"Never, my love."

"Why has my dark prince only come to me now? Why so long?"

He swept the hair from her face and tilted up her

chin to gaze into her lucid blue eyes. Lucid, but for how long, he could never know. "Remember when the faery Cressida chose one of your sons as payment for enchanting my werewolf?"

She nodded. "You promised your firstborn. She took him. We had the other. I know it broke your heart, lover. It did mine, too."

"He's always been in our hearts, even though he was gone. Vaillant wants to get to know you, Viviane. He needs a mother."

"I like being a mother. Trystan was easy to raise. He takes after his father, so proud and kind. But my dark prince…he looks like him."

Indeed, Vail had his father's square facial features, and yet the dark hair and blue eyes had come from both his parents. Pray, he did not develop a malicious streak as Constantine had. And pray, the two boys, Trystan and Vail, could have a better relationship than Rhys and Constantine had.

"He is not his father, Viviane. Vail is quite new to the mortal realm. He needs guidance. But most of all, he needs family. Do you want to be his family, Viviane?"

"I could be. But my heart…" She pounded a fist to her breast.

"I know." Rhys pulled her head to his shoulder. "Your heart bleeds for the travesties visited you by Constantine de Salignac."

"I will kill him."

Would that she could, and then perhaps Salignac would haunt her no longer.

Rhys had had opportunity when they'd been tracking Viviane after she'd been released from her centuries-long prison in the catacombs. He'd held Constantine by the neck, his talons emerging with anger. But no matter the evils Constantine had brought to Rhys and Viviane's life, he could not kill his own brother. The past could never be erased.

In truth, Rhys did not desire a relationship with his brother, but neither would he be the hand to bring him down, as was, he suspected, Vail's focus.

"You're hungry?" he asked, but didn't wait for her answer.

Sitting on the chair, Rhys drew Viviane onto his lap and tilted his head aside. She stroked his neck. Her touch always sent shivers through his system and ignited desire. As a half-breed, his werewolf could not abide being bitten by a vampire. But he was in vampire form now, and though his mind was all wolf, the vampire always won the insistent desire to have his blood drawn out by his wife. It was a sensual experience they both enjoyed.

He gave Viviane strength, and in turn, when he took blood from her, it calmed his raging vampire.

They could not survive without the other.

LYRIC CLUTCHED THE EDGES of the passenger seat. Trystan Hawkes drove exactly like his brother. Did no one take driver's education classes anymore?

The brown SUV sported red and orange flames along the exterior sides and laughing skulls across the back. A gold skull capped the stick shift. The interior was pasted with graffiti of skater logo stickers. All very colorful. As was Trystan.

The man was tall and built like Vail, but where Vail's muscles were streamlined, his brother's were meaty and imposing. As she would expect from a werewolf. One of Lyric's friends was a werewolf—Blu Masterson; she spent the summers in Paris with her husband, Creed Saint-Pierre—but the female wolves, while muscular, were often slender and athletic in form.

Trystan cast her a sideways glance. "I can smell your fear, Lyric."

"Yeah? Who'da thought, a werewolf capable of scenting out fear." She wasn't afraid of him. Well, maybe a little. Lyric had never been this close to a male wolf.

"Don't be afraid of me. I won't bite. You, on the other hand..."

"Wouldn't dream to bite a werewolf. You're not afraid of me, are you?"

He shrugged, and turned onto a different road. "Vamps don't scare me, though I am fearful of the blood hunger I could develop if one ever bit me. Keep your fangs locked and loaded, sweetie."

"Will do. Surprised, though, you'd be offended by me."

"I'm not offended. Hell, my mother is a vampire, and my dad is half-vamp. There's nothing about you that offends me, sweet—"

"Enough with the sweetie. Your brother uses the same tired endearment. I'm no one's sweetie."

"I bet you're not. So Vail got scared by Mother and left you behind?"

She twisted on the seat to face him, and noticed he instantly sat straighter, more alert. Who was more leery of whom?

"Why do you hate your brother?" she asked. "From what I've learned, you two don't know each other enough to form an opinion worthy of hate."

"My mother is insane because of him."

"She is not, and you know it. It was Vail's father who buried her alive. Vail had nothing to do with that."

"He's told you a lot in what—the few days you two have known each other?"

"Something like that. So? Are you going to blame the son for the father's sins? Come on, Trystan, I suspect you're a smart man. Don't give me tired excuses."

The werewolf whistled and gave her an appreciative nod. "I like you. Do you love my brother?"

She bowed her head and looked out at the long ditch grass that blurred as the SUV sped past. "Of course not. Love doesn't come so easily."

"Tell me about it."

That made her smile. "A good friend of mine is a werewolf, but I've never been alone with a male wolf before. Well, I've never been around one at all."

He waggled his brows. "Impressed?"

"I am. You're a tough guy, but I think you want a relationship with Vail as much as he does with you."

"Ch'yeah, right."

Lyric swung her head around. "Make that noise again."

"What? I didn't do anything."

"That sound you just made."

"Ch'yeah?"

"Vail says the same thing."

The werewolf cocked a goofy look at her. "No kidding? Huh."

The brothers had more than a few things in common. It gave Lyric hope that the family she sensed Vail needed was only a few heartfelt conversations and an open-minded understanding away.

"So where we headed?" Tryst asked. "You hungry? No, that was a stupid question. Mind if I get a burger? There's a great little cafe at city's edge just ahead."

"Go for it. My brother's apartment is in the eighteenth. But maybe..."

Maybe she should go to Vail's place. He wouldn't return to Leo's apartment. And much as he thought he needed to be alone, she didn't want the vampire to sit and stew about things too long.

VAIL WALKED FOR HOURS to get into the city. He entered Montmartre around three in the morning. The skitter of wings across his ankles reminded him he'd not worn the necessary ointment to see what he desperately wanted to see.

Didn't matter. This was as close to home as he'd ever get. And they knew him here.

"FaeryTown," he said with a drunken smile.

He wasn't drunk. He was out of sorts and still riding

the wicked high of crashing the car. Easier to destroy than to face reality.

His mother didn't love him? Screw her. He didn't need a mad vampiress mother.

And soon enough he'd plunge a stake through his father's heart, obliterating all ties to anything remotely family.

And what about that werewolf brother of his? The cocky wolf was too busy with his own life to give a crap about Vail. And yet he managed to make Vail feel as though it was his fault Viviane was insane.

Maybe it was. Had he never been born, had he never gone to see her today, she would not have been reminded of that awful night in the eighteenth century when Constantine de Salignac consigned her to hell.

"She said I looked like him," Vail said, and stumbled through the arched stone doorway to an ichor den. "Figures."

Pushing past an overgrown fern frond, he navigated the bright darkness. A tacky replacement for the real Faery, the decor was similar to the Lizard Lounge with wild, verdant plants and bright colors. The colors tended to attack when he was high on ichor—which was the cool part.

It smelled like forest after a sun shower, with a hint of the spices, cinnamon and clove, that faeries loved so much. A low rhythm pulsed, yet it wasn't exactly music, but perhaps the combined beat of the inhabitants' heartbeats. The atmosphere hummed in Vail's senses, pleading he succumb to decadent pleasures.

Beyond the delicate silver chains spilling like

rainfall before various rooms and lounges, Vail heard the satisfied moans of vampires enchanted to a macabre supplication.

It was said after the first taste of ichor the vampire was powerless to stop taking more. Like meth to humans, the drug became the vampire, changed his thinking and made him weak and unpredictable. A vampire could fight real demons barehanded, yet after a hit of ichor, could never defeat the inner demons that occupied his soul.

If Charish Santiago had made a deal with Zett, it would be for the faery women and men who serviced these addicts.

"Monsieur Vaillant." A sweet, heart-faced sprite fluttered before him. She was small enough to fit into Vail's fist, which also made it easy for her to dash when a client got out of control. "Your usual?"

Nodding, he followed her into the azure room. The domed ceiling was painted with cheesy clouds and cupids. He'd come here weekly since his arrival in the mortal realm. It was a home like no other, a reminder of what he could never again be a part of, of the lie that had been his life. And still was.

But he didn't *need* ichor like the dust freaks did. It was something he'd been born to; it was simply a part of him he must replenish and sustain.

*Ch'yeah, right. Tell yourself another one, dark prince.*

Viviane had called him her dark prince. It was difficult not to want to clutch that endearment and make it something it could never be. A declaration of love and acceptance.

It was a silly name. Like the names he gave Lyric.

The sprite fluttered off, leaving Vail staring at a pretty faery sprawled on an orange sofa. Her wings were pale, and one looked broken, though it could have been tucked at an odd angle against the velvet sofa. She was half-drained and smiled weakly at him as she patted the cushion for him to sit next to her.

He peered into her violet eyes and heard Lyric's voice. *What if you got clean? Why do you need to maintain?*

It was what he knew. It was easy. And he did need this. Because if he ever stopped, he wasn't sure how to live. On mortal blood? The idea of it disgusted him not so much as it usually did. And why was that? Vail toyed with the May bells circling his wrist. Protection.

*Home.*

*"Monsieur?"* Her thin fingers grasped for his hand, but he slipped from her frail touch.

"I changed my mind."

"Tut-tut." A cool breath tickled his ear.

Vail did not turn to see who stood beside him. Her presence always lowered any room's temperature by a few degrees. Faery gossamers slipped about his leg and she walked her fingers up his spine.

"My pretty vampire child doesn't want what makes him strong?"

"Get the hell away from me, Cressida."

"You are using mortal oaths now? Oh, Vaillant."

The disappointment in her voice was nothing new to him. "You are in tatters. What's happened?"

"I like to drive fast." He lifted his head defiantly and turned his back to the weak faery sprawled on the couch.

Tiny and seeming frail, though Vail knew otherwise, the Mistress of Winter's Edge hugged him from the side and tilted her head onto his shoulder. Rare had she shown him affection in Faery. It was as if she could not be emotional there, and in the mortal realm she was released from a binding spell.

It was possible. But it mattered little.

She touched the lily bracelet. "Only a few bells left. Poor child."

"Bring me a new one," he demanded.

"I will."

So easy as that? Without asking a boon in return? "Why would you do anything for me, Cressida?"

"I do everything for you, Vaillant. You won't see what you don't want to see. Was your life in Faery so awful?"

"You damned me because I was bloodborn. I was not the child you would have chosen. You wanted my brother Trystan. Everyone loves Trystan."

"I've never known you to be so self-deprecating, Vaillant. You've always been a scrapper who will stand against any who look at you the wrong way. This mortal realm has weakened you."

Had it?

He tightened his muscles, but still she clung to his arm. "If anything it's opened my eyes to the cruelties of Faery. Not that I wasn't fully aware all my life. Cressida, what is Zett up to with the Santiago clan?"

"Oh, now you wish to speak with me? When you've important business you seek my knowledge, but never to simply wish me well or want a visit?"

"I can never return to Faery. You know that."

"Zett does rather despise you. You had no right doing what you did."

No right to make things better for one innocent shifter sidhe whom Zett had marked in his sights? Vail would do the same thing and take the punishment over and over again.

"What's done is done, Cressida."

"Yes, and done so well. I may not approve, but you know I admire your courage, Vaillant."

She shuffled him against a wall so plush his shoulders settled into the softness of fabric, or perhaps foliage, he couldn't determine which.

"What do you ask of me to answer my questions?" he asked. With the sidhe, a bargain was always demanded.

Her violet eyes twinkled. Wings like a dragonfly's, yet three on either side, fluttered at her back. Her pale hair always wavered as if the sea about her lithe form.

"I know why you are after Zett," she said. "It is to ultimately bring you to Constantine. Your mortal stepfather holds you in wicked supplication with a bargain made in blood."

Like it or not, they had a connection, and always Cressida knew his mind.

"You've made it clear over the years you hate Salignac," Vail stated. "Won't you help me now to find him?"

"While it would please me immensely to see you stake that bastard, I'm not entirely sure I wish my pretty vampire child to commit such violence."

"Cressida, do not affect love toward me. It is something you and I both know the sidhe cannot embrace."

"Admiration." She cooed against his ear, her cool touches gliding down his throat and chest, yet remaining chaste. "Pride. Even respect, I have for you, Vaillant the Dark. I do not believe destroying your father will put you in a right place."

Vaillant the Dark. *My dark prince.*

False affection, all of it.

"Then be gone with you. I don't need you. I don't need…"

He glanced to the faery on the couch. The frail thing smiled and tilted her head to reveal her long neck, which was unscarred. Was it possible no one had yet supped from her?

Vail inhaled, testing the cool allure of ichor at the back of his tongue.

"Yes, Vaillant, you need what she offers," Cressida cooed. "You will never be like them. They are bloodthirsty fiends who feed upon unclean mortals. You are starving for ichor. Take her. Be the man you are and can only ever be. My Vaillant."

She'd not told him he disgusted her. She'd not hissed at him or demanded he leave. Cressida, in her own twisted manner, would always be the mother he could never have yet pined to love.

As he focused on the tender stroke of Cressida's finger along his cheek, Vail inhaled the spiced forest scent. A heady dizziness swirled his thoughts. He nodded and bent to sit beside the faery. Cressida kissed his head and whispered some unaffectionate endearment. The whoosh of her wings crackled in his brain as Vail leaned in to bite the faery's neck.

# *CHAPTER EIGHTEEN*

DESPITE KNOWING IT was the safest place in Paris, Lyric hadn't wanted to return to her brother's apartment. And if Rhys Hawkes would not accept the gown from her, then she needed to find Vail and settle things once and for all.

She couldn't fathom innocents getting hurt because of a deal her mother had made with the Unseelie lord. Getting the gown back in the hands of the Seelie court would stop that from happening. And then she'd go to the Council with the information she had about her mother's dealings in FaeryTown.

Maybe. She wasn't sure she could turn in her mother.

Connor must be behind this. Charish would not stoop to such low tactics to make money. Would she?

Lyric realized now she knew her mother not at all. On the other hand, maybe she was lying to herself. She'd grown up in a family of thieves; why suddenly expect morality?

Trystan had dropped her off at Vail's building.

Before he drove off, he gave her the address for his penthouse in the second quarter, and had given her the entrance code, in case Vail was not home and she needed somewhere to crash.

That confirmed Trystan Hawkes as one of the good guys.

Without thinking to knock, Lyric started to enter the code on the digital box outside Vail's loft door—Leo had taught her to pay attention whenever someone entered a code—when she noticed the door was ajar. Listening for noise inside, she carefully pushed in the door and slid along the inner wall, carefully pushing the door closed.

Someone could be inside right now, or else Vail had left the door open when he'd gotten home, which didn't seem likely. Then she noted the upturned couch, the shattered coffeepot and the scatter of kitchen drawers strewn about.

Had he been robbed? Was the thief still here?

Something glittered all over the living room floor.

"Faeries." They'd found Vail's home but hopefully not Vail.

The steel floors would announce her presence, so she slipped out of her high heels and crept along the kitchen counter, being careful not to step on Green Snake, whose branch had been broken and tossed in a corner.

The white shirt Vail had borrowed from her brother's closet lay crumpled on the floor before the bathroom. A peek inside found it was empty and dark.

"No faeries," she muttered. If Vail was home he had to have seen this mess and…

The cowboy boots abandoned in the bedroom doorway gave her a stumble, but Lyric caught herself with a balancing sway of arms. Her gymnastics training gave her impeccable agility.

There on the bed, sprawled facedown in a beam of pale moonlight, lay Vail. Was he injured? Beaten?

Moonlight slashed the white bedsheets. Trails of faery dust glittered everywhere. Vail's back looked as though a faery had spread its dust into it. His hair shimmered, and there, at the base of the bed below his head, it looked as though he'd spit out ichor.

Lyric gasped. "He's high on ichor. Did the intruders do this to him? But why?"

And then she knew that couldn't be the case. Faeries would have killed him, or forced him to take them to her. Vail had to have arrived after his place was trashed.

Cruelly rejected by his mother, he had gone straight to FaeryTown, possibly the only place in this realm that provided some means of sanctity for him.

"Oh, Vail."

Unsure what to do, wondering whether it would be better to dash out and leave him alone in whatever crazy realm his brain traveled right now, Lyric couldn't force herself to turn away from him.

She knelt on the bed, careful not to touch the dust that spilled like talcum across the sheets with her movement. "Vail?"

He stirred, and she stroked her fingers through his

hair, but quickly wiped the dust off on her skirt. The last thing she needed was a contact high.

"Vail, it's Lyric. Did you see the faeries who did this?"

He grunted and smirked, turning his face aside to give her his ichor-dusted cheek. "Lyric," he said drunkenly. "Pretty vampire who I love to fuck."

It was the ichor speaking, she told herself. He was high, stoned, whatever they called it. A dust freak.

"I'm sorry, I shouldn't have made you see your mother."

"You can't make me do anything." He rolled to his back.

His chest was wrinkled from the sheets, and his pants were unbuttoned and shoved down his hips, and his muscles pulsed and tensed with the movement. A sheen of dust coated him as if he'd sweated it from his pores. It was at once beautiful, and then horrible.

"Fucking faeries," he spit. "Trashed my place."

"I'm sorry, they were looking for me."

"Need more," he murmured. "So sweet. Ichor. Lyric?"

"Did you do this because of your mother?" she asked, wanting to curl up next to him, to hold him and make it all better. What a lie. "Vail, this won't make things better."

"Makes everything better," he slurred. "You don't understand."

"No, I don't. But I think you'd see more clearly…"

How dare she preach to him while he was in such a state? He'd never remember, and it was foolish to argue with an addict. Words would fall on deaf or defensive ears.

"I thought of you," he said, reaching out, but his hand dropped to the sheets. "Wasn't going to do it. Heard your voice telling me to get clean."

Lyric swallowed. She felt so helpless. Could she have prevented this?

"Then she showed up."

"She?"

"My faery fucking stepmother. Heh." He laughed deeply and turned to his side, coughing. "Hot in here."

He did look hot. If the ichor was sweating out of him, he could have a fever. But how was that possible? Would an overdose cause it? He must have taken too much. She didn't want to think about the faery that may have provided him this high.

She remembered the ichor-addicted man who had worked for Charish. He'd been a literal zombie, and had puked ichor and stank, all the while screaming for more ichor. Charish's demon guards had wrestled him out of the mansion and taken him—Lyric had no idea where he'd been taken. Most likely they'd dumped the hapless wreck in FaeryTown.

She would not allow that to happen to Vail.

Lyric dashed to the bathroom and ran cold water over a towel. She squeezed it out and caught a gasping sob in her throat, searching vainly for her reflection in the mirror.

Why the hell did she care at all for the stupid vampire who thought he was a faery? It wasn't as though they meant anything to each other beyond a means to get what they wanted, both in life and sexually. He was arrogant and cocky. He didn't have a clue how to exist in the mortal realm. The guy stood alone, and he liked that. He didn't need anyone.

Oh, but he did. Just as much as she needed someone. Anyone. One single soul she could relate to. And Vail, for good or for ill, was that soul.

Rushing into the bedroom, she crawled onto the bed, wary of the dust. A little skin contact shouldn't hurt her. As far as she knew, a vampire had to imbibe ichor to get high.

She pressed the cool towel over Vail's forehead and he moaned pleasurably. The skim of his iron rings tickled her thigh.

"You're good to me, vampiress. Why?"

"Because you deserve good. Because I like you."

"Not like this." He pushed away the towel, but she persisted, and sopped it along his neck. "Feels good. Too good. I don't deserve you."

"Just close your eyes, lover. I'm going to take care of you."

VAIL SLIPPED IN AND OUT of consciousness. His brain had been floating through a loopy dream since taking the faery ichor. But he'd regretted it the moment he'd seen Lyric standing in his bedroom doorway.

He should have resisted. *For her.* He could be different for her.

Hell, he must still be high. He didn't do anything to please anyone.

Except, apparently, Cressida.

*You did as she asked you. You succumbed to the addiction you've always had, much as you deny it. It is how she kept you all those years. It is how she will always keep you.*

Close by, his vampire lover fretted, "I don't understand why the dust doesn't seem to go away."

The cool towel annoyed him when Lyric pressed it against his neck, and across his shoulders and chest. He'd felt feverish after taking the ichor, yet now he shivered.

He'd taken too much. He wasn't sure if the faery had survived. He'd left her… *I didn't kill her. I would never.*

And yet, he didn't know. He just didn't know.

If only he'd come home earlier, when the faeries had been trashing his place. They would have beaten him, perhaps killed him. *One less thing for Lyric to worry about.*

"It sticks like nobody's business," Lyric complained softly. "How do I get this stuff off your skin?"

*Keep it there. Don't take away the one means to oblivion I have left.*

*She wants to help you. Let her.*

Resisting what he wanted most took too much out of him. Vail groaned and shoved away the towel.

"Rain," he muttered. Outside the patio window, rain battered the small iron deck hugging the penthouse. "Faery dust repels mortal tap water," he murmured. "Rain…can drown a faery."

Lyric slid off the bed and opened the patio door.

A gush of raindrops whipped in on the wind, and the cool spatters tickled Vail's face.

Did she think she could save him? Dredge him up from the mindless oblivion of the high? Hell, *the high?* He'd not been high on ichor since he'd first started drinking it. He must have taken a lot.

But he hadn't killed. No. The faery had been smiling, waving to him as he'd stumbled out from the ichor den. He'd left her all the money he'd had in his pocket, which was probably a thousand euros. Much more than the den charged, but he sucked at math, and didn't care about paper money.

A heavy, wet glob of towel landed on his stomach. "That's cold!"

"I'm sorry," Lyric said sternly. "But if you want to get clean, this is the way to do it."

"Who said anything…" About getting clean?

She'd decided for him? Hell. Why hadn't he forced her to give him the gown that first night? He'd be done with her now.

And all alone.

*You don't want to be alone. Alone sucks. Lyric makes life right.*

He admired her courage, and yes, he did want to get clean. To purge the dust from his system.

And after that? He wasn't sure. He'd take things as they came.

"You're shivering."

"You noticed?" he said sharply. "I need another fix. I'm coming down. Fuck!"

The towel washed over his hips, and now he realized he was naked.

"You took off my clothes? What are you up to, woman? I don't want this. I don't..."

But again, he couldn't force himself to speak the lie.

Some achy part of his tattered soul did want this. He needed this. Lyric's touch worked a balm to his pain. It was the first and only touch he could endure since leaving Faery.

"You're right, the rain takes this stuff off your skin." She returned to the patio, and he heard her wringing out the towel.

Tilting his head, Vail saw through blurry eyes the image of a beautiful vampiress, her thin pink dress damp with rain clinging to her skin. Red ruffles spilled below her curvy ass, which segued into long, gorgeous gams. He wanted to lick the rain from her skin—but only if it was shimmering with ichor.

Gripping the sheets, he growled and tore the sheet from the bed. Ichor dried to dust spilled over his face. He lapped at it like an animal.

"No!" Lyric grabbed the sheet and wrestled him for it. "You idiot vampire. I'm trying to help you!"

"Fuck you!"

She gaped at him, bewildered by his violence.

His heart pulsed. "I'm sorry, Lyric—no, I'm not!" He did not release his hold on the sheet. "I want another taste. I need it!"

She pulled so hard, he reneged and she won the

sheet. Vail turned his back to her. He was hurting her. And she only wanted to save the wib vampire.

"You don't know how to save me," he muttered. "This is what I am. I—" He bent double, wincing at the pain clamping his stomach. It radiated through his muscles. Clawing at the dust sprinkled on the mattress, he pressed his fingers into his mouth.

"Just try it," whispered from the sodden angel. "Give it a chance, Vail. If not for me, then for your own sanity."

"Why? You think I will go mad like my crazy mother?"

"No, I didn't mean that. Don't you want to see clearly?"

She was an angel he didn't deserve, but, oh, did he desire her. And not just for sex. He desired her admiration, and her trust. But most of all, he desired her respect.

Smashing his fist against the headboard averted some of the pain tracking his nerves. With a shout to curse all the sidhe in Faery, Vail surrendered to his lover's selfless determination.

IT WAS WORKING.

Lyric had no idea about addicts and how they functioned, but she had seen a few television shows. Denying the addict the drug and helping them through withdrawal was the way to do it. And now that she had gotten Vail's skin wiped clean of dust, he seemed to be in less pain. His tight abdominal muscles had relaxed, his chest now rising and falling as if in sleep. And he'd stopped insisting on more ichor.

The fact that no more dust emerged on the surface of his pores gave her hope. Had the vicious fever racking his body expelled all the dust within his veins?

Blinking and catching the heel of her palm against the headboard, she cautioned herself not to fall asleep. It couldn't have been more than forty-eight hours. She only needed a few hours of sleep. But she couldn't risk Vail waking and leaving to get more dust while she was catching a few Z's.

If he wandered out now, it was likely the Unseelie would find him, and she was in no position to protect him, since they would take her, as well.

But sleep teased. Or rather, some kind of loopy bliss begged her to surrender. She couldn't keep her lids from fluttering, yet the sensation humming across her skin was like tiny kisses, electrifying her nerves and sparking them erotically.

So what if Vail didn't come clean? She could understand the desire for the high that ichor promised. She'd never drunk it herself, no—but she could completely relate right now.

Funny. That seemed…not right.

"You need blood," she whispered. "So hungry."

She scanned the room. A pile of sheets mounded in the open doorway. The mattress was exposed, the green satin fabric glinting here and there. She leaned forward and wiped a finger through a smudge of dried ichor and held it before her to examine in the full moonlight that shimmered through the rain.

So pretty, and yet so addictive. Of course a vampire who had lived in Faery all his life could handle the stuff. He had known nothing else. Certainly wasn't a replacement for fresh, hot blood.

It had no scent. It tickled her nose when she got some on the tip of it. Lyric sniffed and a shock of sensation heated the back of her throat and softened her resistance. Licking the dust from her finger, she settled across the end of the bed, allowing her limbs to loosen, and her mind followed.

HE WASN'T SURE how much time had passed. But the world felt different now. Lying on his back, staring at the ceiling, Vail noticed the hum of traffic outside the open patio door was louder than usual. Bird chirps were sharp and surprising. Clear.

The quilted mattress fabric abraded his skin, and he lifted his arm away from it. Studying the skin on his biceps, he brushed his fingers over it. No dust? Impossible.

And yet, something had changed. The air in the room did not suffocate as it had earlier. His breath sounded plainly, not muted by the fog of ichor. Had he come out of the high?

Impossible. And improbable. But he did feel… different.

He clutched the lily bracelet. One blossom remained. It meant nothing to him right now.

He sat, and his toe nudged a body. Long and lithe, she lay stretched across the end of the bed, the brown hair she hated so much spilling over her face. Green

Snake slithered along her body and aimed for the floor. Her dress had dried wrinkled against her skin, yet it outlined the sexy sinuous form of her.

Lyric Santiago was some kind of dark angel. A rescuing angel. She must be exhausted after nursing him, and had fallen asleep. He owed her so much. He was…yes, he had to be—was he clean?

That was what was different. He didn't feel Faery at all. Gone was the numbing hum of ichor that spoke to him on seductive whispers. The overwhelming knowledge that other sidhe occupied this realm had dissipated.

Gone? And he did not regret it.

"Thank you," he whispered. "I love you for this. I guess you were right. You can't get love until you give it. You gave it to me, Lyric. Now I want to give it back."

He leaned forward and stroked her hair down to her waist. She felt feverish. "Lyric?"

She moaned and slid up a knee, curling her hands under her chin. "More," she murmured.

"More?" He touched her hair. On the curled brown tips, it shimmered. She must have gotten dust into her system after all the contact with him. "No, not this. You can't succumb, Lyric."

He lifted her into his arms, and at first she lolled, but when he juggled her closer she snuggled against his chest.

Was it already too late? She could not have taken it by mouth, only through skin contact. Would that save her?

"Just a little taste?" she pleaded in a small voice that would have seduced him to his knees had she been clear and lying before him naked.

Hell, he was naked. No time to worry about that. Though maybe he should. The mattress was dusted with ichor, and the floor, too.

He rushed to the closet and pulled on a clean long-sleeved shirt and leather pants to protect his skin from absorbing the dust. He'd take Lyric into the living room, which was probably dusted with residue ichor from him, but it shouldn't be as thick as it was in here.

Stripping the clothes from her body, he then eyed the wet towels heaped in the hallway. They sat in a thick ichor puddle.

From the bathroom he claimed a new towel then held it outside to collect the rain. Tossing it over Lyric's shoulder, he lifted and carried her out to the living room sofa.

Kicking the couch, he managed to turn it upright and lay Lyric on it.

She squirmed and moved sensuously as he wiped the towel over her, getting all the places where she glittered, which was the exposed skin on her legs and arms and neck. There wasn't much on her, so he counted that as good.

"Lover, give me some of that ichor-laced blood of yours." She tickled her fingers into his hair.

"You helped me get clean," he said. "There's no ichor in my blood, sweetie. I've never felt better. Ever."

"But I want some." She pouted. "It's so good. Makes me tingly. You like me tingly?"

"No, sweetie, not like this."

How to counteract the ichor's effects? Dust had sweated out of his body. He'd done this to her!

Her clothes glittered with the stuff. He shuffled her arms from the dress and then slid down her skirt, being careful not to brush the skin beneath with more dust.

She hooked a finger around his wrist, below the bracelet, and tugged. "Give me."

She thought he had ichor in his veins? No, he innately knew it was all gone. And yet…

Vail stood and paced to the doorway, near a window. He could help her. Maybe. He had to know for sure.

Biting his wrist, he held it toward the window to study the blood. It was thick and oozed brightly.

"But no ichor," he decided. Not a single glint. "It's gone. She did it."

"Vail!

He rushed to Lyric's side, and eased a hand over her feverish forehead. "You want my blood?" He lifted his wrist to his mouth and touched it to his fangs. "I hope this works."

## *CHAPTER NINETEEN*

THE FIRST DROP of Vail's blood spilled across Lyric's tongue like water to a parched wanderer. She didn't understand how or why he was giving her his blood. The guy refused to accept the fact he was a vampire.

Another drop trickled across her tongue and burst at the back of her throat. Many followed. She pressed her lips to his skin and sucked in his dark glamour. It beamed a heady crimson heat through her system and battled against the loopy dust high.

His blood was not laced with dust, and she could taste it was missing. But what wasn't missing was too good. She didn't want dust—she wanted Vail. Inside her mouth. Streaming through her veins. Filling her.

As she sucked from him, he slipped behind her body and slid a hand around her ribs to cup her breast. He pulled her against him, and she held tight to his wrist.

He nuzzled into her hair and whispered, "Take it all, Lyric. It feels as if you are drawing out my soul. I want you to have it, to bond with me. This is incredible."

The only way they could bond was if he, in turn, took her blood. She sensed that would never happen. The reason he made this offer was he must still be tracking remnants of the high. Because if he were clear, this would not be happening.

It probably wasn't happening. This strange offering was a whacked hallucination brought on by the dust.

Vail moaned and pressed a kiss against her jaw, his fangs grazing her skin. The tease of his hard tooth against her skin pushed her over a sensual edge and Lyric cried out, as if in orgasm. The blood high—the swoon—rushed over her and she arched her body, lifting her chest and tilting her head back against Vail's shoulder.

She grasped his leather pant leg, disappointed he was dressed, and dug in her nails. "You have to have sex with me right now. That was so good, but it can be better. I want you inside me, Vail."

He stood and shuffled off his shirt. "You've my blood on your lips."

She teased out her tongue to lick it off. "You taste better than anything I've ever had."

"Really?" He unzipped and tugged down his pants, which revealed an erection that snapped up to slap his torso. "I want you," he said, and then reluctance washed over his face. "I do and I don't."

He stood there, looking aside, his eyes tracking the floor.

"You don't have to reciprocate," she offered. "I know—"

"Everything I thought I knew, and wanted," he said,

meeting her eyes, "has changed. You brought me into the clear, Lyric. I…I do want us to bond."

"But that means…"

"Yes." A sexy smirk revealed his fangs, descended and ready for action. That meant he did want her. "But I still need some time. You got me clean. And now you've taken my blood. Everything is happening so quickly."

She hooked a foot around behind his thigh and toppled him onto her body, wrapping her legs about his hips. "Come inside me, lover. With this." She grasped his cock and guided him into her depths. "We'll save the fangs for later."

The thickness of him thrusting inside her brought her to the precipice of orgasm so quickly Lyric could but grasp the couch, while one hand clutched air.

He clung to her, his fingers closing over her breast and squeezing the nipple. His hips slapped hers as his rhythm increased. It happened as if the proverbial fireworks were going off in celebration. His muscles tensed and he growled roughly at her ear. Her body reacted of its own volition and answered the call of instinct.

Giddy with the high, Lyric sought more, and sank her fangs into Vail's neck. He moaned, yet did not pull away as she sucked out the glamorous elixir. The vein pumped hot blood down her throat, feeding her his darkness and the magical wonder he tried to hide. She tasted it now—Vail complete.

Crying out with climax, he collapsed upon her, his lips brushing hers, breaths warming her cheek.

"Was it as awful as you expected it to be?" she asked.

"Never," he said, huffing and hugging her tightly. "Too amazing when you bite me. Man, I never imagined it could be like that. Your teeth sinking into me when I came? There are no words."

"Soon, you'll allow me…?"

He nodded and stroked his neck to look at the blood smeared on his fingers. "Yes, but don't push, Lyric, please."

"I'll give you all the time you need." She stroked the hair from his face. "Your eyes are so clear. I think the dust is completely gone from your system."

"It's a giddy feeling."

She nodded. "Let's not stop the giddy."

"You want to do it again?"

"And again."

He swiped a hand over a couch cushion and showed her the dust. "In the shower. It's probably the only clean place in the apartment. And then we're leaving this place behind so we don't risk touching any more dust. Deal?"

"I'll race you to the shower."

ONE OF THE LORD OF Midsummer Dark's men had just left the Santiago mansion. Charish sniffed the air, and brushed at her bare arms. She shivered. Felt like faery dust had gotten all over her and her home, but in reality, she could find no trace of a glimmer anywhere. She hated dealing with the sidhe. They were far more sneaky and malicious than any who had ever served her.

She hustled down the hallway toward the garage. What the faery had told her was remarkable. They'd located Lyric! Yet Zett had commanded his men not to intervene, but rather to merely report back to her. That was thoughtful of the man. So maybe faeries weren't all bad.

Her lover swung around the corner and caught her in his always-too-rough embrace. He smelled brutish and spicy. "Charish, where are you off to? You never leave the house in the daylight."

"It's raining, so the sun's hiding behind clouds. Connor…" She clutched his shirt.

Just as she was ready to spill the details the faery messenger had relayed to her, something made her pause. Normally, she told Connor everything. Trusted him implicitly with the Santiago finances, despite the mysterious losses they'd incurred lately.

She loved him for his simple desire to please her, for his devotion and his sexy, sometimes overwhelming, strength. But he had never shown Lyric much interest. That bothered her.

"Out with it, my dear."

"It's…shoes," she decided. "You know how I adore shoes. A pretty new pair will take my mind off things."

"She will be found," he reassured, in a surprising show of compassion. "I've sent a couple tracking demons out, as you requested, though your daughter's scent confuses them when it's masked with perfume.

But you mustn't worry. We'll have that gown back in no time, and hopefully will be able to resurrect the deal with the Unseelie lord."

"Thank you, Connie. I love you." She kissed him, and he kept their contact brief. She had decided it was because he was always moving, too busy to sit still, or remain in a liplock for longer than a few seconds, and not because he didn't care to kiss her. Perhaps? No, Connie loved her as much as she him. "I'll see you in a bit."

"I'll want to see those new shoes on you," he said, as he strode down the hallway, away from her. "And nothing else."

Charish blew him a kiss, then turned and raced to the garage and the waiting driver.

LYRIC SORTED THROUGH the bedroom, looking for her clothes, while Vail collected the things he didn't want to leave behind, such as Green Snake and his Johnny Cash CD collection.

Carefully, she picked up her pink dress and shook it, watching the flakes of dust shimmer as if particles misting out of a thick wool blanket. Finally she decided to hold it out the patio door and give it a good whack against the wall.

"That should do." She slipped it on and stood a moment, testing to see if she'd feel a tingle. Nothing. "Good deal."

Noticing the thin green stem on the dust-littered floor, she plucked it up. "Vail's lily bracelet."

All the flowers were gone, which meant, well, she wasn't sure what it meant.

Stepping outside onto the patio, she propped her elbows on the iron railing and played the stem between her fingers. The afternoon breeze kissed her cheeks and brushed fine hair strands across her nose. In the distance a crowd rushed toward the metro station near the Opéra Bastille and the scents of chocolate pastries and savory meats wafted up to her.

Vail had allowed her to drink his blood. The realization sent a thrill up her spine and a wave of goose bumps rippling across her skin. It had been such an intimate clutch, one she'd never before experienced with another vampire. Vail's blood was sweeter than mortal blood, yet had been thick with darkness, much like a chocolate truffle. If she never tasted any other blood the rest of her life, she could be satisfied.

Now if only he trusted her enough to drink her blood. He did trust her. She sensed he wished to, but he had an entire lifetime of revulsion against vampires to overcome. She wouldn't push him. He had to take things slowly. He'd just gotten clean. They needed to celebrate that.

As soon as they'd ditched the faeries chasing them and returned the gown, Lyric intended to do just that, by taking Vail out and treating him like the powerful vampire he was. She'd take him to the vampire club in the second and introduce him to some of the more honorable vamps she knew, like Vincent LaPierre and Blu's husband, Creed.

"The flowers are gone."

Lyric startled so frantically at the soft female voice, she slammed a shoulder against the brick wall and slapped a palm to the iron railing.

A petite woman with white hair curled high upon her head in a style that looked set for an eighteenth-century salon, stood beside her looking over the city, as if they'd been having a casual conversation and she'd not just appeared from out of nowhere at Lyric's side.

"Who are you?"

And then she knew the woman was faery. Not because pearlescent wings jutted from her back, between the folds of the shimmery red gown, but because she inhaled the lure of dust that glittered within the woman's hair. It would taste so good…

"Mistress of Winter's Edge," she offered, without looking at Lyric.

"Vail's faery stepmother?"

"Be quiet, child. I don't wish him to know I'm so close. When did the last bell fall?"

"The bell? Oh." Lyric looked at the bare stem she held. Vail had called them May bells. "I'm not sure. He's been out of it the past few days, and I—well…it must have happened then. What does this mean? He said the flowers were supposed to protect him. Is he in danger now?"

*Stupid question, Lyric.* He'd been in danger since meeting her. Suddenly conscious of her faery mark, she tilted her head to ensure her hair hung over her ear. Would any faery pick up on the mark or did it only attract Zett?

"Has he been quick to anger? Brooding?" the faery asked.

"No. He just got clean. There's no ichor in his system now. He's feeling better than he ever has."

The faery hissed inwardly. "Has he taken blood?"

"No, he's—" *Afraid.* "—unsure."

The fairy's wings tightened, then rippled with a shiver.

"Vaillant has a dark hunger that can never be sated, but it can be disguised. All his life I have seen that he is protected. Then you come along, and now, see? He is vulnerable."

"I didn't do this."

"He is clean of all ichor?"

Lyric sensed the faery was not pleased. Had she kept Vail addicted to ichor during his life to keep him complacent, a captive in Faery? If so, she was as cruel as Vail had alluded to.

"He is vampire," Lyric stated firmly, not about to kowtow to this woman regardless of whether she was mistress of something or even a queen. "He belongs in the mortal realm. Blood is his sustenance."

"He does belong here, but he will never be like you and your breed."

"He already is. Yet he needs to pull himself free and see beyond whatever lies you've fed him."

"The sidhe do not lie," Cressida stated plainly. "It is beyond our means or necessity."

"Then tell Vail where to find his father."

"That is not for me to interfere."

"But you know?"

"Not exactly. Vaillant the Dark has already a means to learn that information here in the mortal realm."

Yes, Rhys Hawkes, who had been frustratingly tight-lipped with the information, as well. Why deny the man information about his father? What harm could simply meeting him cause?

*As much harm as meeting his mother.*

The faery turned to face her and Lyric felt her blood chill. Bold violet eyes conveyed a sad sense of disgust as she looked over Lyric's wrinkled dress, and sex-tangled hair. She suddenly felt self-conscious that she had only buttoned one button and her cleavage was revealed.

"I adore my vampire son," Cressida said. "I, above all others, love him most."

"You cannot—he said you wanted his brother Trystan, that you were so angry with your incorrect choice you made him feel unwanted. Unloved."

"Enough," the faery muttered. "You listen to words, but do not look into Vaillant's heart. Here." She thrust something toward Lyric. "If you love him you will make sure he wears this."

It was another lily bracelet. Lyric took it, and the moment her fingers touched the stem, Cressida shimmered away. The air cooled drastically, and Lyric smelled ice and hoarfrost, and then nothing.

VAIL ALLOWED Green Snake to curl about his arm—then gripped his chest. A unique, ferocious stab pierced at his organs. It attacked so suddenly he could not disregard it as a simple ache. Staggering, he steadied himself against the back of the sofa.

What was it? He…needed something. Something to feel…what?

"Too much dust in this place," he muttered through gritted teeth. That was it. The cravings were acting of their own volition. "I'll never be completely clean until I get away from it. Time for us to leave, Green Snake. Today is the day the Seelie will come for the gown. I need to call Rhys."

He looked for his cell phone in the collection of personal items he intended to take with him. Green Snake slithered over his arm and across the stack of CDs.

"Where's the phone?"

"It was in your bedroom," Lyric said, walking out to hand it to him. "That's all you're going to take along? Have you nothing of value?"

He shrugged. "What is valuable?"

"That you own? Your car, for one thing."

"Drove it into a river on the night I met my mother."

"What? Vail, that thing was worth hundreds of thousands. Didn't Rhys give it to you?"

"Listen, I may not know the value of mortal material things, or even care…" He slid a hand along her cheek. "But I do value one thing, and that is you, lover. You are priceless to me. There's not a faery gown in this realm that could begin to match your worth to me."

Just as he kissed her, the living room window

shattered inward, scattering glass shards everywhere.

Vail pushed Lyric against the wall and yelped as a glass shard cut through his forearm. His body crushed hers, their eyes searching each other's, and he gripped the glass sticking out of his arm and dropped it to the floor.

She stared at his bleeding arm and ran her tongue along her lip.

"No time, my hungry vixen," he murmured, yet regretted the refusal. Glancing aside he noted the fist-size rock on the floor. "Someone wants our attention."

"I recognize that stationery." Lyric bent over the rock. "It's my mother's."

## *CHAPTER TWENTY*

WALKING OUTSIDE TO talk with Lyric's mother could be nothing but a trap. But Vail took comfort that the gown was still hidden. It could be used as a bargaining chip. The mother would never take back the daughter without that valuable item, or so he suspected.

Although, now that he thought on it, Lyric should prove more valuable to Zett than the gown. Unless he no longer cared if anyone discovered his mistake.

No, Zett would not stop until Lyric was dead. It would humiliate the faery lord should anyone discover he'd marked a vampiress for his bride.

Slipping his hand into hers, Vail paused in the building's foyer doorway. "Will you have me?"

"What deep thoughts are rushing through your brain, lover?"

"You've taken my blood." He kissed her hand and rubbed the back of it across his lips. She in turn, inspected the cut on his arm, which had healed but left behind a smear of blood. "I want you to be mine. Forever. If you'll have me."

"Yes, forever, vampire." She touched a smear of his blood to her tongue. "I will have you."

That answer put him over the moon and into the stratosphere. Vail didn't even register descending the stairs to street level, until he stepped out into the overcast sky and rain droplets trickled from the roof onto his shoulders. A white limousine waited at the curb. Rain drooled down the darkened windows. He clasped Lyric's hand and tugged her next to him, kissing her on the forehead. "I'm here for you."

"Touching." The voice sounded from beside them, tucked in the shadows of the building's overhang. A petite blonde woman stepped forward as they looked toward the car and street. "You found yourself a pretty toy, Lyric."

"Mother," Lyric said sharply. Her fingers tightened about Vail's until he winced.

"This is Vaillant," she said. "Vail, my mother, Charish."

"We've met," Charish said. "I see you've done the job you were hired to do, Monsieur Vaillant. You've found my daughter. But I suspect you have no intention of returning her. Is that Hawkes Associates' standard operating procedure?"

"I haven't yet located the gown," he said, knowing the woman would not be such a pushover as her small frame suggested. "I never do a job halfway."

"Well, I thank you for your work, *monsieur,* but now that my daughter is safe, she can return home with me."

"Perhaps you should ask Lyric if she wishes to go home?"

"Don't be ridiculous."

"Mother, he's right. I'd prefer not to return."

Charish Santiago's jaw dropped open, but she snapped it shut. "I don't understand."

At that reaction, Vail took a step back from his rigid suspicions. Was it possible Charish did love Lyric and really had no clue what she may have gotten her daughter involved in?

"I can't go home now, Mother, not while Zett is looking for me."

"Because you have the gown we agreed to give him in the bargain. Just hand it over to him, dear. You know I will send protection for you."

"The bargain," Vail said. "To see the gown handed over to Zett in return for faeries? That's a crime punishable by the Council."

Charish sucked in a gasp. He'd been right on one part. The woman was trafficking in faeries. He'd figured out the mystery. Yet, why couldn't he feel the satisfaction he should feel?

"You make assumptions. I'll not abide such accusations. Do you know who I am?"

"Yes, you're the matriarch of a family of thieves, murderers and liars."

Lyric squeezed his hand, as if to warn. He saw in her eyes a misty plea. She didn't like his harsh manner with her mother. And he shouldn't be so cruel. She was Lyric's mother, and Lyric worried she was involved with a tyrant. The deal with Zett could have been a desperate attempt to free herself. Would both women succumb and return home?

"Let's go, Lyric." Charish stepped onto the sidewalk. "Tell Monsieur Hawkes he may keep the fee I paid even though the job was not finished."

"You don't want me to find your precious faery gown?" Vail asked. "Zett won't like that."

"I don't know what you're talking about, and if you continue to accuse me, you'll never live to see the next sunrise."

"Mother!"

"Sunrises are overrated." He put an arm around Lyric's shoulder and she melted against him. She was on his side—for the moment. "Nor will Lyric live to see another dawn should you allow her to go anywhere near Zett. There's nothing easy about leaving Faery."

"I know that."

"And yet you would have sent your daughter to Faery to make the exchange."

"It wasn't required she go *into* Faery. The meeting was just outside a portal."

"Come on, Charish, you know better. If you'd trusted Zett to not take your daughter why did you intend to send along demon guards? Be truthful. She was bait to sweeten the deal."

"No, I—"

"For a vampiress who wears a faery mark, she would have stood on Faery ground less than a mortal minute before Zett slayed her."

"A mark?" Charish flickered frightened eyes at her daughter. "What mark?"

Hell, Vail had forgotten the mother wasn't aware of the damning mark.

"There's something you need to know, Mother. I met the Lord of Midsummer Dark the last summer of camp before my blood hunger developed."

Charish gasped. "You never told me that."

"I was young and thought if I ignored it, nothing would come of it. He…marked me. I didn't know what it meant until much later when I dared to tell Leo."

"You told your brother but not me?"

"I never dared tell you. You were so strict, and only let me date people you knew. I thought you'd keep me a prisoner forever to protect me—"

"You're damned right! I can't believe this. Lyric? Oh, my baby, if I had known, I would have never agreed to such a bargain. I would have never put you in harm's way. Oh."

"I know that. I'm sorry, Mother. I thought I could buy some time by disappearing while Leo searched for a way to have the mark removed, and then still have the gown for you to hand over. I had no idea you were dealing in such horrid crimes."

"I'm—"

"Don't deny it, Mother. We saw the Santiago crest on a faery in FaeryTown."

"What were you doing there? You took her to that vile place?"

"Does it matter?" Vail countered. "Are you involved in the heinous crime of trafficking faeries?"

Charish hung her head. Arms clasping across her chest, she shook her head and touched Lyric's arm. "Your father has trafficked in faeries for decades. It's an easy way to make money. And Connie insisted."

"Connie?" Vail asked.

"Connor," Lyric explained. "Her fiancé."

"Connie, Connor, Constantine." Charish waved the matter away with a gesture. "He goes by so many names. Well, you know our breed has to change our names every century or so. He insisted this could be the deal to save our family."

As if shot in the chest by a high-powered rifle, Vail staggered. What the Santiago matriarch had so casually revealed. Could it be?

Blinking, as if surfacing from a fog of dust, he gripped Charish by the lapels of her fitted suit coat. "Constantine?" He revealed his fangs to the woman, but she didn't flinch.

"Pretty," Charish commented snidely, "but just for show, eh? I've heard about you and the faeries."

"You called him Constantine?" he insisted again. "Your fiancé. Constantine de Salignac?"

"Well, yes. How do you know his last name—" The woman stiffened suddenly, eyes going wide, and clutched her throat. Crimson trickled over her grasping fingers and spilled onto Vail's hand.

Reacting, he shoved Lyric behind him. She stumbled, bracing herself against the wall. He leaped to catch Charish as she collapsed in his arms. The tip of a wooden stake pierced through her bleeding throat.

He reached to pull it out, but retracted, not knowing if the stake had been poisoned.

Down the street a dark fog billowed. It thickened and expanded, like darkness clouding over a midsummer revel.

"Lyric, get in the car!"

"What happened?"

"Just get in the car. And don't come out, no matter what."

"But my mother?"

"I'll get her onto the backseat. Get in there. Now!"

She scrambled into the car and Vail kicked the door shut. With little time to make sure the mother was safe, he gently laid Charish on the sidewalk and spun up to meet the fog, which quickly formed into the shape of a man.

Thin yet regal, the silver-haired sidhe lord's violet eyes locked on to Vail's fierce gaze. Zett's red coat was open to reveal bare skin, covered over with luminescent marks that resembled mortal tribal tattoos, yet these pulsed and glowed as if alive, and some could even produce magic if touched with alternating fingers in a coded manner. At his hip a weapon belt revealed another wooden stake. The faery had the skill to throw the stake from long distances and hit his mark.

"Why the mother?" Vail called. "It's not her you want."

"Exactly." Zett's voice slithered silver upon black waves. His long fingers weaved before him as if concocting a ritual, yet he did not make a move to strike with what Vail knew could be powerful dust. "I need the vampire bitch's daughter. But she decided to renege on our bargain, and so she must be punished."

Vail fisted his hands and spread his feet, thrusting back his shoulders. He stood before the fallen vampiress, prepared to block any magic Zett should send at him. "You made a mistake when marking Lyric. Let her go. She'll not tell anyone."

"You know about the mark? That's two vampires too many who possess such knowledge, Vaillant the Unwanted."

The word was just a word, but it never failed to strike at Vail's soul when issued in Zett's scathing tone.

"What if I offer the gown instead of Lyric?"

He had no such right, but he wasn't thinking on game, and was allowing the faery to make him nervous because his thoughts were ruthlessly divided. Charish was engaged to Constantine? And Lyric had known, except she'd never associated the name Constantine to Connor. All this time, he'd been so close!

Zett sucked in a breath, and Vail felt the air grow heavy. The Lord of Midsummer Dark could command the elements. The very earth would rise up as his throne if commanded. "Where is the fucking gown, Vail? I need it."

"Enough to sacrifice the one you marked?"

Oh, he did like to see Zett riled. Rarely did a sidhe resort to using mortal oaths. Zett stood as high as Vail, yet his slender frame looked awkward and spiderish. However, Vail knew that delicate bone structure hid a powerful mien, and Zett would not stop to harm anyone who stood in his path to power.

"That gown would grant you power untold. And a certain status amongst the Unseelie. Still trying to steal the lost king's throne?" Vail put out, and then braced for Zett's retaliation.

The Lord of Midsummer Dark did not disappoint.

The faery touched the luminescent symbol just below his throat with his middle finger, sliding it around the circumference of the design. With a hiss, he commanded the rain puddles on the street, water slicking across the rooftops, and all the rain yet spilling down the windows and gutters into a hurricane that swept toward Vail.

Vail was hit with sharp, piercing water that cut open the skin on his face and hands. The water swirled about him, crushing him in a liquid cage that he could not penetrate with a punch or kick.

Gasping, he swallowed icy water and sputtered. A shout sucked in more water and he choked, heaving up gasps. He put up a hand, but before he could command his own dust, he remembered he was now clean. Defenseless against sidhe magic.

The cyclonic spin of water dropped to the sidewalk, splashing up around Vail. Had Zett given up so easily? Never.

Thrusting back his shoulders, Vail marched toward the faery prince. Zett gestured to the building exterior, and with his other hand tapped a mark at his hip. Bricks loosened from the wall and aimed for Vail.

The vampire blocked them with an elbow or a punch that shattered them into dust.

"You can do better than that," Vail taunted.

"I see the mortal realm has been good to you," Zett said, stepping backward.

"I'm clean of ichor now. It makes me strong," Vail corrected. And indeed, he did not feel defenseless, as he had expected.

"So you've come into the taint of mortal blood?" Zett spit to the side, showing his disgust. "No surprise. You always were just another filthy longtooth."

Vail lunged and delivered a fist to the faery's jaw. Ichor sprayed the air, yet Zett snapped back with an evil grin. "You want to play it that way?"

"I'm still owed a duel against you."

"You think you have a claim to stand against me after I rightfully banished you for your crime against me? Ha!"

"Hell, yes." Zett would deem it a crime that he'd been denied his way, though Faery did not mark it as such.

The faery lord narrowed his piercing eyes. The symbols on his skin glowed fiercely. "Why are you protecting Lyric Santiago? Have you finally bonded with your own kind? Have you taken her as your lover? I would congratulate you, but I'd rather rip your veins out through your throat and strangle you with them."

"By your leave." Vail offered an arm and tapped the thick vein. "Begin with this one."

Zett blew faery dust into a billowing cloud.

Vail dropped to the ground, avoiding the cloud but sensing it would rain upon him in seconds. He snapped his legs forward and came up on the other side of the cloud as it dispersed and settled. Wheeling around, he grabbed Zett by the back of his neck and willed down his fangs.

"Go ahead, Unwanted One." Zett chuckled. "Bite deep and drink well."

How he would love to bite into the man's neck and tear out his veins. But he was clean now. And getting stronger, thanks to Lyric's support. He would not risk succumbing to the addiction after all her hard work. And yet the faery smelled sweet…so sweet.

"Vail!" Lyric leaned out the back window.

"Ah. There is the beauty who will become my bride."

"You would sooner die than marry a vampire. You requested she deliver the gown so you could do away with your mistake."

"True. Well then, I'll have to rip out her veins instead and tie them into pretty bows about her body."

That horrible image zapped Vail's fall into the sensory allure of the faery and made him wish for an iron stake so he could plunge it into the faery's heart. He rubbed fisted fingers in his palm, testing the edges of his rings. "Like I said, the gown for Lyric."

"You don't have the gown."

"She knows where it is. We can complete the deal, if you dare."

"If I dare?" Zett cocked his head to the side.

"You bastard, you are selling your own to the

vampires! I don't believe the Unseelie court would abide that."

Zett kicked, landing Vail on the hip. He staggered, but lost the pain of the hit immediately, and delivered a solid right hook, catching the faery on the jaw and tearing through his skin with the iron rings. Zett screamed as the iron burned his skin.

The faery lord leaped away from Vail and hit the brick wall and clung to it, a foot off the sidewalk. His jaw smoked and oozed ichor. "You will not win this one. I will have the gown, and the miserable vampire bitch," he cried, then pushed off and leaped into the sky. He slipped through to Faery, leaving behind only a glitter of dust.

Vail didn't give him a moment's bother. He scooped up Lyric's mother and slid into the back of the limousine, and ordered the driver to take them to the Santiago home.

THE CAR PEELED ONTO the pebbled driveway before the Santiago mansion. Lyric sat next to Vail but hadn't looked at her mother. He sensed her fear and confusion. She was returning to the one place she had escaped, and with the one person who had betrayed her.

Though, it hadn't directly been Charish. She'd been pushed by Constantine to put her daughter into a dangerous position. Vail was not surprised at all.

After the car parked, he lifted Charish, who felt much heavier than when he'd initially picked her up from the ground. He swung his boots out onto the dew-dappled grass, aware of Lyric exiting out the other side.

The stake still stuck out of Charish's throat. Fingers to the woman's neck, he felt for a pulse and could not find one. Her chest did not rise and fall. Impossible. The only way she could perish from being staked in this manner was if Zett had used poison on the wood—then Vail realized this wasn't a stake, but rather, elf shot, which always contained poison.

Even so, the blood that spilled from her neck glittered. *Like ichor. Take it.* Vail winced as the strange hunger clenched his gut.

"Hurry," Lyric said. "We'll bring her inside. She keeps a doctor on staff."

"Lyric."

"Vail, why are you sitting there?"

He bowed his head, and Lyric stopped. She stood straight, hands once fisted, falling loose at her sides.

Moonlight glinted on the toes of Charish's red shoes. The vampiress's head hung limply over his arm, spilling blond curls under the silvery shine.

The world stopped breathing. Everything was silenced. No wind shimmied through the tree canopies. Not a cricket chirped in the tall grasses. A night bird fluttered its wings in the fountain, stirring up a noiseless spatter.

With "I'm sorry" on his tongue, Vail stood, yet when he opened his mouth, Lyric said, "No, don't speak. Just—come this way."

She turned and, wobbling once on her high heels, she inhaled a breath, seeking composure. Lyric walked toward the mansion, her shoes the only sound. Click, click. Click, click.

Vail carried Charish's body in his arms, but it suddenly felt airy, almost as if…

Flakes of black ash fell over his arms and down his thighs to land on his boots and the sidewalk. Her clothing dropped in a pile. All vampires older than a century ashed with death. She must have been alive after taking the elf shot. The poison had worked slowly, and she'd only expired as they'd arrived at the mansion.

"Lyric," Vail whispered.

He didn't want her to turn around. Didn't want her to see, to associate her mother's death with him. He should have been more alert. Could have grabbed Charish from the sidewalk before being injured. He could have done so much more.

Zett had won this round.

Lyric stopped and looked over her shoulder at the ash at his feet and the traces littering his arms. She did not turn completely around, only bowed her head.

He stepped over the ash and pulled Lyric in for a hug but she shoved him away. "I don't need that. I don't even—"

*Love her* were the unspoken words Vail heard louder than his heartbeats. "Yes." He pulled her unresisting body against his. "You do."

She nodded that she did, and tucked her head against his shoulder. "Take me inside."

## *CHAPTER TWENTY-ONE*

"GATHER THE ASHES," Lyric heard Vail direct the limo driver.

A chill breeze sifted through her hair, icing her skin. The world had changed. She needed…

She needed.

Vail lifted her into his arms, and she melted against his neck and chest, threading a hand up to clutch his hair. She didn't speak. It was hard enough to keep from sobbing loudly. It didn't feel right to cry, yet mutinous tears streamed down her cheeks, and her fingertips sought the dark she wished would swallow her whole.

Vail didn't speak or ask her questions, but instead silently carried her inside. His strength buoyed her. He had sensed correctly she could not stand on her own.

The mansion was dark and quiet, morbidly so. The vampires who had previously occupied it in the nineteenth century had chosen the dark woodwork and wallpaper. She'd never liked the foreboding atmosphere.

Vail walked down the long hall in the south wing that was lined with windows overlooking an English garden. He stopped and Lyric felt his muscles tense against her slack body. A long mahogany table stretched before the garden window, covered with blue cloth and centered with a burst of dying white roses. Her mother's favorite.

She wanted to cling to him. She and Vail. Forever.

*He will never betray me as others have.*

He set her down on the table, but did not back away. Instead, he arranged her legs to hug his thighs and pulled her close, bowing over her head to kiss it. His fingers slipped through her ugly brown hair, but his tender attentions made her feel a princess with gorgeous locks. He stroked along the curve of her spine, reassuring, soothing.

She nuzzled her face against his neck. The bite marks she had pierced into his flesh were healed, but the scent of him, rich, vivacious and dark, crept through her pores on a glamorous sigh. She'd never known such quiet strength. It felt like a gift, empowering yet peaceful. With his silence Vail gave her acceptance and courage. She had lost her mother. But she had not lost hope in the eyes of her lover. This man would protect her always. Perhaps even, love her always.

She wrapped her arms about him and surrendered to what would be, and lost herself in Vail's quiet calm.

"Love me," she whispered.

"Always."

And that reminded her. Lyric took the lily bracelet

out from her pocket and gave it to Vail. "Your stepmother gave this to me."

He didn't touch it. "When did you speak to Cressida?" he asked urgently.

"Earlier today, right before we left your place. She warned me you'd be tormented by a dark hunger, and if I loved you, I should make you wear this."

He nodded but didn't touch the bracelet. Instead, he simply asked, "Do you want me to wear it?"

Inside, Lyric was shouting *no, no, no,* and she found herself saying, "Asking you to wear this doesn't feel right to me. I think the dark hunger she was talking about is your innate blood hunger, the vampire's desire to drink mortal blood. Something you insist on denying."

She placed the bracelet on the table beside her leg. "I don't want you to wear it, but I would never dream of asking you to do as I insist. It is your choice. I need to be alone," she said. "To sit in the gym in the east wing. It's where I go when I don't want to talk."

"With your silks?"

She smiled at him, but it was forced. "Will you wait for me?"

"Yes, go, do what you need to and take as much time as necessary. I won't leave, Lyric, I promise."

She kissed him and padded away into the dark mansion.

VAIL WAITED until Lyric disappeared around a corner, and then strolled outside to the small groomed garden. In the center of the cozy garden, surrounded by a cobbled patio, a fountain dribbled rainwater. A jade cricket sat on the toes of the cherub holding center stage of the fountain.

He dangled the lily bracelet from a forefinger. He could feel the vibrations of Faery in the simple stem of May bells. He could feel the power. Crave it. Yet what power was it?

*You have your own power now. Or you can. You need to take it.*

And what then? What would drinking mortal blood do for him? Give him power? To do what? Rhys insisted he claim such power, yet he couldn't figure why it mattered.

Lyric had understood him. She knew exactly what he'd been taught to believe, and that he'd chosen to believe those things, knowing they couldn't possibly be true.

He had desperately wanted to ask her about Constantine, but now was not the right time. She'd referred to him as Connor. Why hadn't she made the connection?

*Don't blame her. She couldn't have known.*

What twisted joke was this realm playing on him, to put him so close to his father and yet deny him that knowledge?

He tapped the circlet of May bells against his mouth. This bracelet had protected him from the blood hunger, that much he did know. Cressida's sly means to keep him forever a prisoner of Faery, though he could never again set foot there.

He believed Cressida did care for him in her own

twisted manner. But he also knew she would have been happier had she chosen Trystan instead of him.

Had Vail been the baby left behind, he would have grown up with two vampire parents and may have been in a very different place right now.

Trystan may have had a time of it in Faery. Or not. The Unseelie held a tentative truce with werewolves, and allowed them free rein in Faery. Trystan may have enjoyed growing up there, and who knew, he may have been promised to Kit. But he wasn't a half-breed, so Cressida would have been angry about that, as well. He did not wish Faery upon his brother.

Vail dropped the lily bracelet onto the water's surface. It floated, dancing around the circle of the fountain.

It wasn't difficult to admit now that he was glad Trystan had not been chosen. Trystan was Rhys Hawkes's blood child. The two deserved to be together.

*And you deserve no one?*

He tilted back his head and closed his eyes. The dark roil in his being had not let up. It commanded he take action. He fisted his fingers. *Kill Constantine.* He'd not forgotten, nor would he ever. It was what he most desired.

And yet. He wanted something more now.

All of her. Her kisses, her body and her blood. Inside him, outside, all over him. A part of him. He'd never wanted anything more than Lyric Santiago. He would sacrifice it all, die for her, even.

A hot burn clutched him from the inside, pulsing

the ache throughout his system. And then he knew he could wait no longer.

"I want her blood."

LYRIC LAY on the thick gymnasium mats in the east wing of the mansion staring up at the streams of red fabric suspended at the ceiling from carbon swivel hooks. The three-story room was quiet and she'd turned on one light, which spotlighted the silks. She'd changed into soft yoga pants and a formfitting shirt and had washed away the tears that had fallen unbidden once alone in the bathroom.

Now she closed her eyes and a tear trickled down her cheek and landed on the mat. She mourned her mother's passing, and was calm with it.

Charish had lived over a century. She'd done the best she could with the knowledge and habitat she'd chosen for herself. Lyric loved her, and knew Charish had loved her in return. She would always remember her bubbly laughter, her inability to walk by a spider without shrieking and her joy for shopping in cosmopolitan cities.

Saying goodbye was easier than she expected, perhaps only because Lyric was now frightened for her future. It should feel easy now, she mutinously thought. But her heart told her that her world had been flipped. Everything Charish had begun while alive would require reckoning.

Like her mother's deal with the Unseelie lord.

Spreading her arms out across the mats, she breathed deeply. *Don't think,* she reminded herself.

It was how she moved beyond tough situations. This room was meant for serenity. When working with the silks she could only feel peace.

She toed an end of dangling red fabric. Years ago, when Leo had been training, Lyric had become fascinated with the aerial silks used in the course of his training. While Leo had mastered the skill to utilize during break-ins to steal, she found the acrobatics calmed her, returned her to the innocence of her childhood, when summer camps and stolen kisses in the forest had ruled.

Grasping the strong yet giving fabric, she pulled her body up and, hand over hand, worked her way upward until she was suspended twenty feet above the landing mats. A swing thrust her body toward the other hanging silks, and she grasped another.

Hooking an ankle in the fabric with a deft twist, she dropped her handhold and hung upside down, gliding an arm along the silks to grip. Closing her eyes, and spreading out her arms to bring out the fabric like butterfly wings, she surrendered to the graceful art with pleasure.

Much like surrendering to the faery dust had felt.

"Never again," she murmured. She would never put herself in a situation where she might imbibe dust. And she intended to be there for Vail should he decide the same.

VAIL WANDERED THE DARK HALLS in the Santiago mansion. It was a real castle, with musty stone walls and old tapestries on the floor and the walls. The furniture was dark, heavy, and reeked of ancient times. He had no idea how far back the Santiago lineage went. He sensed Charish had touched every part of this home, and it wasn't a good sensation, but not repulsive either. Just different.

He didn't want to impose on Lyric's privacy, because he'd meant it when he'd told her he would wait as she took as long as she needed. Much as he should be looking for Zett—who was now a murderer.

And Constantine.

And find the gown to save his uncle's ass.

But he could no longer deny the aching hunger. He'd felt the pain in his home just before the rock had smashed the window. It had returned as a hollow ache below his breastbone. Now that he was clean of ichor, he needed blood.

Cherry jasmine perfume led him down the hall. It tickled his veins, teasing his yearnings into desires. Saliva wet his mouth. A hot pulse burned around the ache. Everything he touched, every chair rail, wall or slip of fabric heightened his senses and opened him up to receive.

So this was the blood hunger?

What he'd once feared, he now craved.

Was it merely a replacement for his previous addiction? Vampires could become addicted to blood.

No, he mustn't rush ahead of himself. He hadn't tasted blood yet.

"But soon."

*You will step down to join the ranks of filth? Vampires are lesser than you.*

No, he couldn't subscribe to Cressida's beliefs now. He wasn't a faery and he didn't belong in Faery. He'd never belonged there. It was time to claim his heritage from the person he trusted most.

He traced the stone wall with his fingers and strolled through the darkness. He sensed her presence as he took the stone stairs and knew she was in the room ahead with the door cracked open. Dim light crept along the door frame and veiled the stone floor.

Stopping outside the door, he put his back against the wall and wondered if he dared intrude. He should not. She'd been through too much the past few days. He owed her this time alone.

They were both alone now, without family. No, he could no longer cling to that tired excuse. He had family—he simply needed to embrace it. He would do so, with Lyric in his arms.

A swish of fabric tickled his curiosity, and Vail could not resist peeking inside the room. It was a gymnasium fashioned after something only the Addams family could appreciate, with dark stone walls, a dusty buttressed ceiling and low lighting.

An incredible sight stilled his breath.

A beautiful vampiress performed a ballet in the air, suspended by rich, red fabric strips. Must be the aerial silks she had mentioned to him. Her hobby, a means to relax.

Captivated, he carefully pushed open the door and walked inside. Low light lit only the center of the mat-carpeted room where Lyric worked out. The slide of her hair along the red silks whispered to his cravings, but he resisted in favor of the visual satisfaction. Graceful muscles pulsed and elongated, strong limbs belied her delicate beauty.

"You're staring, vampire."

"So I am." He splayed out his hands. "I didn't mean to intrude. You looked so beautiful. I'll leave."

"No." She slid down one strip of fabric, stopping about six feet from the mat. "Join me."

"Ch'yeah—no." Vail thumbed his jaw and shook his head. "Sweetie, you were literally flying. You looked more graceful than any faery I've seen in flight. There's no way I could—"

"Quit grumbling, and give it a go. It's just strength and knowing when to grip and when to trust yourself."

Sounded complicated, and off the chart for his skill level.

"I shouldn't infringe on your—"

"Mourning? I've had a good cry, said blessings for my mother's passing. I need to connect right now, Vail. Please—" an ache rasped her voice "—don't leave me alone."

No, he couldn't walk away from her. Not from the heady scent of life that tormented his wanting soul. But more so, he wanted to hold the hand she held out, and never let go.

Vail took off his boots and mounted the foot-thick blue vinyl mats, finding a new balance to navigate the cushy surface. Lyric dangled a silk over his head and he pulled it down to inspect. It was flexible and stretchy and he didn't believe it could support his weight. His lover was a bird compared to his bulk.

"Take your shirt off or the buttons will get caught on the silks."

He did so, tossing it over by his boots, and doubting his sanity as he complied with her request. "You want me to strip naked?"

Her laughter felt good. "Maybe. But let's try a few easy moves first." She performed a move that worked her gracefully up the fabric, supporting most of her weight by twisting the fabric about one foot. Lyric called down. "Just pull yourself up. If you catch me, you can have me."

With a teasing challenge like that, Vail bit hard on the bait. He had climbed ropes and vines a lot when he was younger. Faery was a literal jungle gym for the adventurous youngster who'd always dreamed of having wings. More than a few faeries had teased him and called him a monkey when he was little. It was better than the longtooth epithet.

He impressed himself as he climbed hand over hand, using his feet to guide. Not so difficult when he relied on the strength of his arms. Could he have done this while mired in the hazy fog of his addiction? Probably, but he wouldn't have had the determination to win the prize like he did now.

When he was about five feet off the ground, Lyric slid down, upside down, to meet him face-to-face. "Wrap the silk around your ankle and foot to hold position."

He did so, and looked to her for further instruction.

His muscles were taut and stretched, and he liked the feeling. But even more, he liked the position of her hanging before him, her hair tied back and dangling in a ponytail.

She hung by one ankle that held a sure grip on the silk. With her free hand she slid her fingers through his hair. And then she kissed him upside down. Vail pulled her closer and deepened the kiss. Her lips were salted with what he knew had been tears. Taking away her pain fed the ache that haunted him. His ankle became unloosened from the silk, and he slid down—he caught himself with a clutch of fabric.

Lyric giggled. "My kisses make you lose your cool?"

"Give me a break. This is my first time."

"And you're doing well."

He found a position next to her again and this time divided his concentration between holding on to the fabric and kissing her. "This rocks, kissing like this."

One of her hands strayed down his chest and flicked across the fly of his pants.

"You think so?" he asked.

"I need you, Vail."

He blinked, understanding. His grip on the silk was tight and not at all sure. "I warn you, this could end disastrously."

"Trust me," she said, and she lashed her tongue up his bare abdomen. "Trust yourself, Vail."

WHEN WITH VAIL, the world slipped away and a blissful peace overtook her. It wasn't wrong, in the wake of her mother's death, to want to connect, to feel, to seek confirmation that she was loved.

She unzipped Vail's pants, and he let them slide down to land upon the mats. Ten feet above the ground, they hung suspended, their bodies relying upon each other for support.

Lyric fitted herself in the silks so her support was a cradle of fabric bracing her elbows. Spreading her legs, she wrapped them about Vail's hips and lowered onto his cock. "Don't let go," she whispered.

"Let go? I'm trying not to come right away. Lyric, this is incredible. We're flying and having sex."

She tilted back and jerked her head to the right, which set them to a sway, and then Vail felt her intention and moved his body with hers. They spun out widely, joined together and flying.

He spread out his arms, completely supported by the silks twisted at his thighs, and cried out as climax shuddered through his body. She wrapped her arms and legs tightly about him, feeding off his tremors. And they spun slowly and descended to the mats together.

They settled onto the thick mats in a tumble of arms, legs and laughter. "That was amazing."

When she laughed, Lyric tilted her head to the side to expose the sweep of her pale neck.

Vail stroked his fingers along her neck, sweeping aside strands of dark hair that she preferred golden but knew he would admire in any color so long as he could touch it.

Bending, he touched his nose to her neck, beside the pulsing vein.

"Thanks for being here when I needed you most," she said. "I feel like I could get through anything with you. You're the rock I've never had."

Kissing her neck, he licked her skin. "What if I need you to be my rock? Lyric, I feel something…. I've felt it since we left my place. I think it's the blood hunger. I know now is not the right time—"

"Now is the best time, lover." She curled her hand at the back of his head and gently pulled him to her neck.

Brushing his lip over the tender vein, he gauged the steady thrum of blood beneath the surface. Her life.

His sustenance. If he would take it.

Did he want it? Could he release all the years of lies and deception Cressida had instilled in his soul, the idea that ichor had only ever sustained him?

Dare he?

"Take what you will," she whispered. "I'm yours, Vaillant."

## *CHAPTER TWENTY-TWO*

VAIL WILLED DOWN his fangs. The tingle in his gums always stirred his hunger, and this time was no different, save for the tight clutch in his gut. Nervous, then. But some inner beast roared forward and demanded it be fed what it had always been denied.

The darkness Cressida had tamed, he would now set free.

Pricking a fang against Lyric's flesh, he did not open the skin, only testing as he dragged it over the thick, enticing vein. She hissed with pleasure. Her body arched against his, making him instantly erect. He clasped her breast, filling his palm with her roundness. And still, he lingered, pointed fang to smooth skin.

Could he do this?

He'd been inside her with his cock, thrusting deeply and taking from her what he desired, and giving pleasure in return. They knew how to satisfy one another. But the sex was not a means to bond.

Only the blood could forever entwine them.

"I love you, Lyric."

As she whispered, "Yes," Vail sank his fangs into her skin. They entered with ease, and hot blood spurted against the roof of his mouth. It dripped onto his tongue, and he retracted his fangs to swirl the flavor about his palate.

He moaned as the intensity of Lyric's being struck him. Hot. Bold. Sweet. Sexy. It was like no ichor he'd ever consumed.

And he wanted more.

He pressed his mouth over the entry points and fed upon her life. Her hand slid up his torso, clinging but not demanding, just touching, the curves of her nails cutting a gentle claim into his soul. She tilted her head farther back and he caught it with his palm, holding her in an embrace three mortal decades in the making.

An embrace that would have been impossible had he decided to put on the May bell bracelet. This embrace fed him the strength and power he'd not known he was missing until now.

Straddling her hips, he knelt, drawing her up in the cradle of his arms, and fed on his lover's blood. Swallowing it, sucking it, savoring it for the perfect blend that it was. Falling into the crimson salvation of Lyric.

Lyric inside of him.

Lyric becoming him.

He, becoming Lyric.

"Lover," he whispered against her neck, dashing out his tongue to slick over a droplet. "Lyric, mine."

She hugged him, melding her body against his. As

he moved, the hanging silks brushed his bare back. And the darkness within Vail expanded. It pulsed with a life of its own, a beautiful darkness that he snatched out to claim.

His fangs descended again, and he bent to bite into the high curve of her breast. Lyric cried out in pleasure. Her fingernails gashed his back and shoulders, but she did not break skin. He wanted her to. He wanted to bleed for her.

"This is what I've hungered for," he muttered against her breast, licking, and then sucking. "You, Lyric. Your blood."

"I love you, Vail."

He laughed against her skin, and kissed her over the bite marks that swelled the flesh. "Yes." Another kiss along her throat. And one kiss to each puncture on her skin. "Yes, and yes."

And he sank his fangs into her neck again, below the previous bite, and let the blood flow down his throat and sweep him to oblivion.

HE HELD HER in the cradle of his arms, and she floated beyond the moment and into another space that could only ever be occupied by Vail and her. That he'd trusted her to take her blood was beyond words, but the way he claimed her now took away her breath.

A fierce gentleness held her captive. At her neck he mastered her. At her breast he teased and tasted her. At her lips, he now kissed her, the taste of her blood on his tongue. She devoured his need, his urgent want and desire. It was all she desired.

Sliding a leg along Vail's hip, she opened herself to allow him to penetrate her doubly. The swollen head of his cock intruded into her wetness at the same time his fangs pierced her breast. Vail growled that delicious wanton tone.

She was his.

AFTER A SHOWER, Lyric slipped on a red jersey dress that clung to her curves, then eyed the thigh-high black suede boots in her closet. Vail's hands slid down the fabric from behind her, and he kissed her neck where the bite marks had already healed, but she still felt tender. His touch reignited the hum of pleasure the bite had given her, and she wanted him to do it again, and again.

But they needed to reconcile more important things before they could lose themselves completely in this new and lasting bond.

"I can see your red, ashy aura now," he said.

"I can feel your shimmer."

"I'm completely vampire."

"You are. How do you feel about that?"

"Yippi-i-oo!"

Laughing, she slipped on the suede boots, which tied up the backs with a bright red ribbon. She posed for him and he nodded approvingly. Slicking his fingers through his soot-dark hair spiked it and gave it an Elvis swoosh. Her sexy lover waggled his eyebrows and delivered the bad-boy smirk that had attracted her even when she'd been afraid of him.

She loved the goth look on him now, but wouldn't

call it that. He had a style all his own. The steel-gray shirt studded in hematite buttons, the dark jacket that sported a line of spikes along the seam of each arm. All of it played into his appeal. Had he the faery ointment on his eyes, she would have to shove him onto the bed and take him again, so powerful was his dark glamour.

"What?" he asked, pausing from his preening to glance over his shoulder.

"Just looking at the sexiest man I've known," she said. "Make that the sexiest vampire."

"Vampire," he said, as if trying on the word for the first time. "It works for me. I think Hawkes was right about me claiming my power. I feel great, Lyric, like a new man since taking your blood. It's weird, but I feel I can conquer nations and leap tall buildings, and—"

"Look through women's clothing with your X-ray vision?"

They laughed and sealed their shared happiness with a kiss that only lovers could share. Tongues danced and fangs pricked at lips. Sips of blood, sighs of pleasure led to her pulling down Vail's jacket and him sliding up her dress.

A courteous knock at her open bedroom door startled them. "Miss Santiago?"

The door opened inside and they turned to the driver, who stood holding a small box. It had to be Charish's ashes.

"Not now," Vail said.

The man, a vampire Charish had turned only a

few years earlier, nodded and backed away, but Lyric sensed he wasn't sure about Vail.

"He'll want instructions," she said, finding no sadness for the death of her mother now. She was in a better place, far from the aggressive command of her fiancé. "From the one in charge. Who is probably me, for now. I'll need to contact Leo. Not sure he'll want to step into my mother's role. Hell, I can't remember where he said he was going."

"Berlin. You should call him. The two of you can create a new beginning for the family, if you wish," said Vail.

That sounded wonderful. But she had no idea how to make the first step. And she knew Leo had no desire to take position as a leader of the Santiago clan. Her brother liked his freedom and his lack of alliances.

"Is there an advisor or someone your mother trusted who can assist you until you can get your bearings?"

"No, only…" Connor.

Vail nodded. "Constantine."

"If I had known, I would have told you, Vail."

"I know." He kissed her forehead. "How could you have known? You should talk to the driver. I'll wait for you."

"What are your plans now?"

"Today is the day the Seelie come for the gown. I have to find it."

She kissed him quickly. "Give me a few minutes, and then we'll end this crazy gown chase for good."

TEN MINUTES LATER, Lyric returned to her room and found Vail putting the faery ointment under his eyes. She dallied with the idea of tearing off his clothes and kneeling before him to pleasure him until his fingers gripped in her hair and a moan followed, but she couldn't erase the uneasy feeling she'd had since talking to the driver.

"The driver told me he thought he saw someone enter the mansion through the garden doors."

"When?" Vail clasped her hand as they walked toward the south wing. "An intruder?"

"No, he said he entered with purpose as if he had a right and obviously an invite wasn't necessary, so it's someone who has been in the Santiago mansion previously. Many of Mother's men and the guards she employs have free run of the mansion. Whoever it is, they'll need to know what has happened."

Ahead, the door to the conference room hung open. It was where Charish had held weekly meetings with her closest advisors, and where she kept, in a wall safe behind a treasured Dali painting, all the Santiago family's important financial information.

Lyric quickened her steps. When she rounded the door and entered the conference room's hazy morning light, her heart fell.

It was him.

Vail crowded up behind her in the doorway, but she stayed him with a hand to his arm. She hadn't expected it to happen this way, but now that they both stood here, she must act as liaison for this incredible meeting.

Lyric approached the man who stood at the far end of the conference table with caution. He waited, arms behind his back. Only once she'd seen the flash of broken fang he tried to keep concealed. Charish had told her it was the result of a tussle between him and another vampire. He may have been an imposing tribe leader centuries earlier, but now he looked tired, defeated. Desperate.

"Your mother is not around?" he asked, noting with vague interest Vail, who lingered in the doorway.

Lyric could sense Vail's increased heart rate. His heartbeats matched her own. A condition they would experience thanks to sharing each other's blood. "There's something I need to tell you, Connor."

"Constantine?"

The room grew cold as Vail marched inside and stopped at the opposite end of the table from where the old vampire stood. Lyric would have never wished for the meeting to go this way, but there was no stopping it now.

"Constantine de Salignac?" Vail asked.

"Yes," Salignac answered, unimpressed with the vampire who had charged in. He was always dismissive toward Charish's men. "Who are you?"

Lyric felt Vail's sudden nervous tension stir her blood. His fists formed on the table. The pulse of his jaw intensified.

"Vaillant," he offered, as if a question. "Do you know me?"

"Why should I?" Constantine tossed out. He narrowed his eyes, inspecting Vail too briefly, then dropped his interest. "Where is your mother, Lyric? She's always here. We've business to attend."

"Why don't you know me?" Vail insisted.

"Is this the man your mother hired to find you?" Constantine asked Lyric. "I'll pay you for your trouble if that's what you're waiting for," he said to Vail.

"I can't believe this." Vail clasped the air, and Lyric swung her hand to catch his. His fingers trembled. Were those tears in his eyes?

She glanced at Constantine, and for once, she really looked at him instead of trying to avoid his often leering gaze. His dark hair held no sheen, and was as dense as a moonless night. His blue eyes reflected none of the sunless daylight that forced its way through the bamboo shades. His square jaw and thick brows…she had touched many times when admiring her lover's face. This man was indeed Vail's father.

Vail whisked her out of the room before she could offer an introduction. Lyric twisted her arm from his grasp, yet followed his hasty retreat. "Where are we going? Don't you want to speak to your father?"

"Don't say that," Vail said. "Don't give him a title he does not deserve. He doesn't know me. What the hell?"

"We should go back and talk to him. I'll introduce you two. I have to tell him about Charish."

"Lyric?" Constantine called down the hallway. "Where's your mother?"

Vail ran toward the front door, Lyric's hand clasped in his. "I need to be away from here."

Of course, if he'd found the one man he'd wanted

to meet all his life—and that man hadn't a clue who he was… Hadn't Rhys Hawkes told his brother he'd a son?

"Sorry!" she called back to Connor—Constantine, or whoever he was. "There's an emergency!"

Lyric ran along with Vail to the limo parked haphazardly in the driveway.

"I'll drive," she offered, and Vail got into the passenger side. The sun was masked by gray clouds, yet she flipped on the UV protection, which slid over the windows. She spun out of the driveway.

"Fuck!" Vail punched the dashboard, cracking the hard plastic. "He doesn't know me? How is that possible? Didn't Rhys tell him?"

"We could go back and ask—"

"No! Just get me away from here."

"Where do you want to go?"

"Anywhere. Just drive."

## *CHAPTER TWENTY-THREE*

THE FIRST ELF shot pierced the windshield and stuck in the front seat next to Lyric's shoulder.

"Step on it!" Vail shouted.

"Where are they?"

He twisted on the seat, scanning the sky. "Above!"

Out of the corner of her eye, Lyric spied the glitter of wings—a lot of them—and turned the hulking limo down a narrow street. The car was too big to navigate with ease, and she cursed this alley, which was lined with garbage cans that buffeted the chrome bumper as the vehicle stormed through twice as fast as the speed limit allowed.

"You want me to drive?"

"Are you kidding me?" she said. "I do have a driver's license, thank you very much. I don't see them anymore. How did I see them?"

"Must have caught a glimpse of them from the corner of your eye."

The passenger window broke and Vail yelped. He pulled the arrow from his shoulder. "They're using elf shot. Get inside a building, or parking lot. Someplace we can ditch the car and go on foot."

"Are you okay? Is that going to hurt you now you're not a, you know?"

"Dust freak?" He tossed the arrowhead out the window and shuffled off his jacket. "Here, put this on. It might help you see them."

She struggled into the inside-out jacket. The spikes were dull but they still poked. Meanwhile Vail squeezed the wound on his shoulder, wincing as he forced out the blood. "If there's poison in it, I might be able to get it out."

"You feel woozy?"

"No, and the wound isn't deep. I'll be fine. Don't take any more narrow streets, or you'll crush me."

Before she could protest, Vail leaned out the passenger window and sat up on the door. What he was doing, without any weapons, was beyond her.

She wished she had some of the faery ointment around her eyes. If she could see the enemy, they would be easier to avoid. Would a reversed coat really work?

A piece of newspaper stirred up by the wind slapped onto the windshield and blocked her vision. Lyric swerved right. Vail's boot kicked the car roof and he swore. Something cracked the windshield. A body rolled off, leaving behind a wing wedged in the broken glass.

Now *that* she clearly saw.

"Tell them I'll give them what they want!" she yelled. "If I can get there quick enough."

She headed toward the Gare du Nord in the tenth arrondissement. The midafternoon traffic wouldn't allow her to go much faster than thirty kilometers.

"How do they dare attack in daylight?" And then she realized mortals would not be able to see what she initially hadn't been able to see.

A clatter of wings slashed into the car as Vail dragged in a faery, or some gray creature that was the size of an infant and squealed like a rabbit. One of its wings cut Lyric's arm.

"What is it?" she frantically asked, keeping her focus on the road, and not hitting the biker up ahead.

"Fucking sprites. Who sent you? Zett?"

The squirming faery spit ichor at Vail. He managed to block the spittle with an arm, and whipped the faery out the window. "I hate sprites!"

"Did any of that get on you?"

"No." He inspected his sleeve, which oozed with ichor. "Wait! Stop!"

Lyric pulled the car to an abrupt stop. Vail jumped out and ran toward a business building. What was the guy up to?

Then she noticed Rhys and Trystan Hawkes walking toward the building, as well. And with them, a woman with long dark hair.

"His mother?" Lyric got out and read the sign on the five-story steel building: Hawkes Associates.

TRYSTAN SPUN AROUND and at the sight of Vail took a defensive stance before Viviane. What was his mother doing out in daylight? Could she withstand the sun if it slipped out from behind the clouds?

Rhys extended his hand to shake with Vail, but instead Vail shoved him at the shoulders. "Why didn't you tell him? He doesn't know I'm his son!"

Lyric touched Vail's shoulder, possibly to calm him, but he shrugged her off. Viviane peeked around her werewolf son's shoulder.

"You've seen him?" Rhys asked. "Where? Vail, I had no idea where he's been. I knew he was in the city, but—"

"He's been right under my nose, colluding with Charish Santiago all this time."

"Are you serious?" Hawkes gave Lyric a scathing look, but dropped it quickly to focus on Vail. "If I had known…"

"If you had known you would have still kept this information from me. It was just a ruse, wasn't it? You get me to do your dirty work, and I get the shaft." Vail rubbed his palms together furiously. "He didn't know me. And I look just like him!"

He turned, and Lyric stood waiting for him to step into her embrace. He was in no mood for a pity hug. He snarled at her and she stepped aside to allow him room to vent and pace.

"Is he talking about Constantine?" Trystan asked.

Rhys swung a warning look at Trystan, then turned to Vail, and said, "I have not seen my brother since the day we found Viviane wandering the streets, mad and bloodthirsty, after over two hundred years of being buried alive."

Vail tightened his jaw. He didn't want to hear this. Didn't need to hear Hawkes's lies!

"I would have told him, if I'd had opportunity, but I have had no desire to seek him out all these years. After what he did to me and Viviane, well, I wanted to start fresh, give your mother the best future I possibly could. You must believe me, Vaillant."

"Constantine?" Viviane nudged aside Trystan and stepped up to grip her husband's arm. "Is that bastard still alive?"

"Yes," Vail said.

The vampiress gaped. He bowed his head, feeling the despair at his mother's rejection curdle in his gut. He could not look at her now.

Why had he ever sought to know either of his parents? He should have been content with Cressida's twisted affection. At least with Cressida he knew where he stood: she hated him, and she admired him. No lies, no hiding or madness. Just bald truth.

Viviane railed. "No! He cannot be. You told me he was long dead. First this…this man who you claim is my son, and now…?"

The look Viviane gave Vail burned the remnants of his desperate heart to ash. He would never know her love. He was not worthy of it.

Vail said to Rhys, "Enough secrets. The Unseelie are after Lyric and me, but all I want to do is return to Constantine and rip out his heart."

"Yes!" Viviane stepped up to Vail and pressed her

hands to his chest, sharp fingernails cutting through his shirt. Her wide eyes darted back and forth between his. "Rip it out and give it to me, will you?"

"I, uh…" Vail swallowed. He would rip out his own heart and give it to Viviane if he thought she could learn to love him. But he would not infect her further with Constantine's taint.

"Who is she?" Viviane did not look at Lyric, but he knew that's who she asked about.

"She is Lyric Santiago," he said, clasping his mother's hands to keep her nails from doing him further damage. The contact shimmered boldly through his system. "I love her."

A light brightened Viviane's mad eyes. "My dark prince is in love?" She tilted softer eyes upon Lyric.

*Dark prince?* Vail mouthed to Rhys.

"It is what she called you after you were born," Rhys confirmed. "And what she calls you when she dreams of you, which is often."

Having such knowledge wrapped around him like a long-desired hug. It clasped about his shoulders, and Vail slapped his arms across his chest to hold on to the strange feeling. Fragments of his ashy heart coalesced and grew stronger, pulsing surely.

"Where is he?" Viviane pleaded him. "Tell me where he is!"

Rhys said, "No, Viviane," while at the same time Vail said, "The Santiago estate."

"We can find the bastard later," Trystan said. "Ever since I was attacked, I've been able to see things I'd rather not see. Are those gray things faeries?"

Vail turned to spy the dark cloud of winged creatures swarming closer. "Sprites. They're nuisance sidhe, unless they're armed with elf shot, which they are. Take her inside and keep her protected." He shoved Viviane toward Rhys.

Trystan pulled out a pistol from the back of his jeans and fired, dropping one sprite in a squealing splatter of ichor on the sidewalk.

"Nice," Vail said to his brother.

"You know it, but we have mortal observers, and I've not enough bullets for them all. We need to stop this."

"I can do that," Lyric said, and she grabbed Vail's hand. "We have to get the gown."

"Viviane!" Rhys, his cheek bleeding from scratch marks, pointed down the street. "She took off. When she's manic like this, she is very strong. I'm going after her. Tryst, help me."

Firing five more shots, and taking down five more sprites, Trystan holstered the weapon under his arm and took off after Rhys. "They're all yours, brother!" he called back.

Vail shoved Lyric toward the car. "We can outrun them, but this time I drive. You're too light on the gas."

She slid into the passenger side, brushing out the broken glass, but when she heard the squeal of oncoming sprites, she stopped and closed the door. "Head west to the train station!"

Vail shifted into Drive and sped down the busy street, swerving to pass another car. The Mercedes kissed the back bumper of a delivery truck but didn't miss a beat.

They squealed onto a busy street and Lyric saw the cloud of sprites flicker away. "I can't see them. Are they gone?"

Vail scanned the rearview mirror. "For now. Where are we headed?"

"Just ahead. That big building at the end of the street."

Shifting down and pulling the emergency brake, he spun the Mercedes into a parking space that gave but half a foot on bumper to bumper.

Lyric unclenched her grip on the door and opened it. "Come with me!"

"What the hell do you need in a train station?"

"Just follow me."

The Gare du Nord, one of the largest train stations in Paris, was never empty, and right now it was rush hour. People leaving work crowded into the station where the imposing facade gleamed with rain.

Lyric rushed inside and took in the scene. Mortals wandered about, some listening to music, others rushing to catch a train. The air was cooler in here and she felt less safe surrounded by so many mortals. Vail clasped her hand. She wanted to hug him, to hold him and never let go. Because together they had flown to a place that existed only for them.

Now Lyric wasn't sure they'd ever go there again. Not unless she could make things right.

"I'm sorry. I wish I could do something to make

things right between you and Constantine," she said. "I had asked Rhys."

"You what?"

"When you fled after meeting your mother. I told him I'd give him the gown for information on Constantine."

"He wouldn't do that. The bastard has been lying to me."

"He said you needed to bring the gown to him yourself because it would give you answers. And he was speaking the truth about not knowing where his brother was." He'd specifically said Vail had believed himself unwanted by all, and she knew that belief had changed. He'd learned a lot about himself in the past few days. "I trust him, Vail. I wish you would, too."

He sighed and pulled her to him, hugging her against his chest, which pattered rapidly from his angry heartbeats. "Forgive me. But there's nothing you can do to make things right, because they're not meant to be right between me and Constantine."

"Perhaps not. Just because he is your blood doesn't mean he deserves, or will ever earn, the title of father. But I have something that will make things better." She slid her hand into his and led him toward the lockers. "At least, it may get those wicked sprites off our backs."

VAIL WAS IN NO MOOD for anything other than doing damage to sprites right now, but he stalked after Lyric into the shadows between the aisles of lockers. She located a locker and punched in the digital security code. From inside she pulled out a case perfectly fitted to the locker's dimensions.

It was so heavy she almost dropped it, but managed to heft it onto the wooden bench before the lockers.

"It's iron," he noted.

"Leo had it fashioned specially for this purpose," she said.

"Smart brother. No wonder the Seelie weren't aware it was missing, nor could the Unseelie track it. The iron acted as a shield of protection."

"That's Leo."

Looking around first to check for mortals, she didn't worry about the woman snoozing in the corner not ten feet away with a half cup of coffee near to tipping over onto her pants. Lyric pulled the digital combination lock around and punched in a few numbers, then slapped her palms on the face of the box and looked at her lover.

Vail remained stoic, arms crossed, legs straddling the bench. "Five seconds," he offered.

"What?"

"Remember you asked me for a five-second head start after I get the gown?"

"Oh." But it didn't matter now that Charish was dead and that Vail knew where to find his father. Did it? "I don't want to run away from you, Vail. I meant it when I said I love you," she told him, her clear blue eyes nailing him with a truth so deep it softened his raging heart. "Can this work?"

"Us? Yes," he answered from his heart, steering

clear of reaction. "I love you, too, Lyric. We can work."

He cupped her head and bent to kiss her, not realizing he'd needed this kiss until it happened. Here was home, at her lips. His fingers tangling in her soft hair. Their breaths coexisting. Their heartbeats synching. It was all home.

They'd taken blood from each other. They shared a piece of one another's soul. They were a part of the other now. And he did want it to work, to last, and to be real.

Dragging his tooth across her lip, the skin opened and blood dripped into his mouth. A sweet taste. It infused his system with courage.

"Forever mine," he said against her mouth. "Promise me you'll never run away from me."

"I promise. I can't imagine being without you. We can start our own family?"

"I'd like that."

"I want you to talk to your father. To hear him out, before…"

She knew what drove him, and he wasn't proud of it. "I want you to be there when I do finally talk to him. So open the box?"

She punched in a few more numbers, released the lock and opened the hinged lid.

Vail felt the hum of Faery permeate his pores. It was the glimmering, the knowing when one was in the presence of Faery.

The faery diamonds shimmered and caught light that did not exist on the mortal plane. Lyric drew out the gown slowly, reverently, lifting her arms parallel to her head to let the skirt sweep down. It moved as if blown by a breeze, but Vail knew the gown was literally alive with faery glamour. It was fit for royalty or one who wielded great sidhe power with skill, grace and knowledge.

He dared not touch it. Not because he worried about getting faery dust in his pores, but because of what it meant. It was power.

"It's so beautiful," she whispered.

*Beautiful* was a lacking word for it. "Vast," he tried. "All-knowing. Can you feel the glamour?"

She looked at the gown she still held high. "I don't think so."

"Did you wear it?"

"I did try it on. But only for ten minutes."

"I would have loved to see it on you. But I also would have feared what the gown would do to you."

"It didn't do anything. I'm the same."

Maybe. He was surprised she hadn't gotten an ichor high from it. Hmm…perhaps it had made her more susceptible to the high when she'd been nursing him? It was very probable.

A mortal teenager wandered up to a locker not far from the one from which Lyric had taken the gown. He didn't acknowledge Vail and Lyric.

"Can he see the gown?"

"I—he should be able to. It's got glamour, but has no need for protection from mortal eyes. Unless…"

Vail squinted and peered across the vast stadium-like building. And then he realized the glimmering had increased.

He batted at an insect that buzzed his ear—then noticed the stir of violet wings. Dodging, he avoided the zooming sprite that dive-bombed toward the gown.

"Bloody Herne."

"What?"

He noticed the vibrations now. A rumble in the floor as if from a minor earthquake. The walls shivered, yet the mortals rushing about gave it no notice. An ominous foreboding darkened his blood and he spun about to spy the first wave of soldiers marching in rank on the ceiling above.

"They're here."

## *CHAPTER TWENTY-FOUR*

LYRIC STEPPED AROUND the bench to clasp Vail's hand. He squeezed, hard. Feeling his anxiety increased her worries. No longer did a mere cloud of sprites linger before them, but instead, a band of faeries in all shapes, sizes and colors marched toward them.

"Unseelie," Vail whispered to explain.

They wore silks and gossamers, carapaces and horns, thorns and petals. Some wobbled close to the floor, others stretched to thin heights, many soared on tiny wings, and a few hovered on large sails. Myriad shades and tints of wings clattered like a hive of deadly insects.

That Lyric could see them was startling. They'd dropped their glamour. Yet did that mean the mortals walking through the station could see them, as well? The man huddled near the men's bathroom door at the opposite end of the arrivals platform didn't even look when a faery walked right before him.

"I can see them," she whispered. "Is it your coat?" She still wore his jacket inside out.

"No. They want you to see them now. Don't worry, the mortals are oblivious."

Lyric suddenly recognized the leader, heading the crew of oddities, clad in jade armor strapped to his shoulders and knees and wearing a studded gold faceplate—she knew it was the Lord of Midsummer Dark. He had killed her mother.

Lyric clasped Vail's hand harder and leaned against him in case her knees should bend. "Keep him away from me."

"Shh," he cooed. "No one is going to harm you."

Mortals unaware of the sidhe invasion moved in slow motion through the train station. It was as if time had slowed, and likely it had. Though Lyric's movement had not changed.

"They're controlling time," she whispered. "Have to be."

"It is glamour," Vail said. "There."

She followed his gaze upward to the curved train station ceiling. A crowd of faeries clad in red walked the ceiling, avoiding the iron rafters with a determined regal manner. When the female in the lead swept a hand through the air, they all followed her, descending upside down, wings fluttering, until they were but five feet from the floor, then turned in midair and gracefully landed on their feet.

The aisle between two trains wasn't very wide, and was delineated down the center with globed streetlights that flickered now the faeries had landed. Two trains departed within minutes of each other, leaving the rails open. The Unseelies stood in rank down one side of the lights, the Seelies down the other. Each troop was headed by an armored leader.

The female who led the Seelies must be their queen, Lyric decided, for the interesting crown of roses and horns upon her bold red hair.

"The Summer Queen," Vail whispered to confirm.

What Lyric had first thought was armor wrapping the queen's arms and torso in articulated red leather was actually some kind of fabric that corseted her figure, which was so narrow even death would look away.

And yet, she was gorgeous, her violet eyes luminous and seeing all through the red and golden leaf mask that conformed to her face. A crown of lush roses danced gallantly about her red hair and two stag horns were placed at the pinnacle. Whether the horns were for decoration or real, Lyric did not know. Her arms swayed with her movement, her hands curving and gesticulating with a flamenco dancer's grace. All over she shimmered.

Lyric swallowed. There was so much faery dust in this place, it was a wonder the mortals did not fall to their knees in supplication. Yet the sidhe expended little energy in cloaking themselves from mortal eyes. What mortals did not believe in they could not see.

The two factions exchanged words Lyric couldn't hear and when she asked Vail he again shushed her.

"She has it!" Zett pointed to Lyric and, for the first time, the two faery courts noticed she and Vail standing off by the lockers. "The vampiress is the thief."

"Only because you ordered the gown stolen in the first place." Vail stepped forward, pushing her gently to remain behind him.

"You don't know that," Zett defied.

"Zett plots to own the gown so he may become the Unseelie king, isn't that so?"

"The king is lost. We need a king," the Unseelie lord insisted.

"And what respectable sidhe king would mark a vampiress as his own?"

Zett blanched, as did the entire ranks flanking him. A hum of whispers silvered the air.

"You marked her," Vail continued. "To take her as your wife."

"Abominable!" cried Zett's closest officer.

Vail stretched back an arm and gestured Lyric join him. She remained, defying her lover's command. Would he throw her to the lions? He'd promised no harm would come to her. This didn't feel right.

And in that moment, the scales shifted, as Zett realized his secret could not be proved unless Lyric showed her mark.

The Seelie queen tutted, and tilted her horned head regally. "This is of no concern to me. I simply need to know who shall be punished for thievery?"

"No one." Lyric stepped forward and dragged the iron case along with her. "Because you can have the gown back."

"She does not—" Zett started.

Vail stepped in front of Zett, keeping him from

Lyric. With a nod to her, Vail gave her leave to do as she must.

Lyric pulled the heavy gown from the case. The faery diamonds flashed and danced upon the high ceiling where some Seelie court minions remained at post. They dodged the glimmer as if they were lasers that might burn them.

Most of the factions stepped back until they stood at the edge where the rails tracked, yet the queen and Zett stepped forward as Lyric held it to display.

"It is mine," Zett said forcefully, and Lyric thought she felt something akin to persuasion tickle her brain. *The gown did belong to Zett, the faery who had given her her first kiss....*

Vail clasped her shoulder and the seductive thoughts dissipated. She focused on his eyes, sure and strong, and felt his strength enter her. He was on her side. He'd never stopped being on her side.

"Give it to me, vampire!"

"It belongs to the Seelie court," the queen's second in command stated calmly. The thin squire's sleeves dusted the air with hawk's feathers as he made a gesture toward the gown. "Yet it has been tainted by the vampires."

"Exactly," Zett said, and then to the Summer Queen, "You would not touch the thing now."

"Apparently you would, eh?" Vail volleyed, not about to let Zett off the hook with the faery mark. "Ah, Cressida, so nice you could join the vile festivities."

The white-haired faery fluttered down in violet silks, yet her feet did not land on the concrete. She must have been tucked among the few remaining on the ceiling. With a wave of her hand, the air took on an icy chill.

"Your favorite wants to steal the Seelie gown and claim a vampire as his wife," Vail said.

"I do not wish to marry her, but render her breathless ever after!" Zett announced.

One would expect a stunned silence to follow that announcement. Instead, Zett's Unseelie troops snickered and nodded approvingly. Even the Seelie troops nodded, accepting it was the only method to do away with the Unseelie lord's mistake.

"You will not lay a hand on her," Vail announced.

"That will be decided in good time," Cressida said, taking command of the exchange.

A mortal walked through her and the Mistress of Winter's Edge flinched, while the mortal suddenly shivered and clasped her hands to her arms as if a brisk wind had blown under her T-shirt.

"Your Highness, please, if you will?" Cressida gestured toward the gown.

All fell silent as the Seelie queen looked over the gown, her violet eyes unkind and cold. Lyric thrust it forward for her to take. She wanted nothing to do with the thing. Leo should have never stolen it. Yet she corrected her wish. He'd only wanted to help Charish. As well, if he had not taken the gown, then she would have never met Vail. And that was all she wanted to take away from this fiasco.

In a flutter of wings, the queen moved toward Lyric, *through* the gown. The red raiment she wore dissolved and the diamonds shivered until the gown fit her body perfectly and glittered madly with her graceful movements.

"No!" Zett struggled against Cressida's remarkable hold, yet she but held him by the wrist with one hand. "She has tainted it! A common vampire!"

"Indeed," the Seelie queen said, closing her eyes as if to take in the essence of the gown through her skin, "it is lesser now." Tilting her head, the stag horns glittered under the artificial streetlights. She flashed her bright gaze onto Lyric, but it wasn't kind or even calm. Lyric felt the Seelie queen's disappointment crackle through her veins like trapped lightning. "You will be punished, thief."

"No, I didn't—"

The queen's second in command took Lyric in hand, while five red-coated guards held Vail back with halberds as he struggled to protect her. It was plain he was outnumbered and outpowered. A vampire could not battle a faery and expect to win. Vail had no faery ichor in his system now. He had no skills or advantages, such as weapons, to help him win the fight.

"No!" Vail put up his hands in surrender, but his captors did not step from the tight circle they maintained around him. "The gown has been returned," he said to the Seelie queen. "If it feels lesser it is only because you are in the mortal realm. No faery garment, weapon or sidhe of any breed is as strong in this realm as they can be in Faery."

"Perhaps," the queen provided. "You think me lesser, vampire?"

Without waiting for the answer, the Summer Queen thrust out her hand, sending a direct current of faery dust toward Vail. It circled his throat and tightened, as if a noose.

Lyric fought to get free, but her captor held her with strong and sharp fingers, much like a hawk's talons. Vail was lifted from his feet by the rope of dust, and then dropped abruptly to stagger against one of the guards, who shoved him off.

"I do not think you lesser," Vail croaked, rubbing his bleeding neck. The dust had cut through his skin as if a blade. "You are supreme, Your Highness. Your beauty warms the mortal realm."

"Just so. But I still want to punish someone."

"You cannot take her," Vail said. "I beg of you, leave Lyric Santiago alone."

"Because you love her?" Cressida interjected.

The ground began to rumble beneath Lyric's feet. Another train was pulling into the station.

Vail bowed his head. From what Lyric knew of Faery, they did not know how to love, and so how could they accept it as a viable reason for protecting someone? If Vail confessed his love for her, it would mean little to the factions holding them in peril.

"Love is a precious thing. It comes in so many forms, a man might never live long enough to experience it fully. What can I do for you, Queen of Summer, to forgive Lyric Santiago the crime of theft?" Vail asked. "It was not she who stole the gown, but her brother, in an attempt to stifle Zett's threats against the Santiago family."

"I did no such thing!"

"You plotted to have Lyric delivered to you so you could murder her," Vail countered.

The queen flashed a malevolent gaze at Zett, who noticeably shrank. "You marked her as your bride?"

Zett's face whitened. The luminescent tattoos on his neck darkened. "I had no idea she was vampire."

The queen looked over Lyric, her eyes not missing a portion of her anatomy. Her hair blew away from her face as if a summer wind stirred through the silent building. And when the faery queen's eyes fell to Lyric's heart, it felt like corpse worms moving within the rapidly pounding muscle.

"You should be forced to marry her for the mistake," she said to Zett. "That would teach you a lesson in caution."

Zett lifted his head. "I will do so only if the Unseelie command it of me."

"But then you'd murder her in the marriage bed," the Seelie queen stated. She flicked her fingers over the gown. "I feel the power growing." She leveled her gaze at Zett. "I could do so much while wearing this gown."

Lyric squirmed within her captors' hold. Of course punishment was deserved. And if Leo could not be here to take that punishment, she would gladly accept it on his behalf. They had only wanted to help their mother. But she feared what the faeries might dole out as punishment.

She would not survive it, surely.

"You did not answer the Mistress of Winter's Edge's question, Vail the Unwanted," the queen said. "Do you love the vampiress?"

"Yes," Vail answered with certainty. He shoved off his guards and, shoulders back, lowered his gaze on the queen, fangs down and threatening. "She is mine."

The Seelie queen appeared to favor his bold threat with a nod. "I see that she is. Vail the Unwanted has found a proper mate, one who shares his same vile blood hunger. You've tainted yourself with the mortal world, vampire. You know you can never return to Faery."

"I've already been banished by the Unseelie."

"And today the Seelie banish you, as well, vampire. Very well." The queen nodded and her seconds released Lyric. "You may win the mortal woman's freedom."

"How?"

"By becoming my champion."

"To wage what battle?" Vail asked.

The Seelie queen looked down the ranks of Unseelie court. Zett straightened and pounded his spear on the floor. Behind them, mortals clambered onto the train.

"Very well." Vail bowed before the Seelie queen. "You wish me to fight the Lord of Midsummer Dark? I will, gladly."

## *CHAPTER TWENTY-FIVE*

SINCE ARRIVING IN the mortal realm, Vail could think only of tracking down his bastard father and killing him.

Now, as he stood before Zett, holding the ash-wood quarterstaff one of Cressida's men had provided him, Vail cared little about Constantine de Salignac. The one enemy he had dallied with over the years stood not six paces away, armored in adamant jade and sneering at him.

Zett had stolen the innocence from many females on the night before they were to wed. He'd tormented Vail all his life because he was different, a filthy vampire. He wished to steal the throne from the missing Unseelie king. And he was trafficking his own kind to the mortal realm to be brutally used by vampires. He didn't deserve death, but he did deserve to be taken down by the one breed he hated most. And Vail was just the vampire to do it.

Swinging out the ash-wood staff, he met Zett's staff, tip to tip, in the traditional salute. Someone called out,

"Begin!" and Zett soared into the air, wings flapping. He would use an aerial attack to his advantage.

But Vail had the advantage of the mortal realm. Faeries did not spend a lot of time in this realm. And confined inside this huge iron and stone building? Couldn't be advantageous for any of them.

Blocking a smart stab to his left shoulder, Vail swung and, with a leap, managed to clip Zett's armored ankle. The faery shook it off, and landed on the concrete floor, swinging a furious figure-eight pattern in a blinding attack that forced Vail down the long arrivals platform between two resting trains.

The white globes from the streetlights that queued down the row glowed yellow in the twilight hour. A swing of Zett's staff nicked one of them, sending shards from the globe across the floor and onto the tracks.

"Is it so important to you," Zett said as he deflected a blow from Vail, "my doings? I am not your competition, vampire. Or is it that you've not a home here, either?"

"I fight for the honor of all the women you have stolen from their wedding beds," Vail said. "And for the one woman you will never have."

"I wouldn't dream of it." Zett spit to the side, and then leaped into the air, flipping a somersault over Vail's head and landing on the opposite side of him. "She is filthy."

"At one time, you thought she was worthy of your hand. Worthy enough to mark her as your bride."

"We all make mistakes. Some of us are bold enough to correct them."

"Is it so easy to take a life to make your life better?

"Says the vampire who is on a quest to slay a man for no more reason than he is his father."

"Enough!"

Vail slapped the staff through the air and landed it across Zett's neck, which pushed the man, flailing, against an iron support beam. The faery's hand slapped to the beam and his skin sizzled and smoked from the iron burn. The crowd of sidhe observers hissed and cringed at the sight.

Zett tore off his face mask. "You deny your bloodlust for your father?"

"No."

The faery lord's laughter pricked up Vail's spine. "Then you are like me, vampire. You do as your heart demands."

Zett rammed his staff upward, crushing it through one of the glass globes. Glass shards again rained over their heads, and Vail dodged to avoid the cutting weapons. He blinked, felt the thin glass tear his eye, and knew the hot ooze was blood. His right eye filled with blood and blurred his vision.

A sharp thwack pounded across his back. He stumbled forward. He dropped his quarterstaff and it rolled onto the tracks. Landing on hands and knees, Vail shook his head but couldn't clear his right eye of the blood. A woman shouted and he knew it was Lyric.

*You don't need your father's blood on your hands.*

*It will change nothing. Don't forget the real fight is for Lyric's freedom.*

Hearing Zett charge from behind, Vail dropped to his side and rolled to catch the faery lord with his boots. A well-placed kick sent Zett soaring away from him at such speed that the faery ended up on the iron rafters four stories above.

Using this opportunity, Vail took a running leap and, thanks to his new vampiric strength, was able to soar as high as the rafters. He landed on an iron crossbar and shoved a hand to Zett's neck, pressing the back of it against the iron.

The faery struggled and yowled. The iron burned his exposed hands, neck and the backs of his thighs. Vail tore off his chest plate, and shoved the faery over, burning him onto the iron.

"Enough!" Cressida shouted from below. The Mistress of Winter's Edge held the highest standing while they lacked an Unseelie queen.

But as her champion, Vail answered only to the Summer Queen.

"Do you yield?" Vail asked the struggling faery lord. "Do you swear you will never return for Lyric Santiago, nor send out your minions after her?"

Zett growled and lifted his chest, but the iron was eating through muscle now. The sickening smell of burnt ichor made Vail wonder how he could have ever consumed it. The wound would become irreversible within moments.

"Yes!" Zett cried.

Vail pulled the faery off the iron rafter and dropped

him. The Unseelie lord was caught by a sidhe and helped to stand.

Vail leaped to the concrete floor gracefully beside the Seelie queen. Going to one knee, he bowed his head, blinded by the dazzling gown, and offered himself as her champion.

"Vaillant the Vampire," the Seelie queen said. "You have shown great skill and represented me well. Your banishment remains."

"I accept that. And Lyric?"

The queen glanced at Lyric, who was still held by two armed guards. "By besting the Unseelie lord, you have fulfilled my need for retribution, and won the thief's freedom. We are gone."

And with a flutter of wings, the entire Seelie court ascended upward.

VAIL REMAINED on his knees, quarterstaff held with one hand, his head bowed. Blood dribbled down the side of his head. Faery dust glittered in his hair. Her hero had won her freedom. But at what price? Would the dust tempt him back to his addiction?

Lyric ran to him and plunged to his side, hugging him and kissing him. Wrapping his arm about her shoulder, he hugged her against his chest. Blood scent tempted her, and she nuzzled her face against his, so close to the crimson trickles. But even more, she needed the embrace to feel his heartbeat thundering against her own.

"You're free now," he said. "Free to do as you wish, go where you please."

"You're not still suggesting I take five seconds?"

He shrugged and exhaled. He was exhausted from the battle. "It would please me to be yours, lover."

"You are mine," she confirmed with a kiss to the corner of his eye. "You're bleeding."

"I'll heal."

"And there's dust..."

"Ch'yeah, it's tingling like hell. I...I want to taste it."

"Don't, Vail, please."

"It smells great. I know it's bad for me...." He studied his forearm, sparkling with dust.

Lyric cast about for assistance, for a friendly face in the throngs who stood witnessing their fallen lord's defeat. Foolish to think any would care about a dust-riddled vampire.

"Please," Lyric called, but not to anyone in particular. She didn't know how to help him now. If he tasted the dust she might never get him back as she had before. The addiction would steal into his heart and change him forever.

Off near the lockers, Zett sneered, while the gaping wound on his abdomen was attended by a second.

Cressida was the one who finally stepped forward, bringing a cool breeze upon all. She touched Vail's head. "Look at me, my vampire son."

Vail tore his attention from the faery dust on his arm and looked into his stepmother's eyes. The Mistress of Winter's Edge bowed to kiss him on the mouth. And as she inhaled, the faery dust lifted from Vail's skin.

It fluttered out from his hair, dazzling the air about the two of them, and shimmered to nothing.

Lyric sighed with relief.

"Having defeated Zett," Cressida said, "your banishment no longer stands."

Vail stood and helped Lyric up with him. "I prefer to adhere to the banishment, if you don't mind. I belong here, with Lyric."

The faery's lips curved into a sad moue.

"Though I would ask your favor to visit you on occasion," he added, and with a bow, pronounced reverently, "Mistress of Winter's Edge."

"Of course," she said gleefully, and bowed to him, as if she were the one accepting the gift instead of him. "It pleases me you've found someone like yourself, Vaillant the Dark. She will give you the love your dark heart craves."

Vail laid a palm over his heart and looked into Lyric's eyes. So much love lived in his eyes. She swallowed back tears at the tremendous feeling.

"One more thing." Cressida addressed Lyric. "Where is Zett's mark?"

"Behind her right ear," Vail said softly when Lyric could but shyly lower her head.

The faery ran her fingers along the shell of Lyric's ear. Her touch felt like needles of ice, and when she pressed firmly over the mark it was almost as though frost had affixed to her skin.

"Take care of my vampire son," she said to Lyric.

"I will."

"I know the sidhe do not take kindly to thanks,"

Vail said to Cressida, "but…thank you, Cressida. For all the years, and everything betwixt and between."

Her wings fluttered with what Lyric suspected was unabashed joy, then the faery stepped back and lifted, soaring high toward the ceiling, where her troops, clothed in red, waited.

The remainder of Zett's troops followed in kind, leaving the train station exactly as it had looked an hour earlier, and with but a few frazzled mortals flapping at the air over them as if being dive-bombed by invisible insects. Some believed.

Vail kissed Lyric behind her ear, and infused warmth where Cressida's touch had frozen it. "It's gone," he whispered. "You're safe from Zett."

"Thanks to you, lover. Is it over now?"

He pressed his forehead to hers and nodded. "But there's something I still need to take care of."

"Your father." She slid a hand along his cheek. "You don't need to kill him."

He kissed her, a sweet promise. "I know that now."

Vail's cell phone buzzed and he answered. "Yes? It's Rhys and Tryst," he said to her. "They're tracking Constantine. What's the address of the Santiago mansion?"

Lyric gave it to him. "Did they get hold of your mother?"

"Yes, but Rhys thinks it best to let her see Constantine, to put it all out in the open. Come on." He grabbed her hand, and they rushed outside. "I want to get there before they do."

# *CHAPTER TWENTY-SIX*

CONSTANTINE MET LYRIC at the door, and Vail lingered behind, assessing the situation. A week ago he would have rushed the bastard and staked him without a word.

But now? Constantine de Salignac wouldn't know the pain he'd caused Vail or his mother, because he hadn't known Vail existed. He did know Lyric, so it made sense to let her go ahead—bearing the bad news.

And while he clutched his fingers into fists, and fought to keep his heartbeats calm, Vail knew it wisest to play this carefully. At the least, he was thankful Rhys, Trystan and Viviane had not yet arrived. He wasn't sure what seeing Constantine would do to Viviane, but suspected nothing good would result.

No moon lightened the sky. The estate grounds were deathly silent. And when he thought he should be tight with anger, standing at the edge of the vanguard waiting to inflict some damage, Vail realized he was surprisingly calm. It was Lyric. She calmed the incredible new power he had gained, and he liked that just fine.

"Why didn't you tell me about Charish?" Constantine's voice wavered as he stood in the entry hallway talking to Lyric. His tone was angry, but edged with a sadness Vail knew too well. "Who did it to her? Tell me!"

"Connor." Lyric sighed and, with a glance at Vail, drew in a breath. "Constantine."

"I asked Charish never to use that name," he said. "Why would she tell you that? And who is this vampire with you? I thought he worked for Hawkes Associates. Lyric, your mother is dead!"

"Charish didn't tell me your name," she said, and, with an acknowledging gesture to Vail, added, "Vaillant did. Constantine, I know you're upset about my mother."

"And you are not?"

"I am. I've had some time to work through it. An amazing convergence of events has kept me from truly feeling grief. I know it'll hit me hard soon enough. But right now, the most important thing is that I introduce you to Vaillant."

"I can't do this. If he means something to you—I just can't." Constantine caught his head in his hands and turned away, obviously stricken with the news about his dead lover. "She was my world."

So his father could feel deeply about a woman? At first Vail wanted to shout at him, *How dare you? When you harmed my mother irrevocably?* And then a small part inside him could understand the pain the old vampire felt upon losing one he must have loved.

Had the centuries changed him?

Lyric held out her hand to Vail, not pleading, but merely waiting to see if he would take it. He could not resist her allure, the desire to connect with her, even knowing what she intended. Having her here with him, a liaison of sorts, made what he had to do easier.

He placed his hand in hers and joined her side. She kissed his mouth softly and gave him a confirming nod, which he nodded in return.

"Constantine, this is Vaillant," she said to the sorrowful vampire who leaned against the wall, his arms slack. "Listen to me. You'll want to know this man. He is your son."

The older vampire turned. His eyes, a pale blue, not so bold as Viviane's, locked on to Vail's. And Vail felt the man's intense and acrid scrutiny burn into his very soul.

"My son? That is…" Constantine looked Vail from head to his boots. "I have no children," he offered sadly. "I have tried through the centuries to create progeny, but it was not to be. I don't know where you get your information, boy, but I am sorry."

"Rhys Hawkes told him," Lyric said quietly.

"Hawkes?" Constantine looked to Vail for verification, his eyes narrowing cautiously. "Of course, if you work for Hawkes Associates. What lies has my brother been telling you?"

With an inhalation to draw in the bravery he knew

he would need, Vail spoke, "You raped my mother, Viviane LaMourette. I am the result of that crime."

Constantine's jaw dropped open, exposing a chipped fang.

"You violated her in 1785." Vail relayed the story Rhys had told him. "As a result of some pissing match against your brother. And then you imprisoned her in a glass coffin, bespelled her and buried her alive beneath Paris for over two centuries."

"I…" Constantine clasped his chest. "She was found? Alive? When last I talked to my brother…"

According to Rhys, Constantine had defied Rhys only hours before Viviane had been found, hissingly telling him he'd gotten what he'd deserved. That was the last time Rhys had contact with his half brother.

"Alive and insane," Vail confirmed, finding that the vitriol he feared would make him irrational did not emerge. That allowed him to speak calmly. "Viviane gave birth to two boys, who had germinated within her over the centuries."

"Two?"

"Myself, and my brother Trystan, who is Rhys's blood son."

"But how is that possible? Two children from the same womb, yet different fathers?" The vampire breathed out and stumbled against the wall. "You tell me true? But why did not my brother? If you are my son… My son?"

Vail felt Lyric's hand at his back and it strengthened him. Standing straight, he nodded. "Before he'd met Viviane, Rhys unknowingly promised his firstborn to a faery in exchange for the enchantment of his werewolf nature. When the Mistress of Winter's Edge came for her boon, she chose me over my brother Trystan."

"Cressida took you to Faery? You've grown up there? How long?"

"All my life. I've been in the mortal realm a few months. Since arriving, I have thought only to find you."

"Truly?"

"And then kill you."

Constantine nodded, accepting, and then a broad grin stretched his pale mouth. The man drew up his shoulders, exhibiting a shadow of the great tribe leader he must have once been. "Vaillant. That is a fine name. You, who are my son. Do you know how I have longed for a son over the centuries?"

"It doesn't matter," Vail said.

And it didn't. He didn't care what his father had thought of, strived for, or suffered over the years. None of it could ever erase the horrors Constantine had visited upon his mother.

"So you've come to kill me?" With a resolute nod, Constantine pulled a dagger out from a sheath behind his hip. He set it on the table beside him. "You would take away your only family, son?"

Vail cringed at the label. Constantine had no more right to call him son than he had to call him father. If anyone deserved the right, it was Rhys Hawkes, for his kindness and unconditional support.

He stepped forward, and touched the hilt of the dagger. Such close proximity to Constantine allowed him to sense the elder vampire's heartbeats; they were slow and tedious. He smelled dusty, like something long forgotten in a dark corner.

Gripping the dagger hilt, Vail drew it up to inspect the blade. He eyed the flash of silver, but on the one side of the blade his father's deep blue eyes distracted him. "They are the same," Vail said softly. "Our eyes."

"Boy," Constantine said. "Take your revenge, if you dare."

Vail held his father's eyes just one moment longer, then flipped the blade expertly in his hand, caught it and placed it on the table.

He took a step back and nodded, confirming what he'd known all along but had never the sight to believe it. "This is not my revenge to have. You may be blood, but you are not family. You have been cruel and malicious to Lyric's mother. You drove my mother insane. You have never accepted your own brother—"

"Because he is a bloody half-breed! An abomination!"

Vail winced at his father's vehemence. For a moment he had hoped there was a chance, the slightest possibility of mutual acceptance, but it was not to be. "And what of your son who grew up in Faery and believes all vampires abominations?"

"You've been poisoned by the faeries! I, your blood father, am vampire." He pounded a fist against his chest. "You, Vaillant, are bloodborn, the most regal and powerful of our breed. Come, my son." Constantine held out his arms.

Vail felt the gentle pressure of Lyric's hand upon his back. She wanted him to step forward to embrace the man he could not conceive of loving? Blood was one thing, but he'd meant what he'd said about family. Constantine was not. Lyric, Trystan and Viviane, they were his family. He knew that now.

A shout outside alerted them. An SUV parked in the yard, the headlights still on. Figures moved in front of the lights, and Trystan rushed inside but slapped his hands on the door frame and paused on the threshold.

The brothers exchanged glances. Then the huffing werewolf asked, "That's him?"

Vail nodded.

"Who is this?" Constantine demanded.

"It's Vail's brother," Lyric provided. "Trystan Hawkes. Your nephew."

"Viviane is in a mood," Tryst said. "Rhys thinks it best to allow her to see him, but I'm not so sure, man. You didn't kill him?"

Vail almost laughed. He did like where his brother's head was at. "No."

"So this is your half-breed brother," Constantine said from behind Vail, not disguising the contempt.

"I'm one hundred percent werewolf," Tryst said. "Want to test my talons, longtooth?"

"Tryst." Vail shook his head subtly.

The werewolf was shoved forward into the hall as Viviane pushed by him and clambered into the room. Her azure eyes were bright and seeking. She held beauty captive in her pale skin and dark features.

*No,* Vail thought, *I have my mother's eyes.*

He stepped aside to clasp Lyric's hand and hold her beside him. He couldn't know what was best for his mother right now, but if Rhys wanted to allow her this moment, he would not interfere.

"Viviane," Constantine said on a gasp.

Rhys Hawkes stepped beside his werewolf son. The two exchanged tense nods.

"It is you." Viviane, her long, midnight hair bedraggled, and the hummingbird pin hanging low near her shoulder, boldly stepped forward and slapped Constantine's face. "Two centuries!"

Emboldened by his mother's brave approach, Vail hugged Lyric closer to him. Finally, Viviane would be granted the revenge she deserved. He could never understand her suffering, but would stand behind her no matter the outcome of this bizarre reunion.

"You bastard," she hissed at the cowering vampire. "I am not dead! Do you know I thought of what I would do to you every day I was imprisoned within that hideous coffin?"

"Viviane, I wanted you," Constantine pleaded ineffectually. "You were cruel to me, ignoring my affections, my kindnesses, my gifts! I would have given you the world."

The vampiress snarled and slashed her clawed fingers across Constantine's neck.

Vail stirred at the blood scent. His brother growled lowly. Rhys held an emotionless expression.

"Yes," Constantine offered quietly. He stroked a finger through the blood on his cheek and wiped it along a pant leg. "You must take your anger out on me. I deserve it. And yet, you've given me the greatest gift. A son."

"Never for you," she murmured. "He is *my* dark prince. Not yours!"

Constantine winced and bowed his head. "What can I do to atone for my crimes against you?"

"I want to win this time," Viviane said, head bowed and eyes raging.

Vail sucked in a breath. He felt his mother's rage swell in his heart and fill his lungs with a smothering heat. And he knew she had held that rage far too long; it was what had made her insane.

The vampiress shoved her pointed fingers into Constantine's chest. The vampire howled and gripped the vampiress's wrist. Viviane was too quick. She twisted her hand inside his body and yanked out a heavy mass of bloody muscle.

Vail pressed back Lyric when he felt she wanted to rush forward.

"I have your heart, Constantine," Viviane pronounced coldly. She held up the pulsing muscle and squeezed. Blood spattered her face and Constantine's. "I win now."

"So you have."

The vampire Constantine de Salignac ashed. His body, formed of ash in human shape before Viviane, hung there momentarily, then dropped into a pile.

No one had moved to stop her. Vail, every muscle in his body tight, released Lyric and slapped his hands to the wall behind him for support. He thought he heard Lyric whisper "Sorry," but the thud of his heart drowned out noise.

Viviane turned and dropped the heart, which ashed before it hit the floor and dispersed in a gray cloud that settled upon Vail's boot toes.

The vampiress's bold stare sought everyone in the room, moving slowly from Lyric, to Vail, and then to her husband and werewolf son. She had destroyed her tormentor. A rightful death.

Reaching out, she gestured for Trystan to approach, and he did without pause. She hugged him to her chest. "My son. It is over."

Vail swallowed, holding down his heart for fear it would dredge up a scream. He grasped blindly at his side, and Lyric's hand slid into his.

Viviane's bold blue eyes found his, and she smiled. It seemed genuine. Real. She smiled at him? A gesture with her free hand beckoned him forward.

Vail took a step. She wanted him to approach her? He rushed into his mother's arms, beside his brother.

"My boys," she cooed. "I love you both."

# *EPILOGUE*

DOMINGOS LAROQUE, a vampire friend of Vail's, played cello in the background as Lyric walked down the aisle in the garden behind the Santiago mansion.

Clad in a long white sheath of silk, Lyric, newly blonde, walked barefoot through the grass toward her destiny.

Destiny resembled a man who wore black and silver as if royal raiment, and who sported Green Snake—a symbol of change—curling about his left trouser leg. His bare feet curled into the soft grass strewn with rose petals. He was her rock 'n' roll faery vampire lover, and she wouldn't have him any other way.

Forgoing the dramatic walk to the cello's wedding march, Lyric tossed the bouquet of red roses aside and ran up to Vail. He caught her and kissed her deeply before the new family they would now share.

Rhys and Viviane Hawkes held hands beneath the cherry tree, both with irrepressible smiles. And Trystan, Vail's best man, tapped Vail on the shoulder when the officiant waited for them to say their vows. He handed Vail a ring encircled with black diamonds.

"Mortal diamonds," Vail said, as he slid the sparkler onto Lyric's finger. "This makes you mine."

Lyric leaned in and kissed him. "And that makes you mine."

They promised to love each other. Forever.

Vampires.

* * * * *

*Are you curious about Rhys and Viviane's story?*
*Read more in*
*SEDUCING THE VAMPIRE,*
*in stores now.*

*Visit Michele's website for information on current and upcoming releases, and stop into Club Scarlet for details on all the characters in her Beautiful Creatures world: clubscarlet.michelehauf.com.*

Harlequin®

# nocturne™

LOOK FOR *NEW YORK TIMES* BESTSELLING AUTHOR

# MAGGIE SHAYNE

&

*USA TODAY* BESTSELLING AUTHOR

# MAUREEN CHILD

THIS JULY WITH:

# VACATION WITH A VAMPIRE...

## *and Other Immortals*

Nothing says holiday quite like a walk in paradise with a gorgeous vampire...or spending a twilight eve with a charismatic highlander.

Don't be afraid to dip your toes into these two seductive and enthralling stories from Maggie Shayne and Maureen Child. Come on in and leave your cares behind....

**Available June 28 wherever books are sold.**

www.Harlequin.com
www.ParanormalRomanceBlog.com

HNMS0711